T0304801

FRIENDS OF DOROTHY

FRIENDS OF DOROTHY

SANDI TOKSVIG

virago

VIRAGO

First published in Great Britain in 2024 by Virago Press

1 3 5 7 9 10 8 6 4 2

A CIP catalogue record for this book is available from the British Library.

Hardback ISBN 978-0-349-01901-7
Trade Paperback ISBN 978-0-349-01900-0

Typeset in Sabon by M Rules
Printed and bound in Great Britain by Clays Ltd, Elcograf S.p.A.

Papers used by Virago are from well-managed forests
and other responsible sources.

Virago Press
An imprint of
Little, Brown Book Group
Carmelite House
50 Victoria Embankment
London EC4Y 0DZ

An Hachette UK Company
www.hachette.co.uk

www.virago.co.uk

To my beloved wife, the love of my life and my secret weapon;
to my gorgeous kids and grandkids who I adore;
and to my fabulous feisty friends who I could not do without.
You are my family.

One

Number 4 Grimaldi Square did not look like the sort of house which might surprise. It was just one of the identical terraced properties lining three sides of a Victorian square long past its best. Narrow brick places, often with a small bay window beside a less than stout front door. The only unusual thing about Number 4 on that November afternoon was a police officer who had been pacing outside for at least half an hour. Dressed in immaculate uniform, including a stab vest, there was something about her which suggested she was prepared for anything. She carried a small black duffel bag.

Constable Stevie Baxter did not 'do' late, so it was with some agitation that she continually checked her watch and tapped her mobile to see if perhaps a message was struggling to appear. Finally she reached for the radio on her left shoulder, hesitated and then pressed to connect.

'305 to Control, are you receiving?'

There was a moment's pause before a crackling voice replied, 'Control to 305. Yes, yes, go ahead.'

Stevie bit her lip before continuing.

'Uh, any message for me?' she asked. 'Over.'

'Negative, 305. Airways clear, please, 305. Out.'

Stevie nodded but took a moment to let go of the radio. She clapped her hands together, uncertain what to do next. She was a handsome woman of thirty. A good height, strong looking with an asymmetric haircut shaved on the left side with a neat parting and then a great flop of hair hanging down over her right eye. Whenever Stevie became anxious she found that thoroughly assessing a situation helped. She always started with an overview and then homed in on detail, so she began by turning her back to Number 4 and planting her feet firmly as she swept her practised eye across the whole square.

It was only a couple of hours or so past lunchtime, yet the sky was surprisingly dark. One of those afternoons when the grey weather oozed damp. A large 1980s tower block several streets away loomed above and stole any sunlight which might have tried to break through. One very elderly woman, bent almost double, was making staggeringly slow progress round the gloomy perimeter with a set of walking poles. Otherwise the place was deserted. Grimaldi Square wasn't a shortcut to anywhere, so few people chose to put it on their route. Bits of rubbish swept in from the nearby high street and lodged in a couple of scrubby bushes. Once there had been four nice benches in the centre from which to admire the day but all that was left were some upright metal struts cemented to the ground.

Directly across the square on the opposite side, someone was already putting the lights on for evening trade at a very large Victorian pub with the unlikely name of The Price of Onions. Filling an entire side of the square, it looked more like a house where the lord of the manor once held sway. It had a wide and welcoming double front door with a substantial series of windows on either side. Above, a generous first floor was topped with an attic with three dormer windows. The whole place had clearly once been extremely grand but like everything else in the neighbourhood it was now weary, its heyday long gone.

Stevie checked her watch again and gave a great sigh before shaking herself into action. She turned back to the house. The previous occupants of Number 4 had not been big on fuss. The only attempt at décor consisted of a rusting metal hook for an unrealised hanging basket. As she made her way up the short path Stevie noticed that Number 5 had made more of an effort; artificial turf lay across the small front patch, which was choked with plastic flowers in tubs. The containers varied in shape – some were like ducks; another was a plastic wishing well which stood cheek by jowl with a violently coloured windmill. The effect was somewhere between a garden and a seaside mini golf course.

Stevie was surveying it all when suddenly the front door of Number 5 banged open and a woman appeared. Bad temper had aged her. She appeared to be anywhere between middle age and death. The woman carried the air of the 1950s with her floral apron, a pair of beige slippers for the wider foot and poorly dyed hair; the sort of person you used to see in old ads for the health benefits of suet. She was not in the mood for niceties.

'Female police?' was her opening gambit.

'Uh, yes, but—'

'Sure you're not a traffic warden?' she barked. 'Look more like a traffic warden. Right, what's the trouble, officer? I've watched you hanging about. Has she popped her clogs? I shouldn't be surprised.'

As if to complement her mad look, the woman now gave a slight grimace and revealed truly terrible teeth.

3

'Sorry, what? Is who dead?' Stevie managed in the face of these challenging features.

'Wretched nuisance.' The woman grimaced again before adding, 'Mrs Haggerston.'

'A Mrs Haggerston is dead?' Stevie was hoping she wasn't going to have to deal with it.

The woman harrumphed and shook her head. 'No! *I'm* Mrs Haggerston. Do I look dead? Why they couldn't send a proper policeman I don't know,' continued Mrs Haggerston disapprovingly. 'Pay my taxes same as anyone. Haggerston.' She began to spell her name out. 'H ... A ... G ... Don't you want to write this down?' she asked.

'No,' said Stevie.

The woman harrumphed again. It was a noise she was clearly practised at. 'All on computers, I suppose. You probably don't even have a pencil. Let me know!'

And with that she turned back into her house and slammed the door.

Stevie shook her head and in an attempt to get back on track clapped her hands again, as if scaring away demons, then looked through the windows of Number 4. The place was empty. Not a stick of furniture. She nodded. She was surprised to find the door ajar. Why was it not locked? Had someone broken in? There was nothing to steal. Her anxiety levels rose and instinctively she ran through her almost choreographed dance of checking her routine equipment, tapping the radio set on her left shoulder and then swiftly round her body, lightly feeling each piece of her kit.

Work mobile: left pocket of her stab vest, with rubber gloves and pocket notebook. Right pocket: personal mobile, pens, first aid kit. Duty belt from left to right: irritant spray, multitool, extendable baton, torch, Taser holster, rigid handcuffs. She patted her belt one more time, looked over her shoulder and gently pushed the front door open. It squeaked slightly onto a narrow corridor, off which lay a tiny sitting room. Stevie walked in slowly, conscious of the heavy tread of her boots. She put her head through the entrance to a small dining room with the world's tiniest kitchen extension off the back.

A miniature downstairs loo had been crammed in under the stairs in an old cupboard. The place hadn't been touched for years. Stevie went back into the hall, where she stopped momentarily to pull up a piece of the terrible carpet – swirls of claret with gold, the sort of carpet often found in pubs as it shows neither dirt nor vomit. She tapped the wooden floorboards below with her toe and it echoed through the empty house.

At the end of the hall, stairs rose to the first floor. Stevie began to climb slowly, her footwear continuing to resonate. She looked into the main bedroom; a good size, with two windows looking out over the square where she saw an older man pissing into a dead bush. He glanced up and waved with his free hand. Stevie stepped back into the corridor, where she took a deep breath and noticed a faint smell of lily of the valley. The door to the second bedroom was closed. Stevie hesitated with her hand over the doorknob and was suddenly overcome by the ominous stillness all around her. She flung open the bedroom door to find a very old woman sitting on a small red sofa, staring straight at her. This caused Stevie to do something utterly out of character and unofficer-like: she screamed.

The elderly lady screamed in response and put up her hands, so Stevie screamed again. Once more the woman returned the call then dropped her arms and thrust her wrists under Stevie's nose. Stevie paused in a slight state of shock. Her own scream was not a sound she had ever made before, and it didn't really suit her. There was a moment's silence.

'Your turn,' said the unexpected woman.

'What?'

'Your turn to scream, I think,' the woman said as if she were giving it quite some thought. 'You screamed first,' she explained, 'then I did, then you again then me, so if we're going for a third time, I think you're next.'

Stevie shook her head. 'I don't want to scream.'

The woman smiled. 'Oh good. It's exhausting.' Once more she put her arms out towards Stevie. 'Right, pop the cuffs on.'

Stevie shook her head before replying, 'No, sorry, I'm not the police ...'

'Bloody good costume,' sniffed the old woman. 'Breaking and entering, is it? Clever. I'd never have thought of doing it in uniform. Shame everything worth nicking's already gone, now you've gone to all that effort.'

'I mean I am police but ...' Stevie took a deep breath before saying, 'OK, can we start again?'

'I doubt it,' replied the old woman. 'The door closed behind you. No handle this side. It's how I got stuck in here. Used to make my husband sleep in here when he'd had a few.'

Stevie and the woman stopped speaking to eye one another. The now silent old lady was ancient yet fit and even rather elegant in a black blouse and matching trousers, with a small orange silk scarf tied at her neck. Her grey hair was in a neat short cut. She looked nice but Stevie had had a long shift and was not handling things well.

'Are you a ghost?'

The woman chuckled. 'Any day now.'

'Sorry, sorry, obviously not.' Stevie tried to slow her breathing and be more reasonable. 'What are you doing here?'

'I live here,' came the confident reply.

Stevie decided to be calm. 'No, that can't be true. I live here ... I mean, we *will* be living here.'

'We?' enquired the woman.

'My wife Amber and I.'

'Amber,' the woman repeated before adding, 'That's a nice name.'

'Yes,' agreed Stevie.

'Good looking?' asked the woman.

'Yes.'

The woman nodded. 'I mean, they say looks aren't everything, but it doesn't hurt first thing in the morning. Well done.'

'Thanks.'

There was another silence before the old lady smoothed her trousers with her hands and enquired, as if they had met at a party, 'And you live here?'

'Yes, well that's the plan,' replied Stevie, although she sounded uncertain.

The woman reached out for Stevie's hand as if in sympathy. 'I don't think so,' she said, giving her hand a slight squeeze. 'Did you live here yesterday?'

Stevie shook the woman off. 'No ... no,' she answered.

The woman smiled as if she had been right all along. 'Well, it doesn't sound like much of a permanent arrangement.'

Stevie stood in the middle of the room holding her duffel bag.

'What's in the bag?' asked the woman.

'Uhm ... champagne,' Stevie managed.

The woman gave a slight snort. 'And they say the police are underpaid.'

'It's for Amber.'

The woman nodded. 'I see. And where is she, then?'

'Who?'

The woman sighed. 'Dear god, how do you interrogate anyone if you can't follow a conversation? Amber! Where is the lovely Amber?'

Stevie's anxiety rose to the surface in an instant. 'I don't know. I keep calling and calling.'

The woman nodded sympathetically. 'You're worried.'

'Yes,' admitted Stevie.

The woman patted the small sofa beside her. 'Have a sit down,' she suggested.

'What?'

'I can move up,' she said, shifting along the sofa to make room.

'No, I . . .'

'I would if I were you. I told you: you've allowed the door to shut. Follow the clues, Poirot – there's no handle on the inside.'

Stevie looked behind her at the door and saw it was true. It was closed. There were just screw holes where a handle ought to have been. The woman tapped the small velvety sofa once more, and Stevie found herself sitting down. It was a tiny two-seater and their knees touched.

'How did you know about the handle on the . . .' Stevie began.

'I live here,' repeated the woman quietly. 'I'm Dorothy.' There was a pause which Dorothy allowed before continuing, 'And you are?'

'Stevie.'

They made a strangely matching couple, the very old woman and the youngish one. Stevie had dyed her own hair grey last year because Amber thought it was cool. She appeared to be aping Dorothy's more natural tones.

8

'I met the neighbour,' Stevie said quietly. 'Are there nothing but old women around here?'

Dorothy laughed. 'Fucking loads! Place is heaving with women who'll crumble before you even open the oven at the crem.'

'Crem?'

'Crematorium. It's only round the corner. Very convenient,' Dorothy added helpfully.

Stevie nodded. 'I don't think the estate agent put that on the particulars.'

'I say, best to desiccate the old birds and sprinkle them on a cake.'

The two captive women fell silent once more. After a few minutes, Stevie sensed a change in her companion and turned to see that, like a child or a kitten, Dorothy, clearly done with conversation, had fallen asleep. Her flat chest rose and fell gently. It was oddly calming. Stevie looked again at the door without a handle and then around the room. There was nothing obvious to use as a lever. All the room contained was the modest sofa and, besides Dorothy, a small wheeled suitcase closed with a padlock. Stevie was patting her pockets to see what she might have in her kit which could help when her phone rang.

'Fuck! Fuck!' Stevie scrambled to pull her phone from her pocket, wondering why the hell she was suddenly worried about waking the old woman.

'It's Jack!' chirped a cheerful voice.

Stevie got up from the sofa and moved towards the door, keeping her voice low. 'I know it's Jack!' she whispered. 'Your name comes up on my phone, you idiot. Jack, I need your help! There's a woman in my house!'

'Come now,' replied Jack, not lowering his exuberant voice in the slightest, 'that's no way to refer to Amber.'

'Yes, but it's not Amber. An entirely different woman. Someone I don't know.'

Jack's delight in any kind of gossip was instantly aroused. 'Ooh, and where is this mystery woman now?'

Dorothy stirred and Stevie turned away, speaking even more quietly. 'On the sofa.'

'I'm sorry, Stevie, can you speak up?'

'No, she's asleep.'

Jack was impressed. 'Blimey, you don't hang about. One minute you're buying a house with Amber and the next you're changing horses on the merry-go-round. Where did you meet this bird? Oh!!!' Jack took a giant deep breath. 'Please don't tell me you want me to give Amber the news. You know I'm not good with drama. She won't take it well. For reasons I can't fathom she likes being married to you.'

'No, I ... oh Christ. I picked up the keys after work and came to meet her like we arranged but Amber never showed and then the front door was open and when I went in this old woman was in here on a sofa upstairs.'

'That is unusual,' agreed Jack.

'You could say that.'

'You don't often get a sofa upstairs.'

'Jack!'

'Well, where is Amber?'

'I don't know! We've been planning this for months. I can't get hold of her. I'm worried something's happened.'

'You could ring the polic— Oh, yeah. I'm at work. I'll come over,' he said. 'What was the number again?'

'Number 4. You know it's Number 4. You can see it from the door of the pub.'

'I'm your friend, not your secretary,' retorted Jack. 'You know

10

how I hate detail. I'll try and find Amber; you get rid of the other woman. Go on!'

'I don't know who to call,' said Stevie rather plaintively.

'I'm like a fairy godmother to you,' Jack sighed. 'Try the estate agent!'

It was actually quite a sensible idea, so Stevie hung up and placed the call.

The estate agent was shutting up shop for the day. Because both Stevie and Amber worked shifts and the agents kept hours often known only to themselves, there had been several days' delay in arranging for the handover of the keys. There was now relief all round – not least at the office, as Number 4 Grimaldi Square had not been an easy sale. The place needed everything doing. The small team of three house sellers were off to the pub to celebrate. Stevie reached the manager just as she was putting her coat on.

'Pixie Lee and Partners!' she said brightly. 'Pixie speaking.'

'Oh hello, Pixie. It's Stevie Baxter.'

As Stevie had seen her only hours earlier, she half thought Pixie might remember but there seemed to be nothing coming back. 'Stevie Baxter? And Amber Delaunay? We bought 4 Grimaldi Square,' Stevie continued.

'How nice,' came the reply. Pixie finished all her sentences on a rising note, as if she were constantly trying to convey optimism in a very uncertain market. 'Very nice!'

'It is, but the thing is – there's an old woman in the house,' Stevie began.

'Oh, yes?' replied Pixie in the professional voice she used whenever she pretended to be interested.

'I mean really old.' Stevie lowered her voice to a whisper as she looked at Dorothy sleeping. 'Like nearly dead old.'

11

'Hmm.' The estate agent put her hand over the phone mouthpiece and Stevie could hear her whisper 'Gin and tonic!' to her colleagues. 'Hmm,' she said again. 'Really old?' she echoed.

'Yes. Grey hair, black clothes ...'

'Oh yes. That'll be Dorothy Franklin, the vendor. I don't think you ever met her.'

'No,' agreed Stevie.

'Lovely woman,' opined Pixie.

'I'm sure,' said Stevie, 'but still here.'

'Hmm. I'm afraid that if there are any problems with the handover you will have to speak to your solicitor. Thank you for dealing with Pixie Lee and Partners.'

And with that she hung up.

Stevie rang her solicitor.

'Maisie Pilkington and Associates!' came the answer. 'I'm afraid we are now closed for the evening. Please leave a message after the beep.' Then there was the unmistakable sound of a woman saying the word 'beep'.

Stevie was not in the mood. 'Stop it, Maisie. I know you're still there.'

'I'm not here. That was the answer machine.'

'You don't have an answer machine. You don't even have any associates. It's just you in your kitchen.'

Maisie was Stevie's cousin, otherwise she might have looked elsewhere for legal representation.

Maisie sighed. 'What do you want, Stevie? I thought you were moving in today.'

Stevie explained and Maisie listened.

'Hmm,' she said, as if she worked for Pixie Lee. 'Right, well, that's not what's supposed to happen so we'll have to see what we can do in the morning.'

Stevie was aghast. 'In the morning? But—'

'Yes, Stevie, it's after hours.'

'It's four o'clock.'

'I've got a date. Actually a *second* date!'

Dorothy gave a slight snore, as if to remind Stevie of the reality of her presence.

'Maisie?' Stevie said into the phone but Maisie, with her high hopes for her evening, was long gone.

Stevie heard someone downstairs.

'Stevie?' called a male voice. She had left the front door open. It was Jack. She could hear him on the stairs.

'I'm in here!' yelled Stevie, banging on the inside of the door, no longer caring about waking the old woman. Dorothy awoke as the door opened.

'Jack!' Stevie called out. 'Please don't scream because Dorothy's really good at it.'

Jack entered. He was the same age as Stevie. A large, hand-some lad whose body entirely filled the doorway. The moment he appeared he screamed. Stevie turned sternly to him, demanding, 'Why are you screaming?'

Jack smiled, saying, 'I wouldn't have if you hadn't mentioned it but once you'd said I couldn't think about anything else.'

Stevie took a deep breath. 'Have you found Amber?'

'No,' he replied, 'but who have you found?' He looked engagingly at the old woman.

'This is Dorothy,' explained Stevie.

'Hello Dorothy, I'm Jack. And what are you doing here?'

'We bought the house from her,' said Stevie.

'From her or with her?'

But Stevie was checking her phone for the hundredth time. 'Where the hell is Amber?'

Two

If Stevie could have seen Amber at that moment it might have caused her to do a second uncharacteristic thing and faint because Amber was covered in blood. This is not a happy look for anyone, but at least Amber was a paramedic so it was not entirely unexpected.

Still dressed in her dark green uniform, Amber, who had just finished her shift, thought she had time to buy new towels as a surprise housewarming gift for Stevie. They had once stayed in a hotel on holiday where Stevie had loved all the high-quality linen.

'One day we'll have towels like this!' she had enthused. 'Feel that! The luxury of it! Imagine!'

It was typical of Amber to think of a practical but thoughtful gift, and she had enjoyed going to John Lewis and choosing two large bath towels in bright orange to make Stevie smile. It was her favourite colour. As Amber left the shop with her purchase she glanced up at the large ornamental clock over the central stairway and was pleased to see she was going to be exactly on time for the much-anticipated rendezvous outside their new house. She had been reading a Henry James novel in the queue at the till and was still trying to finish her chapter as she walked briskly across the shiny tiled floor with her shopping. She moved quickly and with practised skill managed to both read and avoid bumping into anyone. All she wanted was to finish the chapter and get to Stevie. As a consequence she did her best to block out the distressed voice which was echoing through the mall.

'Oh my god! Oh my god!' it cried.

An exceptionally pregnant woman was in the middle of the concourse, screaming for help. She was wearing a bright floral dress under a wool coat, and it was easy to see that her knees were buckled. She crouched in fear above a large puddle. Clearly her baby was on the way. The woman was alone, calling out:

'Help!'

That single word caused most shoppers immediately to head in the other direction. For once in her life Amber nearly walked on but she just couldn't. Partly because she was still in uniform and that was not a good look but mainly because she did not have it in her to ignore anyone in trouble. She stopped, sighed and went to help.

'All right, love, you're all right,' she soothed. She had thought she would call for an ambulance before heading off, but the newly arriving human clearly had other ideas.

'It's coming, it's coming!' the woman cried.

Maintaining her usual calm Amber managed to get the distressed woman out of the flow of pedestrians and over to the side of the shopfront of a newly opened branch of Screwfix. Temporary display banners on stands framed the doorway, boldly offering 'Click and Collect in as Little as One Minute' and the reminder that 'Timing is Everything'. It was not Amber's first delivery, but usually she had at least a partner and medical equipment. There was no question that delivery was imminent and so professionalism took over. She laid her shopping bag on the floor and tucked her paperback in her back pocket.

'What's your name, love?' she asked the somewhat hysterical woman.

'Sarah!'

'OK, Sarah, I'm Amber. I'm a paramedic and it's all going to be fine.'

The woman's screaming response suggested an element of doubt on her part.

'Sarah, I need you to take your coat off,' said Amber.

Sarah seemed incapable of doing it herself so Amber almost wrestled the garment from her and laid it on the floor. 'Now we need to lie you down on your coat and take your tights off,' she instructed.

'I can't take my tights off here!' Sarah yelled.

'Yeah you can,' Amber said. 'We don't want that baby bouncing back in again.'

A young man in a bright blue T-shirt emblazoned with the Screwfix logo appeared from the shop. He had clearly drawn the short straw among his colleagues to go out and see what was going on, and wanted nothing to do with whatever was happening. He was extremely young and wore a name badge which read 'Mo'. He arrived just as Amber managed to lay Sarah down and begin removing her tights.

'Excuse me!' he called bossily. 'You can't do that here!'

'Tell that to the baby,' replied Amber. She looked up at the youngster and clocked his name badge.

'Mo, I need you to call an ambulance and then I need you

to move some of those banners over here to give Sarah some privacy.'

By now Amber had managed to remove both the tights and Sarah's underwear. The delivering woman lay on her back with her knees raised. Mo looked right at her.

'Oh my god!' he cried.

Amber tried again. 'Mo!'

Mo stood staring. 'I can see all her ... *business*,' he whispered in shock.

Amber nodded. 'If this is your first sight of a vagina it may not be the best introduction, but I still need you to call an ambulance and move the banners. Mo!'

The young man finally shifted himself. He began to move one of the advertising boards to create an illusion of privacy. The baby did not care and just kept coming.

'Sarah, do you have someone I can call?' Amber asked.

Sarah was now panting so hard it was difficult to understand her but she did manage to say that her husband, Trevor, was in the Wetherspoons further down the mall.

Mo moved a second banner into place as Amber looked up at him.

'Right, call the ambulance and then go to Wetherspoons and get Trevor,' ordered Amber. 'Tell him his partner has gone into labour.'

'I don't know what he looks like,' said the horrified young man.

Amber had no time for him. 'Go to the door and yell "Trevor, your baby is coming!"'

Mo did as he was told and returned with Trevor.

'She can't have the baby here!' he shouted immediately. 'Everybody can see all her business!'

'I said that,' agreed Mo.

17

Without looking up Amber said evenly, 'Grab a towel out of that John Lewis bag!'

Trevor had had a few and was minded to do more yelling, but suddenly he felt involved. He pulled the brand-new orange towel out of the bag and thrust it toward Amber. Meanwhile she remained utterly calm and got him to kneel beside her as her near decade of experience took over. The baby was in a hurry and the sight of his new-born son appearing and crying shut Trevor up completely.

'I need something to cut the cord with!' Amber yelled at Mo.

'Like what?' he asked.

'A sharp thing!' she managed. 'And a bucket!'

'Right,' said Mo. 'Metal or plastic?'

'Nobody cares!'

In the end Amber helped Trevor cut the baby's cord with something usually used for tiles and the boy was wrapped in a luxurious towel just as the ambulance crew arrived. Trevor wiped his hands on the second brand-new towel and got up to greet them. The new paramedic team checked Sarah over and then lifted her on to a gurney, with Trevor now being quite the attentive husband. Amber and Mo were left sitting side by side on the floor, leaning against the shop window. In one arm Amber held the baby, safely wrapped in a bright orange towel, while with the other she held Mo tucked into an embrace. Amber smiled down at the newborn, who seemed entirely content. Tiny, probably less than six pounds, but perfect. She kissed the miniature human on the forehead.

'Welcome to the world, little one,' she whispered and hugged the child close. Her delight at a job well done was interrupted by the reappearance of the new father, who seemed to have only just realised he was missing a child. He awkwardly reached for the baby, which Amber gave up reluctantly.

She dug out her phone and was about to call Stevie when she noticed Mo was crying.

'It's all right, Mo,' Amber soothed. 'It was just a shock.'

Mo shook his head and between tears chokingly said, 'That's the most beautiful thing I've ever seen.'

'Yes,' agreed Amber, 'yes it was.'

3

Moving-in day was not the only time Amber was late. The first time they viewed 4 Grimaldi Square she was also delayed. It was August 10th. A cloudy day. The place lay in shadow, grey with disuse apart from one tiny bright spot of colour. In a crack in the pavement outside the house a bright yellow dandelion was growing.

It was Amber who noticed it.

'Oh look, Stevie,' she exclaimed. 'Isn't it wonderful?'

'It's a weed,' said Stevie, looking at her watch. Amber reached out and touched her arm gently.

'Take a minute,' she said. It was so like Amber to have noticed the one single piece of colour in a monochrome landscape, and in that moment Stevie loved that her wife found the good in everything.

'I want this flower,' declared Amber, 'so I say it is not a weed. Back in the day, dandelions were used for all kinds of medicine. Fever, boils, eye problems, diabetes, diarrhoea.'

'Did it give you those things or make them better?' laughed

Stevie. 'Maybe take some with you on your next shift. Car accident? Don't worry, I've got a dandelion!'

Amber smiled as she gently plucked the flower and held it out to Stevie.

'The Victorians thought of the dandelion as the flower of faithfulness and love,' she said softly. 'No matter how hard you try to get rid of it, this sturdy little thing will always come back. Just like me.'

Amber reached up and kissed her wife, who took the flower and slipped it into a buttonhole on her shirt.

Amber loved the small house with an alarming passion from the second she clapped eyes on it. She and Stevie were only a few months married and Amber could not wait to start what she continued to think of as their 'grown-up' life. The estate agent showed them round with a lot of 'in need of some modernisation, etc.' but Amber just knew this was the place for them. Stevie, being intensely risk averse, worried about the money, the commitment, anything else she could think of, and did all she could to delay the moment of decision, but in the end they made an offer that very day which was accepted.

After that Stevie was on a mission not to be surprised by anything. This move was a massive life milestone and she wanted to be ready. There was not a fact about the house available anywhere which she did not gather and carefully place in a green folder imaginatively labelled '4 Grimaldi Square'. From her research Stevie could tell you normal stuff, such as that the house had three small bedrooms, a sitting room, kitchen-diner and a small but soon to be perfect garden, but she also knew things like the width of the place (11 feet as per regulations from the Local Government Act 1858). It was this habit of checking everything which one day might make her rise up through the ranks of the police and become a great detective.

Preparation was key to everything yet none of it was helpful now.

Jack eyed the old woman on the red sofa. 'Wait! Wait! Wait!' he suddenly exclaimed, banging his fist on the door jamb. 'Oh my god, I'm an idiot! What a prat! Dorothy! It's Dorothy Franklin! Is that really you? Oh my god, Dotty.'

He bundled over to the elderly woman and scooped her up in a great embrace, then he turned to Stevie and declared, 'This is Dorothy ... Dotty. She saved my life when I was growing up.' Not letting go of his new prize, Jack immediately sat down next to Dorothy, nearly knocking her off the small sofa as he said, 'I'm Jack! Birdie's boy! Her grandson!'

'Hello?' called a voice from downstairs. 'Dave de Van? I've got your furniture.'

'I think the furniture is here,' tried Stevie.

'Nan is going to be so thrilled!' Jack enthused to the room.

'Jack? Hello?' Stevie tried to stop the flow.

'Furniture!' yelled a man, sounding irritated.

Jack turned to Stevie and explained: 'Dorothy used to take my grandmother to her rheumatism appointments. It was the only time Nan went out and I had the place to myself. All through my teenage years Dorothy was like an emergency service for me.'

'I *do* remember you: we used to call you Wanker Boy,' reminisced Dorothy fondly.

'It wasn't all wanking,' protested Jack. He looked at Stevie as if to explain. 'I mean, it was a lot.'

'I don't want to hear about it!' Stevie half shouted.

Jack put his hands up in mock amazement. 'I couldn't do it while Nan was in the flat, could I? Dotty saved me.'

Two men appeared in the corridor carrying a headboard.

22

Stevie, beside herself, said, 'You can't just bring that up here! There's a plan. Oh, where is Amber?'

'It's a bed,' retorted one of the men, looking into the room. 'Did you want it downstairs? I mean, you've got a sofa up here. Topsy-turvy it is, if that's what you want. Queer, I call it.'

'Dorothy, the furniture is here so you really have to . . .' began Stevie.

'Oh, hello Dotty!' said the other guy, noticing Dorothy and seeming most surprised. 'You still here? Haven't see you for yonks. Thought you might be dead.'

'Dave de Van!' replied Dorothy, delighted. 'How's your dad?' She turned to Stevie to fill her in. 'Lovely man. Dutch.'

'Flemish,' corrected Dave.

Dorothy nodded. 'I get that when the weather's bad.'

'He's bad with the gout again,' continued Dave.

'Too many trips to the *pub*,' nodded Dorothy, getting up and taking charge. 'Right, stop chatting and get on. You mind that wallpaper! Plenty of wear in that yet.'

Stevie looked at the ancient floral wallpaper in the corridor and hoped that wasn't true. Dave nodded and asked again, 'Which room?'

'At the front. The big bedroom,' replied Dorothy.

Stevie tried to pull herself together and stop what was happening. 'Hang on! I'll decide!' She turned to Dorothy. 'Why are you bossing everyone around? You were asleep five minutes ago!'

There was a moment's pause, then Dorothy said, 'Asleep? Was I? About bloody time. You wait till you get to my age. All right, decide then.'

'Yes, go on then, decide!' encouraged Dave. 'This thing's fucking heavy.'

'Right,' said Stevie reluctantly. 'At the front. The big bedroom.' She went to show them.

'I'll make tea!' called Dorothy.

'No!' shouted Stevie. 'We need to talk. Anyway, I don't know where the kettle is.'

'Don't be silly,' replied Dorothy, heading downstairs, 'it's in the kitchen. Jack, you can help.'

Stevie tried once more to take charge.

'I've made a floor plan of where everything goes,' she cried, taking sheets of paper out of her duffel bag along with a large roll of tape. She went downstairs to fix them to the front door but they didn't last long. Dave appeared with a small table and knocked the lot off onto the floor. Meanwhile Dorothy made tea for everyone, and Jack fussed over the exact positioning of some cushions. There seemed to be plenty of mugs, a kettle, and milk in the fridge. Dorothy even conjured up some biscuits. Halfway through all the commotion Mrs Haggerston appeared from next door.

'Not dead then!' Mrs Haggerston said to Dorothy, making it sound like an accusation. She turned to Stevie. 'I thought you'd come to see if she was dead!'

'On All Saints' Day?' asked Dorothy. 'Are you mad? Why, we wait all year for this much choice.'

'Oh no you don't!' said Mrs Haggerston sharply, wagging her finger at Dorothy. 'My saints are very important to me.'

'Oh, and me,' declared Dorothy, clutching her chest, wide-eyed with innocence.

Jack grabbed Stevie's arm and leant against a box. 'Ooh, I just know this is going to be marvellous,' he declared.

It was quickly clear that these two older women had a history, and it was not a happy one.

Dorothy turned to Stevie and Jack to explain. 'Today: November 1st. So hard to know what to celebrate. All Saints' Day!'

'Don't start,' tried Mrs Haggerston.

'It's not the starting that's the problem. It's knowing when it's enough. All the saints! We are awash with choice, but I quite fancy St Lawrence.'

'Do tell!' exclaimed Jack but there was no need for encouragement. Dorothy ploughed on.

'King of barbeque. Griddled to death over hot coals for being too nice to the poor. That'll teach you.'

Dave and his mate continued bringing in what appeared to be never-ending boxes of books.

'He was laid out on the flames and after a bit called out "I'm well done on this side. Turn me over!" What a laugh!'

Mrs Haggerston tried several times to interrupt. 'Please will you—'

'It won't surprise you to learn he's the patron saint of cooks, chefs and comedians,' continued Dorothy across the incoming traffic, 'so he's one to hang with in the afterlife. The best bit is that the whole thing may be a spelling error. Apparently, leave a single letter p off a sentence in Latin and you go from "he was martyred" to "he was roasted". May just have been beheaded, which does seem more likely than a barbeque.'

Mrs Haggerston crossed herself at the thought. 'Have you quite finished?' she managed, white with suppressed rage.

Amber came up the front path just in time to hear the words 'beheaded' and 'barbeque' in the same sentence. Stevie almost pushed Jack out of the way as she raced to put her arms around her wife. Amber was considerably shorter than Stevie and slight, which usually made Stevie feel like a giant. Now she clung on as if she would never let go.

25

'Oh my god, I thought something had happened to you,' wailed Stevie, hugging Amber and stroking her hair. 'Where have you been? I've been sick with worry.'

'I'm so sorry,' soothed Amber. 'I got caught up and then I've been calling.'

Stevie patted her pocket. 'Oh, I must have left it on the sofa. I'm sorry.'

Jack moved to hug Amber before pulling back and almost shrieking, 'Oh my god, what is that smell?'

Stevie now noticed that Amber's uniform was covered in dried blood and unidentifiable fluid.

Stevie's voice rose in panic. 'What the hell happened? Are you OK? Is that blood?'

'Yes, but I'm fine. It's not mine,' Amber replied calmly, looking down at her dishevelled state. 'Mostly amniotic fluid.'

'Oh dear Lord,' managed Mrs Haggerston, who no doubt could not recall ever being this close to someone else's bodily effluence.

Amber looked up at Stevie. 'I'm so sorry, Stevie. A woman decided to give birth outside Screwfix in the shopping mall. I was off duty but, you know – she went into full-on labour literally as I was passing. I couldn't just leave. There was no time to think. I couldn't even text. And then the bloody car wouldn't start for ages.' Amber pulled back from Stevie and held both her hands. She squeezed them and looked her straight in the eye. 'I'm all right! You know what it's like sometimes. I'm so sorry I missed going into the house with you.'

Dorothy gave a slight chuckle before holding her hand up and declaring, 'Can we all just take a moment to enjoy how pleasing Screwfix is as a birthing location?'

Amber couldn't help but smile as she raised an eyebrow at her wife and turned to look at Dorothy. 'Stevie?' she prompted.

Stevie let Amber go for a second in order to make introductions.

'This is Mrs Haggerston – she lives next door – and this is Dorothy.'

'She lives here,' added Jack helpfully.

'Well, we bought the house from her,' explained Stevie, 'but she hasn't—'

'Gone?' said Amber, who was quick.

'No,' agreed Stevie.

'Well, either we're having a fun training event for all the emergency services,' Dorothy said brightly, 'or you must be Amber.'

Dorothy turned to Stevie, saying, 'You're right. She's a catch.'

It was true. Amber was beautiful, with dark skin and blond-tipped curly hair. Matched with Stevie's more robust figure, pale face and very straight steel grey hair, they made a handsome couple.

Jack was still thinking about St Lawrence. 'Where would you get a barbeque that big?' he asked Dorothy.

'She doesn't know anything about it!' said Mrs Haggerston through gritted teeth.

'I don't know. It seemed like quite a lot,' commented Jack, who had been gripped by the exchange.

Mrs Haggerston tried to get onto a firmer social footing. She looked at Stevie.

'Why are you still here?' she asked. 'This is not a police matter. And we certainly don't need a medical person. She's clearly not dead.' Mrs Haggerston could barely look at Dorothy.

'Not so far, no,' agreed Dorothy. 'Although if there is any uncertainty we could get a second opinion.'

Stevie felt as if she were having an out-of-body experience. Amber took charge.

'OK, let's just try and sort this,' she began. 'I am Amber. I am a paramedic. I mention this in case anyone is actually having some kind of mental health episode and needs help. None of this makes sense. This is Stevie. She is a police officer but that is not what she is here. She is here because she is also my wife, and together *we* have bought this house. To live here' – she looked at Dorothy – 'by ourselves. No offence to anyone who thought they might also live here.'

Mrs Haggerston looked pale. 'Your wife? What do you mean, your *wife*?'

'God almighty,' exploded Dorothy. 'They've only been here two minutes and even I've got the hang of it. Both Stevie and Amber have a wife, who happen to be each other,' she explained impatiently.

Mrs Haggerston looked appalled. She crossed herself, muttering, 'And are you friends of Dorothy?'

'A question which I feel at some point may require a longer answer,' murmured Jack.

Dave and his mate appeared on the path with a sideboard.

'Where do you want this?' they asked in a kind of Greek chorus.

'Sitting room,' answered Dorothy, waving them in before continuing calmly to Mrs H, 'Having a wife means you are not a lonely old bugger like yourself.'

Dorothy turned to Jack as if he might be the most interested and gestured to the flabbergasted neighbour, saying, 'She calls herself *Mrs* Haggerston, but no one has ever seen a Mr Haggerston. I've been here for ever and I don't think there was one, but if there was, he is long dead and buried under that bird bath in the back garden shaped like Notre-Dame.'

'No!' exclaimed Jack, clapping his hands. 'Notre-Dame! The cathedral? Next door?'

Dorothy nodded with a grin.

Jack almost gave a little leap of excitement. 'Sounds fabulous!'

'Jack!' said Stevie sternly. She was really struggling to find a moment to join the conversation.

Mrs Haggerston was beside herself. 'It is not a birdbath. It is a bird *feeder*,' she hissed.

Dorothy crossed herself and muttered how sorry she was for the error. Jack was incandescent with delight at this correction.

'A bird feeder!' he cried. 'The birds must be enormous and blessed, obviously. Let's go look now!'

Whether it was lesbians moving in or the insult to her bird feeder that proved too much, Mrs Haggerston gave one of her clearly trademark harrumphs and departed. Everyone watched her go. There was a brief silence before Amber turned to Dorothy.

'Dorothy, we never met but I gather we bought the house from you.'

'Yes!' replied Dorothy cheerfully.

'Hmm,' replied Amber. 'I don't mean to be rude, but did you want to go as well?' she asked.

'Did you want me to go?' asked Dorothy, looking frail and tearful.

'Well,' said Amber finally, 'it is ... traditional.'

Dorothy nodded. 'I'll get my things,' she said quietly.

Just then Dave and his removal friend announced that they had finished bringing everything in, but rather spoiled the delight of that statement by wanting payment in cash. Jack's phone rang.

'Hello? Who? Agnes? Oh yes, of course. Be right there.' He smiled at Dorothy. 'Got to go. I'm on shift at the Onion. You know, the pub across the way.'

Dorothy nodded as he left, and Stevie went to find an ATM.

*

It was some time before Amber and Stevie were finally alone in their new front room. The place was filled to capacity with boxes.

'Are these all your books?' asked Stevie, peering at them.

'Don't be silly,' smiled Amber, 'I think there's also some in the kitchen.'

Stevie grinned and took Amber's hand, leading her out to the hall. They stood outside the adjacent doors leading to the dining room and sitting room, and Stevie nodded sagely and said, not for the first time,

'I do think we should knock through. I made some plans which . . .'

Amber reached for Stevie and gently pulled her close. 'We can do whatever you want, my love. This is our home. Just you and me.'

'And a dog! I'd like to get a dog,' enthused Stevie. 'Now that we're finally alone . . .'

The happy couple looked at each other and frowned in the same moment.

'Dorothy,' they both declared.

Neither of them had seen her for a while. She wasn't downstairs. They looked in the small kitchen at the back and saw that everything had been washed up and neatly put away. Stevie led them up to the first floor and they looked into the small room where Dorothy had first been found. She was fast asleep on the sofa. Stevie started to speak but Amber put her hand on her wife's shoulder and held her back.

'It's late,' Amber said gently. 'Past nine. We don't know if she has anywhere to go.'

'You're soft, you are,' grumbled Stevie.

'And that is why you married me,' replied Amber tenderly. 'Can you find a pillow?'

Stevie gave a slight sigh and went to look while Amber went into the front bedroom and came back with a blanket which she gently placed over the sleeping old woman.

Stevie returned with a small pillow in rainbow stripes. 'There's only this,' she said. 'I think we got it at Pride when you wanted to sit on the ground and have a picnic.'

'It's fine.' Amber gently lifted Dorothy's head and placed the pillow for her to rest on.

'Amber!' began Stevie. 'We can't . . .'

Amber stopped her. 'We'll deal with it in the morning,' she said firmly. 'Let her sleep.'

As they left the room Amber went to shut the door. Stevie stopped her.

'No, don't,' she said.

'Why not?' asked Amber.

'She won't be able to leave.'

4

So far nothing had gone to plan but Stevie was sure all was not lost. She finally found time to get out of her uniform and into a pair of jeans and a flannel shirt. She was annoyed to find the bedding in a box marked 'crockery' and made the bed while Amber showered off the day's adventure. Stevie opened her duffel bag to produce a bottle of champagne and two Vera Wang Love Knots Gold Toasting Flutes which Jack had given them as a wedding present. She unwrapped the glasses carefully and placed them on the windowsill, covering the surprise with a sheet hung as a temporary curtain. Amber appeared in checked pyjamas, smiling and yawning as she got into bed.

Stevie smiled at her, saying softly, 'I'm so glad you're OK.'

'Where are your pyjamas?' asked Amber.

Stevie sighed. 'I can't find them. The boxes are all badly labelled. I told you I should have done it myself.'

'They were not the most expensive removal people,' said Amber, and then laughed.

'What's so funny?' said Stevie.

'I was just thinking Dorothy will know where they are.'

Stevie managed a half grin.

'Turn the lights out and come here,' instructed Amber, holding out her arms.

'I got champagne,' said Stevie, moving to the window and drawing back the sheet.

'You are lovely.' Amber paused, wondering whether to mention the towels, but decided against it. 'Why don't we have it tomorrow when we have the place to ourselves?' she suggested.

Stevie looked at the celebratory bottle on the windowsill. Amber was right. It could wait. They had a lifetime to look forward to in this house. A light rain fell against the window. Stevie looked out across the square. They were home. This was it. Married life began now, in this moment.

Stevie turned out the lights and, not even bothering to get undressed, nestled into Amber's embrace as her eyes adjusted to the dark. A small rivulet of light from a street lamp made its way onto the floor. Stevie's eyes became accustomed to the shadows and she took in the walls, the floor, the ceiling of her new home. She sighed with a mixture of contentment and anxiety and murmured, 'I'm sorry it all went wrong. I'm worried nothing will be where it's supposed to be. My floor plans got ...'

'It'll all work out,' soothed Amber. 'We're here now. That's all that matters.'

Stevie nodded and stayed in Amber's arms. Her wife's embrace made her feel safe and protected. For a while they didn't speak, didn't need to until Amber kissed Stevie on the head and said,

'It's been quite a day.'

'I was sick with worry,' admitted Stevie.

'I'm so sorry ...' Amber paused. 'Stevie? Something happened to me.'

Stevie almost jerked upright. 'Are you OK? What was it? What are you not telling me?'

'Nothing,' Amber almost whispered. 'It was just ... the baby. The whole thing was a nightmare, and I wasn't expecting it. I know we've talked about maybe in the future and all that but suddenly I just knew. It's not tomorrow, it's now.' Amber took a deep breath before saying, 'Stevie, I want us to have a baby.'

Stevie lay in the dark, thinking she had misheard. 'You what now?'

'I want to have a baby. Our baby. Soon. As soon as possible. I want ... No, I think I *need* to have a baby.'

Stevie lay in silence.

'You OK?' asked Amber after a while.

Stevie sat up slowly, trying to compose herself. 'Yes, of course. I mean, yes of course I'm OK, not "yes, of course, let's have a baby". A baby?' Stevie moved away from Amber and sat on the edge of the bed. She looked intently at Amber. 'I mean, you've mentioned it,' she said. 'We've mentioned it but we're not ... I'm not ... We haven't even moved in yet properly!'

Amber nodded. 'I know, and maybe it's not sensible but I feel like I've been hit by lightning. I promise I'm as surprised as you are. It was just this evening something happened. I don't know why but I suddenly knew I need to get on with it.'

'Lightning? Amber, you have to have been thinking about this. This is not how we do things. We don't keep things from each other.'

'That's why I'm telling you. I promise I haven't been keeping anything from you.'

'A baby? Whose baby?'

'Ours, of course. I don't want anybody else's. I'm married to you, in case you'd forgotten.'

34

'How can it be ours?'

'Lots of lesbians have babies. That lesbian on the telly – whatshername – she has kids. We have had this discussion.'

'I know, but there's so much we haven't talked about.' Stevie struggled to think of other reasons that this was not a good idea. 'What about our shifts? And what about all our plans of just being together? And what about—'

'Stevie, I know you always need to think everything through. Make a plan. All I'm saying is that something has shifted for me and I want to talk about it.'

By now Stevie was pacing up and down at the foot of the bed, lightly clapping her hands.

'This is not OK,' she muttered. 'You can't just spring this on me.'

'I sprang it on myself. We can take our time.'

'You say that like it's not really a discussion. What do you mean, you *need* a baby?'

Amber nodded. 'I don't understand it myself yet,' she answered gently and calmly. 'It came fully formed into my head. I want a family.'

'Oh, like that's a good idea! My family is . . .'

'I know. Families aren't always perfect. The dad today, he . . . Anyway, we'd do it differently. Make it work for us. You know what they say – have a logical family not a biological one.'

Stevie leant towards the bed as if she had misheard. 'I'm sorry, who says that?' She was becoming agitated. 'Nobody says that. I've never heard that. You shouldn't surprise me like this. I don't like surprises. It's not OK. It's not OK at all.'

Stevie pulled the sheet hanging at the window back a little, as if she needed air. As if the night were not happening at all. Across the way the pub lights glowed.

35

'I'm going out,' she announced.

'Babe, please?' Amber knew she should stop her but she was exhausted and there was no pleasing Stevie in this mood. 'Where will you go?' Amber whispered.

'For a drink.'

As soon as she got downstairs Stevie regretted her decision, but she couldn't face going back upstairs either. She wasn't ready for more conversation. Nothing about the day had panned out as she imagined and she was still feeling the rush of emotion from thinking something had happened to Amber. Her precious house file lay on the sideboard in the sitting room. She picked it up and flicked through it. It was incredibly well organised. Its sensible system helped soothe her. She tucked it under her arm, let herself out and walked with her usual long strides across the scrubby central space in the dark toward the lights of The Price of Onions pub. As she got to the front door she turned and looked at Number 4. Despite the continuing drizzle a low light over the front door meant you could see the house clearly.

Three bedrooms! thought Stevie. Amber wanted three bed-rooms. Why did we need so many? She didn't want to consider it but perhaps Amber had been thinking about a baby all along. It was too painful to contemplate. This was not how they treated each other. This was not the person she had married.

Stevie stood for a second, staring at the house, before pulling her phone out of her pocket and checking for messages. There was nothing new. She had thought her parents might have wished her good luck. She moved as if to ring them and then changed her mind, putting the phone away as she entered the pub.

Oddly no one had thought to hold an All Saints' Day event that evening and the Onion was, as ever, pretty empty. A faded sign over one door read 'Hotel Residents Only', suggesting the place had once been more than just a pub, but now it was without residents. Jack had been working there for the last couple of months so she had been before, but she was always a little taken aback at how enormous the old place was. The Victorians knew how to do grand and this watering hole could have been amazing, but not without considerable money and effort. The downstairs contained two gigantic public rooms. On the left-hand side Stevie could see the vast entertainment hall had no one in it. There was a small stage at one end but the faded red theatrical curtains and an exhausted-looking upright piano were all that was left of any showbusiness potential. Stevie walked through some stained-glass double doors to the second cavernous space, where Agnes, the landlady, and Jack stood behind an extensive but scuffed mahogany bar. Stevie had a choice of seat. The room was packed with a range of torn and worn chairs and what appeared to be a permanently blank specials board.

Jack smiled when he saw Stevie walk in and pulled her a pint.

'Well, that was something!' he called, laughing to himself. 'I didn't think I'd see you tonight! I couldn't believe it was Dorothy. I can't bear that I lost touch with her. I mean, she's only just across the square. She must stay indoors all the time – I haven't seen her since she stopped coming to see Nan. What time did she leave?'

Stevie sat down on a stool and waited for her beer. Jack placed it in front of her and watched her sit silently staring at it. Jack looked aghast.

'Ah, she didn't go, did she?' he said in mock horror. 'Where is she now?'

'Asleep.'

Jack hesitated before asking, 'Where?'

'On the sofa in the spare room.'

'And where's Amber?'

'Asleep in our room.'

Jack looked impressed. 'Wow, Stevie! You and the women in your life! All asleep. No wonder you came out for a few sparkling moments in the heady night life that is The Price of Onions.'

Jack banged the bar with the palm of his hand and nearly woke the only other customer. Agnes gave Jack a look and moved to place some small ceramic bowls on the bar. She was a tall, slim woman in her middling years, immaculately turned out. She wore a well-fitting dress with matching heels. Her exquisite nails clinked against the bowls as she carefully lined them up.

Stevie picked up her beer and placed her green folder in front of her. Jack eyed it and frowned.

'Oh good, we can talk about your house a bit more,' he sighed. 'I don't feel we've paid enough attention to the shower curtains.' They had been through every detail of Stevie's new home for what had felt like months. 'Shouldn't you be home in bed in your new house with your young bride and your not so young tenant?'

Stevie said nothing but her depressed mood couldn't have been clearer.

Jack eyed his old friend, trying to guess what the problem was. 'Did your mum call? She knew it was today, right?' he asked softly.

Stevie shook her head. 'She probably forgot.'

'Did *you* call *her*?'

'They'll be on the road somewhere.'

Jack was unimpressed. 'They're always on the road somewhere. This house is your dream, Stevie. They should be excited for you.'

Stevie sipped her drink and said nothing. It was clear she had something on her mind, but Jack knew better than to push her. She would speak when she was ready. Jack picked up a small rag and in a show of busyness began cleaning a spot on the wood in front of him. He did not feel he was destined for bar work so his approach was rather casual. There was a very long silence broken only by Agnes counting out loud as she placed olives in the bowls. She had not been in charge for long and was yet to lose her ambition to improve the place. The delicate olive dishes had been acquired on a package holiday to Cyprus and Agnes thought they gave the place a bit of class. Pointless really. It was not the sort of public house where people liked olives, or anyone was expecting class, but Agnes was new enough to dream.

Stevie toyed with the folder, opening and closing it.

'What is it?' Jack asked at last, his patience exhausted.

Stevie looked up and said, 'Amber wants to have a baby.'

'A baby what?' asked Jack, now genuinely trying to get a stain off the bar.

'A baby baby. Human baby.'

'I'd like a baby owl or maybe a pig,' Jack mused. 'A fur baby! Maybe I could go into the fur baby business. Didn't you want a dog?'

Stevie looked at him sternly. 'Jack! Is there any chance you could take this seriously? I need you to concentrate.'

Jack put his hands up in apology. 'Sorry.'

He turned away to pour a large glass of white wine, picked it up along with a bowl of olives and moved calmly from behind the bar to Stevie's stool. Holding the drink and the snack in one hand, he took his friend by the arm and guided her to a small table in the far corner. Jack sat down and took a great gulp of wine before gently asking,

'*Who* is going to have a baby?'

'Us, I guess. Amber. I don't want to have one . . . in me . . . you know, growing, I think.'

'Ah, a logical family not a biological one.'

The comment enraged Stevie. Twice in one evening – it was too much. 'Who says that?' she exploded. 'No one says that.'

'Yes they do,' replied Jack. 'Gay people say that. "Friends of Dorothy" say that.'

Stevie sighed. 'Yeah, maybe use a different expression.'

'Anyway, it's a thing. You're a gay.'

Agnes, who had the ears of a bat, which made her an ideal landlady, suddenly chipped in: 'I think all babies should be brought up by lesbians. I bet even that Putin would have been nicer with two mums.'

'I need to ask you something, Jack,' declared Stevie with a serious note in her voice.

Jack held his hands up in horror. 'I hate the sound of this.'

'Jack, we've been friends more than twenty years. That's a long time and I've never asked you for anything.'

'I gave you that Creme Egg one Easter when I really wanted it.'

'We were ten and you had a forward roll to do in gym class. It was like a public service on my part.'

Jack smiled and shifted in his seat. He was too large a fellow for any chair to ever quite contain him. He picked up a tiny green olive and held it in his hand before bringing it to his eye for intense inspection like a giant hoisting up a fairy for a closer look.

'I gave my mum an olive once,' he said. 'It didn't go well. All part of me living life on the wild side, apparently.'

Jack did not look wild. He looked immaculate. Even his mop of slightly red curly hair had been carefully subdued with sea salt spray. He placed the olive in his mouth with a delicateness that belied his large size.

'I'll have you know I watch what I eat,' he declared.

'Only so no one else will nick it.' Stevie and Jack teased each other with an ease born of long habit, but today Stevie was in a more serious mood.

'I want to ask you—'

'What?'

'I want to ask you—'

'Ah, ah, ah!' Jack cried out. His eyes wide with surprise he said, 'I know! You want my sperm! It's because Dorothy mentioned wanking!' and then began to choke.

'No! Will you stop being so dramatic,' ordered Stevie.

'It's the chili, you tosser,' Jack spluttered before elegantly removing the olive pit from his mouth and placing it on the side of the bowl. He appeared to be in shock. 'You want *my* sperm, don't you?'

Stevie was exasperated. 'I never mentioned sperm.'

Jack looked his oldest friend right in the eye. 'How do you even know I have any?'

'What?'

'Sperm.'

'I don't care about your ... Wait, what? You're a bloke. Isn't it a thing? It's not my specialist area.'

Jack realised he and Stevie had never really talked about this. He was curious. 'Didn't you ever ...?'

Stevie shook her head. 'You know perfectly well, no.'

'What happened with that one bloke?'

'It was a misunderstanding.'

Jack nodded sympathetically. 'Oh, I've had those. You think you're being perfectly clear and suddenly someone is all upset about playing hunt the sausage.'

Agnes had arrived beside them without either of them

41

noticing. She used her exquisitely manicured red nails to rap on the wooden table for attention.

'Oi, Jack, I've been calling you.'

Jack looked up at the elegant woman. 'Agnes, I'm trying to have a conversation with my friend. It's a pub. That's what people do.'

Agnes sighed. 'Yes, Jack, but not when they are supposed to be working. Get behind the bar.'

'All right, all right. So conventional.' Jack got up to leave but Stevie wanted an answer.

'Jack?' she said.

A young couple drifted in the door. 'Can we get a table?' they called to Jack.

'Christ almighty, do I look like a bartender?' Jack responded to them before leaning down to Stevie and whispering, 'Of course I have sperm, but I'm not having a car boot sale. I may want mine.'

'I never asked you—'

'Anyway, I'd be a terrible father.'

'I haven't asked you,' insisted Stevie.

Jack paused before his face suddenly clouded. 'Wait! Remember we did my DNA last Christmas? Oh my god, what the fuck?' Jack almost shouted, gaining a tut from Agnes. The potential patrons decided to look elsewhere and left.

'Jack!' yelled Agnes, exasperated. 'Customers!'

Jack looked up and saw no one. 'What? There's no one here!' Jack leant forward to Stevie before continuing in a rage. 'You gave me that DNA kit as a present. I thought it was to find out if I was French.'

'Well, you're not.'

'No, but I feel French.' Jack held his arms out wide and then embraced himself before almost weeping as he moaned, 'How could I have this much style and not come from Paris?' He paused for a moment as the vision of his obvious Parisian qualities passed through his head and then shook himself back to the horror of the moment.

'You were checking out my sperm! How long have you been planning this?' he exclaimed. 'You told me it was just a fun present to find out about my heritage.'

'And that's all it was. Fun. Solid stock, you are. No hint of genetic problems.'

Jack sat back down. All thoughts of work evaporated. 'Fucking farmers from Norfolk! I thought I might be related to ... I don't know ... at least the actual Duke of Wellington, not just people who wear them. I was depressed for days.' He stopped to think, his mind on farming matters. 'Maybe I could be a farmer?'

'Jack, how many jobs have you had since we left school?'

Jack slightly squirmed. 'A few ...'

'You could not be a farmer. It involves getting up early and dealing with shit. Literally. I do wish you'd sort yourself out.'

'You make it sound like I don't know what I am doing.'

Stevie sighed. 'How did you get this job?'

'He was in here drunk,' contributed Agnes from the bar, 'and started pouring drinks. Jack, please!'

'Alcohol may have been consumed,' conceded Jack.

'That is not a career plan,' Stevie said clearly before trying to calm things. 'Look, everything today has gone off in the wrong direction. I'm not asking you to be a father. I was asking ...'

Jack put up both his hands to stop her. 'A father! Ah!' For a moment Jack imagined a small child speaking to him. '"Hello, Father." I never thought about it. I mean, I could be a donor dad. OMG, sounds like an order at the kebab shop.' Now he was babbling.

'Jack, be calm. I am going to keep saying this – I haven't actually . . .'

He shook his head. 'Ask someone else. You work in the police. Don't you have databases? I cannot be the only man you can find in town. Although you would need someone with class. I do have class.' He stopped to think before asking, 'How would you even know my sperm was any good? Do they check it?'

Jack, horrified, continued. 'Oh my god, what if there's a rating? Like how bad earthquakes are? I can't wait to tell my mother. A whole new avenue of potential failure just opened for me.'

Stevie said, 'I didn't know you were speaking to her.'

Jack shook his head. 'I'm not. Just sometimes I imagine things I would say to her. It's nothing.'

Stevie put her hand on Jack's arm and left it there. They had been friends for ever. First seeing each other every day at school and then holiday visits after Jack had been forced to move away to live with his grandmother. It was a friendship which had survived time and distance. Stevie patted Jack's arm before saying gently,

'I was going to ask you about Dorothy. Amber wants us to be nice, and as you know her, I wondered if you would come over tomorrow and, well, help move Dorothy out. You know, be gentle, but then I didn't know if it was awkward for you what with the whole . . . wanking thing.'

'Is that it? You're not asking me to be a father?'

'No.'

'Just an escort service?' Jack looked crestfallen. 'Can I say I'm not surprised? You deserve someone much better to parent your child. I should have said this years ago.' His face turned solemn as he put his hand on his heart. 'Stevie Baxter, I fully accept I did not get my outfit right that first day of school when we met and I'm sorry about that.'

Stevie rolled her eyes. 'Jack, stop it. Now you're just fishing. *If I were looking for a father for my child, I cannot think of anyone better than you.*'

'Thank you.' Jack picked up the folder of papers and opened it slowly before grinning. 'That room at the top would make a great baby's room.' He flipped to the picture of the small loft bedroom at Number 4. It was sweet with a small cast iron Victorian fireplace and sash windows.

'I wondered why you got three bedrooms. That is very cute. Imagine that room with cerise accents on the woodwork,' he continued. 'Wilhelmina will love it.'

Stevie had taken a sip of beer and nearly spat it out. 'Wilhelmina?'

'My daughter.' Jack sighed and smiled at Stevie before saying, 'Oh, you can have my sperm but I'm not planning on making this easy for you.'

'I never asked for your—'

'Jack! Get behind the fucking bar!' called Agnes, who had finally lost it.

5

The next morning the happy homeowners awoke in their new bedroom. The relationship was not brand new yet both of them felt the same degree of delight they had experienced when they first met. Neither could believe their luck.

Amber traced her finger along Stevie's shoulder blade. A long thin scar ran across it. She kissed it and Stevie turned over.

'I was so frightened yesterday when you were late,' confessed Stevie between kisses. 'What if something had happened to you?'

'You know as well as I do, things happen. You're much more in the line of fire than me.'

Stevie's brow was still furrowed in concern. Amber reached out and tried to smooth away the lines.

'This is what we do,' she said. 'It comes with the job. I worry about you too, you know, but we can't ... won't live in fear. You wouldn't be able to work if you're just anxious all the time.' Amber kissed Stevie once more. 'When do you hear about the new job?'

'Today maybe.' Stevie sighed and then smiled. 'You're right. Even if I do go undercover it's probably nothing. Most likely I'll spend two nights on some street corner pretending I'm trying to score.'

They hugged each other close until Stevie whispered, 'I'm sorry I got upset. I was just surprised ... about the baby, a baby. I mean, I know we've ...'

Amber kissed Stevie gently on the forehead. 'I promise I haven't been keeping anything from you. I don't know what happened. Some bomb went off inside me. I'm sorry. I'll slow down.'

Stevie nodded before beginning, 'Last night ...'

Amber finished the sentence. '... was not the night we had expected.'

'No, I ...'

Suddenly Amber sat up. 'Sorry, darling, but can you smell bacon?'

Stevie sniffed the air. 'Yup. This house is too perfect!'

'No,' declared Amber, getting out of bed at speed.

'Dorothy!' they said together.

'We need to be firm,' said Amber firmly.

'Absolutely,' agreed Stevie, before asking, 'Can you do that?'

'It is perfectly possible to be firm and kind at the same time,' Amber assured her. 'Why do you think she is still here?' she whispered, pulling on her clothes.

'I have no idea, but I mean, we paid for the house or at least the bank did,' replied Stevie in hushed tones as they raced to get dressed, 'so she can't stay.'

'Of course not.' Kind-hearted Amber paused. 'Where will she go?'

Stevie sighed. 'Amber, we cannot worry about it. She has our money. She must be able to go somewhere. It's not our problem.'

'No, absolutely,' agreed Amber, although her face said otherwise.

'Let's start by asking her what the issue is,' suggested Stevie. 'Maybe she's confused,' she said. 'She is very old.'

'Darling,' admonished Amber gently, 'she had no problem dealing with anything yesterday.' Amber thought for a moment before suggesting, 'Perhaps she has some family we can call.'

'Family,' repeated Stevie.

They both got ready for work and went downstairs with clear intent.

'Remember – firm but kind.' Amber repeated their new mantra as Stevie squeezed her hand and asked, 'Can you hear music?'

Dorothy was sitting at the tiny table in the kitchen. She had a laptop in front of her and was looking at a website. Beside her on the floor was the small padlocked suitcase. A portable Bluetooth speaker was in full use, allowing Dorothy to loudly accompany Lizzo singing 'Pink' from the Barbie movie. She showed no sign of being several centuries old. Indeed, she was so bright and chipper that there was also no sense that she felt she shouldn't be there.

Despite wincing slightly as she got up, Dorothy steamed into a litany of questions. 'You vegetarian? You don't look like vegetarians. I do like meat. I always think vegans look weak round the knees. I shouldn't say that. It's like a social hand grenade these days.'

Both Stevie and Amber shook their heads, partly at the question and partly at being wrong-footed.

'Dorothy?' began Amber gently. 'Do you think we could we turn the music down?'

Dorothy smiled. 'Ah! Not a morning person? It's your circadian rhythms. Do you sleep? You should, although there was a Hungarian soldier who was shot in the head during World War One and never slept again. He was like that for forty years, until he died, at which point he probably did switch off. Not that we know for sure.'

Lizzo continued on her track, singing confidently that pink goes with everything.

Amber pointed at the small speaker on the kitchen counter.

'The music?' she asked.

'Of course, yes.' Dorothy swivelled round and turned it off.

Amber tried to get back to the point, although the medic in her would have liked to know more about the insomniac Hungarian.

'Not veggie, no,' she began, 'though we're not anti-veg . . .' but Dorothy was up and about sorting breakfast, saying, 'I made bacon . . . and eggs, bit of tomato to hide the cholesterol hit.'

She took a laden serving dish out of the oven. 'Paramedic and a police officer, god knows when you'll get a good meal today.'

The elderly woman bustled about getting the table ready.

Stevie looked at Amber and whispered, 'Did you know we had bacon and eggs?'

Amber shook her head as Dorothy called out, 'How about toast as well? Amber?'

'Uh . . . yes please,' replied Amber.

'Amber!' admonished Stevie.

'What?' said Amber defensively. 'I like toast.'

'Firm!' Stevie hissed out of the corner of her mouth.

Dorothy gestured to the table. 'Sit, sit!'

'Go on!' whispered Stevie to Amber, who puffed out her cheeks before saying,

'I see you've got your suitcase with you, Dorothy. Where are you—'

'I like to keep it close,' replied Dorothy as she handed a heaving plate to Stevie and then admonished herself, saying, 'Hang on! Needs a bit of parsley.' She plucked a couple of leaves from a small pot by the sink and placed them neatly on the tomato. 'There! That looks much better.'

'When did we get parsley?' muttered Stevie.

Amber tried again. 'Dorothy …' she began before pausing to gather her thoughts. There was a knock at the door. Stevie got up to answer.

'If that's Mrs Haggerston,' shouted Dorothy, 'tell her I'll come round and talk about St Winifred of Wales later.' She turned to Amber. 'There is some thrilling debate on the matter but I am going to go with it being her saint day today. Excellent story of beheading. Patron saint against unwanted advances, combined for some reason with the diocese of Shrewsbury.'

Stevie went to open up. It was Jack at the door.

'Morning!' he called cheerfully, taking no time to head toward the smell of food.

'Jack!' said Amber politely while she bit into her toast. 'I don't believe I've ever seen you with the sun still up.'

'Morning Dotty!' Jack moved to kiss her swiftly on the cheek.

'I think you came too soon,' whispered Dorothy to Jack.

'Not the first time,' he replied under his breath.

'You come for a wank?' asked Dorothy brightly. 'Have breakfast first. Get your strength up.'

'What?' said Amber.

'It's complicated,' mumbled Stevie. 'When he was young, Jack and Dorothy used to …' She trailed off, realising she was making it worse.

Jack did not need a second invitation. 'Is that toast I can smell?' he said. Dorothy immediately began preparing a plate for him.

'No bacon, thanks,' he called out, 'I'm vegetarian. Better for climate change.'

'Oh Christ,' said Dorothy. 'I don't get it,' she continued, 'all those pulses and whatnot. You shouldn't have to soak food to make it edible. There is nothing veggie I've ever had which didn't look like it had been eaten once before. Have some bacon.'

'OK,' agreed Jack, throwing himself down on a chair.

Dorothy served him a full breakfast.

'Jack!' protested Stevie. 'What happened to saving the planet?'

'Everyone knows bacon is my Achilles heel,' he replied, slightly irritated.

Jack took a large slice of streaky bacon in his hand, placed it on a piece of toast and took a huge bite before saying, 'So Amber, a baby, eh?'

Stevie tried to interrupt. 'No, Jack, I ...'

But Jack was on a mission. 'Stevie and I had a little chat. Can I just say that it doesn't have to be called Wilhelmina. What about a Victorian name? How about Abattoir? Or Avarice? Maybe it'll be twins!'

'Jack, please!' hissed Stevie.

'What is happening here?' Amber could not believe what she was hearing. She turned to Stevie in a simmering rage. 'First you are not sure, then you tell everyone?'

'Not everyone. Just Jack.'

'I mean it's hard to *not* know now,' muttered Dorothy.

'I'm from extremely strong stock ...'

'Like a really good soup base,' commented Dorothy, buttering more toast.

Jack nodded. 'Farmers maybe, but from Norfolk. Not French, but there are royals in Norfolk. I definitely have class.'

'You can see that from here,' agreed Dorothy, slipping a fresh piece of toast onto his plate.

'I could look good in a shapely riding boot,' continued Jack, encouraged by Dorothy's intervention. 'One of those posh brands with a little leather strap at the knee.'

'You want EquiClass,' said Dorothy. 'Bespoke. Italian.'

Jack smiled at Dorothy with deep admiration. 'Oh my god, you grill bacon and you know fashion! This is the best breakfast ever.'

'Do you want coffee, Jack?' said Dorothy.

'Yes please,' he replied. 'Black no sugar.'

'Oh, like your nan,' commented Dorothy. 'Do you know she ...'

Amber rose. There was not much to her, but she had a presence which was extremely commanding.

'Stop!' she declared loudly.

It worked instantly. Dorothy put her fingers to her lips to indicate she was zipping them and in a sort of pantomime slow motion moved to get some coffee for Jack.

Amber tried to be calm. 'I'm going to work. Jack, I think it is wonderful that we have moved to be near one of Stevie's oldest friends—'

'Her oldest!' he corrected with pride. He smiled, ready to engage in this delight, but Amber held up her hand in warning.

'BUT do not mistake her love for you for carte blanche to come in here, first of all to relieve any ... frustrations. Ever. And secondly to involve yourself in private discussions between me and my wife.'

'Does she mean the baby?' Jack mouthed to Stevie.

Amber ignored him and turned to Dorothy. 'Dorothy, it has been a pleasure to meet you. Perhaps we might get together for coffee some time ...'

'Do you want a coffee to take with you?' offered Dorothy. 'I can—'

'No!' declared Amber with the resolution she had promised. 'I don't want anything except to find, when I get back, that you' – she pointed at Dorothy – 'and more importantly you' – she pointed at Jack – 'are not here.'

'And me?' asked Stevie quietly.

Amber looked at her wife. 'You ... you have been hopeless, so I suggest you think of a really good way to be sorry when I get back.'

'Right.'

'Absolutely.'

'Of course,' muttered the trio in trouble.

Amber put on her coat and gathered her work bag.

'Can I just stay and see the Notre-Dame bird feeder next door?' asked Jack. 'Do the birds go in the front door or ...' Amber looked daggers at him. 'I'm going to take that as a no,' he said.

Despite her rage, Amber stopped to kiss Stevie.

'You be careful out there,' she said, as she repeated every morning.

'You too,' replied Stevie.

Amber left and there was an awkward silence.

Stevie cleared her throat. 'So, can I help you, Dorothy? With your bag?' she managed, eyeing the suitcase.

'Oh, don't you worry about that!' responded Dorothy. 'Jack and I have got to finish breakfast first.'

Jack and Dorothy carried on eating. Stevie watched helplessly as they began discussing which of them would do better on a Taylor Swift trivia night. Her phone rang. Stevie knew she ought to get on with the eviction but instead answered the call.

A bright voice the other end intoned, 'Maisie Pilkington and Associates, please leave a message after the beep.'

Stevie sighed. 'Maisie, stop it. You rang me.' She moved in to the hall so she could concentrate.

'Oh yes, sorry.' Maisie sounded flustered. 'So let's just get this sorted. You bought a house from a woman called Dorothy and she won't move out? I don't think that sounds right. I mean, that's not what happens.'

'No,' agreed Stevie, 'yet it has happened.'

'Right. Is she still there?'

'Yes.'

'Maybe you haven't been clear enough,' suggested Maisie.

'Amber was super clear, and yet . . .' Through the door Stevie watched Dorothy pour more tea for herself.

'She's still with you.'

'Yes.'

Stevie could hear typing before Maisie recited, '*On completion day you become the legal owner of the property and your seller or other occupant must move out.*'

'And if they don't?'

'Doesn't say.'

'Maisie, stop reading off a website.'

'OK, but I don't really know,' sighed Maisie. 'I haven't really covered conveyancing. It was only coz you didn't have any money and I owed you for pretending you were going to arrest my dad.'

'I did arrest your dad.'

'Oh yes, that's right.'

Stevie couldn't help but be curious. 'Maisie, what law *do* you do?'

'Well, nothing officially, but off the books drink-driving mainly. Unless you get behind the wheel of a Fiesta with a bottle of Bell's inside you, I can't really help. Points and disqualifications, that's my game. Get bladdered and I'll get you off. I seem to have a knack. I'll be honest, Stevie, I have no idea what you should do. Hold on two secs. Just taking an order.'

Maisie disappeared.

'Tea for you, Stevie!' called Dorothy from the kitchen, holding up a cup.

Stevie went back in to collect it and found Jack and Dorothy laughing loudly at an internet video of an Italian greyhound endlessly changing outfits while apparently saying, '*See this? Love it but couldn't wear it!*'

'How did you even know about this?' Jack was asking Dorothy.

She laughed. 'I'm old, not Amish. You young people spend your days doom scrolling, so I might as well try and keep up. I love all the modern tech although I am stuck with the Ender Dragon in *Minecraft*. Seems to exist within its own dimension.'

Jack looked at Dorothy with awe and opened his mouth in shock. 'Is that true?'

Dorothy laughed. 'No, you twat! I read that in the paper, and I've been saving it to say to someone. I've no idea what it means. Should have seen your face.'

Jack nodded. 'Would it be strange to say I love you?' he asked.

Stevie watched all this with utter confusion.

'I'm back,' announced Maisie on the phone.

Stevie took her tea, went into the front room and shut the door.

'Have you asked her why she hasn't left?' asked Maisie, who was trying to be helpful.

'We were going to, but Jack came round and Amber got cross about ...' Stevie realised it sounded ridiculous. 'No, we haven't yet,' she concluded lamely.

'I'd start there,' said Maisie. 'Might just be a misunderstanding

55

or she's got dementia. Strictly speaking I suppose she is squatting so you could call the police.'

'Why does everyone keep suggesting that? You know what I do for a living.'

'Oh yes. Awkward,' agreed Maisie. 'Well … maybe you should see a solicitor.'

'Oh my god, Maisie, that's what we had you for.'

'Graham might help. He's still here. Come round!' she said brightly and hung up.

Stevie looked at her phone. 'Who the fuck is Graham?'

She went back into the kitchen, steeling herself to have it out with Dorothy once and for all and was surprised to find that both Dorothy and Jack had gone. She hadn't heard the front door open and close. She had no idea where or whether it was for good. There was a note on the table written in shaky handwriting.

If anyone comes for me, anyone at all, please call me.
I won't be long.
I haven't gone far.
Dorothy

Followed by a phone number.

Stevie began pacing up and down. Two days in a row she had been this agitated and it was too much. She clapped her hands together, trying to decide what to do.

She would go to Maisie's and see this Graham guy. Maybe he was a proper lawyer and could sort something to guarantee that their lodger did not return.

She opened the front door and saw the old woman with the walking poles from yesterday, making her stately progress around the square across the broken paving slabs. Stevie could see how painfully disabled the woman was. It was clearly a regular ritual, exercise by the inch, creeping along looking nowhere but down. Slow and steady, that's the way, Stevie was thinking to herself when Mrs Haggerston appeared out of nowhere in front of Number 5 and made her jump.

'You sure?' the neighbour began without introduction.

'About . . .?' A range of things ran through Stevie's mind. 'Uh, what can I tell you? Dorothy's not dead, we have moved in . . . I am with the police.'

'You and that other woman, being, you know . . .' Mrs Haggerston could not finish the sentence. 'Never would have happened in my day. Women together! There's no need, you know. I mean, you're not a prize, but that other girl is good looking. She could get a fella.'

'I will certainly tell her that,' said Stevie. 'Such a comfort.'

'Not surprised you're friends with Dorothy,' continued Mrs H without pause. 'Just the sort of misfits she'd make friends with. There's been dark goings-on in that house, you know. The devil's work. I shan't say more but that's the kind of house it is – cuckoo. Very dark.'

6

It was Jack's turn to do the daily chores at the Onion. He was supposed to sweep the floors then take all the chairs down off the tables, check the beer pumps and tidy the glasses and bar. It was not work which suited him but then he had never found work that did. He unlocked the front door of the pub and gave a great sigh before going in. At his insistence Dorothy had walked over with him.

'I think you should give Stevie a minute,' he had told her.

Getting across the urban wasteland of the square had taken a while as Dorothy had refused to leave behind her padlocked suitcase, which had rolled uneasily over the slabs and patches of scrubby grass. She was now pacing up and down outside the small beer garden at the front.

'You sure you won't come in?' asked Jack for the third time as he flicked the lights on.

'No, no ...' Dorothy suddenly was not in a good state. She stood looking across the square to Number 4.

Jack turned and leant against the doorway.

'Do you want to talk about it?' he asked gently.

'Oh yes, let's!' replied Dorothy sarcastically. 'Let's have a really long talk about our feelings and then do some fucking mindfulness. What about some breathing lessons? Isn't that the new thing? Pay some fucker to teach you to breathe in through your fucking nose and out again as if you've not managed it perfectly well since the day you were born. What about a dreaming workshop where we can lie on the floor and dream about the money some arsehole pretending to be a shaman has shafted from us?'

Jack smiled. 'I've missed you in my life, Dotty.'

He went back inside, but instead of heading to the bar he stepped up to the stage and plonked himself down at the piano. He began idly playing chords, displaying a phenomenal lightness of touch. Dorothy appeared at the door pulling her suitcase. Tunes of all kinds were irresistible to her, and Jack's noodling drew her towards him. Slowly she inched inside and eventually arrived by his side, looking around the pub as if amazed to find herself there.

'I shouldn't have left the house,' she said quietly. 'I need to be home.'

'Shut the door, will you?' said Jack. 'There's a draught.'

Dorothy shook her head. 'I can see my house from here. I need to keep an eye on the door.'

'It's not really yours any more,' began Jack kindly but he could see that Dorothy, for whatever reason, couldn't really cope. 'Shall I make you a cup of tea?'

'Tea! Fucking cure-all for the British,' she boomed. 'There's a war on! Let's have a cup of tea! Someone's died! Tea? Fucking tea.'

'Have a drink then,' tried Jack.

'I don't drink.'

Jack crashed his hands down in a great discordant noise. 'You don't drink?' he exclaimed, appalled. 'What kind of a life is that?'

'I don't know,' replied Dorothy. 'You say you don't eat meat. I'm expecting you to pass out any moment. Staying sober seems less life threatening.'

She placed her suitcase by the piano and then stood rubbing her back as she said again, 'I shouldn't go out. I said to myself I wouldn't go out.'

Dorothy glanced across the square once more, and then with surprising strength flipped a chair from its upside-down position on a table down onto the floor. It was extremely impressive and clearly not the first time.

'Sing us a song, Jack,' she commanded. 'Something gay!'

Jack smiled and looked up in thought before beginning,

> *When you look at me*
> *What do you see?*
> *Sometimes I'm camp.*
> *Like Chaplin a tramp*
> *My wrist can be limp.*
> *My clothes I do pimp.*

Jack stopped playing to say, '*This old thing? I've had it for days.*'

> *It's not a phase or a waste.*
> *It's not wizardly based.*

In an American accent he commanded: '*Dorothy, lose the dress – but keep the shoes.*'

I'm gay, I'm a fag, an old-fashioned Nancy,
A queer, and a homo, a tiny bit prancy,
A fairy, a poof, I'm light in my loafers.
I've had actors, builders, a couple of chauffeurs.

He stopped again and said in his US twang, '*How do you know you're not attracted to women if you've never been with one? Oh I know, honey, I know.*'

Jack repeated the words '*I know*' very loudly in song, played a couple of huge chords and finished with a massive crescendo. Dorothy laughed and applauded wildly.

'I meant gay like happy, but you know, whatever. When did you get so good?'

'Many years of my nan, me and a keyboard in a tower block with uncertain lift service. I can play whatever you like. Bit of Bach' – Jack twiddled the keys in a light classical way – 'Wagner!' – he illustrated something much louder and then announced, 'Light tunes of the thirties and forties.' The piano trilled away under his adept fingers.

'Does your nan like the gay song?'

Jack looked directly at Dorothy. 'That,' he declared, 'is not a song for my grandmother. She is four hundred years old like yourself but much more' – Jack pretended to play some light classical air – 'refined.'

'Thanks!'

'For her I play this.' Jack began to play an old song absurdly fast. It was all about mares eating oats and lambs eating ivy but sung so quickly it made no sense. Dorothy hadn't heard it for years but lyrics have a way of lodging in the brain. She sang along until they were both out of breath and laughing.

She looked at Jack and smiled, grateful for the musical

interlude. He had been a lovely teenager and she remembered him well.

'Does she not know about you?' she asked quietly. 'Your nan?'

'That I'm a giant woofter?' Jack emphasised the words with a resounding chord. Dorothy nodded.

'No,' confessed Jack, tinkling two tiny treble notes as accompaniment.

'Why don't you tell her?'

Jack continued gently underscoring as he spoke.

'Because I am all she has. Well, apart from chronic rheumatism. She has me and rheumatism, every grandmother's dream. What she doesn't need is to worry about me when she is gone. The lonely' – Jack played a mournful chord – 'sad' – he played another – 'bachelor.' He began pretending to weep and moved into some Rachmaninov with such passion that his body shook like a blancmange.

'So, how long you been single then?' Dorothy asked.

'Wow,' said Jack, stopping playing for a moment to turn to her. 'You just fire away at whatever you like, don't you?'

'I'm old,' replied Dorothy, 'I haven't got time to piss about. I've got long-life milk that'll outlast me. What do you want me to do? Pretend I'm some decrepit granny who sits about doing needlepoint and worrying about doilies and antimacassars? Antimacassars! When did we stop being anti macassar?'

Jack was in a thoughtful mood. He had forgotten what it was like to talk to Dorothy. It was nice. He couldn't remember why and when she had stopped visiting.

'I haven't had a partner for a very long time so yes, I'm single. Not because I don't get offers but because I won't just settle. The trouble is I want what Stevie and Amber have. I want a house and a husband but every time I meet someone, they're weird or all they want is sex or I freak them out by talking about commitment.'

'Maybe don't mention it on the first date?'

'I don't know how you find someone,' continued Jack. 'I hate the dating apps. I haven't got the right body. I don't have a six pack.'

Dorothy looked at his lovely round body. 'More like a party keg,' she commented.

Jack laughed. 'I forgot how charming you can be,' he said before beginning to tinkle a small romantic song on the piano. 'I just want to meet someone and *boom*, you know it's your forever person, just like Stevie did with Amber.'

'How did they meet?'

'Stevie got stabbed in some sort of fracas and Amber took the 999 call.'

'So much better than an app.'

They sat in companionable silence for a while until Jack asked, 'Why don't you want to leave the house?'

Dorothy hesitated before answering. 'It's complicated.'

'Do you mind me asking? I feel we can ask each other anything.'

Dorothy looked at Jack. 'OK, how did you get so big just eating vegetables?'

'Chips and cheese.'

'Together?'

'Mostly.'

Dorothy thought about it. 'Doesn't sound too bad.'

7

Maisie lived and worked from a shabby flat in the centre of town, opposite the bus station. The tiny one-bed was directly above the GOAT Pizza shop which stood for Greatest Of All Time but was open to misinterpretation. Maisie was on the phone when she opened her door and beckoned Stevie to come in.

'Uh huh,' Maisie said to the caller, 'and did you want extra cheese with that? OK, two secs . . .'

She picked up a knife and banged out a series of taps on a large pipe which ran down through the kitchen counter to the take-away below. Stevie started to speak but Maisie held up her hand until the sound of taps in reply came echoing through the pipe.

Maisie nodded to herself and then finished her call by saying, 'You can pick up in ten.'

Stevie shook her head. 'Are you doing pizza orders? At breakfast time?'

Maisie shook her head and mouthed, 'It's not *really* pizza and I don't *do* the deliveries.'

Stevie put her hands over her ears. '*La la la*,' she sang. 'Police officer. Can't hear you!'

'Stevie! It's fine. I just take the calls. You know they can't have a phone since that business with the—'

'I've told you, they could get a burner phone and leave you out of it. Oh my god, I'm helping with drug deals.'

'It's not drugs, it's *pizza*. I need you to understand it is *pizza*! And we have talked before about you coming here dressed like that.' Maisie waved at Stevie's uniform in disgust.

Just then a man with a suitcase appeared in the kitchen. He was wearing a suit which shone with over-use.

'Teraz idę,' he said as he laid £40 on the counter. He caught sight of Stevie in her uniform and almost ran from the place.

'Who's that?' asked Stevie, bewildered.

'My Airbnb guest.'

'Airbnb? You only have one bedroom.'

'Yes, it's not ideal.'

'Maisie, you'll never finish law school at this rate.'

Maisie sighed. 'I know, but the whole lawyer thing is complicated. Oh my god, there's exams and studying cases, blah blah blah. It's actually quite boring.'

Stevie began to wonder if all this was worse than she thought. She and Amber had only bought the house by the skin of their financial teeth. Maisie had assured her there was nothing complicated about the paperwork and that she was 'very nearly qualified'. Amber had been right. The cheap packers and movers were one thing, but they should never have penny-pinched on a solicitor. She sat down at the tiny kitchen table whispering with deep dread, 'Maisie, what the hell is happening? Did Amber and I even buy our house?'

At that moment a thin man with an equally slim handlebar

moustache appeared in the doorway of the kitchen wearing nothing but a pair of faded turquoise Calvin Klein Y-fronts. He had a surprisingly high-pitched voice.

'I can assure you that the papers are all in order,' he declared.

Stevie had never seen him before. 'Listen, Calvin ...' she began.

He smiled winningly before correcting her: 'Not Calvin. Graham.'

'Yes, I ...'

Maisie smiled broadly as if this were all a rather lovely encounter at a cocktail party. 'This is Graham. He is qualified.'

'For what?'

'Graham, this is my cousin Stevie.'

Graham was a man on a mission. He got a mug down from the cupboard, turning away long enough for Stevie to see that his ancient underwear had a large hole in the rear.

Stevie took Maisie to one side and whispered, 'Y-fronts?'

Maisie nodded before realising her cousin was less than pleased. 'Oh, yes,' she replied comfortingly. 'Trust me, you don't want to see him in boxers. That's a very loosely packaged item.'

'No,' replied Stevie, 'I was thinking maybe trousers ...' but Maisie had moved to put the kettle on.

'I've had a look at your case.' Graham banged his mug down by the kettle and snapped the elastic of his Y-fronts with all the bravado of a gunslinger squaring up for a fight. He reached for a pile of papers under an open box of cereal and wiped a ketchup stain off the top page.

'Eddie Killeen. Sixty-five. Drink driving ...' he began.

'No, next one,' said Maisie, sorting a tea bag.

Graham rifled through the papers before he found what he was looking for.

'Dorothy Franklin ... of 4 Grimaldi Square?'

Stevie wanted to say that she couldn't concentrate with a legal counsel in pants but her shift was soon, and she needed to crack on.

'Well, yes,' she replied, 'but the whole point is that I don't want her to be *of* 4 Grimaldi Square.'

'Relation?' squeaked Graham. Perhaps his pants were too tight.

'No,' said Stevie.

Graham had greasy hair. He rubbed his left hand through it and then seemed to transfer the oil to his moustache. It was clearly part of his morning grooming routine. All the while he continued perusing the papers in his right.

'Seventy-nine. Hmm. Elderly.' He cleared his throat as if he were a judge about to pronounce on the bench, before intoning in a deep voice of experience, 'It will come as no surprise to learn that the law can be an ass. Getting rid of someone who is living in your house against your wishes is not as easy as you might think. So the first question is: are her care needs being met at home?'

'What?'

Maisie's phone rang and she went off into the hall to take a pizza order.

'I don't know,' Stevie said. 'She doesn't seem to have any needs but more importantly she doesn't seem to be at home. She can't be because it's my home. Mine and Amber's.'

'I see. Tricky,' agreed Graham. 'Well, what was her last known address?'

Stevie just knew this was not going to go well. '4 Grimaldi Square,' she answered.

'And where is she now?' asked Graham, who seemed at least to be a methodical man.

Stevie sighed. 'Number 4 Grimaldi Square.'

'And you say she is fine?'

'Yes.'

Graham put down the papers and looked straight at Stevie. 'I'm very sorry Miss, or is it *Mrs* Baxter?'

'Well I . . .' began Stevie.

'Ah! I see the ring, *Mrs* Baxter.' Graham gave a slightly unpleasant grin as he looked at her left hand and declared, 'Lucky fellow, *Mr* Baxter.'

Winking! He was winking! Even dressed as he was and talking to a police officer, Graham thought he could charm any woman. What was Maisie thinking? Stevie shut her eyes, hoping to unsee him for ever. He didn't notice but carried on, pleased with his compliment to her.

'Well, *Mrs* Baxter, forgive me but I'm afraid I can't see what the problem is.'

Stevie was ready to scream. 'Oh my god. She's not my family. She's not my anything. She has to leave.'

Graham was confused. 'But I thought you said she lives there?'

'She used to live there. We bought the house from her, and we moved in, but she failed to move out.'

'Uh-huh.' Graham looked as though he had understood. 'Does she want to go?' he asked.

'No, I don't think so,' said Stevie. 'She shows no sign but usually—'

'So it would be against her wishes?'

'Well I imagine so but . . .'

Maisie came in and stopped the conversation by banging on the pipe for a moment. She waited for the reply before turning to Graham to give her own two pence worth.

'Can't social services do something?' she asked.

'Well, a social worker can decide to move someone into a care home against their wishes or their family's wishes,' agreed Y-front man, 'if their care needs are not being met at home. Is she a risk to the safety of others living in the home? Is she incapable of deciding about her own care?'

Stevie thought about Dorothy. There was nothing incapable about her.

'No, she's fit as fucking fiddle. She just won't go.'

'Well, hmm, unusual. You could apply to the court for an occupation order, but there are certain criteria. Her housing needs would have to be met. She'd have to have enough money. The court would consider if she'd behaved badly, how her health was, safety, wellbeing. It's called a "balance of harm" test. I mean, if she's got nowhere to go then it might be tricky.'

'She doesn't have a legal right. It's my house.'

'So a squatter.' Graham was appalled. 'You should have said. Bloody hippies.'

'No.' Stevie took a deep breath. 'She's just an old lady.'

'With nowhere to go?' Graham was incredulous. 'What a shame. What is the world coming to? Imagine if that was your own mother.'

'I'd hate that if I was old,' echoed Maisie. 'Nobody wanting you.'

Stevie was exhausted. The three of them sat in silence for a moment before Graham started up again.

'You could get an eviction notice,' he offered. Stevie's face brightened until he added, 'But that can take years.' Once more Graham stroked his moustache. 'I mean, her age, she might die before you get it done.'

Stevie gave up and went to work. She was on a double shift, so she took a pizza with her.

*

When Amber arrived home from her long day she came in slowly, and stood in the hallway, listening. She knew Stevie wasn't due back till much later so the silence was a good sign, however Amber was hungry and exhausted and overwhelmed by all the boxes that needed unpacking. She put down her bag, stepped over a pile of clothing and walked through to the kitchen. Neither she nor Stevie had had time to find the local shops so she knew there wouldn't be anything to eat. She sat down at the kitchen table, put her head down and began to weep. She had been a paramedic for years now, but some days were too much. There was a light step on the stairs. Dorothy. The soft tread, the faint hint of lily of the valley . . . but the tears had well and truly set in, and Amber could not stop; she was all out of her morning rage. Dorothy almost reached out to touch her back, but instead she said softly, 'Come on then, you're hungry.'

Amber, her head in her hands, could hear Dorothy pottering about and before long heard a plate being placed on the table. She looked up slowly. Dorothy was sitting quite still opposite her.

'Shepherd's pie,' said Dorothy. 'Comfort food.'

It smelled wonderful.

'I know I shouldn't be here,' began Dorothy, 'but—'

'Did you say shepherd's pie?' asked Amber.

Dorothy nodded as Amber picked up her fork and tasted the food. It was delicious.

'I make it with lamb and beef mixed,' explained Dorothy quietly, 'and then a blend of potatoes and cauliflower for the topping. I think it makes it more interesting.'

'It's like velvet,' murmured Amber between forkfuls. Slowly she ate and the warm food calmed her.

'Tough one?' asked Dorothy.

Amber nodded and tears welled up again in her eyes. She

70

couldn't talk about it. A car accident. A badly injured baby. One day birth, the next near death.

Amber ate until she had finished the plate. She put down her knife but left her right hand on the table. Slowly, so incredibly slowly, Dorothy reached out and gave it the smallest squeeze before immediately letting go. It seemed to do them both good. Dorothy could not recall touching anyone in years.

'I do want to have a baby,' said Amber.

8

'Thanks for the shepherd's pie last night,' said Stevie. Amber, checking herself in the full-length mirror awkwardly propped up against the wall, was wishing it and everything else in the house was sorted. Stevie put her arms around her from behind and looked at their reflected faces.

'I can't say I mind you going all domestic on me. I thought you only opened tins, but I have to confess, this is what I dreamt about. A real house, proper dinner, finding you in my bed when I'm tired. I don't know when you went shopping or what you did to the potatoes, but they were . . .'

Amber turned in Stevie's arms and slightly bit her own lip.

'Velvety?'

'Yes.'

'It's cauliflower. Potato and cauliflower.' Amber paused. 'Dorothy made it.'

Stevie did not let go as she asked evenly, 'In our house?'

'Yes.'

'Of course she did,' sighed Stevie, dropping her arms and moving to sit on the edge of the bed. 'Did you talk to her?'

Amber shook her head. 'No, I ... It wasn't a good time. I thought you were going to.'

Stevie took a deep breath. 'I did try, Amber. Maybe I need to see a better lawyer. There was this guy at Maisie's but he ... he was a bit ... pants.'

'Pants?'

'Yes. It turns out it's really hard to get rid of someone. I know it's weird but there doesn't seem to be an obvious legal way out.'

Amber finished getting ready, saying very lightly, 'She's very nice, Dorothy, and ... I like her.'

'You like everyone.'

'We don't have the full story. There must be something that happened to make her stay. Maybe some trauma or—'

'What is happening here? I thought you were all about being firm. Ambs, for once could we not analyse someone's behaviour and just agree that we don't like it?'

Amber moved to the door. 'Let's just stay calm. We'll start with simply asking her when she is leaving and see what she says,' she said.

'Yes,' agreed Stevie, 'and then, I was thinking we could just ... lie.'

'Lie?' Amber raised an eyebrow at her insanely honest wife.

'Yes. I think we should tell her that we are knocking through downstairs ... which we are, so it's not, you know, a *complete* lie, we're just not doing it *soon* because we've got no money. Anyway, it'll be a lot of dust and she's old so ...'

'She has to go for her own sake,' concluded Amber.

'Yes. For her health. We could be worried about ...'

'Her health,' agreed Amber.

There was quite a loud thump from above.

'What the hell was that?' Stevie got to her feet and headed upstairs to the small loft room, the third bedroom.

The room was not yet in use and had yet more unpacked boxes of books in it. The conversion had been done some years ago by installing walls around the room to a height of about three feet, above which they sloped up to the apex of the roof. A cupboard door in one of the low walls was open to a storage space. A cry could be heard from within.

'Dorothy?' called Stevie.

'I think I'm stuck.'

'What?' Amber had come in behind Stevie and went into practical mode. 'Stevie, your phone! The torch!'

Stevie pulled her phone from her pocket and shone the light into the eaves. Dorothy had crawled in there on all fours and was now completely wedged in the small space.

'Yup, definitely stuck,' confirmed Stevie.

Dorothy's stifled request was nonetheless clear. 'Can you grab my arse and pull?'

'No, I am not grabbing your arse,' replied Stevie, but in the end she had no choice. It was that or leave Dorothy in there. She grabbed Dorothy's haunches and hauled her out. Amber helped her rest against the wall. Dorothy had a slight cut over one eye but otherwise seemed unshaken by the experience. In fact she was rather bright-eyed.

'It's still there!' she exclaimed excitedly. 'No reason for it not to be, I suppose.'

There was no question that Amber had softened a little toward Dorothy since the shepherd's pie.

'What is?' she asked gently as she ran her hand across Dorothy's forehead to check the cut. Dorothy looked up at her

74

and smiled. It was the second time they had touched each other and somehow it now felt fine.

'The cot,' replied Dorothy. 'It's been there since the seventies and I suddenly remembered. Will you get it, Stevie?'

Stevie hesitated. 'Uhm, Dorothy, the thing is, we were going to ...'

Dorothy's lip trembled and for the first time she seemed a little frail. Almost her age. 'Please?'

Stevie looked at Amber, who nodded towards the open cupboard door as if the subject of Dorothy leaving had never crossed her mind. Stevie shook her head in despair as she got down on her hands and knees and crawled into the storage space. Moments later she emerged backwards, pulling a large object wrapped in plastic and an old grey blanket. Dorothy clapped her hands at the sight of it. Stevie pushed several boxes out of the way with her feet and laid the thing in the middle of the room. Dorothy immediately got on her knees to take the wrappings off a beautiful baby's crib, a white wicker basket covered in matching linen with exquisite lace edging. Dorothy was sobered by the sight.

'Oh it is lovely,' she said quietly. 'I remembered it as lovely, but you know ... you forget sometimes.'

'Whose is it?' asked Amber, as she ran her hand admiringly along the basket's edge.

Dorothy smiled. 'It was never used. Now it's yours, Amber. And you, Stevie. I want you both to have it. For the baby. It'll be perfect in here,' she continued, smiling. 'It was always going to be perfect in here.'

The three of them stood looking at the infant's bed in silence before turning to go back downstairs. Amber was last to leave. As she got to the doorway, she looked back at the cot in the middle of the room. Suddenly it was no longer just a space at the top of the house. It was the baby's room. She felt quite giddy.

Back downstairs, Stevie was determined to see the morning's plan through. Dorothy went ahead to the kitchen, where she busied herself opening the oven and removing an earthenware dish.

'Dorothy,' began Stevie.

Dorothy turned and grinned at her. 'It'll be a lovely nursery, that top room,' she said.

'Yes ... we ... Amber and I haven't ...'

'Baked eggs with spinach and tomato,' said Dorothy, putting the delicious-looking food on the table. She reached for plates and cutlery and began setting the table.

Stevie almost clenched her fists. 'Dorothy, you have to stop cooking for us! And shopping! Who is paying for all of this?'

'Stevie!' Amber wanted her to soften her tone. 'Calm down.'

'No, Amber, it's a good point,' said Dorothy. 'Maybe you'd both feel more comfortable if we had a kitty for the food shopping. Big plate or small?'

'Dorothy!' exclaimed Stevie. 'We're not going to have a shared ...'

Dorothy looked up. 'You not hungry?' she asked.

Stevie tried to be gentler. 'No, I mean, yes, but you have to stop cooking in here, in this house. You have to ... move out because—'

'Oh, I almost forgot. We've had a postcard!' interrupted Dorothy brightly as she went to pick up a card from the kitchen counter. 'Came this morning.' She held it out and squinted at the picture. 'It seems to be a caravan park.'

'Yeah.' Stevie took the card and looked at it briefly before putting it down on the table. Dorothy appeared to be waiting for an explanation. 'Mum and Dad,' Stevie said. 'They're retired. They caravan. All the time. Well, motorhome. They sold their house.'

Amber lowered her voice as if she were impersonating some man.

'We drive the Coachman Travel Master 545. Eight metres long. Bit of a beast. Needs a C1 driving licence. Not for everybody.'

'So they spend their time going to caravan parks?' asked Dorothy, laying full plates on the table and indicating they should start. 'What do they do when they get there?'

Amber and Stevie obediently sat down to eat.

'Mostly Dad spends his time calculating the shortest route to the next place so he can save petrol,' said Stevie.

'And your mother?' asked Dorothy.

Stevie realised she had never really thought about it. All she could come up with was, 'Mum likes to make butterfly cakes.'

'Butterfly cakes?' asked Dorothy.

'You remember? We used to make them at school. Fairy cakes but you cut the top off and turn them into butterfly wings. She does them with pink icing, except on St Patrick's Day when they have a laugh with green.' Stevie picked up the postcard again and examined it. It looked like all the other ones she had ever received.

'Dad likes to send a card from each place. I'm supposed to keep them for a ... uh ... book he wants to write.'

'About caravan parks?' asked Dorothy.

Stevie took a huge mouthful of the excellent food.

'Yes,' Amber replied, 'it's going to be called *King of the Road with Malcolm "Camper" Baxter.*'

Dorothy sat down and took the postcard.

'Does he know that the word "camper" can be open to interpretation?' she asked.

Amber gave a slight snigger.

'A bit like people bagging Munros or knocking off all the Wainwrights in the Lake District, Malcolm wants to do all the caravan parks,' Amber elaborated. 'If you meet him, he'll explain it. In great detail.'

The picture on the front of the card showed half a dozen caravans in a large open space. There was no sense of where they might be in the world. Dorothy examined it more closely.

'It says Billericay. What is there to see there?'

'I don't think that's the point,' sighed Stevie. 'He's a "vanlifer". Not my word. They used to just go for holidays but now he's retired they live full time in the motorhome, so he bought a really big one but it's huge and can't go anywhere other than a massive field, so that's it really. It's too big to go into most towns and ...' Stevie trailed off.

'He's doing all the sites in *The Caravan and Camping Guide*,' added Amber helpfully.

Dorothy had never heard of such a thing. 'How many are there?' she asked.

'That accept caravans?' replied Stevie, '5,978. If he moves on to the tenting grounds as well there are another—'

'1,319,' Amber and Stevie said in unison.

Dorothy nodded and looked at the back of the card.

'It's dog friendly,' she pointed out. 'Do they have a dog?'

Stevie shook her head. 'No.'

'It just looks like a field. Still ... nice your family keep in touch,' she said.

Dorothy got up to put the card on the fridge with a magnet shaped like an elf. Stevie wondered where that had come from, but she didn't ask as she saw a sadness had swept over Dorothy. It made Stevie forget she had been in the middle of evicting her. Amber picked up the thread.

'As Stevie was saying, I'm afraid you have to move out be-cause ... because ... we're going to have building work done,' she explained.

There was a long pause as the lie hung in the air.

'Yes,' said Stevie, who hated not telling the absolute truth and felt mortified that it had been her idea. She felt sure Dorothy must know it was nonsense but tried to carry on. 'We're going to knock through,' she said. 'The sitting room and the dining room, so there'll be a lot of dust and you'll need to ... uhm ... not be ... here. So somewhere else. I mean ... do you have any ... family?'

Family. Just the word brought Dorothy to a halt.

'Dorothy?' said Stevie.

'Yes?' she replied, looking at Amber and Stevie and rubbing her lower back.

'Do you have any family?' Amber asked.

Maybe it was the postcard, more likely it was the cot. The three women sat there as slow tears fell down Dorothy's face.

9

'Have you ever been scuba diving?' Stevie had asked Amber early on in their relationship.

Amber smiled. 'I'm from Dudley. I don't think it's possible to live further from the water. There is a canal, but the only life forms in there are the shopping trolleys.'

Stevie had been scuba diving several times in her youth and been very taken with how it worked.

'The thing about scuba is that it can be dangerous, so you always dive with someone else. In twos,' she explained. 'So say I dive with you, then you are my "buddy". Scuba is safe as long as you pay attention. If you and I are paired together then your job as my buddy when we are under the water is to do nothing but look after me. And my only job is to look after you. Nothing else. I have to check you have enough oxygen, that you're not tangled up in something dangerous and that you get back to the surface safely. You have to do the same for me. I put you first always and in return, you put me top of the list. I really like that, and I think we should do it on dry land.

I mean every day. When we're married. I'll be your buddy and you be mine.'

And they had stuck to it. Both going out of their way to give the other the larger slice of cake, the better cup of tea, the choice of programme on TV. Sometimes it was a little silly. They could sometimes stand in a doorway for several minutes, each trying to let the other go through first, but that just made them laugh. The buddy system had stopped any of those arguments about taking the bins out or clearing hair from the shower drain which can gradually wear away a relationship. Up until they moved into Number 4, Amber and Stevie had not been the sort of couple who really argued. Stevie planned everything ahead so any troubles could usually be foreseen, and Amber was a peacemaker by nature, which was often the more helpful trait in finding a way forward.

But nothing had prepared them for dealing with their present situation.

It was Amber who had put her arms around Dorothy when she cried, leaving Stevie patting her hands together with anxiety. In the end she got up and almost ran out to the back garden, where Amber found her walking up and down in extreme agitation. The pacing didn't take long; the shed kept getting in the way.

'You have to calm down,' Amber began.

'Why didn't you just tell her the truth?' Stevie almost shouted.

'I'm sorry,' replied Amber, taken aback, 'I seem to remember lying was your idea.'

'Yes, but you didn't have to go along with it. You're nicer than me.'

'I never wanted to mention the building work,' Amber fumed. 'That was you. Now we have to do it and we don't have the

81

bloody money to knock through, you idiot. We *have* to get a new car and—'

'Who are you calling an idiot? I'm not the one that sat there with her, eating bloody shepherd's pie.'

Dorothy was standing in the doorway. She nodded, deep in thought.

'What kind of car have you got?' she asked, which was not the question that seemed to be in the air.

'Ford Focus,' replied Stevie without thinking. '1.6 hatchback, 2009.'

'Mileage?' persisted Dorothy.

'Thousands,' muttered Stevie. 'I think the odometer's been round twice. It's a shitheap.'

Dorothy took all this in before saying quietly, 'I know this is all wrong. I'm sorry. This is not what was supposed to happen. You see . . .' Dorothy appeared to be about to tell them something but then shook her head at herself. 'I will help you. I promise.'

She turned and walked back into the house.

'Oh god, now I feel terrible,' cried Amber.

'No you don't,' declared Stevie firmly. 'This situation is not OK.'

Amber could not let it go. 'Maybe she has nowhere to go. Imagine.'

'How has she got nowhere?' asked Stevie. 'She's got half a million pounds of our money. I get that you are kind and I love that about you but what the fuck is wrong with us? She just has to leave. It's not like someone left behind an old carriage clock and we can't decide whether or not to keep it. Enough!'

Dorothy had disappeared into her room with the red sofa. The door was ajar as Amber went past and she thought of knocking, but her hand hovered in the air motionless. She didn't know what to say.

Both she and Stevie hated that they had had words, so it was in distressed silence that they both left the house and went their separate ways to work. They were each on shifts which kept them preoccupied but they texted their way toward peace. Then, as chance would have it, they both finished about the same time, so they agreed to meet at the Onion for a quick glass of wine before going home. When Amber arrived, she found Stevie outside the pub, looking across the square to their house.

'Is she in?' asked Amber.

Stevie shrugged. 'There is a light on downstairs,' she replied and looked sheepish. 'I'm sorry about this morning. I don't know why I suggested lying. I wasn't upset with you, just myself.'

'I know.' Amber smiled. 'I know everything about you.'

Stevie frowned. 'And I thought I knew everything about you. I was knocked out by the baby thing. I knew we might one day but ...'

Amber took both Stevie's hands and held them tight. 'I promise I wasn't expecting this ... To feel this strongly. It came out of nowhere. I can't explain it. The only other time this has happened was when I met you. We won't do anything that we don't agree together. Now, let's not fight any more. Promise?'

'Promise,' said Stevie.

'Whatever happens we can figure it out.'

They kissed each other and walked into the pub.

Jack was on duty behind the bar. He waved as they entered and they saw Agnes coming through from the office at the back looking at her phone.

Agnes smiled at the women and said, 'Jack, I've had an enquiry from some clowns.' Then added, 'For a party.'

'Uh-huh,' said Jack and turned to her, smiling. 'So Agnes, what's going to happen now is I am going to tip my head to one side and smile like this, as if what you said seems entirely reasonable.' Jack tipped his head and pointed to his smile before saying brightly, 'Clowns, you say? How many clowns?'

Agnes re-checked the email. 'It doesn't say.'

'A car full? I mean, with clowns that could still be quite a lot.' Jack grinned at Amber and Stevie. 'We've had a clown enquiry. Please don't think this place is anything but hipster.'

Agnes read from the email: '"We wish to pay tribute to the great clown Joseph Grimaldi, for whom your square is named."' Agnes looked up at the others. 'Is that right? Is it?'

Jack shrugged. 'No idea. Maybe. Not everywhere is well named. There's a place in France called Anus, and two in Scotland named Twatt.'

'How do you know something like that?' grinned Stevie.

'He never bloody works,' answered Agnes.

'Dorothy told me,' said Jack. 'I can't remember why.'

'I'll give them a ring,' called Agnes. 'Man the bar, Jack.'

Jack looked around the almost entirely empty pub before smiling again and yelling after his boss, 'I'll shout if I can't cope.' Now he turned his full attention to his friends. 'And to what do I owe this late honour?' he asked.

Amber looked at Stevie with pride. 'Stevie's off on her new job tomorrow!'

'The undercover thing?' asked Jack, delighted, before glancing around the bar. 'Should I even know?'

Stevie smiled sheepishly. 'It's fine.'

'Congrats!' said Jack. 'It'll be great. I've done some of my best work under cover.'

'I don't think that's quite the same,' laughed Amber.

84

'Well, drinks are on me,' Jack declared cheerfully. He poured two large glasses of white and then got himself one. He could almost hear Agnes sigh as she glanced out the office door and saw Jack go to sit with Stevie and Amber. He shook his head at her. Clowns! Fucking clowns.

'Right, ladies,' Jack began, banging his hand down on the table as if to call a meeting to order.

'Ladies?' enquired Stevie. 'What is this, the WI? Are you announcing a jam competition?'

'These olives are nice,' commented Amber.

'Stevie, Amber, if you don't mind,' said Jack. 'I have something to say.'

'I have never known you not have something to say,' murmured Stevie.

Jack tipped back on his chair and took a deep breath. 'While we are celebrating ... Amber, I know you don't want me involved in your personal affairs and that is not what is happening, but I wanted you to know that I have been thinking about this baby thing. I admit I was a little taken aback when you first mentioned it but Stevie, I am your oldest friend. There is nothing you could ask me for that I wouldn't willingly give, apart from actual cash because I don't have any. I think you two would make brilliant mums so ... Of course, I won't be involved in any discussions, but I want you to know that I will do whatever you want, and I don't have to have anything to do with the kid. She ... he ... they ... whatever ... doesn't even need to know my name. I would love to give you my ... whatever you need. I am here to ... uh, deliver. Which we should talk about because I am not entirely sure how that happens. I mean obviously' – he lowered his voice – 'I don't want to play actual mums and dads.'

He mimed having sex just as some builders walked in and headed to the bar.

Over the course of this speech, neither of the women said a word. But Amber had sat listening to Jack with obvious increasing incredulity and rage.

Amber stood up and Stevie half rose to face her.

'I don't know how my life has suddenly become a public free-for-all,' Amber said quietly, 'but it has to stop. I do not want to live with people I don't choose to live with, and I do not want my business discussed in the pub.'

Jack looked at both women before nodding and saying awkwardly, 'You're not ready for this chat, are you?'

'No,' replied Stevie.

'Mm-hm.' Jack stood up and very carefully placed his chair back under the table. 'Well, this has been fun, but I must get back to work.' He swiftly headed to help the men at the bar.

Stevie and Amber were left standing on opposite sides of the table.

'If I can just remind you,' Stevie began, 'as we came in we promised not to fight, and—'

'I'm going home,' said Amber. And with that she turned and left.

Stevie followed her across the square at a slight distance, muttering, 'Please let Dorothy be gone, please let her be gone.'

Stevie could see the evening was not about to improve, for it was immediately obvious that all the lights at Number 4 were on.

Dorothy was not gone at all. What was gone was a huge chunk of the wall between the sitting room and the dining room. An astonishingly large hole had appeared, and it was possible to see right through. Bricks lay scattered on the floor. Stevie and Amber stepped over them and inched into what had been the separate sitting room just as Dorothy appeared beaming through the new opening from the other side of the wall. She was wearing safety glasses and carrying a huge sledgehammer. She had attempted to cover the sofa and packing boxes in plastic sheeting but that had not held back the staggering mess. Dorothy grinned and pushed the goggles up to the top of her head.

'I am so sorry you missed this,' she declared. 'I've not had this much fun in ages. I think I had a lot more rage than I realised. I'm not sure I should have sold the house. Maybe just knocked it down!'

Stevie could not speak at all, and Amber was struggling. There was dust everywhere and a gaping wound in their home.

'You did this?' choked out Stevie.

'Yes!' replied Dorothy in triumph as she stepped back to admire her work. 'Think of the money you've saved! My dad did the loft extension on this place. Did I tell you that? Him and a couple of mates. They didn't have all those regulations in those days and it looks fine so I thought . . .'

Rage began to boil inside Stevie.

'I . . . I . . . I'm done. Out!' She pointed to the door. 'Out of my house! Now! Immediately!'

Amber tried to calm things by putting her hand on Stevie's arm.

'Stevie!' she warned but it was too late. The police officer determined to have order was out and there was no going back. She would be obeyed. Dorothy's coat and her padlocked suitcase were found. There was a momentary kerfuffle in the hall as Dorothy tried to take off her goggles and give them to Amber, but it was all pretty quick and silent. Within a very short space of time Dorothy was out of the house and onto the step. The front door slammed behind her.

Inside the house, the banging door caused more dust to swirl around and for a while neither Stevie nor Amber could speak nor see very well. When it settled a little they both found themselves in the sitting room, able to look through to the dining room and kitchen. Amber picked up the abandoned sledgehammer.

'Wow!' she said, feeling the weight of the thing. 'At her age!'

'She just knocked a great big fucking hole in our house!' yelled Stevie, trying to get Amber to focus on the important stuff.

'I know, but . . . I mean, look at her!' Amber was incredulous. 'What the hell does she eat to have that kind of strength?'

Stevie refused to discuss it. She refused to speak, she was so angry. She set about cleaning with intense rage. She located the vacuum cleaner and hoovered, swept and dusted like a demon. Amber knew better than to get involved. She pottered in the kitchen, made calming tea, stayed out of the way. Finally, Stevie took a breath. She appeared in the kitchen doorway.

'I don't know if we should sleep upstairs,' she said quietly, 'or even go up there. There's no way of knowing if that's a supporting wall Dorothy has knocked a hole in. I imagine it is, but we need to get someone to check.'

'What does that mean?' asked Amber.

Stevie stood looking up at the ceiling above the hole. Large cracks now ran right across the rooms.

Stevie shook her head. 'I'm not sure. I don't know how safe the house is.'

Now she began to cry. It was enough to make anyone feel sorry for Number 4. In a very short space of time it had become a shrine of tears.

'Ambs, I am so sorry about everything. I don't know how to sort Dorothy and I'll try again but I need you to know that I didn't actually ask Jack. He misunderstood and I was upset that first night. The truth is I don't know what to think about the baby and we should talk, because I'd give you anything. I just don't know about this because ... I mean, a baby is a really big deal. They're so ... needy. And now we don't even have a proper house.'

Stevie began to sob. Amber put down the tea towel she was holding and went to put her arms around her. They were standing holding each when the sound of rain broke the silence. Heavy rain. Amber tried to continue as if she hadn't heard it.

'Do you want to get someone to look at the ceiling now?' she asked.

Stevie shook her head. 'No, it's past midnight. We'll have to sleep down here.'

The rain hammered down.

'Where is she?' asked Amber.

Stevie let Amber go with reluctance and went to the front door. She opened it and by a faint street light she could just see Dorothy sitting on her suitcase in the square. She was facing the pub as the rain fell in great sheets. Silently Stevie went to fetch her. When she brought her in Dorothy was shivering and clinging on to her bag. Stevie insisted on being the one to tiptoe upstairs to get dry clothes and blankets. She would not risk her wife or even Dorothy getting hurt. No one spoke as they made the trembling old woman as comfortable as they could. She kept mumbling, 'I just wanted to help. I heard you say you didn't have the money. I'm so sorry.'

'It's all right,' soothed Amber as she wrapped another blanket around Dorothy. A fever was on the way. She had caught a bad chill.

That night they all slept on the floor. Stevie got the cushions off Dorothy's upstairs sofa and laid them out with a blanket for their old cuckoo in what had once been the separate dining room. Dorothy was not well but she still fussed about and carefully positioned her suitcase near her head before she would lie down. Meanwhile Amber and Stevie set about getting comfortable in the sitting room. The hole in the wall meant the three residents were not entirely separated. Stevie pulled the plastic sheeting off their own settee. It was their pride and joy. Second hand but still in very good shape. Deep blue velvet and not intended for overnights.

'You sleep here, Ambs,' she said.

Amber shook her head. 'Oh no, you're not doing this. I'll be fine on the floor.'

'It's only a two-seater. I won't fit. Besides, I won't sleep if you're not comfortable,' retorted Stevie out of habit but she was also beginning to shake.

'Stevie, are you ill too?' asked Amber, concerned.

'No – oh Amber, I nearly killed her,' Stevie whispered, horrified by her own actions. 'I sent her out in the rain. I mean, she's just an old lady and . . .'

'Oh, shush, you two,' muttered Dorothy from her makeshift bed.

'Oh my god,' exploded Stevie, her brief moment of regret evaporating. 'She just shushed me!'

'Sssh,' replied Amber. 'Just an old lady. She's just an old lady.'

Dorothy dropped off first and the quiet sound of her steady breathing calmed their house.

10

As luck, or lack of it, would have it, Dorothy woke up quite unwell. In fact she was ill for some time. High fever and at times a little delirious. Amber insisted on getting her a put-up single bed from Argos to go in the dining room.

'Where's her own furniture? She must have had furniture,' Stevie protested but her wife was clear there would be no discussion.

'We can't worry about that now. She can't sleep on the floor. Not at her age,' she said.

'At her age?' fumed Stevie. 'Can I remind you this is the woman who knocked down most of our house?'

'One wall!' objected Dorothy quietly.

Amber and Stevie went out into the garden to argue. There seemed to be less and less space to be alone.

'It's enough now!' raged Stevie.

Amber nodded. 'I know,' she said soothingly, 'but she's not well. And look, now you're going away for a couple of days ...'

Stevie sighed. She had been so excited about the new job but now she didn't want to go. She hated leaving Amber. 'Maybe three. I don't know. I don't know what the operation is exactly and ...'

'Let me get her better and I'll have figured something out by the time you get back.'

Amber reached up and stroked Stevie's cheek, saying,

'I know this is not how you thought all this would go, but I have to help her get better. It's what I do. Remember when we met? Who looked after you?'

'You did,' replied Stevie reluctantly, because she knew where this was going.

'And what about the guy who stabbed you before tripping over and banging his head? Who looked after him?' persisted Amber.

Stevie paused like a child being reminded of the rules. 'You did.'

Amber took a breath. 'Dorothy is not what either of us expected when we bought this place but there's not much in our lives which follows an easy script. Let me sort it. I'll speak to her and find an answer by the time you're back, I promise.'

Stevie smiled at her beautiful partner. 'I really love you.'

'Yeah, you do,' Amber smiled back, pulling Stevie into her arms. They were a good team but anything requiring extra patience was, yet again, best left to Amber.

Over the next few days alone with Dorothy, Amber was surprised to find how quickly they settled into a quite comfortable evening routine. Amber would unpack more boxes and then they would eat together. The young paramedic was not much of a chef and when she was on her own usually resorted to tinned soup.

'Don't you cook?' asked Dorothy on the second evening facing a liquid diet.

'No,' confessed Amber. 'My mother has many skills but none in the kitchen. Food is just fuel to her, so I never learnt growing up and haven't bothered much since.'

'Christ. OK. What you got?'

Amber looked at the tin. 'Minestrone.'

'Right. Here's what you do.'

From her bed Dorothy taught Amber how to make even the most boring tinned soup into something more interesting. She instructed her in turning toast into croutons. How to add a dash of chili sauce and a few fresh spinach leaves. It was Amber's baby steps into cooking, and she was surprised to find she enjoyed it. The following night she 'freshened up' the soup and then sat beside Dorothy's bed for a chat. Dorothy had really caught a nasty chill and was slow to recover. It had gone to her chest. Amber wanted to use the time to try to figure out Dorothy, but Dorothy was too tired to talk so Amber read to her instead. It made them both happy.

Stevie had never been away before and Dorothy was nice company after a long shift.

Amber and Stevie had settled on Grimaldi Square through price not passion. Jack was their only real connection with the place. In fact, it had been his suggestion to look in the area.

'Dead cheap coz no one really wants to live there,' he said.

It wasn't a great selling point, but it was a first step on the ladder. Stevie got a transfer into the area and then Amber followed. They did like it, but so far it was not yet their home patch. Away on her undercover work, Stevie realised Dorothy being ill in the house was also weirdly comforting for her. She was indeed sitting on a street corner pretending she wanted to score and everything about it was odd. She hated being away from her beloved and had to admit she liked the idea that Amber was not alone.

'What's the soup tonight?' asked Dorothy from her small bed on the fourth of her evenings with Amber. She was sitting up, propped on many pillows.

Amber looked at the tin. 'Chicken and sweetcorn.'

'I always think sweetcorn is pointless,' commented Dorothy. 'Straight in and out again. Try adding noodles.' She was reading the evening paper. 'What do you think about this? Big story: "Are clip-in hair extensions really worth it? Our beauty team investigates."'

Amber glanced over at the accompanying pictures. 'She looks nice.' She pointed to one of them.

'She looks vacuous,' scoffed Dorothy. 'Our beauty team investigates! What the fuck is wrong with the world? Surely if you are a journalist that means you want to write. Who grows up wanting to investigate hair extensions?'

Amber smiled as she divided the tin of soup into two bowls. She put them in the microwave and got out a sprig or two of parsley to serve on top.

'Never just serve white food,' Dorothy taught her. 'It never, ever looks fresh. Add a sprig of something green and you'd be amazed what you can get away with. Fools the fuckers every time.'

Amber brought over her creations and sat down cross-legged on the floor beside the bed to eat.

'Postcard from California Chalet and Touring Park today!' Dorothy said brightly, holding up the card, which featured another photographic display of caravan parking.

'Where is that?'

'Wokingham.'

Dorothy read from the back of the card. 'It's one hundred acres, established in 1931 as "California in England" by a presumably poorly travelled man called Alfred Cartilage. One of the main features is a swamp called Longmoor Bog. I don't know which I am more obsessed by – the surname Cartilage or the bog.'

'Any message?' asked Amber.

'It says, "Dear Stevie, Hope you're all settled in. We'll see you at Christmas! Mum and Dad".'

Dorothy looked at the card once more and then put it down on top of a large, very tatty book which lay beside her bed.

'Are you reading to me tonight?' Amber asked, pointing to the book.

'Oh, that? No, that's my "Saint of the Day" book. I check it every night before bed.'

'Are you religious, Dotty?'

'God, no. I mean, just no. Leave God out of it. I bought it to annoy her next door. She loves her saints and I'm beginning to see why. It's mad. Such good stories. When's your birthday?'

'May 22nd.'

Dorothy thumbed through the ancient tome. 'Ah!' she said with glee. 'Excellent one. Saint Rita.'

'Could you précis?'

'Yes. Rita. Fifteenth-century Italy. Grew up wanting to be a nun but you know what parents are like. Can't read the room so they married her off to an ill-tempered man with whom she had two sons. Old grumpy husband kept feuding with another family. She decided to work on making him more agreeable and it was fine for a bit. He calmed down his rivalry but sadly the other family didn't get the memo and killed him. Surely, you ask yourself, Rita was now free to go to the convent?'

Despite herself Amber was caught up in the ancient soap opera. 'Was she?' she asked as they ate their soup.

'No!' replied Dorothy dramatically. 'No, she was not because her sons were very cross about daddy dying and they started to plot revenge. This was a terrible idea because they might do something stupid and get sent to hell, so she prayed and prayed. It sort of worked because they didn't get their own back but instead both died of dysentery, which apparently is not sin related. When she died she became patron saint of mothers, abuse and impossible causes, a trio which so often goes unremarked upon.' Dorothy closed the book. 'I read this stuff at night, and I think my life is not so bad after all.'

Amber smiled. 'And is there not something of the feud in your own relationship with Mrs Haggerston?' she asked softly.

'Thank you, Dr Freud,' muttered Dorothy, turning her attention to the soup.

'How long has she been next door?'

'Fifteen years of unrelenting misery. Mrs *Haggerston*.' Dorothy almost spat the name in disgust.

'Do you not even call her by her first name?'

'I don't believe she has one. I believe she turned up on her first day of primary school registered as Mrs Haggerston.'

She and Amber sat companionably sipping until Amber softly said,

'Dorothy, how long have you lived in Grimaldi Square?'

'All my life.'

'Always in this house?'

'No.'

'You know you can't stay here, don't you?'

Dorothy nodded. Later Amber reflected that even though she wanted to find out more about Dorothy, instead she seemed to end up speaking about herself. Stevie wore her whole heart, mind and soul on her sleeve but Amber was not inclined to give a lot away, so this was surprising.

'I get that home is hard to give up,' Amber said. 'I miss the place where I grew up. I miss my mum.' Amber sat in a reverie before saying the single word 'Dudley'.

'Your mother is called Dudley? How did that work out for her?' asked Dorothy.

Amber laughed. 'No. It's a place. In the West Midlands. I grew up in Dudley. My mum is called Faith.'

'She must be proud of you.'

Amber gave a slight smile. 'Absolutely. She is nothing but supportive, and she never says a word but there are days when I feel she has to crush her disappointment.'

'The gay thing? Surely not? Who cares?'

'No, not at all. She often says she wishes she had the urge herself. No. The paramedic thing.'

'Oh yeah,' scoffed Dorothy. 'Paramedic. That's just one up from pickpocket. You're practically on the streets. You're kidding? It's a fantastic job.'

'My mother works in medicine. I was supposed to be a doctor. When she sees me, I live and breathe not being a doctor.'

'Only child?'

'Yes.'

'Accident?'

'No, design. I think I was more of an experiment than a child. My mother—'

'Dudley.'

'Indeed. She's lovely, really lovely, but she's also ... formidable. A genius, probably. Super smart and very driven. Her own mother grew up in care. What's the expression people use? She

97

bounced around the system, struggling to survive, hardly any education, so when she became a single mum there was nothing going to stop her daughter. She pushed and pushed, my mum, and eventually she went to Oxford. Considering where she came from, her achievements are remarkable. I'm so proud of her. Anyway, she reached forty and was ticking off life's accomplishments. She decided she needed a child and went out to get the best sperm possible. My father is also very clever, but the deal was always that he would be nothing to do with me. I met him a couple of times. I suppose I was curious, but now he lives in America. He told me he had been "happy to help" and I knew we weren't going to have a real relationship. It was fine because I had Mum and she was enough. She loves me. She really does and I love her, but my childhood was . . . intense. She hot housed me.'

'Hot housed? Like tomatoes?'

'Reading, writing, flash cards – endless flash cards – art galleries, museums . . . I was going to outshine not just all the other kids but her and every teacher she had ever met who told her she would never make it. And despite all that effort, here I am. Paramedic. Para – "next to" or "not quite". She never says but I feel she's disappointed. The thing is, we're actually very alike. We both want to help people, just in different ways. She does it on paper and I do it in person.'

'And what is this paper stuff that she does?'

'Runs a lab working on the world's first wearable magneto-encephalography system.'

'Not a moment too soon. I hate the unwearable ones.' Dorothy finished her soup. 'Sorry, is that a good thing?' she asked.

'Of course, what else would it be? Potentially life changing. I expect we'll be in some hall soon, listening to her say "I accept this Nobel Prize . . ." She's working on understanding things like epilepsy, neurodegenerative disorders like Alzheimer's, mental health conditions such as schizophrenia.'

'Excellent series of health options,' commented Dorothy. 'At least I'll know where to go.'

'Her work is her life and I admire that. Now I'm all grown up she feels she can just get on. It means she's not always ... present. I was supposed to follow in her footsteps. Instead I just put plasters on things.'

Dorothy looked at her and said firmly, 'That's not all you do and you know it – and I expect she knows it. Is she coming for Christmas? Will I meet her?'

Amber shrugged. 'Always hard to say. She knows I want her to but there's some conference in Helsinki, a book to finish ...'

Dorothy was impressed. 'That's a lot.'

Amber smiled. 'Yes, except there is always a conference, always a half-finished book.'

Dorothy put her bowl down on the floor and leant back against the pillows. 'Delicious,' she said, 'your best tin-opening to date.' Amber grinned as Dorothy looked at her. 'Do you want to be a doctor?' she asked.

Amber bit her lip and gave a small sigh. 'Maybe ... I don't know. I never applied. I think I lack the confidence. My mother is very impressive.' She looked at Dorothy and frowned. 'How do you do this, Dorothy?' she asked. 'I'm trying to find out about you, and you always get me treating it like my own therapy session.'

Dorothy nodded. 'Minicab driver.'

'What?'

'Last ten years I worked as a minicab driver. I don't do it much these days. You'd be surprised how well the drunks behave with an old git behind the wheel. I think they worry I can't see. Which

99

I can't really, but once they realise I can drive then they relax and start telling me everything. I'm no threat, you see. I even took the odd wrong 'un home. No doubt been up to all sorts. None of them hope to get lucky with me either. You'd be surprised what I've heard or pretended not to see. One-eyed Billy left a gun in the back once.'

Amber laughed. 'One-eyed Billy? Do you call him that to his face?'

'No!' cackled Dorothy. 'Well, unless I'm standing on the side where he can't see.'

Dorothy continued to surprise.

'Nice job, minicab,' she continued. 'I don't sleep much anyway.'

'When did you stop doing that?' wondered Amber.

Dorothy shrugged. 'Well, I've not been out this week.'

'I meant sleeping.'

Dorothy clapped her hands once, loudly and firmly like a full stop to the conversation. 'Are we finishing that book or not?' she demanded.

Amber smiled. 'I did finish it, but you fell asleep. Miles died, remember? Such an interesting story. The question is, was there really a ghost or was it all in the governess's mind?'

'I think it can be both,' answered Dorothy quietly. 'I think you can have ghosts in your mind.'

By the time Stevie returned Amber and Dorothy had spent four happy evenings chatting away, reading and cooking, and there appeared to be no moves whatsoever to alter any living arrangements. It was late as Stevie opened the door to find her wife and the interloper curled up watching TV like two cosy roommates. BBC2 had run out of original material and were showing Dorothy's favourite film, the 1945 black and white classic *Brief Encounter.*

'Hi!' called Stevie from the hall, pleased to be home.

'Shush!' said Amber and Dorothy together.

The television was on very loud.

'The train now arriving at platform four . . .'

Trevor Howard was just leaving for the last time. Stevie sat down as Celia Johnson uttered her thoughts with a clarity of diction rarely heard any more.

'I felt the touch of his hand on my shoulder for a moment and then he walked away . . .'

The agony, the near attempt at suicide, swelling Rachmaninov filled the small room. Many tears. No one said a word until all the credits had rolled.

'Oh Dorothy,' sighed Amber.

'I'm an ordinary woman,' replied Dorothy dramatically. *'I didn't think such violent things could happen to ordinary people.'*

Stevie smiled. 'Well, I see you two have kept yourselves cheerful.'

'Oh Stevie! I loved that film!' declared Amber, full of emotion. 'Sometimes the oldies are still the best, right, Dorothy?'

Dorothy smiled and flung her arms out. 'Living proof!' she declared.

Amber was a romantic soul, and her heart was full of the un-requited passion of the film. She had missed Stevie and hugged her so tight it seemed she would never let go.

'You're late back.'

Stevie heaved a sigh. 'The car finally died. Just outside work.'

'Fuck,' responded Amber.

Stevie carried on. 'I had to get it towed and then catch the bus. It is very, very dead.'

'Have a word with next door,' suggested Dorothy. 'She knows a man who can work miracles.'

Dorothy was well enough to get up and make tea. She then climbed into her bed while Amber and Stevie sat on the sofa. The three of them talked through the hole in the wall, with both Amber and Dorothy asking questions about Stevie's new job. She hadn't really liked being undercover but thought it would be disappointing to say. She let the murmurs of concern lap around her like soothing waters. Neither Amber nor Dorothy mentioned any possible future plan about accommodation and Stevie was too tired to bring it up. They all went to sleep, Dorothy in her small bed, Amber on the sofa and Stevie on the floor. The next morning, when Dorothy was in the downstairs loo, Stevie, a little sore from the night, asked if there had been any movement on their lodger leaving but all Amber said was,

'It's just not as easy as I thought.'

'I see that,' replied Stevie. 'Actually, I had a chat with the sergeant while we were waiting for things to kick off and he had some excellent ideas, so I did make one or two calls ... I might have a plan.'

The three of them had breakfast and Stevie, seeing Dorothy was better and up and about again, cleared her throat in preparation to put a new idea into motion. All she had managed was 'Dorothy ...' when the doorbell rang.

'How is it that every time I try to sort this nonsense out there is someone at the door? Hmm?' Stevie looked at Dorothy accusingly. 'We don't know anyone here and yet the doorbell keeps ringing.'

Dorothy shrugged. 'Nothing to do with me.' Except it was. Amber looked out the front window, where she could see that a beaten-up bright green panel van had pulled up. On the side of which was emblazoned *Bobby Twoc—s Builders*. A large piece of black gaffer tape had been placed between the C and the S to cover over part of the name.

'Oh, they're here!' cried Amber with delight.

'Who are here?' wailed Stevie.

'The builders. To sort out the hole in the wall. Dorothy told me about them. They're local. Been here forever.'

'Bobby Twococks!' bellowed Dorothy as a man appeared in the doorway.

'Hello Dotty!' he replied, giving her a great big bear hug. 'Where the hell have you been?'

Dorothy grinned. 'Keeping to myself.'

'Yeah right,' sniggered Bobby. 'That's like J.Lo deciding she's had too much publicity. You all right?'

Bobby was a bullish sort of fellow. He looked like an archetypal British builder – white, balding, mid-forties with trousers which struggled to stay up below his bulging waistline – but there was nothing run of the mill about Bobby.

Dorothy looked out at the van with its partially concealed sign. 'You not using Twococks any more?'

'Not sure, Dots. Just trying Twocs for a bit.' Bobby had a strong local accent and he spoke with care. Although he had left school at fourteen he was sorry about that. Later in life he had discovered that he liked learning, so when he did know something he adopted a slightly professorial way of speaking. He turned to Stevie and Amber to explain.

'Bobby Twococks. It's my surname. Twococks. Old English name with a long history of existence in both house painting and domestic service, as it happens, but sadly, some of the ladies find it a bit aggressive. A bit ... what do we call it, Dorothy?'

'*Toxic masculinity*,' replied Dorothy instantly.

This was not where either Stevie or Amber, now silenced, had

103

thought the conversation would head. Bobby took this as them being impressed. He nodded confidently at his new employers and winked to indicate that he was on side with whatever they might be thinking.

Bobby concluded his musings on his surname by sighing and saying, 'Fact is, some women just find Twococks too much.'

'Even that sentence is ...' began Stevie, trying to regain control, but Bobby was on the move.

'Right! Here's the team. This is Young Justin.' A pale, thin whippet of a boy who looked about twelve arrived wearing headphones and a faraway look. He put down a large ladder and immediately sat on the sofa and took out his phone.

'I inherited him. I mean not actually. I don't think that's a thing, is it? My neighbour's boy. When she died of cancer, I felt bad. Not my fault, obviously. Cancer ... in her lady parts,' he concluded, mouthing the last few words of the sentence. Bobby gave a slight cough as if he had said too much, then carried on. 'But you know how it is. Took him on. *Social* responsibility. Nice lad but between you and me not sure he's got what it takes. You need stamina in this game. Not entirely confident he cares enough about the work.'

Everyone now looked at Young Justin, who was watching and listening to something on his phone while his fingers constantly twitched. He appeared to have even less interest in the building trade than Bobby suggested. Stevie looked at Amber questioningly.

'I think he's fine, but I'll keep an eye,' muttered Amber.

'And this is Arun,' Bobby announced as a rather round, not terribly tall Asian man entered laden with equipment.

'Right then, let's be having you ...' Bobby said, marching straight in to survey the damage.

Dorothy smiled at him. 'Are you not going to say, "Dear oh dear, who's done this then?"' she asked, almost laughing.

Bobby sucked on his teeth and shook his head.

'No need. I'd know your work anywhere. Impressive, Dotty. I can't tell you how many times my dad told me the story of you taking that window out in the pub.'

'Wasn't my fault that donkey got in there in the first place.' Dorothy and Bobby left the tale of the pub window and the donkey hanging in the air as they both stood looking at the hole in need of repair.

'Knocking through,' Dorothy explained. 'Just thought I'd get it started.'

'Not bad.' Bobby looked up at the large cracks above. 'Well, apart from nearly bringing the ceiling down. Bittersweet. Bittersweet. You want to come work for me. Do better than Young Justin. Eh, Young Justin, what d'you reckon to that?'

Bobby picked up the sledgehammer Dorothy had used and handed it to Young Justin. For a brief moment the lad looked up from his phone as Bobby thrust the hammer at him. He took the extremely heavy tool in his free hand and then immediately dropped it on the floor with a massive thud.

'Blimey, careful,' exclaimed Bobby, 'or we'll go through the floor and all.'

'Could everyone stop playing with the sledgehammer, please?' said Stevie.

'It *is* impressive, though,' commented Amber. 'I mean Dorothy using that thing.'

Amber could see this was not the moment for Stevie to be in awe of Dorothy, so she quietly went to begin round two of 'British builders arriving', which is to make the tea.

So far Arun had said nothing but had been systematically

viewing the scene of destruction. 'RSJ,' he finally stated. It was his only contribution but clearly the right one.

'Indeed, indeed, Arun,' agreed Bobby, 'and not a moment too soon.'

'When can you start?' called Amber from the kitchen.

'How much is it going to be?' Stevie asked.

Bobby went over to the wall and looked through the hole to the kitchen before replying to Amber,

'"The beginning is always today." You know who said that?' he asked.

Amber looked shocked. 'Mary Shelley? You've read her?'

Bobby grinned, delighted. 'Indeed. Indeed.' He turned back to the others to give a short explanation. 'Amazing woman. Her mother, Mary Wollstonecraft, tried to end her life by jumping off Putney Bridge. Saved by a couple of boatmen. One of them took her home to his wife, who persuaded her of the "rightness of living". Imagine that. An almost certainly illiterate boatman's wife helping the cleverest woman in Britain to live. Hard to believe.'

'Bobby goes to evening classes,' explained Dorothy.

'Tuesday evenings. It's the only night I'm free, so some of the subjects have been surprising. I said I'd do anything that didn't involve wearing lycra. Take what you can get. Dorothy's idea. My wife said I was an ignorant slob and Dot said she was absolutely right. Needed to up me game.'

Amber appeared with the teas and Bobby took a mug before sucking on his teeth and saying, 'Changed my life. I'm doing Introduction to Women's Studies this year. Fascinating. I'd no idea you ladies have had such a tricky time.'

Dorothy shook her head and turned to Amber, saying quietly, 'He's only just started.'

'Can we talk about costs?' Stevie tried again.

106

Amber couldn't help but be drawn in. 'What does your wife think about this?' she asked Bobby.

'Oh, she left me for the cheesemonger at the market but ... bonus' – Bobby tapped the side of his nose confidentially – 'she gets a very good price on the cheddar ... I do love a bit of mature ...' winking at Dorothy as he said before concluding, 'And for me, I had no idea: turns out the ladies down the pub love a bit of feminist rabbit. Works every time.'

Dorothy pretend-slapped Bobby across the back of the head. 'God, you're a work in progress.'

Stevie stared at Bobby and then at Dorothy before saying to Amber, 'I think I'm having some kind of collapse. We have been here a week. One week! We've only just unpacked and got things sorted and then the wall ... What is happening?'

'When can you start, Bobby?' asked Dorothy.

Bobby grinned. 'As it happens, Dorothy, it's your lucky day – and when wasn't it?' He winked at her again. 'We've had a little cancellation so ... kick-off asap. You'll want this sorted before Christmas.'

'Is he any good?' whispered Amber to Stevie. 'I mean, when are builders ever available?'

Stevie looked pale. 'Yeah, but Christmas!'

Bobby was looking at them, smiling, and Stevie felt awkward. 'My parents are coming! For Christmas.'

'Best crack on then,' he said. 'How would they feel about a house with a hole in it? And the dust has ruined this hall carpet too. Shame. That'll have to go.'

Stevie began to mutter something about silver linings just as Mrs Haggerston appeared. She had been in the middle of one of her daytime soap operas and soon let it be known that she'd been torn between following the storyline and the arrival of a builder's van next door.

107

The mess at Number 4 was so shocking that she briefly forgot about her beloved soap family. Immediately she had a list of questions. When it would be sorted, how much noise was there going to be and was planning permission required?

'Permitted development,' said Arun quietly, causing Mrs Haggerston to notice him for the first time.

'Steady, everyone,' Dorothy called out, 'mild racism incoming.'

This made Mrs Haggerston cross. 'That's not fair, Dorothy,' she said. 'I am not a racist. One of the three wise man was black, you know.'

Dorothy smiled sweetly and nodded. 'And Jesus.'

Mrs Haggerston immediately left to ring the council about unplanned work taking place in her street.

'I really need to know how much this is going to be,' Stevie insisted. 'Only our car broke down and ...'

No one was listening. Before Stevie knew it, she and Amber were living not just with Dorothy but with three men who never seemed to leave. The RSJ had to be ordered and no one thought it was a good idea to spend too long upstairs until it was in place, which meant a semi-permanent life on the ground floor. Meanwhile there was endless preparation which involved even more banging and bricks flying.

The chaos made it increasingly difficult for Stevie to bring up her new plan for Dorothy.

'Look, I've made some calls and ...' Stevie would begin, at which point someone would interrupt and ask about resident parking permits for the square or whether anyone would be in for the skip delivery. Dorothy did not move from the house. During the day her 'temporary' bed was pushed as far into the kitchen as possible to get her away from the dust. From there, when upright she seemed to be able to manage a constant flow of teas and coffees and when lying down provide a further flow of suggestions and instructions.

Before it seemed possible it was the beginning of Christmas party season, which meant Amber's shifts were full of the cuts, bruises and occasional breaks that go with excessive alcohol. Stevie found herself doing longer hours and the odd overnight as well. Their car had gone for scrap so they both had to leave earlier than usual to catch the bus. Neither woman dared say it out loud, but it was obvious that it was actually quite useful having Dorothy at home managing Bobby and his men.

She knew how to deal with them.

'Oi,' she would yell out in the midst of a jackhammer in use. 'No hot drinks on the wooden table! What have I told you?'

'Sorry Dotty!' would come a deep chorus of reply.

Dorothy and Bobby were often in the kitchen chatting when Amber or Stevie got home. One day they overheard the two of them just as Dorothy said,

'Thanks Bobby. I knew you'd help.'

'I don't like it, Dot,' he answered, 'but if it's what you want. Anything for you.'

'I can handle myself,' she assured him.

He sucked in a deep breath. 'Fair enough. You know what they say: "*To see a candle's light, one must take it into a dark place.*"'

'You quoting Ursula Le Guin, Bobby?' smiled Amber as she and Stevie wandered in.

'Possibly the greatest American writer of her generation,' he replied confidently.

Amber smiled. 'I think I told you that.'

It seemed to Stevie that Amber was no longer in any rush to get rid of their house guest, so she instead tried to enlist Bobby's help. She took him to one side.

'Not only is Dorothy not showing any sign of moving, she won't even leave the house. Couldn't you take her out?' Stevie pleaded. 'Get her used to the idea of, I don't know, other spaces?'

'Leave it with me,' assured Bobby.

The following day Jack popped in for a cuppa.

'You better yet?' he asked Dorothy as she opened the front door.

'Fit as a fiddle,' she replied.

'Don't tell them that, Dorothy,' said Jack. 'They'll have you out of here.'

Dorothy gave a rueful grin. 'I know. I am going. Soon.'

Bobby called out from the sitting room. 'That you, Jack? RSJ coming in today. I have told her,' he boomed. 'Best if Dot pops out for a couple of hours, 'less you want her hit in the head with half a ton of steel. Have a word, will you?' Bobby glanced back at the job in hand. 'Going to need a bit of elbow room in here. Oi, you, get off your arse,' Bobby yelled at Young Justin, who was sitting on the plastic-covered sofa as, yet again, he watched a video and moved his fingers in a bizarre flowing motion.

'What is he watching?' asked Jack.

'Hard to say,' replied Dorothy. 'He never speaks. I'll try nicking his phone.'

Dorothy was definitely better. Much better, so Jack did his best to lure her out of the house.

'Come on,' he suggested gently. 'Let's go see my nan. She'd love to see you.'

Dorothy almost looked shy. 'She won't want to see me. Not after all this time.'

It took some persuading from Jack and Bobby combined

110

to get her out of the house. Eventually she agreed, muttering maybe she could go because Bobby had her number and could ring if anybody came to the house for her . . .

'Much as I doubt we can manage without you, Dots, I do not want you going flying coz our Arun has been too swift shifting a metal beam,' said Bobby.

'I've told Nan you're coming,' lied Jack.

'I need my suitcase.' Dorothy disappeared into the kitchen and as Jack waited in the hall Arun came in with breakfast for the lads. Jack turned and instantly felt an odd feeling. Tingling and trepidation. It was strange. He had never felt it before and wasn't entirely sure what was happening. They were both men on the larger side and there was no way they could pass each other easily in the narrow corridor. With their eyes fixed on each other's faces, Arun backed up out the door just as Jack did the same up the hall. Then they both moved forward at the same time and almost crashed into each other.

'Sorry,' they said in the same instant.

Jack's face flushed and Arun looked awkward.

'Bacon?' asked Jack, sniffing the air and pointing to the sand-wich bags.

Arun nodded awkwardly. 'I'm veggie except—'

'When it comes to bacon,' Jack finished.

When Dorothy returned with her bag the two men were still standing facing each other not saying very much.

'Come on, Tweedledum and Tweedledee, stop blocking the hall,' she said as she bustled her way through, pulling her suitcase behind her. Arun had to brush past Jack, which took longer than anyone might suppose. Once past him he turned and smiled a half smile before going to hand out the food. Jack stood dazed for a moment before he left the house. Bobby called out after them,

'*You're off to great places! Today is your day!*'

'Wollstonecraft?' wondered Dorothy.

'I'm pretty sure that's Dr Seuss,' said Jack.

Jack and his grandmother lived in the Soros Tower, the top of which could be seen looming above Grimaldi Square. It wasn't far, just a few streets away, so Jack and Dorothy walked, with her insisting on pulling her suitcase all the way there. He offered to help but there was no talking to her about it. There was no talking to her about anything. Dorothy was unusually agitated.

'She won't want to see me,' she kept repeating.

Jack marched on. His grandmother was increasingly isolated and anything to distract her was a good idea, plus Stevie, he knew, was getting desperate. Maybe he could help all the women in his life?

Dorothy hadn't been to Soros for about five years and the decay was a shock. Built in the early 1980s, the place had once been seen as a shiny new solution to pressure on local housing. Each flat had a small balcony and communal gardens down below were supposed to provide any exercise space residents might need. The design on paper was very different in reality. For years the tower had been plagued with problems – asbestos, dangerous cladding and, lately, mould. The council had included Soros in its 'regeneration' programme fifteen years ago, with a timeline of four years for completion. It was a prediction which had slipped and slid from election to election. So far anyone in charge had resisted knocking the whole thing down because of cost. The solutions provided had been piecemeal and haphazard. For some years now residents had slowly and intermittently been rehoused. Most had gone but

112

some still called the decaying place their home. Jack's nan was one of them. He loved her beyond all measure but could not get her shifted. She stayed, so he did too.

'Surely she should have been top of the list with her troubles?' said Dorothy.

Jack bit his lip and sighed. 'For some reason Nan's decided she needs to be last out. Maybe coz she's been here the longest, but it's like living on the fucking *Titanic*.'

'Perhaps she just doesn't want to go,' said Dorothy. 'It's her home.' But Jack didn't hear.

'Our flat has been rehoming central,' he continued. 'We're like the Battersea Dogs Home for stray locals. She's been helping everyone get a new place except herself. There's still four flats in use. Four out of hundreds. It's like a fucking ghost town.'

They headed up some concrete steps past two teenagers in hoodies so focused on their attempt to get high that they didn't even look up. The much-trumpeted balconies of the apartment block had been designed with each one clad in a different shade of brown. Perhaps it had looked smart in the original drawings; now it was just miserable. Dorothy looked up and could see that whole floors had been left to rot. They passed the empty ground floor, sealed off from the public by metal shutters.

'Harry Flite and a small gang of pals live on the third,' said Jack. 'They love it. Call it Freedom Tower. Smoke dope to their heart's content and play Monopoly for reasons I can't fathom.'

They wandered past piles of rubbish and a faded notice of demolition which had been stuck to the cracked glass panel of a door. They stopped in front of graffiti-decorated lift doors and Jack pressed the button to go up.

'Ida Kovak is on floor seven. She's only been here two years. She arrived long after the demolition order, but she has stage four cancer and I think the council thought she'd be dead before they had to deal with her. She's alone and mostly too scared to answer the door. There are some Ukrainians on floor nine, who the council keep referring to the Home Office and say are nothing to do with them. Then me and Nan. Whatever they offer she says no. She says she's holding out till we get a ground-floor place with a garden.'

The lift arrived.

'Still working, then?' commented Dorothy.

'Sort of.'

'What's that smell?'

'I have a list of possibilities,' Jack replied, before the wretched lift screeched and rattled its way to the twenty-second floor, making speech impossible. At the very top of the tower Dorothy and Jack stepped out into a dingy and poorly lit corridor. Crumbling concrete framed the place. A filthy window looked out across the whole city. Dorothy stopped.

'I forgot about the view up here,' she said.

Jack nodded. 'Feels like you're flying.'

It was magnificent. Up here you could see sky for miles. Far below them, it was possible to make out the large roof of the Onion and most of Grimaldi Square, where the men were busy rebuilding Number 4.

'Makes the square seem so small,' mused Dorothy. She looked at the young man beside her. 'How long have you been here?' she asked.

'Well, Mum kicked me out when I was fifteen, so just about half my life.' Jack took a breath and enjoyed the view before adding, 'It won't surprise you that she caught me wanking.'

'All boys do that.'

'Over her signed photo of George Michael. It was her most

114

prized possession. Well, more prized than me anyway. I tried to talk to her, but she couldn't handle the gay thing at all. Ironically, her last words as she threw me out were "What would George Michael say if he knew?" Hasn't spoken to me since.'

'How could she not know about George Michael? And your nan? How is she with you being gay? She must be fine, right?'

Jack turned in a panic to Dorothy. 'Dorothy! She doesn't know! Don't tell her, will you? I'm not . . . She's not ready. She's old.'

Dorothy gave a short laugh. 'Your nan? She doesn't know? How is that possible? Anyway, she's the same age as me. You don't seem worried about me coping.'

'You're different.'

'Thanks. I think.'

'I haven't told her, and she's never asked.'

'But she can't be completely blind?' replied Dorothy. 'I mean, I've not seen her for a few years but honestly, Jack, even your clothes are practically singing Broadway tunes.'

Jack looked genuinely horrified.

'This is a perfectly nice Harrington jacket.'

Dorothy calmed him. 'Of course I won't say anything. I don't even have to come in. I could just go home now and—'

'Oh, shut it, you offensive old bat,' huffed Jack, striding off down the corridor to the flat in mock fury.

The decrepit front door had been kicked in and repaired many times with pieces of ill-fitting plywood. It was a dreadful thing, but it was a kind of magic portal for it opened up from the dank, dismal corridor into a place of glorious green. There was sunlight and there were plants everywhere you looked.

'Welcome to Oz,' beamed Jack cheerfully.

Dorothy had forgotten how wonderful the place was. An

oasis. There was fresh life everywhere. It was a small Kew Gardens in the sky. Jack's nan, Mrs Birdman – Birdie to everyone – was sitting in her wheelchair watching television.

'They found that cash in the attic yet? Feels like they've been looking for years,' Dorothy boomed, covering her anxiety as she entered.

'Is that you, Dorothy Franklin?' Birdie turned off the TV. 'What you doing here, you old loon?'

Jack went to make tea. Being of a substantial size clearly ran in the family for, apart from living up in the sky, Birdie was not well named. If she were a bird, it would be quite a meal. She had been unwell for a very long time, yet her well-filled body gave the mistaken impression of robust health. Birdie had always had naturally bright red hair. Now a box of dye from the supermarket, applied by Jack, kept her curls vibrant. Dorothy had not seen her for five years but somehow she looked the same. The two old friends smiled at each other. Dorothy sat down beside Birdie and took her hand. They sat for a while before Dorothy whispered,

'I'm sorry, Birdie. Really sorry.'

Birdie squeezed her hand. 'I'm sorry too. We were idiots,' she said, and then in a very English way neither one of them said another word about whatever had caused them to fall out. They just sat holding hands in silence for some time before Jack brought the tea.

'Biscuits,' commanded Birdie, letting go of Dorothy's hand and waving Jack away to find them.

'You know Jack's gay, right?' Dorothy asked as they watched him go.

Birdie nodded. 'Of course. Since he was about five. He'll tell me when he's ready. I'm not the one who needs more time.'

'I don't dare ask – his mum?' said Dorothy.

116

'Still a twat,' replied Birdie.

Jack returned with the biscuits and sat with the two old women. It made him happy to see them together.

'Right,' said Dorothy, getting down to business. 'What you doing still living here? Surely you should have been first to leave, what with all your medical troubles?'

'I know all the reasons to go.' Birdie pointed round the room. 'That window doesn't close, which is fine in the summer but a nightmare in the winter. It would be an easy fix if we weren't so high up. Since Grenfell everyone has been afraid of fire. We have the same kind of cladding, but the government and the council didn't immediately shift their backsides. Lots of residents had trouble sleeping, mental health problems, litter, graffiti, too many people to know who is supposed to be here, we're too poor for a porter, no safe outside space for kids, we had two people take their own lives and now they are all rehoused except us dregs, but—'

'But?'

'It is my home, Dorothy. I've been here for ever, and I love it. No one can see it now, but it was nice. I knew my neighbours. We helped each other. Used to have parties. This was our community. Now we're all spread out, it isn't the same.'

'Fine, but that doesn't explain why you are last to go,' said Dorothy.

Jack laughed. 'Nan's a pain in the arse. The council hate her.'

'I don't know if I'll ever leave. I don't go out any more. It's too hard. What is it you say, Jack? "I shall die in the clouds,"' laughed Birdie.

Eventually Birdie fell asleep in her chair and Dorothy joined Jack out on the balcony. It too was an Eden of plants. Jack picked up some secateurs and went to tend some large, leafed growth at the far end.

'Brownies or joints?' asked Dorothy. Jack looked shocked. 'Your nan may not come out here, but I've still got my legs and, unlike her, I can spot weed a mile off.'

'Brownies mostly. I give them to Nan. They really help with the pain.'

Dorothy looked at the plants.

'How long does it take to grow these?' she asked.

'About six months. Of course, if I could do it indoors then they'd flower in a few weeks, but Nan likes to pretend she doesn't know and—'

'How good are the brownies?'

'Excellent.'

Dorothy nodded. 'Go on then,' she said.

Jack was confused. 'What?'

'Let's have one.'

Jack had perfected the small cakes over some years and, as well as being 'medicinal', they were delicious. He woke his nan gently and they all had one each. Then Jack and Dorothy left Birdie to doze again and walked back to Number 4, both extremely relaxed. Some would say stoned off their faces.

Bobby and his men had gone for the day. The metal RSJ supporting the new archway between the dining and the sitting room was in place and for the first time it was possible to see how nice the arrangement was going to be. Dorothy was beyond mellow.

'I like Amber and Stevie,' she said.

Jack agreed. 'Yes. Very nice.' He was filled with love for them, and suddenly he had a genius idea. 'Let's make them a baby!'

Dorothy shushed him elaborately. 'Yes, but shush in case they hear.'

Jack looked around. 'I don't think they're here. They can't

118

hear here. Hear here. Nobody can hear here. Here can you hear.'
He kept repeating his pleasing phrases and sniggering.

'Yes,' agreed Dorothy. 'You go upstairs.' She pointed to the newly installed beam. 'It's safe now. Upstairs, and I'll stand guard.'

Jack nodded enthusiastically. 'Like the old days. I'll wank and you watch the bank.'

Dorothy looked very serious and took Jack by both arms. 'I have no idea what you are saying.'

Jack went upstairs and came straight down again.

'I need something.'

'What?'

'No idea.'

They both stood, trying to think.

'Glass or something,' Jack finally managed. 'You know, to put *it* in. The whatnot for the baby.'

Dorothy went into the kitchen and returned with a glass. Jack took it and went back upstairs to the bathroom. Dorothy stayed downstairs but not for long. She was really not together at all and now she decided she needed to be excused. The door to the downstairs loo was entirely blocked by bags of plaster. She tried to move them, but in the end decided it was easier to go up to the first floor. The bathroom door was closed and somewhere at the back of her mind she remembered to knock.

'What?' cried Jack, sounding a little more awake than before.

'I need to wee!' shouted Dorothy.

'You can't wee now! You know why I'm in here. You sent me in here, you old bag.'

'It's because I'm an old bag that I need to wee. I have a seventy-nine-year-old bladder that's not feeling too clever, and this may shock you but nothing about it is as tight as it used to be. I'm coming in!' yelled Dorothy and opened the door. Jack's face appeared from behind the shower curtain. He was standing in the bath with the curtain pulled closed. He looked horrified.

'I do not need to know that about your bladder. I'd be fine not knowing you have a bladder at all.'

'Don't be ridiculous.' Dorothy was in a rush so she headed straight for the toilet, lowered her trousers and pants, and sat down. 'Oh my god that's good,' she sighed as an astonishing stream of pee emerged from her. She was very chatty. 'Everyone has a bladder except, *ironically*, gnats! People say "I've got the bladder of a gnat" but they can't have. There's no such thing. Flies don't have one either. They just pee and poo all day long. Like a nightmare resident in a care home.'

Jack, who, living with his elderly grandmother had seen it all, instead of leaving stayed looking out from behind the dreadful seascape shower curtain.

'Your head looks like it's floating,' Dorothy noted. 'Floating away on the ocean.'

Jack stared at her. 'How do you know about gnats?'

'I wee all night long, so I take an interest in these things, and weirdly the internet does not have an age limit. I think it should. I have seen some terrible things. There's a man whose head is in a toilet. He gets attacked by robots.'

The stream of wee had stopped but Jack and Dorothy were attuned to the ways of the older body. They also both suddenly found the sound of weeing utterly fascinating. They waited in silence until another final burst hit the pan. Dorothy gave another great sigh as the pee finally stopped. Suddenly she recalled the name of the online fellow in the loo.

'Skibidi Toilet,' she said.

'Skibidi,' repeated Jack.

'It's videos with singing human-headed toilets,' explained Dorothy. 'We could never have imagined such a thing when I was young because ...' She tried to think why. 'Because we didn't have the technology and also ... we weren't arseholes.' She pursed her lips and mused before saying once more, 'Skibidi.'

They both repeated the word 'skibidi' for some time before Jack, with all the excitement of a eureka moment, exclaimed,

'There's a toilet downstairs!'

Dorothy nodded. 'Blocked.'

'The toilet?'

'The door.'

Despite the fact that she had finished, Dorothy carried on sitting as she looked around the room.

'Where is it?' she asked as Jack slowly got out of the bath and sat on the edge.

'It's definitely downstairs,' he replied.

'No,' replied Dorothy sternly. 'What you came in here for.'

Jack frowned. 'What was that?'

They both stopped to think before Dorothy burst out with,

'Baby! Sperm!'

'Sperm,' repeated Jack and then shook his head. 'Couldn't do it. Couldn't do it. That's right. I don't think we should do this without asking. They're both quite ... particular.'

'It's supposed to be a nice surprise,' said Dorothy incredibly carefully. 'If you ask someone then it isn't a surprise.'

'Stevie hates surprises.'

Jack and Dorothy carried on quietly bickering about surprises without hearing the front door open. They also didn't hear Stevie and Amber climb the stairs. Indeed they didn't know anyone was in the house until the owners of the place were standing in

121

the doorway, looking at Jack sitting on the bath and Dorothy on the toilet.

'Hi,' said Amber tentatively.

'What ... uhm ... the actual fuck?' said Stevie slowly.

'We thought it would be nice for you to come home to ...' Jack ran out of steam.

'Some sperm,' said Dorothy brightly, getting up to slowly pull her pants and trousers back up. 'It was that or dinner.' She turned and pressed the flush.

'We couldn't decide,' finished Jack rather lamely over the noise.

'What is that?' Amber pointed near the toilet.

'Toilet brush?' suggested Dorothy, grinning and still high from the brownies. 'Bleach? I love this game. What does it start with?'

Amber pointed again. A Vera Wang Love Knots Gold Toasting Flute stood on the floor. 'That is one of our best glasses. It's from our wedding. You gave them to us, Jack. What were you doing with it?'

'It was for the ... you know,' Jack said awkwardly. 'I said they wouldn't like it,' he whispered to his elderly accomplice.

Dorothy tutted, 'Oh for goodness' sake, Jack had to have something to ... uh *receive* in. Nobody wants their first child started in Tupperware.'

'Nothing but the best for Wilhelmina,' added Jack. 'Do you not think "Wang" sounds a bit like—'

'Stop now!' insisted Stevie.

Amber could hardly speak. 'Who the hell is Wilhelmina?' she eventually managed.

'Doesn't matter,' mumbled her wife.

Amber tried to stay calm. 'Stevie?' she said. 'The bedroom, please?'

Stevic nodded and followed Amber.

There was silence in the bathroom.

'Do you think they thought I was helping you?' mused Dorothy.

'Oh urgh,' replied Jack. 'Now I feel sick.'

'Skibidi,' said Dorothy.

The calming effect of the brownies seemed to be wearing off. The clue was that Dorothy screamed. Stevie knew the sound well. Everyone could hear it. If you had been at the Onion, you would have heard it. Amber and Stevie came racing back. Dorothy had left her suitcase at Birdie's place.

11

Dorothy's suitcase was entirely full of money. Brand new, shiny money. It was packed to the brim with neat ten-pound notes. A sea of cash. Stevie had gone with Jack to collect the case and had returned without him. She had insisted he stay home with his grandmother.

'Don't you want my help?' he asked slightly plaintively, knowing he had some making-up to do.

'You've done quite enough,' snapped Stevie.

'I meant well about the ... *present* for you ... the sper— I think we'd make nice babies. The more I think about it—'

'Jack, it is *not* ... *your* ... *decision*,' said Stevie, emphasising each word.

'No, obviously, but are you saying that ...'

He hadn't finished his thought before Stevie slammed the decrepit door and left.

On the way back with the suitcase Stevie had been determined to discuss Jack and Dorothy's endless interference in her and Amber's private affairs, but now the suitcase lay open on their kitchen table, and the money trumped everything. Stevie had given Dorothy no option other than to show her what was inside. Stevie and Amber were speechless.

'How much is in here?' Stevie finally managed.

Dorothy looked a little sheepish but replied clearly: 'Just under half a million pounds. Bundles of a thousand each. The woman was most particular.'

Amber was aghast. 'Wow, OK. This has to go in the bank.'

'Don't be silly,' replied Dorothy, 'that's where I got it from. I can't say they were best pleased.'

'Robbery?' asked Stevie calmly.

'No, from the house, you idiot.'

Stevie dug deep for more patience. 'Could you not call me ...' she began but Amber was trying to get a grip on things and interrupted.

'This is *our* money?'

'No!' Dorothy sounded annoyed. 'It's *my* money. You paid me.'

'Yes, but why do you have this in cash? People normally ...' persisted Amber.

Dorothy looked away. 'I don't trust anyone,' she muttered.

'You can trust us,' said Stevie defensively. 'I'm a police officer.'

Dorothy raised one eyebrow as if her point had just been made.

'Stevie, just a minute.' Amber turned to Dorothy and got her to sit down. She pulled up a chair opposite her and took both her hands. 'Dotty,' she began.

'Dotty?' exploded Stevie. 'When did you start calling her Dotty?'

'It's just a nickname. Everyone round here calls her Dotty.'

Amber tried again. 'Dotty ... Dorothy, what were you going to do with the money? Why do you have it?'

Dorothy sighed and answered quietly, 'I was going to go backpacking but now with one thing and another I really need to stay and ...'

'What?' Stevie thought she had misheard. 'Did you say back-packing? OK, I'm done here. Amber, I love that you are so nice but I'm calling a taxi.'

'You don't need to leave,' said Dorothy.

'I am not leaving!' shouted Stevie. 'This is my fucking house. You are going.'

Dorothy looked bewildered. 'Where am I going?'

'I don't actually care.'

'Well, I'll have to give them some kind of address,' persisted Dorothy.

Amber indicated to Stevie to calm down.

'Dot,' began Amber carefully, 'do you have anywhere to go?'

Dorothy shook her head.

Stevie took a deep breath. 'Fine,' she announced. 'In that case I am going to take you to a care home where someone else can be paid to *care*. 'It's not like you can't afford it.' Stevie waved at the suitcase of money. 'I already looked into it and there are several near here. One of them said we can drop in any time.' Stevie looked at her watch. 'It's half past four. Not too late.'

'I don't want to go to a care home,' said Dorothy evenly as her head was now clearer.

'No, but you don't seem to want to move out either. You cannot stay, Dorothy. Backpacking? You're clearly not well. What were you thinking? Eat Love Go Grey? What the fuck is the matter with you? Amber, do you know the number for a taxi?'

'We don't need a taxi,' said Dorothy quietly. 'I have a car.'

'You have a car,' repeated Stevie.

'Dorothy is a minicab driver,' explained Amber, as if it were the most reasonable thing in the world.

'Dorothy was a minicab driver?'

Amber shook her head. 'No. No. She still is.'

'Actually, if you call a taxi round here it might just be me who gets the call, which could be awkward,' mused Dorothy.

Stevie was officially unable to cope. She put her hands up in the air and shouted, 'OK. Everybody out.'

Dorothy had no happy buzz left and was becoming increasingly agitated. 'But someone has to stay with the house,' she wailed. 'Look, I just need a tiny bit more time.' She swallowed hard and set her face into a very determined look. 'Right, family meeting!'

'What?' managed Amber.

Dorothy turned to her to explain. 'When something important came up or sometimes even something unimportant my father would call a family meeting, and everyone would get a say. So I think we should do that.'

'We are not a family ...' protested Stevie but Dorothy was not listening.

'I will look at the home, I promise,' she said contritely. 'I will try to sort things out. If it's nice then maybe I could stay there for a while. I just need someone to watch the house while we're gone. I haven't told you, but someone is coming and I've been waiting. I can't explain. Please don't make me.'

'No one is going to make you do anything,' soothed Amber.

Stevie was exasperated. 'Don't tell her that! When do I get my say in this meeting?'

Feeling they might be heading toward a solution, Amber

remained calm. 'Why don't I ask Mrs Haggerston?' she suggested. 'She never goes out. I'm sure she'll watch the house.'

'It's what she does anyway,' fumed Stevie.

Amber went and knocked on Mrs Haggerston's door. She took a while to answer, which was unusual.

'Yes?' she barked.

'I'm Amber from next door.'

'Are you?'

'I was wondering if you could do us a favour? We have to pop out and Dorothy is a little anxious. She is expecting someone. If you see anyone come to our door, will you tell them we'll be right back?'

'You want me to help you?'

'Yes.'

Mrs Haggerston seemed so taken aback by this idea that she found herself agreeing to watch the house. It was the first neighbourly thing she had ever done. Maybe, thought Amber, it was the first time anyone had asked.

'Will I need a key?' called Mrs Haggerston as Amber headed off. Amber wasn't sure but gave her one anyway just in case.

Amber, Stevie and Dorothy, with her suitcase, headed out across the square, waiting a few seconds while the regular walker inched past with her Nordic walking poles. Round the back of the Onion there was a large courtyard, off which were three shuttered garages. Dorothy moved to pull up the heavy metal door on the left.

'Let me help you,' began Stevie but Dorothy lifted the great weight in one swift move, with no trouble at all. She grimaced slightly as she did it, but it was impressive.

'No ... OK, you got that,' managed Stevie.

Inside the garage was Dorothy's car, but this was not just any

128

car. It was a classic Ford Cortina convertible, bright orange with a white roof. To anyone at all interested in automobiles the car was a thing of rare beauty. To anyone not interested, it was still a magnificent machine. Stevie couldn't help but give a long, low whistle.

'Eighty-two?' she asked.

'Seventy-eight,' replied Dorothy.

'Fuck me.'

It was Dorothy's car, so Dorothy drove.

'Are you sure you're OK to drive?' asked Stevie anxiously. 'Cataracts? Seizures? Anything we should know about?'

Dorothy reversed out of the garage at high speed and did an impressive handbrake turn as she roared out of the pub yard.

'I think she's got this,' said Amber quietly.

Dorothy was a good driver. Really good. Driving with one hand on the wheel and one resting on the open window, she knew every short cut in the neighbourhood. Stevie gave her the address and without even looking it up she had them there in no time at all. Stevie was impressed but refused to let that shake her determination to sort matters. The situation they found themselves in could not continue.

The care home consisted of fifty-one ensuite bedrooms spread out across three very sad-looking Edwardian houses joined together by low prefabricated corridors. None of it was in a good state of repair. Hung with half tile, the older parts had something dejected about them while the modern additions were already not long for this world. Dorothy had pulled up outside with an unnecessary screech and insisted on bringing in her suitcase. Now that they knew what was inside, no one objected.

'You can pay up front,' suggested Stevie.

A large dark blue plastic sign on the wall declared it to be the Jane Topper Care Home.

'Jane Toppan,' said Dorothy.

'No, I think it's Topper,' corrected Amber.

Dorothy stood looking at the sign with one hand on her beloved suitcase. 'Jane Toppan was a famous American serial killer,' she explained. 'She was a nurse who killed more than thirty of her patients.'

Stevie was not in the mood to be distracted. 'That sounds perfect. Let's see if they've got room.'

Stevie spoke with a receptionist and as it happened, the duty manager was free to show them around.

'Hello, I'm Rochelle. And are you Stephanie? I think we spoke on the phone. Hello everyone!'

'Who the fuck is Stephanie?' Dorothy asked Amber.

'Stevie!' hissed Amber.

Rochelle wore a very tight pencil skirt with extremely high heels and a closely fitting cardigan. She said to Amber,

'You must be Amber and ...' She gave Dorothy a watery smile before saying slowly and clearly, 'And who do we have here?'

'I'm the village idiot,' replied Dorothy, 'but the village is going digital so we're looking to expand.'

'This is Dorothy,' said Amber. 'You can talk straight to her. It's fine.'

'Of course, of course.' Rochelle turned her professional attention to Dorothy.

'Hello Dorothy,' she said, still very slowly but brightly, 'I'm Rochelle, with an e.'

Dorothy looked unimpressed. 'Really? With an e? And where would you put the e? I mean, doesn't it have to have an e? Can you spell Rochelle without an e? I would venture to suggest you are underselling yourself and need two.'

130

Stevie sidled up to Rochelle and mumbled, 'Can I just say I am sorry before we even start?'

Rochelle, with another of her range of professional smiles, said, 'You have nothing to be sorry about. Dementia care is one of our specialities. This way, please.'

Stevie and Rochelle went on ahead down the corridor, leaving Dorothy fuming to Amber.

'I do not have dementia! Who the fuck says I've got dementia? Dementia with two Es. Just like Rochelle. See? No dementia.'

An ancient female resident was sitting outside an office. A plastic sign hung out from the wall, marked Weekend Discharge. She had her back to the wall and for some reason sat with her legs wide apart. She was attached to an oxygen cylinder and was wearing a face mask. The fog of her breath on the plastic obscured her mouth. Dorothy leant down to her and whispered urgently, 'Do you want to make a run for it? I could get you out of here.'

The woman lowered the mask and managed to rasp, 'I was in love with Edward Heath, and I believe he loved me,' before replacing the mask and going back to just breathing.

Dorothy stood up straight before saying quietly, 'OK, she may have dementia.' As they walked under the sign Dorothy couldn't help but look up and remark, '"Discharge" is such an unpleasant word.'

'So you're both here with your grandmother?' Rochelle was in full flight.

'No, we're not related,' replied Stevie politely. She was determined to make this work.

'Oh, of course. I can see that.' Rochelle took in Stevie's pale and Amber's dark skin. 'You and Amber ... not related.'

'No,' replied Stevie, 'Amber and I are related. We're married.'

131

'I see,' nodded Rochelle. 'And are your husbands not able to view the home?'

Stevie tried to be calm. 'No, Amber and I are married to each other. We're not related to Dorothy.'

Rochelle and Stevie were not really getting anywhere and yet the conversation continued.

'I see,' said Rochelle, not seeing at all, 'and where is Dorothy living at the present time?'

'With us.'

'And yet you are not related?'

'No.'

'At all?'

'No … except me and Amber to each other because … we're married,' replied Stevie, who was beginning to despair.

Amber could see Stevie was struggling. She did not do well with people who refused to acknowledge their relationship.

'Yes, it's possible I'm not following,' admitted Rochelle and moved on. 'I see your grandmother has a suitcase with her. I'm afraid she wouldn't be able to move in today. There's paperwork, you know. What's she got in there? Favourite bits and bobs? Things she can't bear to be without?'

'Half a million pounds,' declared Dorothy loudly.

'Shh!' hissed Stevie.

Dorothy looked stern. 'Stevie, we've talked about the shushing thing. Not nice.'

Rochelle gave a tinkly laugh. 'Half a million pounds! Oh ha! Good joke! I can see you must have had a lot of laughs in your family. How lovely that Grandma still has her sense of humour.'

Stevie's responses had been reduced to just extremely quiet sounds.

'So this is where everyone gets together, is it?' Amber tried cheerfully as they entered the sitting room.

'Yes. Nice, isn't it?' smiled Rochelle, pleased someone was taking an interest. 'For those residents that are struggling to live independently but still want to engage in the sociable and friendly atmosphere, this room provides a lovely location.'

Amber, Stevie and Dorothy looked around. The quite large room was painted cream, with a thick brown stripe of gloss paint at waist height forming a faux dado rail. Two strip lights illuminated the place, which was lined with identical high-backed upholstered chairs standing on thick red carpet. The chairs were in a very pale brown imitation leather with a single red cushion placed at a considered angle, and had small wings, as if designed to hold in any resident who might unexpectedly pass away while seated. A television was on but the sound had been muted. It stood on a smoky glass table in front of double doors which looked out onto the car park. The doors were framed by thin pink floral curtains and hung with brown vertical blinds. The bright light from outdoors glowed around the TV set and made the picture on screen difficult to discern. Depending on the viewer's angle to the television you could either see nothing but shadows or an occasional glimpse of a blonde presenter who appeared to be talking about hand-knitted leggings.

Rochelle had more to give. 'Nice, isn't it?' she repeated.

Amber didn't really know what to say. She tapped the back of one of the chairs and asked, 'Leather?'

Rochelle smiled. 'Leather*ette*. Easy to wipe down! Here at Jane Topper—'

'Jane Toppan,' interjected Dorothy.

'—we have a dedicated team who personalise and customise each of our residents' care plans to provide the suitable levels

133

of care they need as well as ensuring they continue to live an enriched and enjoyable social lifestyle.'

'There's no one here,' said Stevie.

Rochelle moved on to more of the highlights of her professional pitch. 'Our residential care home is approved by the Care Quality Commission (CQC) and our latest report rated us as "Good" in every category.'

Dorothy turned to Stevie, who was becoming uncomfortable. '"Good"? Is that it? What's just below "Good"?'

'We have art.' Rochelle waved her hand expansively toward a single print of a watercolour scene hung in a gold frame on one wall in the corner. Too high and not centred, it had clearly been put on an existing nail.

Amber kept trying.

'I was just thinking – Christmas is coming. Do you decorate? Celebrate?'

All four stopped to consider the distinct lack of cheer in the room.

'One year we had a Christmas tree,' recalled Rochelle, smiling at the memory.

'I'm sorry, *one* year?' repeated Stevie. 'Don't you have a tree every year?'

'We always have tinsel!' said Rochelle, bright at the thought. 'Tinsel is nice.' She lowered her voice to say, in confidence, 'We had a resident who was allergic to pine, but we are never short of tinsel.'

'That's a thing? A pine allergy? People can be allergic to Christmas?' Stevie whispered to Amber.

'What about outings?' Amber persisted with a smile.

Rochelle took in the view of the car park with a wave of her arm.

'The stunning surroundings make for great fresh air. We also arrange shopping trips, lunches and other activities in the local area. There are a wide range of activities within the home itself, such as bingo, art classes and cookery lessons, but not right at the moment as we don't have the staff ... as such.'

'As such?' asked Stevie. This had been her idea, but she was growing more and more uncomfortable. She clapped her hands and tried to smile encouragingly.

Rochelle frowned but managed to stay chipper. 'I'm sure I won't be the first to tell you that you've entered the care home sector at a tricky time for everyone.'

Dorothy decided to have more fun. 'What do you have the staff for?' she asked brightly.

Rochelle smiled at her and changed her voice to mildly patronising. 'Well, my love, there's three meals a day! Let's have a look at today's menu, shall we? Mmm! Tasty. Creamy celery soup served with homemade croutons.'

'Toast,' Dorothy said out of the corner of her mouth to Amber.

Rochelle moved on: 'Poached chicken in white sauce, and rice pudding.'

Dorothy smiled as if delighted. 'My, what a lot of *white* things. What do you pay an hour? I might just take a job here, although I won't come out for less than minimum wage.'

Dorothy's very reasonable offer went unremarked.

Feeling she had triumphed with the tasty and nutritious dishes on offer, Rochelle now said, 'Bedrooms, I think!'

As she walked, she carried on with her spiel of things to recommend the place.

'We like to think of ourselves as comfortable and compassionate. When we reach our twilight years some of us must move away from a completely independent life and our friendly team

135

can provide that extra specialist residential and nursing care. We also have a wide range of services on offer including a visiting hairdresser, a chiropodist and a large-print library.'

Dorothy had moved on to being her most sarcastic. 'I mean, Rochelle ... with an e ... between toenail clipping and books which scream at you, I'll have no time for anyone to visit.'

'Don't you worry, Dorothy,' soothed Rochelle, 'your grand-children can visit any time. Except Friday evenings, when we do carpet cleaning.'

'Friday?' repeated Stevie.

Rochelle opened the door to one of the bedrooms. It was almost entirely filled by a single bed and yet another high-backed chair identical to the ones in the sitting room. It too bore a single red cushion. She turned back to her group, saying,

'Our residents are welcome to bring a few small personal possessions to make the place their own.'

Amber, Stevie and Dorothy all looked at the room in silence. It was impossible to know where one might find room to put anything.

'They would need to be tiny,' managed Amber.

Stevie wandered over to look out of the window while Rochelle droned on.

'Our luxury care home professionals are on hand to support wherever necessary. All our staff work hard to create a welcom-ing and homely environment for our twilight residents.'

Stevie noticed a moth flapping at the glass. It had a brown, rather drab body, but the most beautiful bright orange markings on the head and a scalloped edge to the wings. Drawn to the light, it tried and tried to find a way out. Its determination held Stevie's attention. Dorothy came and stood beside Stevie.

'Herald moth,' she said. 'They like hedgerows. And the dark.'

136

'Not old people's homes with strip lights?' smiled Stevie.

'No, not really.' Dorothy laughed. The two women stood and watched the small, spectacular creature.

'I love orange. Why a herald?' asked Stevie.

Dorothy shrugged. 'I think the shape is supposed to look like one of those tabards the heralds used to wear.'

Stevie looked closely at Dorothy. 'You have such a head full of stuff.'

Dorothy beckoned for Stevie to come closer before whispering, 'I read a lot of books with very big letters. "Moth" is one of the few words which fits on a whole page.'

Stevie looked at Dorothy, who looked back and smiled before they both sniggered.

'Excuse me? Does this window open?' asked Stevie.

'The window? We don't find the need,' Rochelle answered, clearly having forgotten all about the marvels of fresh air.

Dorothy and Stevie looked at the trapped moth.

'Can I ask you something?' asked Dorothy quietly.

Stevie knew this whole debacle was her fault and was happy to delay returning to the tour, so she said, 'Yes?'

'Who *is* Wilhelmina?'

'Ah, apparently it's Jack's name for my future child.'

'How dreadful.'

'Yes.'

They took a moment to enjoy this agreement before realising Rochelle was addressing Dorothy directly, and reluctantly turned back to the sterile room.

'So, Dorothy, while we like to think of every day as a sunshine day of difference here at Jane Toppan ...'

'Did she say Toppan?' whispered Stevie. 'I swear she said Toppan.'

137

Dorothy giggled but Rochelle was unstoppable.

'... your day would always begin here. Wake up between seven and eight a.m.'

'Christ!' muttered Dorothy and Stevie simultaneously.

'If you need assistance with washing and dressing, a staff member will come to help you. Have your breakfast in the communal dining area then perhaps a morning activity like singing? Lunch! Afternoon activity, maybe some gentle exercise? Do you like clapping? There might be a visit from family members' – Rochelle turned to Amber and Stevie, unable to remember what the family connection was – 'like ... yourselves. Enjoy an evening meal in the dining room, or privately in your own room, maybe some telly and then bedtime. Staff will check on each resident to ensure they are comfy and content.'

Rochelle was done. Time to wrap this up. She ignored Dorothy and spoke straight to Amber and Stevie. 'I think you will find we provide the highest level of care and, of course' – she dipped her head in a show of profound sorrow – 'eventual end of life support to all our residents.'

Dorothy had had enough. She exploded. 'End of life? What the fuck? I'll end your fucking life, Rochelle with an e. Did we bring that sledgehammer?'

Rochelle had dealt with bad-tempered oldies before. 'Now, now, Dorothy. You seem a little tense. What medication are you on?'

'I'm not on any fucking medication.'

'Any pre-existing conditions we should know about?' Rochelle persisted.

'I have bladder cancer.'

Rochelle didn't even flinch. 'I see, and what treatment are you receiving?'

138

'None,' said Dorothy.

Stevie was speechless. 'Wait ... what?' she managed, and then clapped her hands as she took in what had been said.

Amber put her hand up. 'Sorry, stop! Everyone stop.' She turned to Dorothy. 'You have bladder cancer?'

Dorothy nodded.

'And you're not having any treatment?'

'No.'

'What are you doing?'

Dorothy looked awkward. 'Well ... I was going to go back-packing if you pesky kids hadn't got in my way. Which reminds me, I need to wee before we hit the road.'

Amber, Stevie and Dorothy drove away from the Jane Topper Care Home without speaking. There wasn't exactly silence, be-cause the roar of the V6 engine from the still-impressive car was loud enough to wake one or two of the elderly residents. A frail old woman stood with Rochelle, watching out of an unopened window as Dorothy gunned the engine and left behind a scorch-ing tyre mark.

'Lucky fucker,' said the ancient inmate left behind with her romantic thoughts of Ted Heath.

Dorothy parked the car in the garage with remarkable skill before opening the boot to get her ever-present suitcase out.

'Can I take it ... uh, Dotty?' asked Stevie hesitantly. Dorothy looked at her. 'Not because you can't manage,' Stevie added. 'I just want to help.'

'We both do,' said Amber gently.

Dorothy looked at the two young women and nodded. Stevie was tall and strong. She whipped the case out of the car. Together the three of them walked back to the house.

Mrs Haggerston was wearing a thick coat and sitting in a

139

folding picnic chair on the front step of Number 4. She had brought her knitting out with her, and a small flask of tea. She was clearly taking her new duty of watching the house very seriously.

'No one came,' she declared, finishing a row.

'You knitting a friend?' asked Dorothy as she approached.

Mrs H ignored the question. 'Where've you been?'

'Cemetery,' replied Dorothy and no one corrected her.

'Who died?' asked Mrs Haggerston, crossing herself quickly.

'I did,' said Dorothy, moving past her.

Mrs Haggerston did not understand what was happening. She had never known Dorothy to be so quiet.

'You not going to mention today's saint?' she called to her old sparring partner.

'No, you're all right,' said Dorothy, slipping inside without another word.

'Are *you* all right?' Mrs Haggerston asked her neighbour for the very first time in their many years' acquaintance but there was no reply. She turned to Amber and Stevie.

'Is she? All right?' she asked.

Amber nodded. 'Thanks, Mrs Haggerston.'

Amber took back her key and then she followed Dorothy into the house. Stevie, still holding the suitcase, nodded to Mrs H before carrying half a million pounds inside and closing the door.

Mrs Haggerston was utterly baffled.

'Cuckoo House,' she said loudly to the square.

12

It was Stevie who put the kettle on. Usually Dorothy or, lately, Amber took charge in the kitchen but now Stevie set about trying to make them all feel better. At least one thing was very clear to everyone in this bizarre situation: no one, and certainly not Dorothy, should end their days in the Jane Topper Care Home.

While Dorothy made another trip to the loo, Stevie pulled Amber to one side. 'Look, I never thought I'd say this but she's no trouble and in a bad place right now,' she began.

'You're the one that wanted her out,' replied Amber, half laughing. 'I like her being here.' Stevie looked away, not knowing what to say. Amber reached out and turned her wife's face back toward her.

'You just like that she makes dinner every night,' said Stevie softly.

Amber grinned sheepishly. 'It doesn't hurt. Look, we need more information,' she suggested reasonably. 'Let's just talk to her.'

Stevie made the tea and the three women sat down around the kitchen table.

'Maybe that wasn't a good example of a care home,' tried Amber but no one bit at the suggestion.

Stevie sighed and tried to gather her thoughts. 'Right, Dorothy, I have to be honest and tell you I do not know how we have got here but here we are so let's try and sort this. The fact is, you are living in our house and we'd quite like to live here by ourselves but for reasons I can't fathom we seem to be stuck with you, so ...'

Amber picked up the thread, turning to look Dorothy full on, speaking slowly and clearly. 'You need to tell us everything. Why have you not left? What are you planning to do with the money and, most of all, how ill are you?'

Dorothy looked as if she knew the game was up.

'It's not easy ...' she began and faltered, looking down at her lap.

'It's all right, Dotty,' encouraged Amber. 'We are listening.'

Dorothy looked up at the young women, Amber with her gentle face, strong Stevie brushing back the great flop of hair which always seemed to be in her eyes. Dorothy smiled.

'I don't know if you'll understand. I hate when old people say "In my day" but things have changed since I was your age. We didn't take gap years or long holidays. Too bloody busy working. You grew up knowing what you were supposed to do: work hard, get married, buy a house – not some starter home on the way up but somewhere you were going to live all your life – have kids, routine. The most you could hope for in a bumper year was two weeks at the Lansdowne Hotel in Eastbourne on full board, back in the day when orange juice was still considered a starter, high days and holidays at the pub, join the bowls club, die, probably at the bowls club.'

Dorothy gave a slight smile and took a sip of tea.

'I've never been anywhere and so far have avoided bowls. I know every fucking street and dead end around here because I've never been anywhere else. My dad bought this house for £14,500 and that seemed mad at the time. I moved in and, I don't know, muddled along. Every day like the one before. It was OK. Last year, on my birthday actually, I was sitting in this house watching that show *Tipping Point* on TV. What a mindless piece of rubbish that is. Waiting for plastic counters, not even coins, to tip over the edge so you can win £50. Fifty quid? What the fuck? How is that television?'

'Dorothy!' prompted Amber.

Dorothy nodded and continued. 'And I'm watching, and I thought, I need to get out of here. The counters kept inching toward the edge of the drop on that wretched machine and it was like my life. Everything moving so fucking slowly until you just fall off the edge and die. I became quite mad with the thought of just leaving. Putting all this behind me. I started pacing and soon I couldn't stop. Drove myself crazy with the thought but I didn't know what to do. It went on for about six months and in the end I knew I had to do something before I topped myself. Next thing you know, I was up at that annoying woman Pixie Lee's on the high street.'

'She is annoying,' agreed Stevie.

'And I was telling her I wanted to sell my house. Once I'd decided, I couldn't think why I hadn't done it before. I can't just sit watching drivel until I start dribbling, and finish by pushing up the daisies. Drivel, dribbling and daisies – what kind of a life summary is that?'

'Why didn't you go before?' asked Stevie, drawn in despite herself. 'When you were younger?'

143

'Much as I hate everyone banging on about their mental fucking health these days ... How can that many people have ADHD? We are now an entire nation of people who can't sit still or pay attention. It's a wonder they manage to schedule *Tipping Point*.'

Now it was Stevie's turn to try to get their guest to focus. 'Dorothy!' she implored.

'Yes,' agreed Dorothy before pausing and then confessing, 'I think I've been depressed.'

'How long for?' asked Amber.

'Honestly?' replied Dorothy. 'More than forty years. Decades! What a waste of life! I let others leave me here in a great heap but that day, for whatever reason, I think I literally tipped over and decided it was enough. When the estate agent came round and said this place was worth half a million quid, I just couldn't imagine such a thing. Half a million quid! My money! That's like some kind of prize, where that nice Davina McCall says, "Look at that – you could win this!" and they have all this cash stacked up in front of the camera. I started lying in bed trying to imagine what it would be like to actually see half a million pounds and know I could do whatever I wanted with it. That it was mine. Imagine going into a restaurant and having whatever you like and paying cash, or a shop with nice things. Why haven't I had nice things? What the fuck is wrong with me? So once I sold the house to you and they told me the money was in my account, I went to the bank to ask if I could see it – my money. Well, the woman thought I was mad.

'"We don't have half a million quid," she said.

'"Well, I hope you do," I told her, "coz this is a bank. I'm pretty sure this is not just a place to store tiny little pens. That's my money!" Anyway, the bank manager came over and he said they didn't keep that much dough on the premises. Well, I wanted to know where it was. He wouldn't tell me. I don't know where they keep it – maybe the Bank of England – and I started to get anxious, so I told them I wanted it. All of it. Now. Turns out they were telling the truth. They didn't have it on them. It's a tiny branch so I had to go back a few days later. They weren't happy. Not happy at all. I went to the market and bought a suitcase coz I didn't have one. Of course I didn't. I didn't really go anywhere. Well, not for fun.'

Dorothy paused, then said, 'They've come on, suitcases, haven't they? Nice wheels. Not so heavy. I spent ages choosing and there were some lovely bigger ones that matched. Smashing bloke helping me choose, he said, "What do you want it for?"

'"Bank robbery," I said, and being from round here, he didn't even blink. I went and got my money and it just fitted nicely. Who knew there was a right size suitcase for that much cash? The manager looked quite unwell, but I took it home and for ages just sat looking at it. I started thinking about the bigger suitcases I could have bought, and filling them with clothes and buggering off. I wondered how far you could go on that kind of money. I got a map of the world at Smiths and started looking up places I wanted to go – the Colosseum in Rome, a gondola in Venice, a beach in Thailand. Nothing mad, just the sights of the world. Have you ever seen a pyramid in real life?'

Both Amber and Stevie shook their heads.

'Imagine such a thing. I imagined all of it.'

It was an irresistible thought and might have set Amber and Stevie off dreaming had Dorothy not spoiled the moment by going a bit too far.

'Thought I might even have sex. Old men have terrible eyesight, and they can't move well. I could tell them I'm in my fifties and by the time they've worked out it's a lie they won't be able

145

to get away. I'd like to have sex again.' Dorothy waved her hand over her lap in a wide arc. 'I imagine it's all still working.'

Stevie, who had been very drawn in by the tale of travel, now felt she was on some kind of verbal rollercoaster as Dorothy continued,

'I started thinking I'd keep a diary. Thought it would make a good film. I could be played by Helen Mirren or ...' She paused to think of another suitable star. 'Eddie Redmayne. I sold the house, got the money, got rid of all my stuff. Bought a ticket to Paris. I was going to start there. On the Champs-Élysées. I was ready to go; the place was nearly empty. I just left my little sofa upstairs for the last night and then the letter from the doctor came and I ... I don't know. I froze. I'd only been to see the bugger because I can't stop weeing and it's bloody annoying. Fucking bladder cancer. I'm going to die before I've shifted myself and I couldn't stop thinking about it so I didn't do anything and then after a bit I couldn't do anything. This house, this square, this is all I've known. I'm sorry. Maybe I'm not as brave as I thought I was. It's nothing to do with you. I'm nothing to do with you. You're lovely. Both of you. I'm really, really sorry.'

'Do you still want to go?' asked Amber quietly. 'Travelling?'

Dorothy nodded and bit her lip.

'Have you travelled before?' Amber persisted.

'I went to Greece once with Birdie but that was a long time ago. Not a good time. The truth is – now I'm scared, and I don't like it. That's not who I am.'

For a while they all three sat in silence drinking their tea. Annoyingly, it did make them feel better.

Stevie couldn't think of anything to say but Amber had no fear of more personal stuff. 'Do you have any family?' she asked.

Dorothy shook her head.

'No one?'

'I had a daughter ... Connie ... she ... died. A long time ago.'

Amber was gentle in her questioning. 'How old was she?'

'Only in her twenties.'

'I'm so sorry.'

'And there's no one else?' she asked after a while. 'Husband?'

Dorothy paused. 'I have no one.'

Amber had moved into practical mode. The one thing she was certain of in this incredibly uncertain situation was that something needed to change. 'Apart from the letter with the diagnosis, what else have you done about the cancer?' she asked.

'Nothing,' admitted Dorothy. 'I've got no one and I've done nothing. How tragic is that? Chuck me out now! Do you know, there's a grave up at the cemetery which has a woman's name on it – Eliza Buller – and it gives the dates for her life and then it just says "Died unexpectedly in Bournemouth". That'll be me. Died unexpectedly in Grimaldi Square. Anyway, Stevie, you're the police officer. Why is Amber doing all the interrogating?'

Stevie was overwhelmed. 'Uh,' she managed before finally asking, 'What else have you done about the cancer?'

'Still nothing,' said Dorothy.

'Right,' said Amber picking up the thread. 'This is not OK. I'll ring the surgery tomorrow and find out what's next for treatment. Having a diagnosis does not mean you are going to die, unless you just sit here and don't get some help. Cancer is not a death sentence, just a warning. Meanwhile ...' Amber paused before concluding her sentence. She looked at Stevie out of the corner of her eye and said softly, '... you can stay here till we sort this.' Amber turned to Stevie, 'She can, can't she?'

And Stevie surprised herself by saying yes.

*

So Dorothy stayed. Amber and Stevie moved the small sofa to one side in Dorothy's room and promised to upgrade the Argos put-you-up to a proper single bed the next day.

Somehow forgetting that her position in the house was precarious, the next morning Dorothy still managed to be full of instructions for everyone. She was particularly vocal where her suitcase of money was concerned.

Stevie had tried to be adamant: 'It cannot stay here, and you cannot keep dragging it round the neighbourhood. You've already left it behind once. It's half a million pounds!'

'Just under,' corrected Dorothy. 'That bloody Pixie and her commission. Said the house was hard to sell. Can't think why. Look at this lovely knock-through lounge.'

She refused to return the money to the bank because she didn't trust them.

'I'll go again to get it and once more it'll be "We don't have that kind of money, blah, blah." What could be safer than having it right here with a police officer?' she asked. Dorothy looked at Stevie. 'Unless you're not a good police officer. Is there something you want to tell me? Besides, I shall be off any day now. Amber's right. Maybe I'll be fine. Quick pill from the vet's or whatever and I'm off to have sex on the beach.'

Stevie frowned.

'It's a cocktail,' explained Amber.

In the end they put the suitcase of money inside the baby's cot in the loft room and Stevie wrapped the whole thing in the blanket. Then, getting down on her hands and knees, she pushed the lot right back, deep in the dark space under the eaves where no one was likely to look. Stevie wasn't entirely happy with the situation, but it was the best Dorothy would agree to. Stevie shut the door, leaving the most valuable loft conversion for miles around.

That night Dorothy insisted on making roast chicken. She sent Stevie to the shops. All the way there and all the way back Stevie could not quite recall how they had got to this agreement. She was, however, a sucker for a roast and the meal was delicious. Afterwards they all watched a TV show about a retired office manager buying a house on the Costa del Sol. The woman, Marjorie, seemed incapable of making decisions.

'It's a wonder the office she managed ever even had paper clips,' commented Dorothy.

'You could buy a house in Spain,' suggested Stevie after a bit but Dorothy had nodded off.

Amber was sitting up in bed, waiting for Stevie to finish laying out her clothes for the morning. They were finally back in their bedroom and even though everything had been unpacked, Stevie still hadn't got everything as shipshape as she wanted. She liked to have everything exactly so before she could go to sleep. She was methodical and careful. Amber was reading *The Coming of Age* by Simone de Beauvoir. She read aloud:

'"Society turns away from the aged worker as though he belonged to another species ... Old age exposes the failure of our entire civilisation."'

'What?' asked Stevie absentmindedly.

'It's a book about "Society's secret shame".'

Stevie paused to look at her wife. 'Are you having a go at me?'

'No, of course not. I was thinking it might be an interesting book for Bobby. He very much enjoyed the Germaine Greer I lent him.' Amber closed the book and put it down. 'Sorry. I didn't mean anything.'

149

'Drivel, dribbling and daisies,' said Stevie.

'What?' Amber watched Stevie pull clean underwear from a drawer and lay it neatly on a chair.

'Remember? Dorothy said that would be the summary of her life if she didn't do something about it,' explained Stevie. She sat down beside Amber and took her hand.

'Her daughter died,' Stevie said quietly.

Amber pulled her wife close. She could see she was choked with emotion. 'It's awful,' she agreed. 'But we are not responsible.'

'I know, but she has cancer. We can't . . .' Stevie looked up at Amber. 'What if we had a daughter and—'

'All love is a risk.'

Stevie lay back quietly thinking.

'What do you think we'd have?' she asked finally. 'If we had three words to sum everything up for our life.'

'Love,' Amber answered tenderly, kissing Stevie's hair.

Stevie nodded. 'Yes, and that's wonderful, but what else? I want our time to mean something. If you don't have God like Mrs Haggerston, then you only have this life. There's nothing afterwards so this has to mean something.' Stevie thought for a moment. 'How about *Love Laughter Liver Failure*?"

'Good, but four words.'

'Fucking maths!'

Amber laughed. Stevie loved to make her laugh. 'But it is a good question, Ambs. What *are* we doing?'

'Well, we're saving one old lady. That's something.'

Stevie smiled. 'Yes we are. We're saints.' She slipped into bed and nestled into Amber's shoulder. 'Do you think we'll end up in Dorothy's book? Saints of the day?'

Amber grinned. 'Lesbians? Are you mad?'

Stevie smiled. 'I bet you'd be surprised,' she said. 'All those

150

nuns living together? Bet the path to saintdom is packed with ladies who love.'

Amber held Stevie safe in her arms.

'Will she die? Dorothy?' Stevie asked, surprised by how anxious the question made her feel.

'Eventually. Of bladder cancer? Not necessarily, but she can't just leave it. I'll go to the doctor's with her.'

Snug in their bed the two women could just hear Dorothy in the next room, settling in to some gentle snoring. They listened for a short while before Stevie muttered,

'We don't really know her. What the fuck is wrong with us?'

Amber put out the light.

'Fucking saints,' said Stevie. They lay still in each other's arms. The shadows of the street lamp played on the ceiling. After quite some time Stevie whispered into the dark, 'I might like a daughter. Wilhelmina ... Maybe not that.'

But Amber was already asleep.

13

Dorothy needed an operation. Despite the word 'cancer' being involved, the local doctor's surgery was undergoing 'managerial changes' and it took a while to get an appointment. Stevie went with Dorothy. It should have been Amber as it was a medical thing, but the appointment didn't work with her shifts and no one wanted to delay. Dorothy went to get her car out, but having opened the garage door she suddenly turned to Stevie saying,

'You drive.'

Stevie was overwhelmed 'What, your car?'

'No, we'll borrow one from Noddy. Get in!'

Stevie slipped into the driver's seat and turned the key. It was a magnificent noise. The leather steering wheel was a pleasure to touch. It was a beautiful car to drive. On that wintry morning the orange vehicle seemed to bring sunshine to the streets.

The doctor was lovely and painstakingly went through everything, reminding her patient that they had already sent a letter asking her to agree to the operation taking place.

'I can't be reading all your letters,' protested Dorothy. 'We've got postcards of campsites to get through.'

The doctor was kind and clear in her explanations. 'To be technical,' she said, 'what you have is low-risk non-muscle-invasive bladder cancer. It's basically a small tumour. That means it can be treated with minor surgery carried out under general anaesthetic. It's quite a standard procedure.'

'Not to me it isn't,' muttered Dorothy.

'The tumour or possible tumours will be cut away from the lining of the bladder. The wounds are sealed or cauterised using a mild electric current.'

'Christ!' said Dorothy. 'I don't want a shock up my how's your father.'

The doctor turned to Stevie. 'She'll need a couple of days in hospital and a catheter for a few days more but within two weeks I would expect full recovery, although she may still need some help at home.'

'That's fine,' said Stevie and meant it. Then she helped a reluctant Dorothy sign a couple of forms while Dorothy mumbled loud enough to be heard, 'How do we even know she's a real doctor?'

She continued grumbling as they left the surgery. 'Why did you say it was fine?'

'Because it will be fine,' repeated Stevie firmly. 'You are having the surgery and that's the end of it.'

But she could see how shaky the whole thing had made Dorothy. It was a cold December afternoon. Dorothy said she wanted to go home but as they passed a café Stevie claimed she was desperate for a coffee.

'We've come all this way and you made me drive that old banger of yours. The least you can do is let me get a hot drink.'

The windows of the coffee shop were steamed up but as soon as Stevie opened the door she could see it was cosy and festive with seasonal cheer. School was out and the place was busy with mums and kids decorating Christmas cards.

'We won't get a table. Let's go,' moaned Dorothy but Stevie was determined and just managed to get a tiny space for two at the back.

'It's because you think I'm going to die,' said Dorothy. 'You think I'd better have a last coffee.'

'That's right,' agreed Stevie. 'Everyone bangs on about the Last Supper, but they probably had coffee afterwards. No one talks about that. I want a coffee because this may be my last chance to get you to pay for it.'

Stevie ordered and Dorothy did pay. They sat with their drinks, listening to the happy chatter around them.

'Shall we pretend we're undercover?' asked Dorothy.

'We are,' replied Stevie. 'You're a miserable old bat and I'm pretending I care.'

Dorothy smiled and looked around her. She reached for a paper tube of sugar and opened it slowly.

'Am I going to die?' she asked, not looking up as she stirred sugar into her coffee.

Stevie smiled softly. 'Yes, Dorothy, you are, but not of bladder cancer. Much more likely that I'll do you in.'

'I always thought Mrs Haggerston might finally top me on All Saints' Day. I mean, there'd be a lot to talk about.'

It was warm in the café. The two women sipped their drinks and Dorothy dared to take a deep breath. Stevie took her coat off and revealed she was wearing a green replica football shirt.

'Mary Earps?' asked Dorothy.

154

'God, you do keep up,' commented Stevie, impressed that Dorothy knew the name of the England goalkeeper.

'I'm old but not apparently dead,' sniffed Dorothy.

'It's Amber's. I nicked it.'

'Does she play? Football?'

'Used to.'

'Goalkeeper, of course,' Dorothy guessed.

Stevie nodded.

'Is there anything she doesn't want to save?' asked Dorothy.

Stevie smiled. 'Ouch. Well, Dotty, let's just say none of us knew you were going to be on the list.'

Dorothy looked around.

'It's nice here,' she said. 'St Drogo.'

'Are you suggesting that as a new name for Amber?'

'I was thinking what I'd call a café. He was patron saint of both coffee and unattractive people. Hard to know if naming a place after him would be a triumph or a tragedy.'

'You don't really care about those saints, do you?'

'No, but story of my life. Once I start something I can't seem to stop.'

Many of the children in the busy café were dressed for the outing. There was some kind of princess theme among most of the little girls, but one in particular stood out. She was about three and dressed as Superman. She raced about the place, de-termined to be a superhero.

'Baby dyke,' laughed Stevie.

'Do you think?' said Dorothy, watching the child run and then fall. 'Quite determined to have her own way but not entirely sensible. More like a small Liz Truss.'

One of the mums was breastfeeding while at the same time trying to comfort the baby's older sibling, who clearly felt

155

ignored. She looked exhausted. By the counter a boy of about four was deliberately smearing his hands all over the glass display cabinet. It left a great highway of fingerprints.

'Would you mind?' said the café owner to the boy's mother, nodding his head toward the greasy child.

'Sorry,' said the woman, who was typing on her phone. She looked briefly at the child as if he were nothing to do with her. 'Darling . . .' she managed helplessly as he carried on doing as he pleased and she went back to her text messaging.

'Why do you think people have kids?' mused Stevie.

'Religion, upbringing, culture, combination of all three.' When Dorothy spoke it was often with great assurance. 'Sometimes it's just doing what's expected,' she continued. 'The social pressures are enormous.'

Dorothy constantly surprised. Stevie looked at her. 'Did you go to university, Dotty?'

Dorothy laughed. 'I barely went to school. Always helping my dad at work.'

'But you know a lot.'

'Wow, not patronising at all.'

'Sorry.'

Dorothy smiled. 'I know . . .' – she leaned forward – 'it's surprising. Old, working class and yet fully functioning. They should stop leaving the library open so many hours. Terrible waste of council money.' She looked more serious as she concluded, 'Don't think you know anyone, Stevie, until you have tried walking in their shoes.'

Superman raced between the tables and tripped again. Stevie reached out in that exact moment and stopped her from falling on her face. She paused to right the child properly, who smiled at her and ran off, having learnt nothing.

156

'Did you just have the one, Dorothy?' Stevie asked. 'The one daughter, I mean.' She paused. 'Sorry, do you mind me asking?'

'No. No one ever asks. So long ago. She was an accident . . . which is such a bonkers thing to say. I mean, I didn't trip onto the poor man's penis, but we were young, we weren't thinking. I was a teenager. I adored her. Connie. There was no plan.' Then, obviously not wanting to say more, 'Right, my turn. Tell me about your camp parents.'

'They're a . . .' Stevie reached for the right expression '. . . *piece of work*, Malcolm and Barbara. They live this odd life on the road, but I don't think it makes either of them happy. He hates being retired. He can't even think about not having a purpose, so he just arrives somewhere in order to plan to go somewhere else. He is restless with fury at getting old. And Barbara? I'm one of five—'

'Oldest?'

'Youngest, and now we're all off she is living Malcolm's dream, but I think she hates it.'

'Malcolm and Barbara? Not Mum and Dad?'

'Oh, it's a joke. Sometimes they forget who they're sending a card to and sign themselves Malcolm and Barbara. Makes Amber laugh.'

'And they're coming for Christmas?'

Stevie stirred her coffee idly and nodded. 'I have four older brothers, and they take it in turns, but this year – hurrah! It'll be us! They'll be here!'

The small female Superman raced over to Stevie and Dorothy's table declaring 'I brought you sugar!' She handed over a single packet and flew off. They both grinned, neither one wanting to admit how nice this very, very ordinary outing was.

Stevie suddenly put her spoon down on the table with surprising force.

'Amber really wants a kid,' she began, not sure why she was saying all this. 'She grows more certain every day.'

'And you?'

'I wouldn't mind a dog.'

'What kind?'

'Cockerpoo. I wasn't really ready for marriage or a house.'

'Both seem to be working splendidly,' observed Dorothy.

'You think?' Stevie tipped her head on one side and looked quizzically at Dorothy, waiting for a reply, but the old woman seemed focused on her coffee so Stevie continued. 'Amber's always so much more certain about everything. Of course I love her, but this baby idea. It's all so . . .'

'Grown-up?'

'Yes! The thing is, it doesn't matter how much you might want a family, there is no way of knowing if you'll be any good at it. There's so many reasons not to have a child. Amber could do it. She's so smart. She'd sit here and say, "Wilhelmina, what is the statistical likelihood of the next customer ordering cheesecake?"'

'You sticking with Wilhelmina?' Dorothy interrupted, but Stevie was not stopping.

'I can't do maths and then there's all the worries – the planet is dying, food shortages, drought, civil unrest, forced mass migration, homophobia . . .'

'I don't think you're responsible for the whole planet.'

'No,' agreed Stevie before ploughing on, 'but we could lose the house or our jobs or—'

'Dinosaurs are recreated, a meteor lands in the square or . . .' Dorothy said, picking up the list with enthusiasm. 'Dear god, you are full of fabulous horrors today. Alzheimer's, schizophrenia and a dollop of global warming. Shall we just order some cyanide on the side with our cappuccino? Did you think only the homosexuals were worrying about this stuff? Stevie, trust me on this, we can't just give up. Any of us.'

'You were going to,' accused Stevie, feeling got at. 'Before we came. You'd done nothing about your diagnosis!'

Dorothy paused and nodded. 'You're right,' she admitted, 'although I think I didn't give up so much as freeze. You two shook me out of myself. If everyone on the planet decided not to reproduce, we'd be stuffed. Who'd cure things then? Who is going to figure out how to solve this mess we've made?'

'Thanks.'

'The difference between you and a lot of straight people, Stevie, is that you will probably have given the whole thing way more thought. I think the fact that it can't just happen is a good thing. We should all be like that. Not just sex without thinking. Like me.'

Stevie smiled before asking cautiously, 'What did your daughter ...'

'Connie.'

'What did Connie die of?'

Dorothy looked down and waited before saying, 'Innocence, I think.'

The two of them sat listening to the chatter around them. As they got up to leave Dorothy asked,

'Have you worked it out?'

'What?' replied Stevie.

'The statistical likelihood of the next customer ordering cheesecake?'

Stevie grinned. 'No.'

'I have. It's zero. They don't sell cheesecake. None of it is as hard as you think, Stevie.'

14

J ack had taken to visiting Number 4 most afternoons. He would pop in after the lunch shift at the Onion, exhausted from hours of hiding in the kitchen from Agnes. The first time he arrived Arun was up a ladder, patching holes in the ceiling.

'Could you pass me that edging trowel?' he called out without looking down.

There were a number of tools lying on the plastic sheet at the foot.

'Edging trowel,' Jack repeated, blowing his cheeks out in confusion.

Arun looked down from his work. 'The trowel for edging,' he explained.

Jack nodded. 'Yeah. I think I had that much information when you said "edging trowel".'

Arun frowned. 'Are you going to make me get down from my ladder?'

'"Make" is a strong word,' replied Jack. 'I doubt I could "make" you do anything. "Seventy-six trombones led the big parade ..."' Jack hummed to himself as he ran his hands over the selection of tools before picking one at random and handing it to Arun. Arun looked at it for a moment as if unsure whether to comment but finally said,

'That's a hammer.'

'Yes, yes it is,' agreed Jack very slowly, while pointing at the tool in question and nodding with theatrical confidence. 'So that, Arun, was a test, because you are in my friend's house, and now, because of this test, I know that you are a real workman. I'll tell Stevie and Amber that you are worth every penny, and they should not worry about paying you.'

Arun smiled to himself and slowly descended from above. He moved with an agility which was admirable. At least to Jack.

When Dorothy returned from the butcher's with meat for the evening meal she found Arun standing in the middle of the sitting room, carefully explaining the name and purpose of each of the tools. Though reluctant to leave the house, she was going out more easily now that there were people in 4 Grimaldi Square all the time. She knew they had her phone number in case someone came for her. She saw that Jack was listening with a degree of concentration and intensity which Agnes would not have thought possible.

After that, Jack arrived for a 'quick cup of tea' about the same time every day. He would stand at the bottom of the ladder waiting for Arun to ask him for a tool. In between, the two of them chatted. There was a lot of rubbing down before Arun could paint, and the dust was terrible. Some days Bobby would turn up to check on the progress. He was on a new evening course and keen to share. Some of the recently acquired knowledge was driving Arun mad.

'I never heard the word before, Arun, if I'm honest.

161

"Intersectionality". So interesting. All the different forms of minority oppression which you obviously, being of Anglo-Indian heritage, might be particularly interested in. Too often these "micro aggressions" go unremarked, and in that regard I got you this.'

Bobby produced a small notebook with the title *Micro Aggressions! Hate Crimes! Racism! Sexism!: A Notebook of Bad Things!*

'I thought you could write things down and we could discuss them.'

Arun took the notebook. 'Thank you,' he said quietly. These well-intentioned mini lectures from Bobby often led to Arun needing air and taking a break in the garden. He and Jack would get a cup of tea and stand chatting at the back door.

It was mid-December and really too cold for hanging about, but it was private. Their breath hung in small clouds as they fumbled toward shared conversation.

'He's very well meaning, your boss,' commented Jack.

Arun nodded. 'I never met anyone so keen to raise his own consciousness. It's impressive.'

'What you going to write in your new book?'

'I don't know. Maybe that I didn't really like being given it in the first place.'

Jack and Arun enjoyed these chilly chats. They discovered odd points of agreement. They both liked a funny little restaurant nearby which served Venezuelan street food, they deeply disliked baking programmes, loved Anne Murray, adored Celine Dion and rather randomly both knew the entire catalogue of songs by a group from the 1940s called the Ink Spots. The main thing they connected over, however, was a fascination with Mrs Haggerston's bird feeder.

Stevie and Amber's garden was not really a garden at all. Just a space where a garden might one day hope to be. There were broken slabs of old tile and some empty flowerpots but nothing welcoming. A large, almost oversized shed full of old gardening tools took up at least a quarter of the patch, but other than that it was entirely empty. In contrast, Mrs Haggerston's place was a model of horticultural over-thinking. She had laid plastic turf across the entire area and then set about filling it with kitsch. If a free catalogue had arrived at the house suggesting some piece of garden knickknackery then she had purchased it. At the back door a solitary pink lawn flamingo stood beside a neat rubbish bin which inexplicably had a lid like a smiling frog. Mrs H clearly enjoyed her time in the garden for there was a green metal swing seat for two. From here, the lucky seated individuals could admire an array of plastic gnomes smoking pipes as they watched a goblin fetch water from a well.

It was the bird feeder, however, which took pride of place. It was, as Jack had been told, the great Notre-Dame cathedral of Paris, or rather it was Notre-Dame in miniature. Made of wood, it had originally been some kind of architectural model and nothing to do with the avian world, but standing in Mrs Haggerston's garden it had become one of the most astonishing things either Arun or Jack had ever seen. Mounted on a large plinth the two principal towers rose up to flat roofs where bird seed was now liberally spread. Mrs Haggerston was generous with her feeding and the seed spilled down onto the entire base. The large spire which rose from the centre Mrs H used as a spike to hold a fresh fat ball. Over the years many birds had made use of this monstrosity and there was a good coating of white guano down the sides of the building.

163

'I can't decide if it is magnificent or terrifying,' Arun whispered as he and Jack peeked over the fence for the millionth time.

'Where would you even get such a thing?' wondered Jack.

'Where, and *why*?'

The fence between the gardens was just under five feet high and both men were able to rest their forearms on the top of it as they looked over to admire the Gothic construction.

One afternoon, leaning on the fence, Jack realised that by accident his elbow was gently touching Arun's. He felt an utterly unexpected electric charge rush through his body. It was incredibly exciting, but it also caused him to panic. He couldn't decide whether to move his arm away or not. Should he inch his elbow toward himself? Had Arun noticed? Did he mind? A million thoughts raced through Jack's mind and he could feel himself blush. Out of the corner of his eye he looked across at Arun, but his new friend was staring straight ahead, seemingly unaware of their close contact.

For the next week the afternoons were all the same. Arun worked, Jack came over, they admired Parisian architecture, sometimes their elbows touched. Jack rather casually found out where Arun lived, and they talked about what kind of place each of them hoped one day to live in.

'Something like this,' said Arun, indicating Number 4. He had described his very nice studio apartment in great detail but said he longed for something bigger. Maybe a garden. Jack looked up at Stevie and Amber's, and couldn't imagine ever owning such a thing. It was well beyond his or his nan's dreams. Arun went back to work.

'So . . . you and Arun, then?' Dorothy whispered quietly one evening while she made a fish pie.

'What?' said Jack defensively. 'What are you saying? No! What?'

'You and Arun!' repeated Dorothy. 'Oh for goodness' sake, Jack. I'm not blind. You might fool Birdie, but I've got excellent rainbow radar, or whatever you call it.'

'Gaydar,' said Jack. 'It's called gaydar. We've been through this.'

Dorothy waved his correction away. 'Whatever. I'm telling you, there is sexual tension in the air.'

'I think it's mostly plaster dust,' said Jack, a little dejected. 'He doesn't even notice my elbow.'

Dorothy was having none of it. 'I can see it a mile off,' she said with the confidence of a clairvoyant. 'The two of you are perfect together.'

Jack shook his head. 'No you can't and yes, but ... well, he's lovely but he's ... I have Nan to look after, besides I don't think he's ... I don't even know if he likes show tunes. It's nothing. He wouldn't ...'

'You're here every afternoon.'

'I come to see you and he barely notices me. What if—'

'Oh, "what if"!' sneered Dorothy. 'You could waste a lifetime on "what if". I should bloody know.'

'Dorothy, the potatoes are boiling over!'

'Blast!' Dorothy grabbed a tea towel and moved the pan off the heat. She turned back to Jack. 'Ask him out!'

'Where?'

'I don't know. A party. Take him to a party. In my day you could make a party at the drop of a hat in the pub. You do work there, you know.'

Jack snorted with derision. 'When's the last time anyone had a party round here? What have we got to celebrate?'

'Jack!' called Arun from the next room. 'Could you hand me my edging trowel?'

Jack ran instantly to Arun, grabbed the correct tool without hesitation and handed it up while Dorothy watched from the kitchen.

'Time to get Birdie out of her nest, I think,' said Dorothy to herself. 'And free that boy.'

There was no question that something was happening. Not just to Jack but to everyone at Number 4. Dorothy worried less about her money now that it was hidden but she was often preoccupied. She didn't talk about the forthcoming operation, but it did seem to have left her sometimes distracted and sometimes galvanised into action. There was a new urgency and intensity to everything she got involved with.

The other old woman in Jack's life, on the other hand, wasn't doing too well. Birdie was having some really bad rheumatic episodes, and no amount of Jack's brownies could quite ease the pain. Now they were back in touch, Dorothy went to see her most afternoons. Sometimes she would stay for an early supper. The two of them liked to watch *Step into the Spotlight*. It was a talent show in which ordinary members of the public stepped into the spotlight and showed off an often unsurprising lack of talent.

Each show was roughly the same. A dark studio would be illuminated by a single shaft of light from above as an announcer declared,

'Ladies and gentlemen, it's time to step into the spotlight with your host Adam Anderson!'

Adam Anderson would, as advertised, step into the spotlight to reveal some potential new star who had been discovered. All

166

of them had much in common. They had all 'been on a journey', they all had wanted this for their entire lives, most had 'come from nothing' and usually had also overcome some personal horror to get here. Adam was Australian and seemed to think that the shoulder-length hair which had made him look a rebel in the 90s was still working for him. He liked to say what a 'duhlite' it was to meet everyone.

'Today, we're going to meet Derek from Derby. The man is a duhlite. He has overcome throat cancer to become a ventriloquist.'

'Oh, splendid!' Birdie would say.

She loved any acts which were a bit old fashioned, like ventriloquists, jugglers and, on one memorable broadcast, a cavalcade of clowns from Scunthorpe who arrived in a small car and flooded out on to the stage.

Adam Anderson had been beside himself. 'There is literally nothing I like better than a clown.' He pointed at one of the clowns beside him. 'Do you think he looks all right? Looks a bit funny to me.'

Dorothy's enjoyment came from ripping it all to shreds.

'Stop it, Dorothy,' Birdie always said, trying not to smile. 'They're doing their best.'

'I know!' Dorothy would shriek. 'That's why it's so hilarious.'

'Tea?' Dorothy enquired one night during an ad break.

'I've already got one,' answered Birdie.

'Have you? Have another.'

Dorothy got up to head for the kitchen.

'Dorothy!' Birdie halted her friend. 'What is going on?'

'What do you mean?'

'That's the third cup you've offered me. You've got ants in your pants. Why can't you just sit down?'

'I can sit.' As if to prove her point Dorothy sat down on the arm of the sofa.

Birdie stared at her. 'I'm waiting.'

'For what?'

'For you to tell me what's actually going on.'

Dorothy looked at her old friend with irritation. 'What do you think is going on? I'm dying.'

'I don't agree. They haven't operated yet. They are working on you. I believe you will be fine, so could this gloom wait till the end of the show?'

'Can't you take me seriously?'

Birdie flicked the sound off on the TV.

'I have cancer,' said Dorothy grimly.

'I know, and I am here to help you. Do you want to talk about it?'

'No, of course not. I just don't want it to be happening. I'm . . . not ready to die.'

'No.'

On the television two acrobats were hurling themselves around on a trampoline. Dorothy stared at them and then got up.

'Tea, then?' she said.

Birdie sighed.

Both Amber and Stevie thought it was wonderful that Dorothy was venturing out but each time she left the house she would instruct Arun or Bobby or whoever was in that she wouldn't be long: 'If anyone calls for me, I'm only round the corner.'

Dorothy stopped talking about her health and kept her worries to herself. Instead, each time she visited Birdie she interfered in her friend's future plans.

'What's happening? When are you moving? I know you

168

haven't been downstairs for some time, but the rising damp has reached the seventeenth floor. Unless it's using the lift, I don't think that's a good sign. What's the council doing?'

'Truth is,' Birdie told Dorothy one afternoon, 'I don't think they really want to have this place empty out completely. Once we're all gone then they'll have to pay to knock the tower down and think of what to do next.'

'Isn't there a plan?'

'It's the council. Why have a plan when you can have a muddle instead? It's only people's lives we're talking about. I worry. Some of the people who aren't sorted yet are getting so depressed. If the powers that be don't make arrangements, they don't know what they're going to do. They can't carry on living here, it's not safe, but no one will take responsibility. None of my neighbours have the cash to go somewhere else. By the time everyone's got a new place you and I will be brown bread.'

'Cheerful.'

'There's only one thing to do,' Dorothy added.

'What?'

'Have a party.'

'You what?'

'Let's have a party. Christmas party. Like we used to. At the pub.'

'A party? No one's got any money.'

'*What's that got to do with the price of onions?*' replied Dorothy in a gruff voice, mimicking her father.

'Ooh, your dad. He was grand. A good man for a party. Drinks all around and Jim's mince pies!' remembered Birdie before shaking her head. 'We're too old for parties! Anyway, I don't go out.'

169

Dorothy took her friend by the hand. 'The only thing you and I are too old for, Birdie, is wasting any more time. I've been an idiot and sat feeling sorry for myself for too long. Do you remember what my dad used to say was the best Christmas present you could hope for?'

Birdie smiled. 'Just to have a laugh, Dot.'

'Precisely. It's time you and I had some fun.'

Birdie smiled. Dorothy was a good soul.

'But no nativity play!' laughed Birdie.

'No,' agreed Dorothy. 'That fucking donkey.'

'We had fun. He was a good landlord, your dad.'

'The best.'

That afternoon Stevie got in late from her shift. They were no nearer replacing the car and there was some problem with the buses. Amber was still at work, Arun was up a ladder and Dorothy was taking something out of the oven. She put the kettle on as soon as she heard the door. Stevie stopped to admire the sitting room, where Arun had nearly finished the decorating. He stood trying to get blue paint from under his fingernails.

'Looking good, Arun,' she called, popping her head in.

'Me or the room?' he grinned.

Stevie went into the kitchen, taking off her heavy jacket and putting it on the back of a chair. She sniffed appreciatively.

'Smells like Christmas in here, Dorothy.'

'My dad's mince pie recipe. I thought I'd forgotten how to do it. It's been so long, but it's funny how things come back you. You've got your little Christmas get-together down at the station tomorrow, haven't you?'

'How'd you know that?'

'Little bird.'

'Do you know everyone round here?'

'No! But they know me.' Dorothy began putting mince pies into a tin. 'Thought you might like some of these to take.'

Stevie sat down and picked up a postcard from the table.

'Excellent addition to our gallery this morning,' said Dorothy with delight. 'This one, as it happens, is "with love from Malcolm and Barbara",' she added. 'They're at "Coxhill Camping. Just a short drive from the ferry at Dover." Do they go abroad?'

'No,' said Stevie. She stared at the card and then sat tapping one corner of it on the table. 'I don't think I'll go,' she said after a while, trying to sound nonchalant.

'To Dover?'

'The Christmas thing . . . at the station.'

Dorothy eyed her suspiciously. 'Give this tea to Arun and then come up to my room.'

Stevie returned the look. 'Why?'

'It's comfortable, you knob,' replied Dorothy, disappearing upstairs with two mugs of hot tea. Stevie spent a moment trying to get any kind of future timetable about completion from Arun and then headed up to Dorothy's room, where she found her sitting on her red sofa, sipping her tea. She had put Stevie's mug on the floor.

'Why are we in here?' asked Stevie again.

'Because there isn't a man up a ladder splashing blue paint.' Dorothy turned to Stevie. 'Now come on. Spill the beans. Trouble at mill?'

Stevie pulled herself up to her full height and tried to shrug whatever it was off.

'Nothing. It's nothing. Just a weird thing.'

'Ooh! I love a weird thing. Sit down!'

Stevie awkwardly picked up her tea and sat. She hadn't been

171

on the red sofa since the night she'd first met Dorothy. It was surprisingly comfortable. The room was nice. Snug.

'Go on then,' prompted Dorothy.

Stevie had had no intention of telling anyone but somehow . . .

'I was up on Kerviel,' she began. 'Not undercover or anything. Just routine. You know, the estate.'

Dorothy knew it well. A ragged place not far away, made up of old blocks of Victorian flats.

The call-out was horrific. A woman had jumped from the third-floor communal balcony down into the car park. There was nothing Stevie could do by the time she got there. The woman lay twisted on the ground with blood pooling round her head. Her eyes were open and she seemed to stare at Stevie as if asking for her help. Stevie went into professional mode. Called for medical back-up. Checked for a pulse, did all the right things. The woman's handbag had fallen beside her, so Stevie opened it for a name. Inside was a wallet, cheap but really cheerful. Fuchsia pink. Nataliya Bondar. The dead woman was – had been – Nataliya Bondar. Flat 82, Rachman House, Kerviel Estate. Stevie looked in the wallet again.

'There's a kid,' she had said to the officer on duty with her. 'A kid.'

'My partner is new,' she now explained to Dorothy. 'To me, I mean. Not to the force. We don't really know each other. Kevin. He's a bit of joker. You know, says stupid things. I told him about me and Amber straight off. Up front. I didn't want any weirdness or him finding out from someone else.'

'You shouldn't have to explain yourself at all.'

'No. No, I know, but . . . I don't know, the force is not the most woke place on earth. He said he was fine with it but lately he can't stop making jokes. Says things like he's glad I'm a lesbian coz he'll never have to change a tyre, that kind of thing. It's nothing but it wears me down.'

Dorothy said nothing. Just waited.

'There was one of those plastic windows in the wallet,' Stevie said quietly. 'It had a picture tucked into it – a little girl, maybe six or seven, and I knew we had to find her. Our shift was over but we just couldn't leave it. I went to the flat. The key was in the door. Nataliya, the mum, had locked her in but left the key for us or someone. For the kid, I guess. I found her in the bedroom. Tiny little thing. She'd got bored, I think, because she'd put on her mother's dress and high heels. It was black with some lace. Bright red shoes and a long white necklace of beads. She was admiring herself in the mirror.

'"I look pretty?" she asked me.

'I nodded and told her my name. She liked my radio. She asked for her mummy, so I picked her up,' Stevie continued. 'Nataliya is ... was being kicked out of their flat. She had nowhere to go. The girl kept asking for her mother. I wanted to bring her home. I was holding her while I waited for social services. Her mum just died. Kevin came in ... and told me to put her down. Said we didn't need social services making a report about me.'

Dorothy could hardly speak. 'What?'

Stevie looked down at the floor.

'I'm a lesbian holding a little girl. He said there might be talk.'

'What did you say?'

'Nothing. I put her down. She cried. The little girl cried till social services came for her. Later I told him I was upset. He said he was just looking out for me, and I was lucky to have him on my side.'

Dorothy's eyes blazed with fury. 'You should complain,' she said.

173

'About what? I mean, yes, but ... I want to go back undercover and the squad are not going to have me if I can't be "one of the lads". They deal with some really serious shit, and this was just—'

'It's disgusting,' said Dorothy firmly and then held her tongue. She could see Stevie couldn't take any more. The two of them sat for ages drinking their tea and not saying a word until at last Dorothy got up.

'Wait here,' she instructed.

Stevie remained on the sofa, noticing that Dorothy still had the rainbow pillow she and Amber had given her the night they moved in. It made her smile. Dorothy returned carrying a cake tin.

'Take this,' she instructed, holding the tin out to Stevie, who got up to do as she was told. They stood together in the doorway. Stevie looked back at the red settee.

'Why do you have a sofa in here?' she asked.

'It was my daughter's. She saw it in a magazine. This was her room.'

'Was she grown up when she died?'

'Not grown up enough.'

Stevie clearly had something else on her mind, because she had to clear her throat to speak.

'Dotty, I spoke to Bobby today,' she said. 'I wanted to know what we owe him for all the building work.'

Dorothy was staring at the picture on the lid of the cake tin. She appeared not to be listening.

'Dorothy, he says it's all paid,' said Stevie. 'In cash.'

The old cuckoo looked up for a split second and smiled.

'Well, isn't Christmas a wonderful thing?' she said, but Stevie looked displeased. 'Let me do this,' urged Dorothy. 'Please. I need to do something with my money.'

Stevie looked down at the cake tin. 'Why do I have this?' she asked.

'We don't hide, Stevie,' Dorothy replied. 'That's not OK. Tomorrow, you take this tin of mince pies – brilliant mince pies, by the way, my dad's recipe – to the party at the station house, look everyone in the eye and tell them that your wife Amber made them.'

Stevie didn't know what to say. 'Was your dad a baker?' she managed.

'Publican.' Dorothy took a beat before adding, 'He owned the Onion.'

'Right. The Onion? Wow, Dorothy – do you only work in surprises?'

Stevie then surprised them both by stepping forward and hugging Dorothy who, equally surprisingly, hugged her back. It was brief. Almost nothing but at the same time everything.

15

The party at the Onion was happening on Christmas Eve. Dorothy, having first mentioned the idea of a gathering to Jack, then made the thought such a regular subject of conversation with everyone that eventually they all just presumed someone else had decided it was definitely taking place.

'Christmas Eve is in a week!' moaned Jack but Dorothy would not be deterred. It would be at the pub and there would be mince pies.

'How have you made this happen?' he asked.

'I have connections,' she replied.

Considering she wasn't well it was astonishing how Dorothy had somehow managed to kickstart everyone, including Agnes, who was thrilled.

'Do you think Leonardo took this long?' Arun asked as Jack continued the endless refinement of his hand-drawn poster.

Jack blushed before mumbling, 'Sit and help me.' The two men spent hours colouring in and chatting.

Every customer who came into the pub left with a ticket for

the party and it seemed to generate a new energy in the neighbourhood. The only person who was not entirely enthused
about the forthcoming celebration was Birdie.

'What you going to wear?' Dorothy asked one evening while
they watched *EastEnders*.

Birdie grunted and failed to reply.

'I'm sorry, I didn't quite hear you. What are you going to
wear to the party?'

Birdie reached for the remote and snapped off the television.

'I am not going to the party, Dorothy. Look at me! Nothing
in my body works and I can't even walk, let alone dance.'

'I will remind you, Birdie, that *I* am going under the knife
soon and this might be my final hurrah. You may have aches
and pains but I've got an actual trouble.'

'I'm not playing medical Top Trumps with you, Dorothy
Franklin. You'll be fine. I can't believe anything will ever stop
you blabbing in my ear.'

Dorothy snorted. 'Of course you can dance. You danced at
my wedding.'

'That's a very long time ago.'

'What's your favourite song?'

'"Land of Hope and Glory".'

'It's not the fucking Last Night of the Proms. A song for
dancing, you twit.'

'Oh, that's nice.' Birdie thought about it. 'No ABBA,' she
said.

'No.'

The two friends sat in silence. Dorothy had nearly dropped
off when Birdie suddenly said, '"It's Raining Men".'

Dorothy put her head back and let out a loud 'Ha!'

She got out her phone and almost instantly found the hit song by the Weather Girls. She put it on as loud as she could and grabbed the back of Birdie's wheelchair.

'You're supposed to be taking it easy!' bellowed Birdie but it was no use.

When Jack got home that evening his grandmother was dancing in her chair while her ancient friend bellowed out a final chorus about the weather having turned surprisingly male, hallelujah.

'Woo!'

'Amen!'

The two women couldn't stop laughing.

'You'll come,' declared Dorothy firmly.

Birdie was still unsure. 'I don't know, although I do love that song. Do you like it, Jack?'

'Uhm, uh ...' Jack was lost for words. It was an awkward song title for a man in the closet to his nan, but Birdie failed to notice his reticence.

'It was that or "Staying Alive",' she laughed, 'which seemed a bit too much on the nose.' Birdie turned to Dorothy and asked, 'Didn't we have both of those on the jukebox?'

'What jukebox?' Jack asked.

'Not just any jukebox,' his nan replied.

'The Americana II. Wurlitzer's finest music machine,' Birdie and Dorothy said in unison.

'Have you still got it?' Birdie asked Dorothy.

'What do you mean, still got it?' said Jack.

'It used to be mine. A long time ago,' said Dorothy. 'When my dad ran the Onion.'

'You two old birds are a constant mystery,' replied Jack.

'I know!' agreed Dorothy. 'Just think, we used to have lives and everything.'

'We never, ever had sex,' Birdie assured him.

'No, we never had sex,' echoed Dorothy.

The next morning Dorothy took Jack out to the garages behind the pub. She pulled open the metal garage door in the middle and winced with the effort.

'Take it easy! You ...' began Jack, before his eye was drawn to the walls inside the garage.

Most garages are quite dreary spaces but this one had walls that had been whitewashed and then painstakingly painted with fairy-tale characters. There was a host of figures – Old King Cole, Jack and the beanstalk, the Fairy Godmother, Goldilocks and the three bears, Cinderella with her Prince Charming – in bright, cheerful colours. All of the characters were gathered around a pink castle with large wooden doors.

Jack took a deep breath of shock and rather dramatically placed his hand on his chest. 'Be still my beating heart,' he whispered.

Dorothy smiled. 'My dad did them. He called it the magic room. It was for my daughter, Connie. He didn't like her being in the pub all the time.'

Jack threw his hands up in delight. 'Peter Pan with Tinker Bell!'

Dorothy made a small noise of delight. 'That was Connie's favourite.'

'You lived here, at the pub?'

'All my life till I got married.' Dorothy smiled.

Jack looked serious. 'Nan told me what happened. I'm so sorry.'

Dorothy ran her hand across the wall as if to bring the characters to life.

'We came out here on my wedding day. Connie was almost grown up by then but she still loved her magic room. It was a place for surprises. My dad hung the key to my new house on those doors.' She pointed to the castle entrance and smiled. 'It was his present to us. He'd do last orders, clear up and then come out here and paint till all hours.'

They both looked at the walls. It was a vast and brilliant labour of colourful love.

The garage was empty apart from two quite large items, both covered in dust sheets. Dorothy pulled on one of the coverings, only to reveal several boxes and, inexplicably, what looked like an Edwardian wheelchair in dark wood with a cane seat.

'Nope,' she declared, pulling on the second sheet, and there was the Americana jukebox in all its glory. A massive, nearly four-foot-wide music machine with two integral silver speakers. The top was decorated with a large glass pane bearing a picture of some mountains and fir trees, which appeared able to light up. Beneath it lay another piece of glass shielding hundreds of old records.

'They're 45s,' said Dorothy.

'I don't know what you're saying,' replied Jack.

'45s! The speed? Like 33 or 78?'

'Is this like one of those games on Radio 4 which pretends to have rules but no one actually understands it? Do you just say random numbers until one of us gives up?'

Dorothy ignored him. 'You put a coin in here' – she pointed to a slot on the right – 'and then press the right combination of buttons to pick your track. The arm goes across, put the record on the turntable and then the music plays.'

'Wow,' managed Jack. 'I imagine people often passed out, giddy with the speed of the entertainment. What the hell is it doing out here?'

'I think we had a leak and moved it for safe keeping. Then Dad died and there were no more parties.'

'Until now,' grinned Jack.

The Americana was filthy with dust, but all the records were still in place and a quick press of one of the buttons suggested it might all still work.

'What music does it have?' asked Jack.

'I think it's quite specific. Hits from whatever year we got it. Late seventies, early eighties, I guess.'

'ABBA?'

'No, definitely no ABBA. We had all those replaced with Cliff and Elvis, I think.'

Jack was bewildered. 'What? That's mad. Everyone loves ABBA. What was wrong with you people?' He stood back to look again at Jim's wonderful fairy-tale paintings.

'A magic room,' breathed Jack. The work was all still intact. He reached his hand out and brushed a cobweb away from Cinderella's gown.

'He was good, your dad. These are stunning,' he whispered.

Dorothy had not been out here for more than forty years. She looked at her father's artistic present and felt choked.

Jack slowly wandered round the whole garage looking at each art work in detail before he turned to Dorothy and said solemnly, 'Dorothy, can you tell that I am about to be brilliant?'

'Well, it's never obvious with you, Jack, so I'm glad you've given me a heads up,' replied Dorothy, trying to cover her emotion.

'Fairy-tale characters!' he boomed, and clapped his hands.

Dorothy looked confused. 'Are we just saying things we can see?' she asked before exclaiming, 'Jukebox!'

'No!' Jack huffed. 'God, you're slow. You've got a mind like a jukebox. No, let's get everyone to come to the party as fairy-tale characters! Or story books or movies or fiction in general! It's genius!'

Dorothy was not sure but Agnes loved the idea. It meant additions to the poster of course, so Jack and Arun had another busy evening of colouring together.

'We could have a prize for the best costume!' suggested Agnes.

'Like what?' asked Arun.

'How about a free meal for two?'

Despite its name, the Onion was not noted for its food. Agnes bought in ready meals and used the microwave.

'What's second prize?' Jack asked. 'Two meals?'

It took Bobby, Arun, Dave de Van and a few others to get the Wurlitzer back into the pub. Filled with old records, it was very heavy. Bobby volunteered to get the thing going again. Everyone, including Dorothy and Agnes, stood with bated breath while he fussed about, before plugging it in and flipping the switch. The coin box still had a stash of the heavy old coins needed. These could be taken out and used to make it work, and it was Dorothy who dropped the first one into the slot to see if entertainment was back. She stood for a moment, looking at the record selection, and then carefully pressed one alphabet button followed by two numbers. The arm of the Wurlitzer cranked into gear, moved slowly to select the record and then placed it on the turntable. The playing arm slipped across as the needle descended with a slight crackle.

'Oh my god, how long does this take?' asked an impatient Jack.

'Sssh!' said Dorothy.

A disco drumbeat boomed out and no one could help but begin to bop up and down as 'Disco Inferno' by the Trammps filled the room. The speakers were still surprisingly good and loud.

'Burn, baby, burn!' chorused the room as they danced.

'This party is going to be epic!' roared Jack, overwhelmed by dancing so close to Arun.

With the music sorted, now everyone had to select a fairy-tale character for their costume. This should have been easy, but it turned out to be quite the talking point.

'I'll just carry a plant,' suggested Jack to Bobby, Arun and Young Justin. Silence followed the suggestion.

'Jack and the beanstalk?' said Jack.

Young Justin sniggered but Arun was appalled. 'That's terrible!' he said.

'I think you need to work harder than that,' scoffed Bobby. 'Interestingly,' he continued, 'we were discussing this week at evening class how some of the first fairy tales were actually feminist critiques of the patriarchy ...'

Young Justin sat flailing his fingers as usual and not listening. There was much chatter, and everyone was very pleased when it was decided that Arun should be Old King Cole, the merry old soul, complete with crown and sceptre.

'Perfect for you!' said Bobby.

Amber could not think who to be. Drinking tea in the kitchen at home, it was Dorothy who suggested Cinderella. Stevie smiled and immediately said,

'Only if I can be Prince Charming.' She and Amber grinned at each other.

'You two!' mocked Dorothy. 'So in love it ought to be illegal.'

Stevie smiled. 'Not my fault,' she said defensively. 'Who wouldn't love a woman who makes such great mince pies?'

Dorothy's mince pies had been a huge hit at the station and Stevie had done as suggested, telling everyone Amber had made them.

Amber was confused. 'What?' she asked.

'Nothing,' said Dorothy and Stevie together.

Amber shook her head at the two of them. 'Fine, have some secrets.' She smiled before asking, 'And what about you, Dorothy? Who are you going to be?'

'Oh, I'll just make some cakes and have a night in,' Dorothy replied nonchalantly but Stevie was not having it. She rang Jack to come and help.

When he arrived at Number 4 he found Dorothy set in her reluctance to join in.

'I don't think Birdie will go, so I won't either,' she insisted. 'You don't need half-dead old people slowing you down. This party is for you, Jack.'

He would hear none of it. 'It's Christmas, you old fart. As far as I know, there's no age limit. Have some fucking spirit.'

'Well, as you put it so nicely.'

'You must have some old frocks from the war or whatever,' insisted Jack.

'How old do you think I am?'

'I know how old you are but you do seem to have been around for ever. You know about all them saints – I wouldn't be surprised if you knew Jesus personally. Nice guy. Sandals all year round, which is a bold look. Come on, let's see what clothes you've got. We can cobble something together.'

They went upstairs to Dorothy's room, where she proceeded to empty a single plastic bin liner out onto the sofa. There were several pairs of pants, some tights and a grey sweater.

Jack was appalled. 'Is that it? Where's your stuff?' he asked.

Dorothy looked at him as if she couldn't decide whether or not to tell him, and then, without another word, headed out of the house and across the square with Jack following after her.

'I do wish you wouldn't rush about,' he begged. 'You're supposed to be dying. I didn't get this large shifting my arse.'

At the back of the pub, in the same courtyard as the garages, there was a narrow black door in the main building wall. Jack had been working at the pub for some time but had never even noticed it. Dorothy surprised him by producing a key. She opened the door to reveal a steep wooden staircase going up to the first floor. Dorothy grabbed the handrail and climbed up. Jack looked up. It really was very steep.

'Do you not have anything on the ground floor?' he called before sighing and following.

Jack had never been up to the first floor. It hadn't been used for years and he was blown away by how much space there was. A wide corridor led off into room after room, with another slightly smaller floor above up under the eaves. The unused accommodation was staggering but so too was the collection of things it housed. Every inch of every room was filled floor to ceiling with furniture, boxes and knick-knacks.

'What the fuck is this?' exclaimed Jack. 'Looks like how my head feels.'

Dorothy looked around as if seeing it all for the first time.

'It's my stuff,' she admitted. 'I used to ... Doesn't matter.'

Jack put his hands on his hips and looked at her. 'Dorothy, what is going on? I feel like I don't know anything about you.'

Dorothy looked away. 'Everybody doesn't need to know all my business.'

'Please tell me you also have super powers.'

'Shut up and look.'

Jack did not know where to begin.

There were chests of drawers, bed heads, sideboards, lamps with and without shades. Framed pictures in many sizes leant against the wall. On top of the antiques were balanced more modern-looking things – a bookshelf from Ikea, a nest of tables from Habitat. A pretty blue sofa.

Jack was mesmerised by the eclectic mess.

'Where's it all come from?'

'A lot of it is stuff from my house.'

He stopped in front of a full-size model of a *Star Wars* stormtrooper.

'Really? This?'

'Oh, Tony got that for ... some strange trade with the butcher. I can't remember.' She stopped to look at it and gave a small sigh. 'He loved it.'

'Tony?'

'The clothes are in the far room, at the back, I think.'

The place was an Aladdin's cave of treasure which had clearly lain untouched for years and Jack was in heaven. He raced about picking things up and letting out little yelps over pieces of furniture, too busy to ask any more questions.

'Oh my god, we should get them to do *Cash in the Attic* here!' he exclaimed. Not knowing where to look first he headed down the corridor, passing an old bathroom with an avocado-coloured suite and catching a glimpse of a kitchen with an ancient eye-level gas grill, a butcher's block and a scrubbed pine table. At the far end he opened the door to a room entirely devoted to clothing. Jack paused, putting his hand on his chest. He felt as if he had just wandered into Neverland.

'Jack?' called Dorothy, coming after him.

'I need a minute,' he said, taking great gulps of air before practically screaming in delight.

'Is this all yours?'

Dorothy smiled. 'My dad bought the clothes from some

market stall man who was retiring. I think he thought I could start a business. Get out of the pub. Do something of my own. It didn't help that I have no interest in clothes.'

'Oh my god! Is that a Nehru jacket?'

'Just going to repeat – I have no interest in clothes.'

Jack fell on a pile of clothing. Here was heaven, for in this place sartorial time had stood still. Clothes appeared haphazardly grouped in decades. There were tie-dye shirts, ponchos, bell-bottoms, frayed jeans, midi skirts and maxi dresses – anything the 1970s had deemed essential. A large shelving unit held handcrafted neck ornaments and accessories made from wood, shells, stones and feathers. Someone had gone mad at the nature table. Beyond those pieces there were headbands, floppy hats, flowing scarves and even a pair of buckskin moccasins. Digging beyond the 70s Jack found earlier eras including men's clothes from the 1940s and 50s which had belonged to Dorothy's father. There was even a very large, full-length fur coat.

'Don't tell PETA!' Jack shrieked, putting it on. 'Look at it! It's perfect! Not even got moths!'

'It's fake,' said Dorothy from the door. 'A moth would get more pleasure out of a plastic bag. Don't rub your arms together coz the thing will spark.' She picked up an old dress with a lace collar. 'Everything from that man was fake,' she said to herself.

Jack swung round in the fur coat, utterly delighted. It fitted him perfectly. Dorothy smiled at him. 'You look like a baby bear,' she said.

'I do,' agreed Jack. 'I'm going to be the baby bear from Goldilocks and you ...'

He spied a brilliant green trouser suit and wrenched it from its hanger. 'And you shall be Peter Pan!'

187

Dorothy shook her head.

'Of course you should. Connie's favourite. You said so.'

Dorothy sat down on an old wooden box. She looked pale and tired. It was too much. She didn't want to play. But Jack was oblivious . . .

Once they were back downstairs Jack could not keep quiet about what he had discovered. Everyone had to see the magic room and no one could think of anything more perfect than Dorothy dressing as Peter Pan.

'That is just right, Dotty,' said Amber. 'I don't think you'll ever grow old.'

Dorothy agreed but her heart wasn't in it.

It turned out Agnes was brilliant at sewing. Another thing no one knew about her. She adored the newly found rooms upstairs and went through finding odds and ends with delight, ready to make them into party costumes. Customers came in and found out she could help with their ideas and soon there was a flow of fabric in and out of the pub. It was fun. The only downside was Birdie's absolute determination not to attend. Jack worked on her every day, but it appeared to be no use. He was desperate not to leave her out of the fun and Dorothy worried her absence would spoil his big night.

The afternoon of the party, everyone was getting ready. Dorothy was in her room with the door nearly closed. Slowly she put on her costume, an excellent imitation of a boy from Neverland. Agnes had tailored the suit to show off Dorothy's legs, which were a fine set of pins for anyone's age. There was even a little emerald cap with a white feather in it from a dead pigeon Jack had found round by the bins. Dorothy looked at herself in the mirror and for a split second thought she saw Connie and her dad behind her, smiling.

When Dorothy came down Stevie was pacing in the hall wearing a paper crown, breeches and cropped dinner jacket. It had been long on Dorothy's dad, but Stevie was tall. She looked splendid.

'Great outfit,' smiled Dorothy.

'Right back at you!' beamed Stevie.

When Amber came down the stairs as Cinderella, in a ball gown made from sheets and decorated with elaborate frills made from some net curtains, Stevie felt her heart would burst under the weight of love it contained. She put her hand out for her beloved and bowed. Dorothy watched Amber and Stevie stand arm in arm, and there may have been a tear or two. She was about to say something when her phone rang. It was Jack.

'It's an emergency!' he shouted.

'And merry Christmas to you too,' Dorothy replied.

'Nan says she'll come!'

'What?'

'I know!' Jack sounded a little guilty. 'I may have given her an extra brownie. Anyway, she's super mellow but she won't come without a hat.'

'Why?'

'I don't know. I told you, she is super mellow. She wants a hat, but it has to glitter. She won't leave the flat without it. Do you have any tinsel? I can make a hat, but I need tinsel. Dorothy, I don't think you understand. It's urgent and the shops are shut.'

He was very serious. Nearly tearful. Jack could be very intense, even about tinsel. Fortunately Dorothy knew exactly where to find some.

She grabbed her car keys.

'Where are you going?' asked Amber.

'Emergency foraging,' replied Dorothy.

189

Peter Pan, Cinderella and Prince Charming all headed out at the same time. As they left, the curtains next door twitched and Mrs Haggerston looked out to see what was going on. Amber saw her.

'Did anyone ask Mrs Haggerston?' she wondered out loud.

'The last time a witch went to a fairy-tale party Sleeping Beauty missed a hundred years of her life,' replied Dorothy.

Amber and Stevie went to the Onion to help lay out glasses while Dorothy drove off. She went straight to the Jane Topper Care Home. As it was Christmas there were even fewer staff on duty than usual. In fact there was only one, very new, carer in attendance. She was not only absurdly young but significantly short-sighted. The poor child had taken the job in her gap year and been rather shocked to find herself in sole charge on Christmas Eve. She was clearly out of her depth and later explained to Rochelle, and eventually the police, that she had only seen what happened through the window from the corridor and not all that well. Nevertheless, she would swear that Peter Pan had flown in to take all of the tinsel from the hall. It was all very confusing. As well as the decorations he had also spirited away one of the old women, who had been sitting on a bench nearby with her oxygen tank.

Dorothy returned triumphant.

'You take this over to Jack at Soros Tower,' she instructed Amber and Stevie, handing them her stolen tinsel. 'I've left something in the car.'

The meeting on the twenty-second floor of Soros had its own comedy.

'Nan, this is Amber,' said Jack. 'She's a paramedic, and this is Stevie, my best friend. You met her years ago. She's a police officer.'

Birdie eyed Prince Charming and Cinderella.

'I must be more off my head than I thought!' she declared, grinning.

Now armed with tinsel, Jack managed with great speed to create a most marvellous glittering hat.

'You're the Fairy Godmother!' he said to his beloved grandmother as he put it on her head.

'Let's get out of here!' she roared, raising her arm like Boudicca ready to lead troops into battle.

Jack could not recall the last time he had seen his nan out of the tower and suddenly his nerves got the better of him.

'Will you be all right?' he asked.

'I've got a paramedic and a police officer,' snorted Birdie, 'I fucking better be.'

Prince Charming and Cinders used all of their professional skills to bring Birdie and her wheelchair down from her eyrie. By rights she should perhaps have been nervous about this out-of-the-ordinary outing but she was exhilarated by both the novelty of the escapade and her shiny headwear. As the prince and Cinders pushed her through the streets, she kept calling out to passers-by,

'Merry Christmas! Allow me to grant you a wish!'

Jack followed along behind, looking splendid in the old fur coat. He had fashioned some ears out of a brown towel attached to a headband and looked somewhere between Winne-the-Pooh and the crazed bear in *The Revenant*. They got to the pub bright cheeked and ready to enjoy themselves. The sound of Gloria Gaynor boomed out the door as fairy-tale characters flowed in.

Amber took Stevie's arm and whispered, 'Baby, I forgot something at the house.'

'I'll get it,' Stevie offered but Amber shook her head.

'I'll be two minutes,' she called as she raced home.

'Not a book!' called Stevie after her. 'You're not reading. It's a party!'

Jack, Birdie and Stevie were just in time to bump into Dorothy, who was coming round from the back of the pub pushing another old woman in what appeared to be an Edwardian wheelchair. Dorothy was in her full Peter Pan costume while her companion's only nod to a festive outfit was a wreath of tinsel in her hair.

'Birdie, you look marvellous!' said Dorothy, considerably out of breath.

'Is this what you left in the car?' asked Stevie, pointing to the new arrival.

'Yes!'

'Who is it?' asked Jack.

'Wendy Darling, of course,' proclaimed Dorothy.

Four-hundred-year-old Wendy's breath rasped against the mask. It made a heaving, wheezing sound which was almost menacing.

'Wendy, or Hannibal Lecter,' said Dorothy. 'I can't decide.'

Stevie took in Jack's vast display of fur. 'Wow, Jack!'

'Baby bear from the Three Bears,' he announced with pride.

'Christ!' she replied. 'Imagine the size of the rest of them. Goldilocks must have been terrified.'

'Rude.'

Dorothy moved to take her guest in, but the Edwardian wheelchair was not easy to handle and Peter Pan had lost her puff.

'Thank god I am big and strong,' said Jack-bear, taking charge of the new old lady. 'You weedy woman.'

He and Stevie pushed Wendy in through the door as Dorothy called after him, 'I can knock a house down, you know!'

Dorothy sounded confident but the truth was, now the Christmas celebration was a reality she was losing her nerve. She sidled up to Birdie and whispered to her, 'There's no one at the house. Someone ought to be at the house. Maybe I should just stay in.'

'No!' replied Birdie with surprising force. 'What we are doing, Dorothy Franklin, is going out. What we are not doing is worrying about anything else.'

'I haven't been to a party in years,' muttered Dorothy, glancing through the pub door. 'I thought it would be fine, but I think I might have forgotten how to do it.'

'It's like riding a bike,' insisted Birdie loudly while waving her arm in the air as if to dispense magic. 'In fact, I may ride a bike later. Could someone get me a bike?' she yelled out into the dark square.

The extra brownie had clearly done the trick. She had gone from a woman who wasn't at all sure of going anywhere to someone who appeared ready to take on the world.

'Come on, you two!' Stevie returned to push Birdie into the bright pub, while Dorothy followed saying something not entirely nice about bicycles and eyeing her old house.

'Maybe it doesn't matter any more,' she said under her breath.

Agnes had come as Pinocchio, Young Justin ... some kind of sea creature and Bobby Twococks had gone all out, arriving as Humpty Dumpty. He was clearly going to win a prize. Dressed as a giant egg with a bow tie, he was very soon holding court with a couple of women at the bar who were both dressed as Elsa from *Frozen*.

'I don't want to get too deep, but I do think my choice is reflective of my own fragility. I mean, of course we do need to

193

talk about toxic masculinity but there are many mental health warning lights for a modern man.'

The women were entranced and Bobby allowed them to tap his fragile shell.

Dorothy leant down to Birdie. 'Did you ever think you'd miss a builder with sexist chatter?' she asked.

Dorothy hadn't seen the pub this busy or joyous in years. Fairy lights twinkled everywhere and paper stars hung down in great festive loops across both the main rooms. It looked splendid. Dorothy was on the edge of happiness until she saw, with horror, that Amber was bringing in Mrs Haggerston. Amber was being very encouraging to her neighbour, who appeared both terrified and appalled. Amber sat her down in a corner next to some-one dressed as Chewbacca. Mrs H was not wearing a costume and was being incredibly clear that she would not be staying. Nevertheless, she allowed herself to be given a small tonic water.

'I see the Wicked Witch of the West has turned up,' Dorothy said to Amber as they passed at the bar.

'Dotty! Be nice!' admonished Amber. 'It's Christmas. No one gets left out.'

'You're *too* nice,' said Dorothy.

'Well, isn't that just as well for you?'

Most of the old residents from Soros Tower turned up for the party. They were so thrilled to see each other, and Birdie was quite the hero. On top of her calming cake she had by now had a cream sherry and became quite the merry centre of attention. The jukebox was a huge hit and Agnes was rushed off her feet taking orders behind the bar. Jack was supposed to help but his assistance was intermittent. Agnes had clearly predicted as much because a handsome middle-aged man was pulling pints besides her. Clearly she had engaged help for the evening.

194

Soon the level of party noise was at a happy high pitch. Arun, as Old King Cole, was less than merry at first and stood shyly nursing his beer, speaking to no one, until Dorothy gave him a look and nodded furiously toward Jack. The king gathered all his courage and inched over to Jack in his furry ensemble.

'Aren't you too hot?' Arun asked.

Jack blushed. 'No ... I'm just right. Not too hot, not too cold ...' He fumbled to find a sensible answer. 'Like the story ... I'm just ... right.'

'Yes, you are,' replied Arun and they both dared smile at each other before looking away.

Dorothy and Birdie sat together with ancient, wheezing Wendy. They watched Prince Charming and Cinderella dance together, kept an eye on Humpty Dumpty's moves and noticed every detail of Old King Cole flirting with Baby Bear. Nothing escaped them. Young Justin sat with his usual faraway look, twiddling his fingers in the air.

'Why do you think he does that?' wondered Dorothy.

'No idea,' replied Birdie. 'But I bet you find out.'

Dorothy looked a little ashamed. 'Leave it,' she said. 'That's what you're saying, isn't it, Birdie?'

Birdie turned to her. 'Dorothy, I have known you for ever. You are one of the kindest people I know, but not everything can be fixed or even needs your attention. Stop interfering.'

Dorothy knew her friend was right. She nodded and smiled at the Fairy Godmother beside her. 'I am sorry, Birdie. About everything,' she said.

'I know you are,' replied Birdie.

'I was trying to help.' Dorothy had waited a long time to say her piece. 'Jack was so unhappy,' she began, 'I felt sure his mum had just made a mistake. I thought if I explained to her then—'

'I know,' sighed Birdie, 'but you going to talk to her just finished everything off. She had hardly been in touch as it was – birthdays, card at Christmas – but after that she never spoke to him again. She's not a nice woman. I don't know why my son ever married her. If he were still alive . . . Maybe it was too much for her to have a stranger tell her where she had gone wrong. You should have left it alone to mend by itself. She never understood Jack and maybe she was always going to cut him off. I expect you just hurried things along, but I was so angry with you. I am sorry. We should have spoken. Not speaking is not an answer. I know that now. I'm sorry I cut you out. I know you meant well.'

'Thank you,' replied Dorothy and sighed. 'Oh god, I wish I wasn't so hot-headed. I don't seem to get any better with age. I know it sounds pathetic, but I just want everyone to be happy.'

Birdie smiled at her. 'Maybe start with yourself. It's good to see you out. Everyone says you've been stuck in that house for too long.'

'Not every day. I have been doing the minicab business.'

'Of course you have, you bonkers old biddy.'

'Well, maybe not recently,' replied Dorothy and smiled.

'I mean, from a building point of view it's a sobering story,' Bobby was heard to say at the bar. 'You see, the thing about Humpty Dumpty is that when he broke, falling off that wall – which already was a health and safety nightmare – what did they do? Let all the king's horses have first go at fixing him. It's in the rhyme: "All the king's horses and all the king's men." That's never going to work, is it? Horses? You want to get Twococks in there.'

Jack and Arun had been jigging around each other all evening when the jukebox clunked into a record change and rather ironically Percy Sledge started to sing 'When a Man Loves a

Woman'. Everyone began slow dancing and Jack had just shyly taken Arun's hand when a couple of strangers, who clearly didn't know about the party, came in.

'What the fuck is all this?' the first one asked loudly.

'Like some fucking pantomime in here,' said the second.

They had already had a few and moved to the bar to carry on. As they did, they walked past Arun and Jack, who had started to dance. The interlopers stopped and looked at Arun before one of them went right up to him, saying,

'Oi, fatso, who you then?'

Arun ignored them and carried on trying to have his precious dance with Jack but the man was not prepared to be ignored. He moved closer to Arun's face.

'I *said*, who you supposed to be?'

Arun let go of Jack and smiled his usual disarming grin. 'I'm Old King Cole.'

The men laughed. 'Oh yeah, I see that. King *Coal*!' He turned to his friend and pointed at Arun's face as if it were the funniest thing in the world. 'Do you get it? Coal! Like in the fire!'

'Ha, nice!' replied his friend.

'That's enough,' managed Jack bravely, at the same looking to see if Stevie was around to help.

'Oooh, who are you?' trilled the second man in a high-pitched, mocking tone. 'Liberace?'

This was not Agnes's first pub and she had spotted the trouble before it started.

She called out from the bar, 'Come on, lads, have a pint and be off!' pouring out some drinks at speed. She was holding the beers when one of the uninvited guests gave her an intense look and walked slowly towards her. He moved to the other side of where Agnes was standing and then leant across the bar to stare. Agnes

197

did not move but jumped when the man suddenly slammed his fist down, pointing at her and saying very loudly,

'Fuck me, it's Andrew! Look at that, John,' he called to his mate. 'It's fucking Andrew!'

It was enough of a commotion to cause the happy chatter of the party to die down a little. Stevie looked over at the same time as Bobby slowly put down his drink.

Agnes said nothing but her neck muscles tensed, and it was clear she was not happy. She put down the glasses and walked away. The man helping her behind the bar moved toward the intruders but she signalled for him to stand down.

'Oi, Andrew!' shouted the man after her. 'What the fuck happened to you?'

Agnes stopped, waited a moment and then turned back.

'My name is Agnes. *Agnes.*'

Jack moved to the jukebox and put on 'You're the One That I Want' from *Grease*. A few people tried to start dancing but the men at the bar were not to be distracted.

'Agnes? You're fucking Andrew. I was at school with you.'

Agnes did not move, and the man was becoming irritated. Jack turned the music up, but the troublemaker simply went over to the jukebox and yanked the electric cable from the wall, causing the plug to fly off. John Travolta and Olivia Newton-John died and now everyone was aware of trouble in the air. Without saying a word Stevie and Bobby moved closer to the men.

'Stevie!' called Amber from across the room but her wife was in professional mode.

Bobby smiled at them. 'All right, lads?' he beamed. 'Happy Christmas!'

Calmly Bobby suddenly reached out and grabbed one of them by the back of the neck. He squeezed hard. It was clearly a tight grip because Bobby was able to lift the man onto his toes and then turn his head at will without him being able to resist. The man's friend went to move but he had not seen that Stevie was behind him. She pulled his arm up behind his back in a nano-second and held it there saying quietly,

'I wouldn't, if I were you.'

'Perhaps you haven't met our landlady, lads.' Bobby twisted the man's head to look at Agnes before continuing in the same jovial tone. 'This is Agnes. Doesn't she look nice tonight? Say yes.'

Bobby squeezed the man's neck and made his head nod up and down in agreement. The man could not believe this indignity was happening to him at the hands of a man dressed as an egg.

'What's your name?' Bobby continued, turning the man's face towards him.

'Uh, Carl,' the man heard himself say meekly.

'Well, *Carl*,' Bobby continued, 'we'd all love you to stay be-cause we're friendly round here but unfortunately we're full up.' He turned to Stevie. 'Aren't we, *Constable* Baxter?' He turned the man's head to look at Stevie. 'Oh, have you met our local constabulary?' he asked. 'Carl, this is *Constable* Baxter. Say hello.'

Without wishing to, Carl found himself looking Stevie right in the face and saying hello.

'Hello, Carl,' smiled Stevie. 'What a shame you can't stay and enjoy the fun.'

Arun had moved to stand behind the piano. He glanced at the broken plug of the jukebox. Arun's defence was music. He quietly began to sing 'Whispering Grass' by the Ink Spots. It was a beautiful, gentle piece and he was pitch perfect.

Jack went over to the piano and opened the lid. He sat down and began to play a tune he knew so well. Together he and Arun held the room captive while Bobby and Stevie showed the troublesome men to the door and out into the square. Jack and Arun carried on singing until the very end of the piece. It was exquisite. There was wild applause for Old King Cole and Baby Bear.

'I was going to sing "I Am What I Am" but I thought it was too much,' whispered Arun to Jack.

Jack squeezed Arun's hand. 'What you did was perfect.'

After that everyone carried on as if no interruption had taken place. Bobby could be heard saying to a woman dressed as Pippi Longstocking,

'Can you just reach up inside my egg? No, no ... I mean, maybe later, but right now I just want me Swiss army knife. Left-hand pocket.'

The penknife was retrieved and he set about using the screwdriver to bring the jukebox back to life. Dorothy checked on Agnes.

'You all right?' she said quietly.

Agnes nodded as the man with her put his arm around her shoulder.

'Want me to take over?' Dorothy asked but Agnes went back to work.

Having briefly held hands, Jack and Arun parted with both needing to catch their breath. Dorothy returned to Wendy in the wooden wheelchair. Her oxygen tank was on the back, and somehow Dorothy had discovered breathing in blasts of the pure air was rather intoxicating. Now she and Wendy took turns with the plastic mask. Jack sidled up as Dorothy took another puff.

'Agnes is Andrew?' he asked.

She shook her head at him in disappointment. 'No, she isn't,' she replied firmly. 'It's her dead name.'

'Her dead name?'

Jack looked at Agnes behind the bar and it was almost as if one could see the cogs whirring in his brain.

'How did you know that?' he asked.

'I hired her.'

'You hired her?'

Dorothy was getting irritated. 'Jack, is there a world where you could stop just repeating what I say? It was my dad's pub – I told you that. And now it's mine.'

'Yours?'

'Oh my god, you're driving me mad.'

Jack had a lightbulb moment. 'You didn't just hire Agnes! You got her to hire me! You sly old devil. All this time you've been keeping an eye on me. I thought you'd forgotten me.'

Dorothy shrugged. 'From what I was hearing you weren't getting on with anything.'

'So you interfered?'

'I don't know why you and Birdie always call it that. I helped things along. Now, if you will excuse me. I don't drink but' – she held up the mask – 'it turns out pure oxygen may be my thing and I'd like to get back to it.'

'Her *dead* name. Why didn't I know that?' said Jack.

'I don't know, Jack. Maybe it's time you woke up. Stop moping about focused on your own life and start thinking about other people. Why don't you know that Arun wants you to make a move? Wake up, boy. Listen to the two of you singing. Everyone else knows what's going on. Listen to me: I know what it's like. You mustn't let this get away from you. You need to speak to Arun – now. Tell him how you feel. Tell him ... "the sun and moon rise in his eyes. Reach out to him ..."'

Jack was aghast. He put up both hands to defend himself. 'Oh my god, Dorothy. Stop now! That's a Barbra Streisand song.'

'Yes,' agreed Dorothy, 'although let's not leave out Celine Dion.'

Jack pursed his lips and looked at her intently. 'Are you sure you're not a gay man?'

'I don't know. Are you? And now, if you'll excuse us, Wendy and I are going to dance. Can you push her out to the dance floor, please?'

Jack felt he was on some other planet and did as he was told. Donna Summer had just started playing and an astonishing number of old women, including Birdie in her wheelchair and the old woman with the walking poles from the square, were boogieing away to 'Hot Stuff'.

Jack felt ashamed. He went behind the bar and stood beside Agnes, who was replacing a whisky bottle in one of the dispensers.

'Sorry, Agnes. I don't think I've been very nice to you. I didn't know,' he finished lamely. It was only then he saw that Agnes had tears in her eyes.

'You shouldn't need to,' she said evenly. 'It shouldn't make any difference. You of all people. Be nice anyway.'

16

J ack poured himself a large drink and then another before
 seeking out Arun. Arun, who had been so bold with his
singing, was now feeling shaken by what had happened. He
thought that he and Jack might talk about it but Jack was on
his own path.

'Arun, I need your help,' he began. 'I've been horrible to Agnes
and I . . . I think I'm going to go to hell.'

'Do you believe in hell?' Arun asked.

'Not until this minute. I mean, I don't think so but, you know,
I don't want to find out.'

Arun thought for a second and then suggested,

'I don't really know how it works but maybe . . . maybe if you
do a nice thing then it'll make up for it.'

The round king and the cuddly bear were both severely tipsy.
They stood surveying the room, trying to find someone to be nice
to, and unfortunately their eyes alighted on Mrs Haggerston. She
was still at the party but had made no friends. A couple of people
had tried sitting at her table, but she had rebuffed all offers of

companionship. Someone had selected Elvis, who was busy asking 'Are You Lonesome Tonight?' Pop music has an intense potency for emotion and Mrs H was a fool to herself, for now she radiated loneliness.

'Mrs Haggerston!' Jack and Arun said in unison.

'No one likes her,' whispered Jack.

'Exactly,' said Arun. 'I think that's extra points.'

Where these points were coming from was unclear but the two men went over to her anyway.

'Mrs Haggerston?' Jack began.

'And you are?'

'Jack ... Stevie's friend. Stevie? Your neighbour. Next door at Number 4?'

Mrs H harrumphed, as if this was not a good starting point.

'May I get you a drink?'

'Alcohol is the devil's work,' she replied.

'She's very tense,' whispered Arun to his co-conspirator. 'Try crisps!' but this offer was also turned down.

Jack remembered that he had brought one of his grand-mother's special brownies as back-up in case Birdie's courage faded.

'They are really good,' he whispered to Arun.

'I can't believe you have dope cake,' replied Arun.

'Do you not approve?' asked Jack anxiously.

'Only that you've never shared.'

Jack pulled a small foil-wrapped parcel from his coat pocket and went to get a plate. He added a bright napkin and made the small cake look as beautiful as he could. He didn't have high hopes but took it over anyway.

'I brought you a bit of chocolate cake,' he tried with a smile.

Mrs Haggerston looked all set to refuse but she had a great

204

fondness for chocolate, a sweet treat which she hardly ever allowed herself.

'It's home-made,' added Jack, putting the offering down on the table. It did look very good and Jack added a cheery 'Merry Christmas'.

Arun and Jack retreated to the piano and watched out of the corners of their eyes. Mrs H took her time. She turned the plate slowly, examining the cake for any inconsistencies, and then gingerly broke off a tiny corner, which she brought to her mouth. It was delicious. She had been determined not to eat too much but the brownie was beautifully moist and very chocolatey. She broke off another morsel and then another before finally picking the remaining cake up and consuming the whole thing.

Jack and Arun watched and waited.

'I think it's working,' Arun slurred as they saw Mrs H look up and actually smile at Bobby as he passed with a woman on his arm, who was giggling as he said,

'Have I mentioned I'm free range?'

Next Mrs Haggerston began tapping along to the Jacksons, who were blaming it on the boogie from the jukebox.

'It's a triumph!' declared Jack.

And indeed she was so relaxed that her head fell forward on her chest, and after a few moments she stopped moving at all. Jack and Arun stood staring at her for quite some time, hoping for a sign of life, but there was nothing happening. Nothing at all. They moved closer and without wanting to draw attention to themselves, surreptitiously began clicking their fingers in front of her eyes.

'She all right?' asked Dorothy, passing them on her way to the loo for the umpteenth time.

'She's ... FINE,' said Jack.

'FINE,' agreed Arun a bit too loudly.

But the pissed men began to grow uncertain.

'Do you think it was too much?' queried Arun anxiously. 'Do you think she could be ... dead?'

'I don't think you can die from one dope brownie ...' began Jack, not at all sure that he was right.

Agnes stepped up onto the stage. 'Time to announce the best costume prize.'

There was a low murmur of excitement and Stevie and Amber went to join the throng gathering in front of the stage. They stopped by the men. Arun smiled innocently and tipped his glittering crown in greeting. Stevie was suspicious.

'What are you two up to?' she asked.

'Nothing,' Jack answered innocently.

Just then Mrs Haggerston proved she was still alive by beginning to snore. Really loudly.

Jack, thrilled that he hadn't killed anyone, burst out with bizarre delight, 'She's snoring! Mrs Haggerston is snoring!'

'You all right, Jack?' asked Stevie. There was definitely something suspicious going on.

'He's FINE,' reassured Arun before stiffly indicating Mrs Haggerston and adding, 'Because ... *she's* FINE.'

Mrs Haggerston continued making snuffling noises of sleep.

'I've never seen her so chilled,' marvelled Amber.

'We should probably get her home,' Arun mused.

'Really?' said Stevie. 'Don't you want to hear who's won?'

Jack smiled. 'Yes, but taking her home is the right thing to do,' he declared earnestly. Stevie was not certain about this version of Jack she was witnessing but she let it go.

'Would you get a sweater for Amber while you're there?' she

asked. 'I don't want her to get cold when we walk home. Here's the key.'

'I'm OK,' protested Amber.

'Everybody is fine,' agreed Jack. 'But let's do it anyway.'

Jack and Arun were ill prepared to deal with Mrs Haggerston. They tried gently poking her, but she didn't shift her chin from her chest.

'Really, really asleep,' marvelled Arun.

'We could carry her,' suggested Jack. Arun was horrified at the thought but in the end they gently took the sleeping woman under her arms and lifted her to her feet. As they half carried, half dragged her between them, Jack and Arun could hear Agnes announcing 'And the prize for . . .'

Once they got started, Mrs Haggerston almost flew across the square. She was really quite light and gave no resistance whatsoever. She probably had never had drugs of any kind, but this was clearly the one for her. Jack and Arun had no trouble air-lifting her to her front door. A baby bear and a fairy-tale king returning her home. They found the key to Number 5 in her bag and let themselves in.

Mrs H's sitting room was as much of an homage to retail excess as her garden. Both Arun and Jack liked a bit of camp décor but this was a cave of kitsch. Mirrored tile lined the walls above the dado rail, reflecting the backsides of porcelain women who twirled in full skirts on a narrow shelf. There were dozens of them. Each more fey than the next.

'Doulton ladies,' whispered Jack knowledgably.

'Hideous,' said Arun.

The ladies looked down on endless framed signs displaying homilies above a sofa awash with hand-knitted toys. There was a red tin soldier, a hippo in a pink tutu. Arun and Jack deposited the sleeping woman on her sofa between a sunglasses-wearing giraffe and a boxing kangaroo. She flopped forward.

'Push her back a bit,' urged Arun. 'She might fall off.'

Jack grabbed a cushion embroidered with *The Best is Yet to Come*. He hesitated with it in his hand. He pointed to her chest. Perhaps it was the flying across the square but a couple of the buttons on Mrs Haggerston's blouse had come undone.

'Oh god,' he cried, stepping back. 'I can see her … you know …'

Arun paused to have a look at Mrs H's chest. 'Oh yes,' he agreed before looking again. 'Are they meant to be that low?'

Neither man wanted to do her shirt up, so Jack pushed Mrs Haggerston back with the cushion while Arun got a tea towel from the kitchen and laid it over her exposed bosom. It had some text which he read aloud:

'He is Risen.'

'Must be for baking,' said Jack. 'Oh my god, I love this!' he continued, picking up a small china bell emblazoned with the words *Ring for Jesus* off the mantelpiece. He gave it a slight tinkle and put his head on one side as he waited. 'Nothing,' he said, disappointed.

'Come on,' said Arun, who was being marginally more sensible.

As they left the house, the two men almost got stuck in the doorway, each trying to be polite to the other. For a moment they stood face to face, unable to move. Jack felt as though he couldn't breathe. The brief interlude of tension was broken by Mrs Haggerston letting out a huge snore and causing the men to rush outside. They shut the door and headed back to the street, where they could hear the party was still in full swing. The lights from the pub shone out on the square and for once it looked beautiful.

'We have to go back,' said Jack.

'Amber's sweater!' remembered Arun.

They let themselves into Number 4, and Jack fetched the sweater while Arun stayed downstairs. The only light in the room shone from a street light in the square. It was dark and quiet.

'I thought we could have a cup of tea,' suggested Arun nonchalantly when Jack returned.

'Great!' said Jack but neither one of them moved toward the kettle. Instead Arun slowly inched toward his furry friend. He was just about to put his hand on Jack's arm when the lights in the back garden came on and shone through the kitchen window. They both froze.

'She's up,' whispered Jack. 'Mrs Haggerston!'

They tiptoed to the window and looked out. Over the fence they could see Mrs Haggerston was awake and had come out into her garden. She did not look entirely compos mentis. She took two steps and then suddenly seemed to disappear.

The two men went outside to the garden of Number 4 where Jack dared to look over the fence.

'Can you see her?' asked Arun.

'She's asleep on that swing sofa thing.'

Arun paused and looked up at the sky.

'Oh my god, it's going to snow.'

Now they both looked up, as if neither of them had ever seen such a thing before. Great fat flakes of December snow began to fall, slowly but steadily. The really heavy kind which settles in an instant. They were in for a blanket of the stuff. Arun and Jack stood looking over the fence as a fine layer of white began to cover the sleeping Mrs Haggerston. She seemed oblivious to this change in the weather and settled back to very loud snoring.

209

'She'll freeze to death and then it'll be our fault and no one will like us,' predicted Arun, pushing his gold crown back on his head.

'Let's get her,' said Jack, pulling a garden chair toward the fence and beginning to climb over. He practically fell into Mrs Haggerston's garden and was swiftly followed by Arun. Something had happened to the woman. She was now so deeply asleep that she had become a complete dead weight.

'Fuck,' said Arun as they failed to move her.

Jack, who, whenever he had a few, mistakenly believed he was at his most brilliant, declared,

'I know! I'll light a fire. Keep her warm.'

The back door was open, so he went into the kitchen at Number 5 and found some matches. Arun moved the frog-faced bin nearer to Mrs H and removed the lid. As luck would have it, it was full of recycling – paper and cardboard.

'Perfect!' said Jack and lit a match. The flame went up pretty swiftly and Jack turned his back on the blaze. As he did so his fur coat swung toward the fire. The wretched thing was as fake as Dorothy had said and the nylon threads caught fire immediately. The yard was small and the flames from the teddy-bear inferno, having shot several feet in the air, had nowhere to go but hit the twin towers of Notre-Dame. Rather like the real thing, it too began to blaze.

Arun never gave a thought to his own safety. He grabbed Jack and pulled him to the ground, rolling on top of him to put out the flames. Their faces were inches apart and the fire forgotten. Jack was safe now. He didn't need rescuing but neither man moved. They looked into each other's eyes, trying to guess what could or should happen. Neither dared take the next step. Afterwards Jack would believe Arun kissed him and Arun was

210

certain Jack had leaned in first. It was the lightest touch of the lips, but it was electrifying. It was also the moment when Mrs Haggerston woke up.

In the firelight she saw a black king rescuing her from a brown bear and cried out 'Balthazar!'

Arun leapt to his feet with astonishing speed, leaving the fur bear on the floor.

'There was a fire,' murmured Arun, mortified. 'Jack was on fire. Did you see that? I had to roll on top of him because ... fire ...'

The flames continued to leap from the bird feeder. Jack left Arun to it and ran inside to call 999.

Stevie, Amber and Dorothy came home not long afterwards. The party had been brought to a halt by the police arriving to look for an old woman who had gone missing from a local care home. Stevie suspected Dorothy had had a hand in the matter so she went outside to chat to the officers and calm things, and saw the fire engine outside her house.

The fire was put out and the retirement home escapee was found and returned. No one at the Onion was able to help the police with any information about any of it.

Rochelle of the Jane Topper Care Home would always say the illicit outing killed her patient, and perhaps that was true, but when the elderly party-goer passed away they removed her oxygen mask and found she was grinning from ear to ear.

17

'Please don't mention Brexit, or the price of petrol. Don't say a word about gay pride but do know that it's ridiculous we have a parade each year. They're not homophobic but you have to understand, my mum and dad have been married for more than forty years and have never seen the need to show off about it. *They've* never had a parade. Cricket is not what it used to be because not everyone wears white any more, so you don't know where you are with that. Why oh why do *craft* beer people think they're so special and' – Stevie glanced at Amber – 'no one should send a digitally generated birthday card.'

'I was trying to be nice,' muttered her wife. Amber was busy setting up a tiny Christmas tree in the bay window.

'And, dear god, no one mention immigration,' Stevie concluded.

'Or that my mother is blacker than me,' added Amber. 'They've never met her, and we want it to be a surprise.'

'He'll tell you that he's not a racialist—'

'A racialist?' repeated Dorothy, baffled, but Stevie ploughed on.

'—and that when he complains about this country becoming entirely black in his lifetime he obviously doesn't mean Amber, who in some lights almost doesn't look black at all.'

Dorothy finished wrapping a few bits of privet hedge topped here and there with red buttons around white candles. She had covered the dining table – now extended by an old card table from a skip – with a spare red curtain from the pub. The two surfaces were slightly different heights but it looked fine and Agnes had provided some crackers. There was plenty of room for everyone: Stevie, Amber, Jack, Birdie, Dorothy, Malcolm and Barbara, and a seat for Faith, if she made it. Everything was jolly apart from Stevie's mood. The looming threat of the festive day with her parents always put her in a terrible state.

Out of nowhere Dorothy seemed to have magicked some lovely ruby red wine glasses. She picked one up to give it a professional polish as she turned to Amber. 'Did your mum get back to you about coming?'

'She's going to do her best, she said.'

Stevie got up and began removing and replacing books on some new Ikea shelves. The room was really beginning to come together. Painted a lovely light blue with white shelves, it was calm and welcoming. Stevie wasn't at all sure Amber didn't have Scandinavian roots.

'Stevie, what are you doing?' enquired Amber, having finished her seasonal decorating by placing a shiny angel on the top of the tree.

'Sorting, just sorting,' answered Stevie, who needed to be distracted. 'I've done them all by subject matter so you can find what you want really quickly. This is history here, there's a gay section, feminism, gardening and cooking ...' She held up a black leather book. 'Why do we have a Bible?'

213

'It's mine from school,' said Amber. 'Put it away.'

'History or fiction?' asked Stevie.

Dorothy laughed but she was nervous. 'What have you told them all about ... me being here?'

Amber gave a slight sigh. 'My mum, we told the truth. Malcolm and Barbara are a little more ... complicated. You're lodging here to help us with the cost of the building work.'

'And where did you find me?' Dorothy said, curious about this backstory.

Amber looked awkward. 'OK, unusually, Barbara phoned. She phoned me because she couldn't get hold of Stevie and I was caught on the hop. I said I met you at work, but Barbara was enjoying the chat. She wanted to know more. Once I'd started, the story rather grew. I said you've come back from living in Australia for years and looked the wrong way when you crossed the road.'

'Am I all right?' asked Dorothy nervously.

Amber smiled. 'Not a serious injury, thank goodness.'

'Small blessings. And why did I leave Australia?'

'Because you got tired of it.'

Dorothy nodded. 'Fair enough. A woman can only cope with so much barbeque.'

Dorothy thought for a moment. 'Don't they drive on the left in Australia, same as us?' she asked.

'Shit!' replied Amber. 'Well, I don't think she noticed.'

Stevie was pacing up and down, beside herself, still holding the Bible.

'I can't do this, Amber. He makes me crazy. They won't want to be here.'

'Yes they will. It's our turn and anyway, your dad said we're practically on their current petrol loop.'

'Give that to me, Stevie,' commanded Dorothy, gently taking the Bible from her.

Amber went and stood in front of Stevie, holding her by both shoulders to get her to calm down. 'They love you, Stevie,' she soothed.

'No! They love the idea of me, not the actual me. He always says something that makes my blood boil. I promise, he'll tell everyone that I was an accident and that they never should have had me. That they were never sure about the gay thing but only cope because they really like you.'

'I am very likeable,' agreed Amber, kissing her wife and stroking her face.

'OK, party game!' announced Dorothy. 'It's Jesus' big day so let's play "Random Quote" from his book. I choose a Bible verse with my eyes closed and you have to guess what it will be about. Whoever is nearest wins. Amber?'

'Uh, sex.'

'Stevie?'

'I don't know.' Stevie did not want to play but it was Christmas, so she shrugged and said, 'Figs?'

'Figs is good,' agreed Dorothy. 'I can't decide. Serpents or dragons? Serpents.' She closed her eyes, flipped the Bible open and pointed at a page before reopening her eyes and beginning to read aloud.

'Ezekiel 23:19: *Yet she increased her prostitution, remembering the days of her youth when she engaged in prostitution in the land of Egypt. She lusted after their genitals as large as those of donkeys, and their seminal emission was as strong as that of stallions.*'

'Sex! Amber wins!' Dorothy shook her head in mock despair. 'So annoying! I had thought of donkeys.' She looked back at the book with renewed interest. 'Racier than I remember. I might give this another read.'

She put the Bible away on a shelf and went to fetch a mince pie, which she handed to Stevie. 'Stop clapping your hands,' she ordered. 'Have a sugar rush instead. It's only one day. We can do this.'

The front door at Number 4 was open and they could hear the sound of Birdie and Jack arriving. It was early but Birdie had insisted they would come to help. Dorothy went to get the turkey in the oven but it was heavy so Stevie went to help. Jack looked very smart in a pair of Prince of Wales check trousers and a Harrington jacket, today in bright red. He was already wearing a paper crown as he had lost half an eyebrow in the previous night's fiery activities and was keeping quiet about it. He had tilted the festive hat at a jaunty angle to cover his missing facial feature. Despite the jolly headgear he did not look too clever, unlike his grandmother, who was in fine fettle. Having been out once, Birdie now had a taste for it. She had slept exceptionally well and had got up excited to be invited for lunch. She had dressed up for the occasion, wrapping herself in a shawl with Christmas trees woven into it.

Jack and Amber had just managed to get Birdie's wheelchair in through the door when there was a loud beeping from the street. Stevie ran out from the kitchen.

'That's them!' she cried. 'They're here.'

'How can you tell?' asked Dorothy, wiping stuffing from her fingers.

'Dad always beeps. He never rings.'

'Good to know.'

Stevie knew her parents' habits well. Out of the sitting room window it was impossible to overlook the fact that her parents,

216

Malcolm and Barbara Baxter, had arrived in their motorhome with Malcolm unnecessarily sounding the horn. No one could have missed their arrival. It was quite the biggest vehicle the square had ever seen. Just over eight metres long, it managed to cast a shadow over the whole of Number 4, all of Mrs Haggerston's and a portion of Number 6. Now that they were living on the road full time, Malcolm had wanted something with plenty of space, which he had certainly got. The trouble with that was the parking.

'I should probably go and help,' said Stevie, failing to move.

'Go on then, darling,' encouraged Amber. 'I'll get Birdie a drink.'

Reluctantly Stevie went out into the street to assist. Fortunately there was more available parking than usual as a lot of people were away for the holiday but the vehicle was ginormous and still required a lot of toing and froing. Her father wanted to ensure that it was parked exactly outside Stevie's property, where he could keep an eye on it. He could probably have kept an eye on it from space, but Barbara had been made to get out and help. Unfortunately she always seemed to stand where Malcolm couldn't see her in his mirrors. Despite the fact that she was wearing a bright red jumper with an appliqué penguin in a glitter Christmas hat, he could not catch sight of her. There was quite a lot of shouting going on when Mrs Haggerston appeared in the front garden. She had taken her time getting ready and was now fully dressed in a smart hat and coat, and carrying her best handbag. Christmas Day was a big day for her, but she was not feeling entirely clever. A considerable headache plus the previous night's fire had made her less than charitable.

'You!' she hissed, pointing at Stevie and shaking with rage. 'I knew the minute you moved in, pretending to be a police officer to get my guard down . . .'

Barbara spied her daughter and moved to say hello but was stopped in her tracks by Malcolm shouting, 'Am I in at the back?'

Barbara knew she was in charge of being 'in at the back', but she was never sure what that meant and the whole process often left her on the edge of tears. She moved back behind the giant van. Above her head a small, fading rainbow sticker was fixed to the window. She stood underneath it, by the exhaust pipe which was belching acrid fumes and choking her.

Dorothy, who was on best behaviour for Stevie and Amber, came out to say hello to Mr and Mrs Baxter. She spied Mrs Haggerston first and, knowing there might be work to do to calm her neighbour, misguidedly thought she'd head off trouble by launching into her Christmas present of a daily saint.

'Ah, Mrs H! Merry Christmas! What a good day for saints. Everyone talks about Jesus on this day, but I think that is rather overlooking the fact that it is also the feast day of Saint Eugenia of Rome.' Dorothy turned to Stevie and said, very pleased,

'It's her saint day today and she's rather good because she pretended to be a man.'

Malcolm leant out of the driver's window to get Barbara to shift into his eyeline. Dorothy waved at him and found the first thing she said to him was the sentence,

'One of your *gender fluid* saints.'

Dorothy turned back to include Mrs Haggerston, who tried to interrupt but could not get a word in. Unable to see or hear Barbara, Malcolm got out of the van deeply frustrated. He went round the front to check how close in to the kerb he was while his wife stayed at the back, awaiting further instruction. The sound of the engine meant she couldn't really hear what was happening. Dorothy smiled warmly at Malcolm, but she was in full flow with Mrs H and didn't want to stop. Truth be told, she didn't want to give Mrs Haggerston a moment to tell the Baxters about the burning of her cathedral bird feeder.

'You'll know all this, Mrs Haggerston. Eugenia was the daughter of Philip, governor of Egypt. I'll be honest,' admitted Dorothy, as if she were being generous, 'there's something missing in the story. She had run away from papa dressed in men's clothing and I have no idea why. Anyway, as a bloke she got baptised by some bishop and it clearly went well coz she stayed a man and became an abbot, as you do. Climbing up the ranks, Abbott Eugenia then cured some woman of an illness, and the woman thought, Hello, I like this abbot, and she made, you know . . . *advances*.'

These words caused Malcolm to look up from his kerbside inspection and approach the small group.

'Dorothy!' Stevie tried to change the subject, but Dorothy held up her hand to be allowed to continue.

'Not my words. The book of saints. Of course Eugenia said no! Well, the woman was hurt so she accused the abbot of adultery. Eugenia had to go to court, where, still disguised, she came before – what are the chances? – her old dad as the judge. At the trial, her real female identity was revealed and she was let off. Eugenia moved to Rome, where she converted loads of people, especially maidens. Clearly had a way with the ladies. Anyway, in the end Christ appeared to her in a dream and told her that she would die on the Feast of the Nativity, and she was beheaded on December 25th, which is hardly festive, is it? Make a mess of the tablecloth for a start. I've no idea what happened to the woman who first fancied her.'

Malcolm had stood stock still, utterly dumbfounded. He liked to think of himself as a decisive man but had no idea what to do with this tale.

'That's a story they never tell at Christmas,' Dorothy concluded.

'No,' he managed.

'Hello, I'm Dorothy.'

'I'm still at the back!' called Barbara, not sure what was going on.

Perhaps it was the after-effects of the night before or the horror of Eugenia's story, but Mrs Haggerston exploded.

'I have had enough! Enough! You heathen, the lot of you!' She pointed at the whole group outside Number 4 and swept the poor newly arrived Baxters up in her fury. Barbara appeared from the back of the motorhome just in time to have a finger pointed at her and be told,

'Hell will rain down on you. Sinners! Strutting about with your' – she pointed to the back window – 'with your rainbow flags which everyone knows *belong* to the NHS! Babylon! Antichrist! I am going to church, and I will pray for you but there is no point. You will be punished!' She then turned in a great huff and marched off down the street.

There was a considerable pause.

Amber, who had missed the whole thing, now appeared in the door calling out cheerfully,

'Malcolm, Barbara! Welcome! Come on in!'

'Did you want to bring anything in?' Stevie managed.

'I've got everything to make butterfly cakes,' said Barbara weakly.

Barbara collected her baking things while Malcolm checked he was definitely in at the back. Then he fetched a Sainsbury's shopping bag and locked up the motorhome before going back twice to check he had done it properly.

'I do think that is right about the rainbow flags,' whispered Barbara to her husband as they walked up the path to the house. 'I do think they ought to be just for the NHS.'

Jack had been watching all this through the window, too terrified to come out in case Mrs Haggerston somehow knew he had seen too much of her the night before. Suddenly he felt awkward in his paper hat and took it off.

'Jack!' bellowed Malcolm, banging on the glass as he caught sight of 'the boy' who he had known since he was seven.

'Mr B-Baxter,' Jack stuttered.

'Your face looks crooked!' Malcolm shouted through the glass.

Jack waved a hand at his own face. 'Yes. Yes ... I ... lost an ... eyebrow, Mr Baxter,' he said loudly, not wanting to admit how.

'You're all grown up now!' Mr Baxter carried on shouting, uninterested in the eyebrow. 'Call me Malcolm!'

'Yes, Mr Baxter,' replied Jack.

With that sorted Malcolm marched in, nodded to Stevie, who was waiting in the doorway, and went to find a comfortable seat. He plonked himself down on the new navy two-seater sofa with its pale blue striped cushions. His wife followed more slowly, taking her time to stop and hug Stevie tight.

'Hello, love,' she said. 'I've missed you.'

'I missed you too, Mum. Is Dad all right?'

Barbara gave a slight wince. 'His back is bad. Too much driving.'

'Drives you mad, a bad back,' empathised Dorothy, rubbing her own.

'Is yours from driving?' asked Barbara.

221

'No, bladder cancer,' replied Dorothy cheerfully.

This was too much information for an Englishwoman, so Barbara said nothing.

The older Baxters were not blessed with good looks; thankfully their rather handsome daughter looked like neither of them. Malcolm was a short man whose stomach had expanded since they had taken to life on the road. His skin had been bleached pale by endless rain at the caravan sites and blown air from the van's heating system. The hair on his head was now mere wisps of memory but he had tried to even out this loss by growing a thin moustache. It reminded Stevie of the solicitor Graham's terrible moustache, and she wondered why men thought these adornments racy. It was possible that Malcolm had left this facial excitement a little late in life for it was patchy and in no way could really be said to be working. It was as if a small creature had expired on his lip. But at least he had that. There was nothing quite so distinguishing about Barbara. It would be kind to say she was an average woman. Average in every way – height, weight, looks, with a bad short hair style which she must have cut herself.

Stevie had never seen her mother with cropped hair. She had always had the same shoulder-length bob. It was faintly shocking.

'Mum, what happened to your—' she began but Dorothy interrupted.

'Let me take those trays for you, Barbara,' she said.

Introductions were made, flour and cake trays placed in the kitchen, and everyone sat down. Barbara squeezed in beside her husband, who grudgingly accommodated her on the small sofa. Dorothy really was doing her best and tried to turn on some kind of cocktail party charm. Amber made everyone coffee with only Dorothy declining. She had her usual cup of tea and took sips in between bursts of politeness. Mrs Haggerston was explained away as having mental health issues, which even Malcolm knew was a thing.

'She might have that ADAC everyone's got these days,' he commented.

'You've cut your hair, Mum,' Stevie finally managed, still startled by the change.

Barbara put her hand up to her new 'do and nodded. 'It's the travelling. There isn't always as much water as I'd like. I can't wash it as often as—'

'A good vanlifer thinks ahead and saves their supplies,' interrupted Malcolm. A piece of advice to which no one could think of a follow-up sentence.

'Isn't this nice!' commented Barbara brightly, looking around the room. 'I like the colour in here. Different, isn't it?'

'Different?' repeated Amber.

'We knocked through!' said Stevie.

'Nice,' repeated Barbara.

'I gather, Malcolm, that you are retired,' Dorothy tried. 'From what line of work?'

Malcolm cleared his throat with his own importance. 'I was in paperware distribution,' he said as Barbara mouthed the same words.

Dorothy frowned. 'Which is ...?'

'Plates, cups, anything disposable which you might need for an occasion. Actually,' Malcolm said, thrilled by the thought, 'I've brought a seasonal tablecloth for today. Still got my connections to the business,' he declared, very pleased his power was not waning.

Dorothy made a face at Birdie to get her to join in. 'How nice,' Birdie said.

Malcolm handed the plastic bag he had brought to his daughter. She looked inside before saying, 'This is for Easter.'

'Is it?' replied Malcolm.

'It has chickens on it.'

'Aren't we having chicken?' asked Barbara, trying her best to make everything all right.

'Turkey,' said Jack, the single word being his only contribution so far. Jack was terrified of Mr Baxter. He had always found the man overwhelming. He was so frightened of saying the wrong thing and he was also in a daze about Arun. He could not stop thinking about him. Perhaps he might see him later. Was it acceptable to call on Christmas Day? Had the kiss been a mistake? They had both had quite a bit to drink. Might Arun not even remember?

'Of course. Turkey,' said Barbara.

'Lovely,' said Birdie.

'And what about you ... Dorothy, is it?' Malcolm turned his attention to the old woman who had just spoken.

'I'm Birdie,' said Birdie. 'That's Dorothy.'

'Ha!' laughed Malcolm. 'Sorry! Like an old people's home in here. Dorothy!' He faced the correct woman. 'Australia, eh?'

It seemed a random thought until Dorothy remembered she was supposed to have returned from Down Under. 'Yes ...' Dorothy tried to think of anything she knew about the place.

'Australia?' said Birdie, confused. 'Like Adam Anderson?'

Dorothy stared at her friend before saying brightly, 'Yes! Yes! I went ... hoping to meet Adam Anderson, but when I got there I discovered – and this'll make you laugh – he lives here!'

'*Step into the Spotlight*!' beamed Barbara but Malcolm ignored her. He had never heard of Adam Anderson and he hated gaps in his knowledge being exposed particularly by his wife,

224

so he simply said, 'I've never been. Odd, though. I thought they drove on the left like us.'

'Not to be trusted,' Dorothy replied, as if that explained everything.

Malcolm nodded. 'Long way to get bitten by something,' he opined. 'I heard that their houses are not properly insulated.'

It was pretty certain that no one else in the room had ever heard that but Malcolm liked the odd, unexpected fact which made him look widely read.

'And now that you *are* back, *Dorothy*, what keeps you busy?'

'Oh, you know, working the streets,' she replied, smiling.

Malcolm nearly choked on his coffee. He could be heard whispering to Barbara squashed in beside him, 'Prostitute! That's why she doesn't have a proper home.'

'No, Malcolm!' Barbara whispered back. 'You have to say "sex worker".'

Stevie could hardly speak. 'Minicab driver,' she tried. 'Minicab driver,' but her parents were not listening, nor would they have thought it a sensible answer.

Dorothy smiled and gave a slight groan as she got up.

'I'm just going to check the turkey,' she announced.

When she came back to the sitting room Malcolm had moved on to family history and although her father had only been in the house half an hour, Stevie already looked on the edge of blowing up.

'Stephanie was our last child,' he said expansively, smiling at Stevie. 'We already had four considerably older children and had no intention of any more, so she was our little *accident*.'

'Dad, please could you . . .'

Malcolm scowled at some slight back pain and stood up. 'Nice lot of books you've got. You read all these?'

225

'Amber likes to ...' began Stevie. Her father ran his hand along the titles and randomly picked one out.

'What's this? *Islam and Homosexuality.*' The words died on his lips.

'Of all the books ...' muttered Amber.

'Double whammy,' replied Jack.

Stevie looked at Amber and, speaking very slowly, said, 'It's in the ... gay section but maybe we could do with one just for ... religion ...'

Amber raised her eyebrows to Dorothy, who immediately jumped up and clapped her hands.

'Right, family meeting!'

Barbara looked puzzled.

'She wants our attention,' explained Stevie.

Dorothy took charge. 'Amber, why don't you show Barbara where everything is in the kitchen for her cakes? And keep an eye on the turkey. Birdie, you can fold these napkins into nice ... shapes while Jack, Stevie and I go out and ... fetch a bag of coal.' She turned brightly to Mr Baxter, saying, 'And Malcolm, I expect you'd like a bit of shut-eye? I nod off rather well on that little sofa.' She paused. 'Maybe ... pop the book back.'

Everyone did as they were told. Stevie, Jack and Dorothy put on their coats and left the house. Snow was once more gently falling in the deserted square. After the good coating of the night before it looked quite pretty but the three of them were not in the mood for it and walked away from the house in silence.

'Why do we want a bag of coal?' asked Stevie. 'We don't have a fire.'

'It seemed Christmassy. Sort of thing Tiny Tim might've popped out for. We just need a bit of time out,' said Dorothy,

226

taking a deep breath of fresh air. 'Let's try not to explode until we at least get round the corner.'

'Sex worker! He called you a sex worker!'

'And we just managed to turn the corner,' commented Dorothy. 'I'm going to take it as a compliment,' she said, trying to calm Stevie, but her young friend was off on a rant.

'And what the fuck was all that sinner nonsense from Mrs Haggerston this morning?' she almost yelled. 'I don't need this shit from anyone. I am sick of it. I get it at work, in the street . . .' she fumed as they came to a corner where a large Victorian church stood.

It was an impressive edifice which, made into a scale model, might have made an excellent bird feeder. A large sign read 'St Mary the Virgin'.

'It's not all right,' agreed Dorothy, who was in a feisty mood. 'Mrs fucking Haggerston. Judgemental twat!'

'She was probably upset,' suggested Jack, who knew it was his fault. 'I'm so sorry I . . .'

Stevie shook her fist at the church. 'How dare anyone comment on my life and Jack's? I'm not going to take any of it any more!' she shouted.

Dorothy, who felt there was nothing more to lose, responded, 'Good idea. Me neither!'

She marched up the path to the church and opened the large wooden door. Stevie and Jack had no idea what was happening but following Dorothy seemed preferable to going home.

Despite it being Christmas morning there was not a large congregation. Perhaps twenty or so people were gathered. Mostly elderly and entirely white except for the vicar. In another life Dorothy might have fitted right in. The church itself was rather a beautiful building made of grey granite, but the parish was poor and they couldn't justify turning the heating on. The dutiful flock sat wrapped in coats and scarves, listening to a quite rotund woman vicar, who was giving a rather jolly sermon from the pulpit which was everyone was enjoying. Nevertheless Dorothy bursting in with Stevie and Jack in tow was now the more exciting event.

Dorothy led the way, striding up to the front. Stevie had decided this had gone too far and tried to reach for Dotty's arm, but it was too late. Dorothy was already in full flight.

'I'm sorry to interrupt but I need to say something,' she began. The vicar smiled and paused.

'Christmas Day,' Dorothy continued. 'Jesus' birthday, right?' It was an opening gambit which suggested she might have only popped in to learn the basics. Dorothy looked up at the pulpit and noticed a large stained-glass window in the wall behind. It bore a particularly gruesome depiction of Jesus on the cross with a lot of blood and very sharp thorns. The sight of him caused her to pause and she almost found herself giving a slight bow of apology for what she was about to say. Pointing at Stevie, who thought she was going to die of embarrassment, and then at Jack, who was sure he was going to faint, Dorothy took a deep breath and continued.

'I'm upset for my friends, and I want to know if you really think Jesus was bothered about gay people. I tell you what I think: I don't believe he ever said a word about it, but I do remember from school that he wanted us all for ...' Those school lessons were a very long time ago and what Jesus had wanted Dorothy for did not spring instantly to mind. 'He wanted us for ... for ... his sunbeams! Right?'

A couple of the older women nodded. That sunbeam thing, that was right.

228

'Not some of us,' continued Dorothy. 'Not just one or two but all of us and that includes my friends here. You will not find nicer, kinder, more decent human beings in this country than Stevie and Jack. I'm pretty sure the Bible says more about eating prawns than it mentions them. Aren't you supposed to be about love? Isn't that the point? Bring me your tired, your poor ...'

'I think that might be the poem from the Statue of Liberty in New York,' whispered Stevie.

Dorothy waved her arms at the congregation. 'I'm sure you think you're nice people but you're being taught terrible things. Stevie ...' Once more Dorothy pointed at her friend, making it super clear who she was talking about. 'Stevie loves her wife with a passion I have rarely seen. It is a beautiful thing to be around. We heterosexuals should be so lucky. How dare you make it dirty? How dare you put yourselves up on some pedestal and imagine that you are better than her? I do not believe that Jesus would have done that. He seems like a decent guy, and you should all be ashamed of yourselves.'

Dorothy took a breath and the vicar leant down from her pulpit to address her.

'You do sound cross,' she said kindly. 'I am so sorry about that, but I think it's possible you want St Agatha's on the next street. Harper Lane? They are a bit more ... conservative. Might be what you're looking for.'

Dorothy ran her eye across every one of the very focused faces in the congregation.

'Where's Mrs Haggerston?'

'I don't think we have a Mrs Haggerston,' replied the vicar, who knew her flock well. The elderly group murmured their agreement. No, no they did not have a Mrs Haggerston.

'I'm in the wrong church?'

229

The very nice woman vicar nodded. 'I think so,' she said and smiled again as if the interruption had been nothing but a pleasure. 'Everyone …' She looked at Stevie and smiled. 'Absolutely *everyone* is welcome here,' she said. 'Stevie, I am delighted you have someone wonderful in your life. Merry Christmas to you all.'

Dorothy turned to Stevie and Jack, and out of nowhere gave a slight swagger with her shoulders.

'Right. Let's bounce,' she said loudly and headed back outside.

Stevie moved to leave but Jack stood stock still for a moment before addressing the vicar.

'So then,' he said, 'I think we're off. Uhm …' He pointed to a floral arrangement on the altar. 'Nice flowers,' he said as he retreated. 'Excellent colour choices.'

The heavy wooden door clanged behind them as Dorothy, Stevie and Jack exited back into the churchyard. The snow was falling heavily now, and the street was empty. Stevie looked at Dorothy with a mix of horror and awe.

'"Let's bounce"?' she echoed.

'Yeah, I thought they might report me to the police, so I thought I'd confuse them by not seeming so old.'

The three lost souls stood looking at each other. Dorothy appeared almost sheepish.

'Did you want to try St Agatha's?' Stevie dared to ask.

Dorothy brushed some snow off her shoulders before saying, 'No, I think that will do. The carrots will want sorting.'

They headed home but had only gone a few steps when Jack began to snigger. Quietly at first and then he was laughing so much his stomach hurt. Stevie took a bit longer to join him, and finally Dorothy.

'Who knew we had two churches?' Dorothy complained but Stevie and Jack's laughter was infectious.

'Where have you been?' hissed Amber as they came back into the house. She was delighted to see the change in Stevie's mood but Malcolm had not slept long and she was having terrible trouble holding the conversation together while getting the potatoes in and watching the turkey. Dorothy had left her clear instructions, but it was all too much.

'Church,' replied Stevie.

'Did you get the coal?' asked Malcolm.

While the turkey finished cooking, drinks were served and then at last they all sat down. Stevie poured the wine and Malcolm reached for a cracker so everyone else did too. They were all grateful for the pause, putting on paper hats and reading out the jokes. Jack and Stevie loved to guess the bad jokes and raced each other to come up with the answers.

'Why don't you ever see Father Christmas in hospital?'

'Because he has private elf care.'

'How did Mary and Joseph know that Jesus was 7lb 6oz when he was born?'

'They had a weigh in a manger.'

'Why is it getting harder to buy Advent calendars?'

'Because their days are numbered.'

Amber cheered each correct answer, grinning at Stevie who grinned back. It made Barbara very happy to see her child so contented.

Dorothy was a very good cook, they all agreed. There was a slight incident when the gravy went over because the card table was slightly lower than the kitchen table and Malcolm hadn't noticed the join. A brown stain oozed across the red curtain/tablecloth.

'You see, with paper you don't get that kind of trouble,' Malcolm said as if the cloth was at fault.

Barbara did her best to keep things light. 'Amber was telling me she went to a party last night dressed as Cinderella. I love that. Such a nice story – that poor woman being rescued from a life of drudgery by Prince Charming!'

Dorothy looked briefly at Malcolm and smiled as he somehow managed to put a whole potato in his mouth.

Amber opened more wine.

'Lovely glasses!' Barbara tried again.

'Two cups!' said Malcolm rather randomly. 'That's all we have. No space, you see, but you can have wine, beer, tea, whatever you like out of them. Don't know why people make such a fuss about having a different receptacle for everything.'

'I expect paper is the answer,' smiled Dorothy.

Malcolm carried on eating. He had seconds and then thirds of the food and jovially kept egging Jack on in a competition about how much 'the *men*' could eat. The vast amount of food made him sweat, causing him to take off his jumper and reveal a white shirt which had not fully fitted for some years. There were slight stains at the armpits and the buttons strained as he reached across the table for one more potato. He relaxed, pushing his orange paper crown to the back of his head and tipping his chair on two legs against the bookcase. In a rare fit of bonhomie, Malcolm suddenly said,

'So, Jack, what are you up to these days?'

Jack was drinking wine on top of a profound hangover, which is rarely a good move. Malcolm's question caused him to panic.

'I'm hoping to be a father!'

There was a pregnant pause, which seemed suitable. Stevie thought she was going to be sick. Amber grabbed her hand to steady them both while everyone looked at Malcolm, whose face appeared suspended in time. He finally moved, banging his fist down with such force that the card table gave a slight leap in the air and the gravy went over for a second time.

'This is wonderful news!' beamed Malcolm unexpectedly. 'Glorious!' Stevie felt as though she had entered a parallel universe where her dad was much more accepting than she realised.

'Isn't that marvellous, Barbara?'

Barbara smiled. 'I like babies.'

Malcolm was unstoppable. 'Known you a long time, Jack, not going to lie to you. I didn't think you were the type. I'm afraid I had you down as one of those "Oh-oh, here he comes, backs to the wall, boys!" kind of fellas.'

'Me?' Jack replied before repeating the word in a much lower tone. 'Me?' He slapped the table in what he hoped was a manly manner. 'Good god, Malcolm. Ha ha!'

'I'll have another drop of wine, Dorothy,' said Birdie softly.

Stevie was horrified as she watched her friend do his impression of what a butch man sounded like.

'Jack,' she tried.

Jack continued to deepen his voice while looking sideways at his nan's reaction.

'The thing is, *Malcolm*, these lovely ladies' – he indicated Amber and Stevie, both of whom looked away – 'want to have a baby but there's *a bit missing*, ha ha, if you know what I mean, and that's where I come in. Happy to help. Work of a moment. Think of me as the ...' Jack looked around for inspiration and his eye landed on the small Christmas tree. 'As the archangel Gabriel.'

It took Malcolm a few seconds to fully understand what he was being told. As a series of small thoughts whirled around before forming into a larger, more uncomfortable whole his face went puce.

'Stephanie,' he said, turning to his daughter, 'am I to understand from this that Jack is to father a child for you?'

Stevie gripped Amber's hand before saying evenly,

'Yes. Amber and I want to have a baby and Jack might ... I mean, nothing has been decided but he has offered to ... donate. We weren't going to tell anyone yet but ...' Stevie looked furiously at Jack, who focused hard on straightening the tablecloth.

Barbara smiled and gave a small clap of her hands. 'That's nice, isn't it?'

'No, Barbara, it is not,' said Malcolm firmly. 'Donate? Donate?'

The angry fat man clenched his jaw and attempted to stand up. Clearly he planned to make some kind of speech but despite the knocking-through, the room was not expansive and his cushion-like stomach caused him to be pinned in between the card table and the wall. Barbara tried to help him and there had to be some slight shuffling about from everyone before he was able to stand. Malcolm's shirt gave up and burst open revealing a good two-inch gap where everyone could see the hairs on his very white stomach. A dribble of gravy had made its way down one side of the shirt and appeared to point at his right nipple. He still had his Christmas hat on and there was bread sauce in his moustache. It was almost possible to feel sorry for him. He was shaking.

'Stephanie,' he began, speaking slowly and distinctly.

'She prefers Stevie,' tried Dorothy.

'Don't get upset,' pleaded Jack. 'I shouldn't have said anything. It's just biology. All perfectly normal. Clinical, even.'

'Who's Stephanie?' whispered Birdie. She was full of questions, but Malcolm was not to be stopped.

He ploughed on. 'I do not know why you would do this to us.

Your mother and I, we have done our very best to be accepting up till now.'

'*Accepting?*' repeated Dorothy.

'You know we have,' he continued. 'Has there been a single one of Amber's birthdays where we forgot to send a card? And not digital. No. I don't think so and sometimes the sites where we have pitched are not entirely convenient for a post box.'

'Stevie,' prompted Dorothy quietly. Stevie looked at her. In all her years she had never before stood up to her father.

'You didn't even come to my wedding,' she said, looking him in the eye, her voice beginning to rise. 'That is not "accepting".'

Her father gave a deep sigh and turned to Barbara to indicate she should get her bag as they would be leaving.

'What?' said Barbara.

'Your bag! Get your bag!' Malcolm turned back to his accidental daughter. 'Stephanie, we have been through this,' he fumed. 'Why you decided to have your wedding on the same day as the South-East Caravanning Conference, I do not know. We could not understand it, could we, Barbara? I am the *chairman* of the South-East.'

'It was the same day,' echoed Barbara but no one was listening. She had half risen to get to her bag, but it was on the sofa, which seemed an impossible distance in that moment, so she sat back down again.

Malcolm took his time, but he was clearly releasing some years' worth of anger.

'Maybe we hoped when you became a police officer . . .'

Amber failed to see the connection. 'What?' Now she stood too and held Stevie's hand.

'Children are a big responsibility, and they need a father,' decreed Malcolm. 'You needed a father.'

235

'Yes, I did,' replied Stevie, emboldened by Dorothy's silent encouragement. 'On my wedding day.'

'What are we supposed to tell people?' her father asked plaintively. 'Think of your mother. How is she supposed to explain this to her friends?'

'We don't really know anyone ...' Barbara began.

Malcolm moved on to his trump card of Stevie's trouble-free siblings. 'We don't have this nonsense with Mark,' he said. 'Or John or Peter or ...'

'Paul.' Barbara filled in the blank.

'Peter and *Paul*!' admired Dorothy, who was not doing her best to keep out of it. 'How ever did you think of it?'

'Twins,' explained Barbara.

Malcolm moved to get away but he carried on addressing his daughter.

'You just don't think. It's just not ... natural ... and there are financial implications. What if the two of you split up? Bad enough you bought this house together. What if Amber leaves you? What happens to the house then? What if—'

'What if it is the most marvellous thing that ever happened?' asked Dorothy quietly.

Malcolm gave the old woman his best withering look, picked up his sweater and then ruined the drama by having to get Jack to help him push Birdie out of the way so that he could turn in the doorway and deliver his final line with furious intensity.

'There's no talking to you, *Stephanie*!' He said the name with force as he pointed at his daughter and then scowled at Jack. 'We came a long way to be here. It was not on our petrol loop at all. I lied to save *your* feelings. There's no getting through to her, Barbara. We've wasted our time.'

Malcolm strode out. Barbara got to her feet and stood alone

in the sitting room. Stevie felt heartbroken looking at her mother. Barbara looked tragic. Her penguin jumper, something she wore every year, had never been cleaned because she was terrified the glitter would come off the appliquéd creature's hat. Both she and her Antarctic bird looked worn out in every way.

'Barbara!' barked Malcolm from outside.

'Happy Christmas!' Barbara managed as she finally reached her handbag. 'It was really very lovely,' she added and left.

The front door remained open, and a chill afternoon wind blew in across the remaining lunch guests.

'I don't think that could have been worse,' ventured Amber.

Just then a cheerful voice could be heard in the small front garden, clearly hailing Malcolm and Barbara on their departure.

'Oh, hello! I don't think we've met! I'm Amber's mum.'

'My mistake,' said Amber. 'Gays *and* blacks.'

Stevie sat back down at the table with a thump. Dorothy moved to put her hand softly on Stevie's shoulder.

'It'll be all right, Dot,' said Stevie, putting her hand on Dorothy's and sighing. 'Jesus wants me for a sunbeam.'

18

Jack couldn't speak or move. He sat, not even trying to cover up his deformed eyebrow. What was worse? Mentioning the baby or the charade of pretending to be someone else? His oldest friend couldn't look at him and he just wanted to cry. Even Dorothy quickly moving to bring in the pudding didn't really smooth things over.

'I think the baby sounds very exciting,' Birdie remarked cheerfully.

'Nothing is decided,' warned Amber on her way to the hall to receive her mother.

Faith was a lovely woman. Stunning to look at, she was immaculately dressed not just because she had just come from a conference but because she always took the time. She spoke carefully and beautifully, considering each word with the same care she selected accessories for her ensemble. She carried matching luggage and a much-needed light heart.

'Hello darling!' she called, genuinely thrilled to see her only child. They hugged and hugged with Faith constantly saying, 'No, I need one more,' and pulling Amber back into her embrace.

When they were finally able to part Faith turned her attention to Stevie, who also received much love.

'My beautiful girls,' Faith repeated, hugging them both together before turning her smile on the rest of the room.

'You must be Dorothy,' she guessed and put her arms out for a welcoming hug.

'And this is Birdie and ... Jack,' said Amber.

'Jack, I remember from the wedding. Quite a speech! I was still laughing on my way home,' said Faith warmly. 'So naughty!'

'Yeah,' agreed Jack, 'I probably shouldn't have made that joke about the little Dutch boy.'

Wine was poured and Dorothy made up a plate of leftovers for the late guest.

Stevie went to shut the front door. As she did so she looked out and saw that, sadly, Malcolm and Barbara's dramatic exit had been rather spoiled by someone parking a red Mini right up to the front bumper of the Baxters' motorhome. Barbara had done an unexpectedly good job of making sure they were 'in at the back' and the van was almost touching a Volkswagen behind. They were utterly wedged in place. Malcolm could now neither move forwards or reverse. The vanlifers were stuck. Stevie left them to it and went back to the table.

Not long after there was a rapping on the door of Number 4. It was Dorothy who answered.

'Who drives a red Mini?' Malcolm barked.

Dorothy was wiping her hands on a tea towel and took her time.

'Is this a quiz question?' she remarked. 'Is it Twiggy? Oh no, you mean a car! She was mini*skirts*, wasn't she?'

Malcolm pointed to the offending car, shaking with impotent rage. 'There is a red Mini in my way.'

Dorothy looked at the car and then at the enraged man.

'Malcolm, may I ask you, have you thought about the dangers of angina?'

Malcolm could not think at all, and Dorothy was not helpful. No, she did not know who owned the car. It was Christmas and lots of people were having guests. It could be anyone's.

'Did you want dessert?' she continued. 'Only I could bring it out. There's brandy butter. Finish your heart right off.'

Malcolm turned on his heel and went back to his motorhome.

'Have they gone?' asked Stevie as Dorothy returned.

'Not entirely,' she said. 'Christmas pudding?'

'Don't let Jack have the matches,' warned Amber.

'Hmm, seems like a tricky time,' Faith commented. 'I think we need presents.'

She had managed to get something for everyone. Amber had told her who was coming and while her mum had been on her Scandinavian speaking tour she had picked up gifts along the way. Amber and Stevie received a large, beautiful star made of thick paper from Norway which lit up and was designed to hang in the window of their new house. Jack was given some Swedish chocolate called Plopp, because Faith had thought it would make him laugh. Birdie got tan-coloured Norwegian cheese which everyone agreed tasted somewhere between cheese and a pudding. Dorothy was last and hers was a black Danish mug with the single word *Hygge* written on it in white.

'It means cosiness or well-being,' explained Faith. Dorothy loved it.

Faith ate her late lunch and marvelled at every element. Stevie hung the star in the window where Mrs Haggerston saw it on her way back. She had enjoyed a lovely uninterrupted church service and then a communal meal in the church hall. Even she thought the star looked lovely. Hygge, in fact, had she known the word.

240

Birdie fell asleep in her chair and Jack busied himself trying to get back in everyone's good books by helping Dorothy tidy in the kitchen. Amber took her mum up to the loft room, where she was going to sleep. Stevie had carried up the Argos put-up bed that Dorothy had used when she was ill. No one mentioned either the money or the cot in the eaves.

When Amber returned from upstairs, she found her wife standing in the sitting room looking out the window at her parents' still-present motorhome. It was dark out but the light from the new star shone out on the path.

'You all right?' Amber asked as Stevie turned and set about collapsing the card table. Amber stopped her by putting her arm around Stevie's waist and pulling her close. Stevie gave a deep sigh.

'I always feel it's my fault,' she said.

'Why is it your fault?'

'I don't know. Maybe I don't use the right words or I push him too far and he's not ready.' Stevie squeezed Amber's hand and moved to the front door. 'I'll just see if they need anything. It is Christmas.'

Stevie went out and knocked on the door of the motorhome. There was no reply but she could see the battery-powered lights were on, so she tried again. A curtain twitched and a window in the sitting room area slid open, revealing Malcolm.

'Hi Dad,' began Stevie quietly.

Her father nodded but said nothing.

'Look, uhm, I'm sorry,' Stevie continued, 'if you're upset. Jack's sorry. It came out all wrong but maybe if we talk about it ...'

'I don't see the point,' replied Malcolm. 'We're never going to agree.'

241

'You're my dad and I want to find a way for us to—'

'You've been like this for years. There's no changing you.'

'I don't want to change but I do want to ...'

Malcolm disappeared back inside, where he could be heard to say, 'It's *her*. At the window.'

Now Barbara poked her head out.

'Oh love, thank goodness. I didn't like to knock but ...'

'Mum, I want to make things better.'

'Barbara!' came a loud command from inside. She turned to look behind her and then back out the window at her daughter.

'Yes. Your father wants me to empty the cassette,' she whimpered.

'No,' replied Stevie, moving from a conciliatory tone to adamant refusal without missing a beat. 'We have been through this before and it is not happening. You are supposed to empty that thing in a proper place. At a campsite.'

'I know,' said Barbara, 'but there was quite a charge at the last site and your father thought we could save some ... It's full, Stevie, and your father ... well, he's had a big lunch. He needs to ...'

At that moment Dorothy appeared round the back of the motorhome. Stevie had been a while and Amber had sent her out to see if back-up was needed.

'Oh hello, Dorothy,' beamed Barbara as if they were friends and nothing untoward had ever happened. 'I'm afraid we need to empty the cassette.'

Dorothy smiled back. 'I'd forgotten about cassettes. I had those. I remember one was a mix tape. Loved it but I played it so often the tape stretched. You do not want to hear Glen Campbell singing "Rhinestone Cowboy" several inches longer than he ought to be.'

'It's the cassette from the toilet,' sighed Stevie.

Dorothy was baffled. 'Sorry?'

Stevie tried to explain. 'They have a chemical toilet and all the ... waste goes into a sort of box ...'

'It's called a cassette,' explained Barbara helpfully. 'You have to empty it when it's full, and it is full. Really full. I don't think we could get another—'

'All right, thank you,' interrupted her daughter. 'Mum, you know it's supposed to be done at a campsite. There are laws about it.'

'I know, but your father is desperate.'

'Well, can't he come inside and use the toilet?' asked Dorothy.

Barbara pursed her lips and couldn't even speak of the impossibility that Malcolm might go back into the house.

Malcolm's voice could be heard muttering, 'It's the least you can do!'

'Bring it in,' said Dorothy practically.

She went back inside, leaving mother and daughter to the mechanics of whatever it was that needed doing. Barbara looked very grateful. She disappeared from the window and reappeared in the doorway saying rather pathetically, 'I'm afraid I can't lift it.'

'Christ,' responded Stevie.

The cassette could be removed from the motorhome by opening a small hatch at the side of the vehicle. It was a feature of this particular model that the whole thing could be unlatched and removed without having to carry it through the living quarters. Barbara opened the hatch and undid the latches, but it was Stevie who had to tug on the large handle and remove the box. About a foot and a half square, the heavy-duty plastic container was, as Barbara had indicated, full.

243

Incredibly full. So full that Stevie almost dropped it on the pavement. It made a sort of slopping noise. Mrs Haggerston watched from behind her curtains while Malcolm kept an eye from the driver's seat.

Stevie was fit, but the weight of her parents' waste matter was almost too much for her. She struggled up the path carrying the box. It was all very clean and neat but nevertheless the very thought of what she was doing made her feel unwell. In the house she headed for the downstairs toilet, but Jack was standing outside the door.

'Nan's in there.' He grimaced slightly. 'It won't be quick.'

'We need to empty the cassette,' explained Dorothy, pointing to the box. 'From the camp toilet.'

'No!' Jack exclaimed, bringing both hands up to hold his face.

'Please don't make me wait!' pleaded Stevie. 'I cannot have this in the house for a minute longer than absolutely necessary.'

'You'll have to go upstairs,' said Jack.

The box was astonishingly heavy.

'All right!' fumed Stevie. 'But you'll have to help me!'

'I'm not carrying that . . .'

Stevie gave Jack one icy look, which reminded him of his part in the day's disaster.

'Hold this,' he said to Dorothy, taking off his precious jacket and moving to take one end of the cassette.

Between them Jack and Stevie got it up the stairs and into the bathroom. It was one of the tragedies of Stevie's life that she had helped empty the device before. There was a pipe which swung out from the box with a screw cap on it. Stevie pulled up the toilet seat and tried to tip the box so that the open pipe could release the contents into the bowl.

'Help me!' she yelled at Jack.

Jack was pretty sure he was going to be sick. He grabbed the bottom of the box and heaved it up at an angle, at which point a ton of brown sludge mixed with what might have been loo roll began to splash out.

'Oh my god, oh my god!' screeched Jack. 'No, no, no, no!' He let go of his end of the box and Stevie nearly dropped the whole thing. Jack backed up until he got to the bathtub, at which point he got into the bath and lay down full length, moaning, 'Oh my god, oh my god,' before checking all his clothes for any possible brown splashes.

Dorothy came in to see how it was going and found Jack almost passed out in the bath while Stevie bravely carried on emptying and flushing in a sort of relay. Dorothy sat down on the edge of the tub and looked at them both.

'I'm sure you don't need me to point out that you are literally dealing with your father's shit, Stevie,' she said softly.

A great lump fell from the pipe. Jack screamed and covered his ears.

'I can't listen. That's poo, isn't it?' he howled.

Dorothy got up and found some bleach. Together she and Stevie finished the emptying and disinfected anywhere the cassette or its contents had touched. Stevie put the cap back on and took the wretched thing back down to Barbara, who was waiting on the front step.

'I'm not putting it back,' said Stevie.

'I'll manage,' replied her mother and left with the now empty box.

It took a while to persuade Jack out of the bath. They went back downstairs, where Birdie had reappeared and was drinking port with Faith and Amber.

245

'I love your house – such cosy style,' said Faith to Amber and Stevie.

'Thank you,' said Dorothy.

About half an hour later there was another knock at the door.

'How much shit can he have done?' wondered Dorothy as she went to open up, but it was Barbara carrying a small plastic bag from Tesco. She looked tragic. Exhausted and drained.

'I was wondering if I might have a shower,' she said.

'Of course,' said Dorothy gently.

She could see the woman was in distress so guided her upstairs and then took her time showing her where the towels were, giving her some shampoo and moisturiser and a bar of lily of the valley soap.

'I do like the flowered wallpaper in the hall,' said Barbara.

'Yes,' agreed Dorothy.

'I'm so sorry we spoiled your lovely lunch,' Barbara said quietly as Dorothy went to leave her in the bathroom.

Dorothy smiled. 'You didn't spoil anything, Barbara. I'm sure Stevie was just happy to see you. It's a wonderful thing to have a daughter.'

'Yes. Yes it is.'

As Dorothy closed the door, she just heard Barbara call out,

'And I'm sorry about the sex worker remark. It's none of our business what you do for a living.'

Dorothy sniggered to herself and didn't tell Stevie.

When Barbara came downstairs again she was wearing an old nightie and dressing gown. It made Stevie smile. It was the same bathrobe Barbara had worn all through her childhood. Barbara had been thrilled to have an unexpected daughter, but thanks to four boys and Malcolm, they had rarely had a quiet moment together, except after Stevie's occasional bad dream. Then Barbara would lie on Stevie's bed in her dressing gown, soothing the monsters away. In that moment, that is what they both remembered. Stevie gave her mum a slight hug and they surprised each other by clinging on.

Dorothy and Birdie made hot chocolate and Jack handed out marshmallows to bob in the cream.

'What about your butterfly cakes?' suggested Dorothy and helped Barbara hand them out. They all sat eating, drinking and complimenting the baking. Barbara was thrilled.

Dorothy smiled at her. 'Mark, John, Peter, Paul ... and then Stephanie?'

Barbara nodded. 'Malcolm wanted Mary, but I went to the registry office by myself. Stephanie Beacham. *Dynasty*. You remember.'

'And *The Colbys*,' added Dorothy.

'Ooh, I loved Blake Carrington,' sighed Birdie.

The older women smiled at the memory and Barbara looked so happy it made Stevie almost cry. Amber reached out and squeezed her hand before changing the subject.

'How was your conference, Mum?' she asked, turning to Faith.

'Good. I think I might get the funding I need.'

'Mum is working on a new wearable magnetoencephalography system,' Amber told Barbara.

'I would explain it, but I don't want to sound big headed,' said Jack.

Faith produced some pictures showing a bright blue plastic helmet with a lot of wires. A smiling child gave a thumbs up to the camera with her special hat on.

'It's great for kids,' she explained. 'It's basically a wearable brain scanner so we can see what happens when they have an epileptic attack.'

Birdie thought it was marvellous. 'I had a swimming cap like that. Little flowers all over it.'

Stevie could not help but think how far apart her mother and Amber's were in their lives. How far apart their whole upbringing was. She looked at Faith and felt a pang of envy.

'Do you like life on the road?' Faith asked Barbara.

Barbara was having a wonderful time and didn't really want to think about life on the road.

'I like it when we have to stay in a car park,' she said.

'A car park?' repeated Faith.

'Yes, sometimes we stay in a supermarket car park. We were at a twenty-four-hour giant Tesco's recently. I loved it. Malcolm fell asleep and I went round the whole shop three times.'

No one knew what to say to this.

'They had a coffee machine,' added Barbara. 'I had a chat with a nice woman with insomnia who likes to look at the crockery. I liked the crockery but we haven't got room.'

'And Malcolm,' asked Birdie. 'Is he happy?'

Barbara looked away and played with the belt on her dressing gown as she replied.

'I'm sure it seems an odd life, but you have to understand we talked about doing this for years. Thirty years we planned living on the open road, so he has to be happy, but I know his back hurts from all the driving. The bed's very comfy but you have to climb in and out and he's got bad knees. Well, he's put on weight because he eats while he's driving and now I've had to cut my hair so it doesn't use so much water when I wash it.' Barbara ran her hand across the back of her head. 'He's a good man but ...' She looked at Stevie. 'I am sorry about everything, love.'

There was a silence of profound sadness which Dorothy filled by standing up and demanding,

'Do you know what we need? Dolly Parton!'

She put on some Dolly very loudly. It was indeed just what was needed. They all danced. Even Barbara, and Birdie in her chair. Malcolm, whose stomach was not at all right, peered out of his van at Number 4. With the shining star in the window he could see what appeared to be the happiest party imaginable. He pulled the curtains closed.

Jack took Birdie home. When she was tucked up in bed, he brought her medication and sat with her for a moment.

'No one should tell you how to live your life, Jack,' his nan whispered to him as they hugged good night. 'Go get on with it.'

When he was sure Birdie was asleep, he slipped out again. In his whole life he had never been so nervous or determined.

He knew where Arun lived. He went straight there but then paced up and down under a street lamp for quarter of an hour mustering courage. What if he didn't think it was a real kiss? What if he is horrified? What if he has someone with him? What if . . .

Jack's phone pinged. It was a text from Dorothy which simply read 'Ring the fucking doorbell.' He looked around, terrified that somehow she was watching, then he read the text again and realised how well she knew him. He grinned.

'Ring the fucking doorbell!' he said to himself.

So he did. It was late and Arun did not appear immediately. When the door finally opened Arun looked at him and slowly smiled.

Arun reached out for the zipped edge of Jack's jacket and pulled him inside.

'Baby bear!' he said quietly. 'I thought you'd never come.'

19

Maybe Jack's outburst at the big lunch had been a good thing. Stevie and Amber were now having long talks about the possible baby.

'There's nothing to stop you having the baby, Stevie,' Amber was keen to say.

Stevie shook her head. 'I'm finding this whole thing scary but one thing I do know: I don't want to *have* a child. You're so smart. Your mum makes swimming caps into brain scanners, you quote books I've never even heard of and my family . . . I'm scared of the whole DNA thing. What if we're waiting for the baby to be born, all excited, and a mini version of my dad comes out?'

'Don't be silly. It'd be a mini version of you and that would be perfect.'

Stevie shook her head. 'Your whole family is brilliant and I'm—'

'The person I love. You're smart. I don't know anyone who reads a situation better. Please will you stop doing yourself down. It hurts me.'

'OK and what about if we split up?'

'We won't,' replied Amber with absolute certainty.

Stevie wouldn't let it go. 'Ambs, I love you and you love me,' she said, 'but we have to talk about everything. I don't want anything to surprise us.'

They talked and talked and talked. What did they think about discipline, schooling, how many treats were too many. They watched mothers in cafés and supermarkets and commented on their parenting, the way they spoke to their kids. There was nothing Stevie did not consider.

She even talked to Dorothy.

'We can none of us help where we came from, but we can decide where we're going,' advised Dorothy.

'That doesn't help,' moaned Stevie. 'Sounds like a greeting card.'

'Absolutely,' agreed Dorothy. 'Hallmark, I think.'

The decision about who would be the father was the hardest conversation of all.

'Jack has offered,' Stevie kept saying. 'I mean, it is the easiest and he does feel like family to me.'

Amber downloaded information about Viking sperm from Denmark, which was apparently the best, but it was expensive, and Jack was ... Jack. Jack ... Jack ... the conversation went on and on.

Meanwhile Jack was not thinking about babies at all. After that first night with Arun he had utterly lost his heart. Arun was a little older and had been in love before but for Jack what was happening was indescribable. Every fibre of his being was alive with his feelings for his new partner, and he could hardly contain himself. On New Year's Eve he bounced about Birdie's flat full of fireworks but not telling her the reason.

'When are you going to tell me, Jack?' she finally asked him. 'Only I think if you don't you may burst the windows in this place.'

Jack looked at his grandmother. This was a moment he had long thought about. Would it kill her? Would she disown him as his mother had done? What if . . .

'Does Arun feel the same way? Is he in love with you?' persisted Birdie.

'What? What?' Jack snapped and looked at her aghast. He clapped his hands over his mouth and said with astonishment, 'Oh my god! You know!'

Birdie smiled. 'I live with you. You're my grandson.'

'How long have you known?'

'About you being gay or about Arun?'

Jack sat down at her feet and looked up, ready for a good chat.

'Let's start with the gay thing,' he said. 'Did Dorothy tell you?'

Birdie reached out and stroked his hair. 'She didn't need to. How old were you when you asked for the Barbie house?'

'Five.'

'OK, at least since then.'

Jack shrieked. If it weren't for the fact that their neighbours on both sides had already moved out, people would have come running.

'Oh my god, if you weren't half dead already I would kill you.'

'Charming,' replied Birdie. But there was no time for Jack to get violent because Dorothy was at the door.

'Dorothy!' he began as soon as she was in. 'Nan knows I'm gay. Did you tell her?'

'Not necessary,' sniffed Dorothy, taking off her coat and looking at Jack. She waved her hand in a circular motion to take him in completely. 'I'm going to go with just the outfit you have on today.'

Jack put both his hands on his hips. 'Do you know how hard it has been, keeping my gay side down?'

'Wow,' said Dorothy, 'that was you keeping it down. It's going to be loud round here now.'

'He did a very good job at Christmas lunch,' remarked Birdie. 'Malcolm and Barbara were completely fooled.'

'You two old bats!' Jack laughed, both appalled and amused. He kissed them both and escaped.

The women smiled at each other. From out in the corridor they could hear the lift screeching its way to the ground floor.

'Dorothy, I need to find a way to manage on my own,' announced Birdie. 'It's time that boy was allowed to fly.'

Dorothy nodded before saying, 'I want to know more about your brownies.'

'What brownies?' replied Birdie innocently.

'Birdie,' said Dorothy firmly, 'I am not Jack. You can't fool me with your little old lady who knows nothing act.'

Everything seemed to have turned a corner for Jack, even at work. Agnes had been impressed by Jack and Arun's performance on Christmas Eve and suggested that perhaps they might have a music night at the Onion once a month. It would be good for business. Jack was mad for the idea. Apart from anything else, it was another way to spend more time with his beloved. Soon the two lovebirds were rehearsing old songs and thinking of a theme for the first evening. Agnes introduced them to Madame Mimi Beaverhousen, a drag queen she knew, who might compère and the whole show took on a light, gay tone.

After much discussion it was decided that an event would take place on the last Friday of each month, and they would begin at the end of January. They settled on *Fabulous Friday* as the title.

When Jack wasn't working or rehearsing, he spent all his time arranging special dates for Arun: a picnic laid out in the pub after closing lit entirely by candles; tickets for a late-night showing of *Brokeback Mountain*, after which they both cried all the way home; a stroll in the park, where he had hidden a flask of hot toddy and some biscuits behind a tree. At the local Chinese restaurant the waiter brought Arun a fortune cookie. When he broke it open and removed the small slip of paper it read,

'You will fall in love with a man called Jack.'

Arun looked at Jack, who was pretending to look away.

'What's your fortune?' Jack asked innocently.

'It says I will fall in love with a man called Jack, but that's not true,' said Arun, putting the paper down.

Jack looked panicked. 'It isn't?'

'No.' Arun got up from his seat and slowly moved toward Jack, taking his hand. 'The truth is I have already fallen in love with a man called Jack.'

They left hand in hand with Jack asking, 'What are the chances of that exact fortune in that particular cookie?'

'Very slim, I'd say,' answered Arun, smiling.

It was wonderful. They were both smitten.

Dorothy was at Birdie's place one afternoon when Jack was heading off for rehearsal.

'How's it going?' she asked.

Jack looked stressed. 'It's fine but we need to liven the pub up,' he moaned. 'It looks like an old drinking hole.'

'It *is* an old drinking hole,' she replied. 'Why don't you go upstairs and see if there is anything you can use?'

It was the perfect solution. Jack and Agnes found mutual

delight in repurposing some of the wonderful stuff to decorate the Onion. There was a bright old poster with a toucan suggesting it was a 'Lovely day for a Guinness', a mannequin wearing a bright yellow Mary Quant dress with a Peter Pan collar, and a couple of lava lamps. Jack brought down the *Star Wars* stormtrooper, who was draped in fairy lights. Agnes decorated and swept the stage while Arun and Jack rehearsed an entire evening of entertainment.

'We need a big belter at the end,' insisted Arun as they toyed with 'Rose's Turn' from *Gypsy*, or something from *Wicked*. The two of them decided they would do a mixed programme of show tunes and old classics, while Mimi could introduce and open the second half. It turned out she was an excellent mime to both Cher and Donna Summer, performing in a dress made entirely of pink silk bows.

Since the Christmas Eve party the Onion was busier than it had been for years. Dorothy had taken to gathering a group of older women once a week and insisted on Birdie coming with her. Even the Nordic walking poles woman came. Rather like the pub she appeared to have taken on a new lease of life. She was definitely less bent over than usual and at one point abandoned her walking sticks entirely when she got up for a slight hip thrust in time to the music. It was a remarkable transformation. One night Jack played the piano and everyone sang.

'Jack! Jack!' Dorothy called out, 'Play that gay song you wrote about yourself!'

Jack tried to decline but she was so insistent he had no choice. Birdie cried with laughter and everyone liked it so much he had to play it again. Then Stevie put on 'We Are Family' by Sister Sledge and they all danced.

'Have a drink with me!' Dorothy urged Birdie.

'You don't drink,' replied Birdie.

'Champagne I do,' smiled Dorothy as Agnes brought a bottle to the table.

'What are we celebrating?' asked Birdie.

'That we're still here!'

Drinks were poured and Dorothy grinned as if she might never stop.

'Shouldn't she be taking it easy?' asked Stevie, watching her anxiously, but Amber shook her head.

'This is the best medicine,' she declared. Dorothy excused herself and headed off on the first of her many trips to the bathroom. They both watched her walk across the room. 'She got the information about her operation today,' said Amber. 'It's in two weeks. Friday.'

'That's the same day as Jack's show. Shit, I think I'm on shift.'

'I don't think we should delay.'

'No.'

'She'll stay with us till she's better, right?' asked Stevie.

Amber smiled. 'Of course.'

'And then what? She's not really going backpacking, is she?'

'You never know with Dorothy,' Amber laughed. The women sipped their drinks.

'You realise she will have been with us for months? How has this even happened?'

'It's Dorothy,' smiled Amber. 'There seem to be no rules. We do need to think of something long term. I keep saying we'll help her look for somewhere to buy but she says it's complicated.'

'I told her she needed to make some sort of plan and she told me not to worry. She was sure Jane Toppan has vacancies.'

Dorothy returned and there were whoops from her table at something she'd said. Agnes was in her element, thrilled that her once-overlooked olive bowls now needed constant refilling. Everywhere you looked there was a tapestry of bright fashion. It was definitely not the usual crowd, and it was great for business.

By closing, everyone was in a slightly different mood. Happier. More optimistic somehow. Perhaps it was the 'We Are Family' song, but Stevie could not have been more ready for Amber to have a baby on the way.

She whispered to Amber as she looked around the contented room. 'How lucky would any kid be to join in all this?'

'So definitely Jack, then?'

'Jack.'

Arun and Jack were beaming with a heady mix of the show they were planning and love. They went to sit with Amber and Stevie, ready to explain in great detail which of the songs they were planning would be the most spectacular. They were on a high both trying to give each other credit for being the best. Arun went to get another bottle of wine and Stevie leaned forward to her oldest friend.

'Jack, I just wanted to let you know that we're ready.'

Amber nodded and smiled. 'We weren't before ... when you tried to ... but we are now and we're so grateful.'

'You're going to be the most brilliant dad. I can't think of anyone better,' added Stevie.

The two women grinned at Jack, who made lots of movements with his mouth but didn't speak.

Arun returned bearing a bottle of white and laughing because Agnes was already in the office planning the next event. A strange silence had fallen over the table.

'All right?' asked Arun, confused, as he topped up everyone's glass.

'Fine,' replied Jack, trying to act normal.

'Jack, is everything …?' asked Stevie.

'It's fine. Fine,' managed Jack but Stevie knew him better than anyone. A dark cloud had descended.

'You did say …'

'Yes, yes.'

Stevie got up. 'I'm going home,' she announced and without another word left the pub.

Amber and Arun were both a little startled, but Jack didn't even look up.

'Congrats,' said Amber, kissing both men goodnight before chasing after Stevie.

Arun was baffled. 'What the hell just happened?' he asked.

Jack shook his head and changed the subject.

A few days later, just before opening, Jack was in the Onion trying out a new song at the piano.

'Jack!'

He hadn't heard Stevie come in.

'Jack!' Stevie tried again.

Jack smiled at his old friend and stopped playing.

'You've been avoiding me,' she accused.

Jack looked away. It was true. 'I'm sorry,' he said.

He and Stevie had always been straight with each other, so she didn't hesitate to ask, 'Is it the baby thing? Is everything OK? Have you changed your mind?'

Jack nodded. 'No, I just … Look, I haven't told Arun and I …' Jack didn't know what to say. 'I want to do this for you, Stevie, it's just … Well, before it was just me but if he and I … I mean, I think it's quite serious and …'

'Of course. Of course. I am so happy for you, Jack, and absolutely you need to speak to him. I'm sorry. Since Christmas I think I just imagined you were all set.'

Jack slowly played a few notes on the piano and looked down. Stevie was trying to be patient.

'Will you, Jack? Will you speak to him?'

'Yes, yes of course.'

'Soon?'

Having come out to his nan and indeed to the world, Jack didn't want any secrets, but he also didn't want to spoil the wonderful time he was having by suddenly mentioning babies to Arun. It was way too soon but he really loved Stevie and ... Maybe Stevie and Amber were not in a hurry and maybe Arun didn't need to know.

The next day Jack was carefully selecting the finest vegetables you could get in a Tesco Express when Amber appeared beside him.

'Oh Jack, this is so exciting. Thank you. Thank you for everything.' She picked up a melon and focused her full attention on it as she continued. 'Now, I'm sure you never thought I'd give you this much detail about myself, but Stevie has made a chart – you know what she's like – and, well, Wednesday, as it happens, would be a very good day ... for a, uh, donation. Has she told you?'

Jack shook his head. 'Uh-huh. No. Donation?'

'You know, for the baby.'

'Baby.'

'Yes. Wednesday. Day after tomorrow.'

'Day after tomorrow,' he repeated, his head spinning.

Amber hugged him. 'You are wonderful.'

He had come in looking for oat milk and tomatoes and left with an agreement to donate his sperm in a couple of days' time.

'How do you like kids?' he asked his beautiful boyfriend in bed that night.

'Medium rare,' replied Arun sleepily.

*

Jack tried to talk to Dorothy, but she had her own preoccupa-
tions. Her operation was playing on her mind.

'I need your help,' Jack began, regardless. 'You know Stevie
and Amber want me to donate for their baby? Well—'

'Not a problem,' interrupted Dorothy briskly. 'When is it?'

'Uh, tomorrow but . . .'

'I'll come over and take Birdie out.'

The next day Dorothy arrived at the tower block as promised.

'Sorry I'm late!' she called as she opened the door. 'I
stopped to play a quick game of Monopoly with Harry on the
third floor. Amazing what you can do with a bit of property
leverage.'

Dorothy took Jack's nan out, leaving Jack alone to provide
his contribution. He spent ages delaying. He took time to
carefully choose a nice clean jam jar with a screw lid for the
delivery but for the second time in his life Jack found he could
hardly deliver. When he finally succeeded it was a pathetic
amount. He walked over to Grimaldi Square with it tucked
in his jacket pocket, hoping he wouldn't bump into anyone he
knew.

'It's just biology. All perfectly normal. Clinical, even,' he
kept saying to himself.

Stevie answered the door. She and Jack stood looking at
each other as he reached into his pocket and handed over the
jar. Neither of them knew what to say.

Amber was waiting upstairs and Stevie came into their bedroom with the donation. Amber looked at it. She had been so
certain and full of confidence but now the moment had arrived
she too was suddenly unsure.

'I just want it to be us,' she kept repeating to Stevie. 'I love
you so much. I just want us. This doesn't feel right.'

'It will be us. We've been through this. It's very simple. We've got the syringe, Jack has donated and you and I will make the baby alone. In private. Just the two of us. We got this.'

And so they went ahead.

20

The next day Arun and Jack were rehearsing. Jack noodled away at the piano, but his mind was elsewhere. Arun put his hands on Jack to stop him playing.

'What is it?' he asked.

'We need to talk about babies,' Jack began.

'Wow, a month in, you're confident,' smiled Arun but he could see Jack was serious. 'I mean ... uh ... sure ... I ...'

'Not us,' Jack said hastily. 'Stevie and Amber. They want a baby and before we got together, I said I'd ...'

'Donate?' asked Arun. 'OK. We should talk about that.'

'No,' said Jack. 'I mean, we should have.' He didn't know where to look. He had done this all wrong.

'I already have. Donated,' he confessed.

Arun looked shocked. 'When?'

'Yesterday.'

'Yesterday? Why didn't you tell me?'

Arun talked about trust and truth and then walked away.

Stevie was like family, but this was some price to pay. Jack didn't know who to talk to. He tried Dorothy but she was packing a bag for the hospital and was distracted. Jack was distraught.

On the morning of Dorothy's surgery the possibly pregnant Amber awoke in an agitated state. She had read every medical article she could find about the bladder procedure. She knew it was deemed routine, but she also knew the possible problems. She didn't tell Stevie quite how scared she was, as her wife was full of her own fears.

'It'll be fine, right?' Stevie asked for the twentieth time as she got ready for work.

'Of course,' soothed Amber, kissing her and telling her, as she always did, to be careful out there.

Stevie was calmed by Amber's medical knowledge, but both women were in a mild state of suppressed panic. Stevie brought Dorothy's bag down to the hall just as Dorothy was giving last-minute instructions.

'There's a card in the kitchen for Jack. For his show tonight.'

Stevie turned to wish Dorothy good luck.

'Right, well ... uhm ... see you later,' she managed before awkwardly putting her hand out to shake goodbye.

'Idiot,' Stevie muttered to herself as she strode off clapping her hands together with anxiety.

Amber was anything but upbeat as she and Dorothy headed for the Royal Infirmary. Neither of them said anything which might accidentally betray an emotion. There was no parking on site, so they took a taxi. Dorothy could not stop chattering all the way.

'If anything happens,' Dorothy instructed, 'don't tell anyone about the money. If anyone comes just say you don't know anything about it. No matter who they are. Just keep it.'

263

'Nothing is going to happen,' reassured Amber. 'They do this procedure day in, day out. You'll be fine.'

'And what will you do?'

'Me? Be bored to tears, I should think. Good thing I've brought a book.'

Amber said all the right things, but in truth she was in turmoil herself. She had no idea if this first go at a baby had worked but there was also something about how they had gone about the insemination, something about Stevie and Jack which didn't feel right. Neither Amber nor Dorothy was in good spirits as they entered the hospital. Dorothy surprised herself by reaching out to take Amber's arm to steady herself as they walked in. Anyone seeing the two of them together would have seen a young woman looking scared as she helped a frail and elderly relative.

Amber knew everyone at the hospital and the nurses helped make them as comfortable as possible. They were early and Amber read aloud to keep them both calm. '"Which would you rather be, divinely beautiful or dazzlingly clever or angelically good?"'

Amber looked at Dorothy. 'Are you not going to interrupt? I mean, it's a good question.'

'Is this a children's book?' asked Dorothy.

'Yes.'

'Nice' was all she said.

Dorothy was not due to go down until late afternoon and Amber was able to stay with her right up to the door of the operating theatre. Dorothy lay on the gurney, silently holding Amber's hand until the last moment.

'Keep the money!' Dorothy instructed as she was wheeled away.

The staff let Amber wait but even for her the basic rules still applied.

'Phones off!' said the charge nurse firmly, forcing Amber to wait in silence. She did try to read but could not concentrate.

Back at the pub, as evening arrived the newly established queer night got off to a roaring start. Jack and Arun did a splendid job although watching from behind the bar Agnes thought she noticed that there was less of a spark between them. She didn't have long to think about it because customers were several deep at the bar. More and more people had heard about the fabulous fun at the Onion and the place was packed. It was a mixed crowd of every kind of person. Queer people who had heard it was a safe space, straight people who were local or had come with gay friends, young people looking for a laugh they were never going to find on TV, old people thrilled the pub was back on form. A bit of everything, the way it should be. With Jack now part of the entertainment Agnes wished she had hired more help.

Jack and Arun had opened with two huge musical theatre numbers and now Arun was ready to reach out to the heart strings with a rendition of the Sondheim song 'Losing My Mind' from *Follies*. The audience were entranced. They all had drinks and for a brief moment Agnes was able to relax and enjoy the show. She stood wiping out pint glasses, listening to the song. Her focus on the entertainment meant she took her eye off the crowd. She was alone and vulnerable.

No one noticed a small gathering outside as Arun and Jack finished the last number of the first half. While they were still feeling soppy they had settled on closing with 'I Finally Found Someone', a song made famous by Barbra Streisand and Bryan Adams. Jack sang while he played the piano, and Arun duetted beside him. Agnes stood in the doorway watching. She had stepped out from behind the bar, drawn by the beautiful music.

Looking at each other, Jack and Arun held the last note until it faded away. The song worked its magic. There was a profound silence from the large crowd who were touched to their core. There is something about being in the presence of two people who are so clearly in love which warms even a stone heart. Jack reached out for Arun's hand, and he leant down and gently kissed his new love.

'It'll be all right,' he whispered to Jack.

The great cheer that went up from the audience covered the commotion of a group arriving.

'Oi, Andrew!' Agnes looked across as half a dozen rough men entered carrying various weapons. She saw Carl, who had a stout stick which he slammed against the door jamb to get everyone's attention. It worked. Agnes moved slowly backwards toward the bar with Jack following.

'Jack!' yelled Arun but he was not going to let Agnes down this time. Jack managed to get between her and Carl as Agnes opened the top to the bar and slipped behind.

The crowd parted and went silent as the intruder walked toward Jack, his men circling behind him. Jack tried to put his fists up.

'Don't be pathetic,' sneered Carl, pushing him out of the way and onto the floor as he crashed his weapon down onto the bar. He pointed at Agnes, who had reached for her phone and dialled 999.

'Oi, Andrew! I'm talking to you!'

Agnes tried to be calm.

'Police!' she managed just before Carl vaulted over the

266

counter, smashing bottles hanging in the optics with a single swipe and throwing Agnes's phone to the ground.

'Fucking poofs!' he shouted. His words released mayhem. People ran as the violent group split up and went after anything that could be destroyed. Agnes held her arms across her face to protect herself as Carl took a great swipe and hit her hands. Trapped behind the bar, she turned to pick up a large whisky bottle by the neck and swung it at Carl, who ducked, leaving the bottle to smash into the wall behind. A shard of glass hit his arm and he cursed her.

'You fucker!' he screamed as blood spurted from the back of his wrist. Agnes took the opportunity to escape. Carl, enraged, used his stick to destroy a tray of glasses while Agnes pulled several customers into the office with her and locked the door.

The place had descended into pandemonium. Arun flipped up a table and tried to hide behind it with Jack as one of the thugs grabbed the piano stool and threw it high in the air. The stained-glass window above their heads, which had watched over the place for almost a hundred years, crashed to the ground, splintering glass all around them and knocking Arun and Jack over with the force. In the entertainment hall Mimi turned out to be a fabulous fighter, pulling down one of the stage curtains to throw over an oncoming attacker. She wrestled him to the ground before hitting him over the head with an olive bowl. Some of the men gathered behind Carl, who was pounding on the office door, and others were tossing tables and glasses to the floor, terrifying the customers who were pressed up against the walls and trying to edge out of the place.

Agnes's call had gone through and been traced. Stevie was first in the door looking for Jack, Arun and Agnes. Another two officers followed her and ran through the noisy broken pub, going after Carl's men, but they were outnumbered. Stevie spied Carl and two men using wooden sticks as battering rams on the office door, and it did not look like it would be long before they succeeded.

'Police! Stop!' yelled Stevie.

'Stevie!' cried Jack but his warning came too late. One of the men had picked up a bar stool and smashed it into Stevie's side, knocking her to the floor. Jack ran to her.

'Get out of here, Jack,' she shouted as she got to her feet, utterly determined. This was her home. This was her family. Nothing was going to stop her.

Carl turned to see what was happening. He smiled. He remembered Constable Baxter.

'Come to save your paedo friend, have you? Too late, lesbo! Watch this!' He gave one last swipe at the door and the lock gave way. He wrenched it open to find Agnes standing shielding three terrified customers. She picked up a computer keyboard and valiantly stood her ground as Carl moved to swing at her head.

'Oh no you don't!' yelled Stevie, leaping at him from behind. The move saved Agnes. Carl fell forward but somehow managed to right himself. He stood up and swung his heavy weapon back behind him. It caught Stevie in the shoulder and she fell again. He turned and kicked her in her side.

Jack and Arun surprised themselves by picking up chairs and moving like lion tamers towards Carl. Once more he lashed out at Stevie, kicking her in the back of the leg just as she was getting up again. She collapsed back down on the floor, where he stamped on her side. Once, twice. She was like a woman possessed because she still got to her knees.

'You fucking dyke,' Carl sneered, ready to punch again. Now Arun swung at him with his chair, but he missed. Jack did better.

He held his weapon by the legs, swung it over his head and managed to hit the man on the back of the neck. The blow caused Carl to stagger forward but not before he managed a final blow and knocked Stevie out cold on the floor. Her policing partner, Kevin, was behind her and managed to take Carl out with his Taser, but it was too late.

Jack ran to Stevie while Kevin and the other officer finally managed to quell the rampage. He cradled his unconscious friend and wept as if he might break.

'It was my fault. It was my fault,' he sobbed.

'Jack, Jack!' wailed Arun.

'Oh my god,' sobbed Agnes while the police rounded up the invaders. Anyone not arrested stood in a state of shock.

Soon the sound of emergency vehicles filled the square. The paramedics had to cut off most of Stevie's uniform to find the rest of her clearly substantial injuries. By the time she was taken out on a stretcher she looked utterly destroyed. Jack went with her in the blaring ambulance to the Royal Infirmary. He tried and tried to get hold of Amber, but her phone was off. Messages came from Arun – 'I'm on my way!' – but nothing from Amber.

In the very hospital to which the ambulance was now racing, Dorothy had come round. The surgeon had good news. The operation had been a complete success. There would be more tests, of course, and a catheter for a few days but there was no reason why Dorothy shouldn't make a full recovery. Amber couldn't stop smiling. The anaesthetic had made Dorothy feel a little sick, so Amber sat with her giving her sips of water.

'I thought I was going to die, Amber,' admitted Dorothy.

'But you're not going to. You will live on to trouble us some more.'

'I'm sorry.'

'Sssh.'

'Are you shushing me?'

'Yes.'

It was quite a while before Amber took a minute to go outside and turn her phone on to ring Stevie with the good news.

There were a dozen messages and missed calls. She raced downstairs to A&E. Amber had been a paramedic for some years now. This was her home patch. It should have been entirely familiar, but Amber felt as though she had entered a nightmare world. There was no mishap she had not seen or had to deal with but the blood of the person you love most is an entirely different matter. Jack had been asked to wait outside and she could see his face pressed up against the window in the door as he tried to see what was happening. Amber went behind the curtain and found Stevie on oxygen, and there seemed to be tubes and bags of fluid everywhere she looked.

'Blood type?' yelled the on-call doctor.

'O positive!' wept Amber, trying to help, and a bag of blood was fitted.

The remains of Stevie's clothes were removed with scissors. Blue marks could be seen covering her skin. Amber thought she was going to faint, and despite her skills she too was asked to wait outside. It was several hours before anyone came to find her and Jack. They both just sat staring at the wall.

The doctor who finally appeared to update them was someone Amber knew well.

'It's OK, Amber,' she began. 'She'll be all right.'

Amber began to sob with relief.

It was Jack who asked, 'What's happened?'

'She's got concussion. Dislocated knee. Plenty of bruising. We need to monitor for any internal injury we might have missed but mostly what she will need is rest and recuperation. We've given her something to make her sleep right now.'

This was not Jack's world and his knees buckled beneath him. He and Amber sat together crying until Arun arrived. The news from the pub was that Agnes's arms were very bruised where she had defended herself and she was extremely shaken but she didn't need to come in. The Onion was pretty much a write-off and there had been a number of small injuries to customers. Mimi had a sprained wrist but otherwise was fine. Carl and his men were being booked.

Amber was allowed in to sit with Stevie but Arun and Jack insisted on staying in the waiting room. Neither man could speak. They sat in shocked silence with Arun's arm around Jack.

'I think I caused it,' he cried.

Amber stayed beside her beloved wife all night, stepping out every hour or so to stretch her legs and check on Dorothy on the floor above.

In the morning Stevie opened her eyes and looked at Amber asleep in a chair beside her. It took her a few seconds to realise where she was.

'Babe?'

Amber's eyes flew open, and she almost fell on the bed trying to get to Stevie.

'Oh my god, oh my god, oh my god.'

'Don't touch, please!' warned Stevie in pain.

Stevie could see the fear in Amber's face and tried her best to make it all right but she was weak.

'Wow,' she rasped. 'One blow to the head and you find God. Has Mrs Haggerston been?'

Amber would have kissed her for ever if Stevie had been able

271

to tolerate it. Stevie tried to be her usual self – brave and funny and determined not to make a big deal of any of it but her injuries made her speech slow and painful.

'I didn't call your parents,' said Amber. 'Do you want me to?'

Stevie shook her head.

'I don't think the motorhome would fit in the hospital car park,' she managed.

Fellow officers came to see her. She joked about last orders and how she'd only wanted a half. Jack was allowed in briefly and would have hugged her if she hadn't been in so much pain. She demanded he write a song about the whole event.

Bobby and Young Justin came, with Bobby immediately fixing a sagging cupboard door and a broken blind to make the room more comfortable. Amber stayed all day but as night fell Stevie persuaded her that the drugs were kicking in and she should go home. It was only then, left alone in her hospital room, that Stevie allowed fear to overcome her. Paralysing, overwhelming fear. She was lying in shock when she heard the sound of wheels in the corridor. A shadow appeared in the doorway. She opened one eye to see a wheelchair approaching and caught the faint familiar smell of something floral. Dorothy had come down from the ward above in her nightdress. She pushed herself slowly toward the bed.

Stevie watched as Dorothy inched toward her.

'Dotty?' whispered Stevie.

'I'm here.'

Dorothy reached out and took her hand. Stevie clung on and finally allowed the tears to come. Despite her own pain Dorothy managed to get herself out of the chair and onto the bed. Then she reached for Stevie and gently pulled her into her arms. In the dark Stevie cried and Dorothy rocked her as she soothed the monsters away.

21

Mrs Haggerston came by the hospital with a small medal on a chain for Stevie.

'It's St John Licci,' she explained. 'Patron saint of head injuries.'

'Can't hurt,' Dorothy said as she helped Stevie put it on. 'Let's take all the help we can get.' She managed not to grimace as she said, 'Thank you, Mrs Haggerston.'

Mrs H summoned a slight smile. Dorothy was so happy that Stevie was going to be all right that she very nearly asked their neighbour her first name but held back at the last minute.

Dorothy's walk had slowed and she looked pale but within a few days she was back at Number 4, trying to run the place.

'Your grandmother is remarkable,' a junior doctor had commented to Amber.

'Thank you,' she replied, feeling no need to correct him.

Stevie, however, was more worrying. She was in hospital for a week and her recovery was going to be slow. Her knee had been put back in place but it would be about six weeks before all the ligaments healed. She arrived home on crutches and in a knee brace. The bruising meant she did not look at all good. She would be off duty for at least a month and Amber took compassionate leave. The pub was closed and would stay that way until the police and the insurance people had finished their investigation, so Jack had nothing but free time.

Now Amber and Jack endlessly hovered about the house, seeing if she wanted anything. Anything at all. Arun was back at work, but he and Bobby and Young Justin also found reasons to loiter about the place trying to be helpful. Bobby would never forgive himself for not being there that Friday night.

Though the physio was encouraging, Amber knew that Stevie wasn't OK. She was definitely not herself, snapping at the slightest thing. One morning, sitting on the sofa downstairs, she looked up to find Jack, Dorothy and Amber at the kitchen table, all staring through the archway at her in case she needed something.

'Will you all fuck off?' she shouted.

It wasn't the Stevie they knew.

It was early February and not pleasant outside but nevertheless Dorothy and Jack took to being busy by spending time in the garden 'clearing out the shed'.

Amber would sit reading except when she tried to make Stevie do her physio.

'Just do some gentle knee bends,' Amber would encourage. 'You don't even have to get off the sofa.' But Stevie argued at every turn. She didn't want to do it, it hurt or sometimes she would just turn back to the room.

'You should rest too,' Amber would call out to Dorothy, who kept insisting on cooking. 'You have had surgery too, you know.'

'Will you stop making that fucking noise?' Stevie would demand at the mere stirring of a pot.

No one mentioned Dorothy leaving.

No one mentioned the possible baby.

Young Justin would come by when Bobby visited. Bobby found little jobs around the house, bits of snagging which he said needed doing and were, he assured them, already paid for. He helped Jack and Dorothy with something in the garden which required wood and drilling. Young Justin, who had never managed to be all that helpful, would sit at the table not speaking but wiggling his fingers as usual while listening to something on his headphones and looking at his phone. It drove Stevie mad.

'What the fuck are you doing?' she demanded on his third or fourth visit.

Young Justin kept so much to himself that on the whole no one ever addressed him directly. He looked surprised.

'I'm playing the guitar,' he said in a higher voice than anyone had expected. 'I've been learning. On YouTube. I'm doing the fingering.'

'I had no idea you could learn fingering online,' called Dorothy cheerfully as she came into the kitchen from outside, but Stevie was in no mood for jokes.

'Do you even have a guitar?' she barked at the young man.

'No,' he said.

'Get him a fucking guitar,' said Stevie. It was a weird request, but it was also the only thing she had asked for, so Dorothy and Jack went to Argos and got one. It turned out Young Justin had never held an actual guitar. He had just watched instruction videos. They must have been excellent because as soon as he got hold of the instrument he played as if he had never done anything else.

275

'That's nice,' muttered Stevie. This seemed a positive sign, so he started serenading her every afternoon. Classical mostly. The sound of it filled the house and helped bring a semblance of calm.

One afternoon Dorothy and Jack were sitting at the kitchen table. She was answering emails.

'Who writes to you?' asked Jack.

'Lots of people. This one is from a prince in Nigeria. Tea, Stevie?' Dorothy called out, getting up.

'Why aren't you two in the fucking garden?' Stevie replied. 'You're always in the fucking garden!'

'It's raining,' tried Jack but there was no answer. He shrugged at Dorothy who put on the kettle out of habit.

'Let's see what it says about you online, Dorothy Franklin.' Jack pulled her laptop towards himself and began typing.

'Ignore the early porn. I was just learning,' Dorothy said.

Jack found something.

'Ooh look, Dorothy,' he cooed, 'there's an American actress with your name!'

'Am I famous?' Dorothy asked idly as she moved to get out some mugs.

Jack looked more closely. 'No. You last worked in 1998.'

'Sounds about right. What about you?'

Jack entered his name, Jack Parker, and began reading.

'I was an international motorcycle speedway rider but I'm not doing that any more because I'm dead.'

Searching for his name led Jack to discover a heritage website called My Ancestry and delighted to be distracted, he immediately headed down the rabbit hole of researching his family.

'Oh my god, I have one of the eighty-five most common surnames in the world! "Parker: most likely originated from a person who worked in a park." How can someone like me be so boring? I'm one of the most interesting people I know.'

But it wasn't all parks. He carried on researching and found he came from quite a long line of distinguished horticulturists. He was thrilled to discover that he was distantly related to the great gardener Capability Brown, whose real first name was Lancelot.

'Lancelot!' he declared. 'If we have a boy let's call him Lancelot!'

'No,' said Stevie. No one had thought she was listening.

'Why not?' demanded Jack. 'It's a family name.'

No answer came.

At night the well-meaning carers went home and the house was much emptier, but it began to be filled with the novel sound of Amber and Stevie bickering. Amber did not want to fight but absolutely nothing she did pleased her wife. The tea was too hot, too cold, too late. The room needed more air, less air. Stevie needed more fuss, less fuss. She refused to sleep anywhere except the sitting-room sofa but it was too small so Dorothy got Bobby to bring her old one from the Onion attic over to the house. While he was there, he also returned with a couple of lamps and a framed watercolour of the pub by her father. It was a sizeable item which Dorothy placed on the mantelpiece. She tried to give Stevie one of Birdie's brownies, but Stevie said she knew what they were and refused. Dorothy was tired. She had not focused on her recovery as much as she should have, so, encouraged by Amber, she took to going to bed early. She lay in her room listening to the distress.

Agnes came to the door one afternoon with flowers and chocolates. She brought a handsome man with her, who Jack remembered had helped out once or twice behind the bar. 'This is my husband, Frank,' she said.

Dorothy made tea as Agnes told them about her decision to move on.

'So is this goodbye?' asked Jack. Agnes nodded.

'I need a fresh start. I can't go back. I don't want to live here in my past.'

'Don't give up, Agnes,' said Dorothy.

Agnes smiled and looked at Stevie, who lay silent on the sofa.

'Thanks for trying, Stevie,' Agnes said softly. 'I'm sorry. You keep singing, Jack. We need that. We all need that.'

But the attack in the pub had hit Jack hard. He couldn't sing. He found no solace in music, half believing his singing had helped fuel the trouble. Dorothy and Birdie both tutted at his absurdity and pushed him to occupy himself. But all he wanted to do was ancestry research. He carried on, paying extra for more access to the depths of the website, and decided to sign Amber up as well.

'Both parents!' he said gleefully.

'We don't know I'm pregnant,' tried Amber but he was off.

'Ooh Amber! Get your family.' They were extremely impressive. The Delaunays were awash with scientists, engineers and entrepreneurs, many high achievers. There was even a duke and a prime minister amongst them.

'Think of the child we've probably made, Amber!' said Jack, sitting back in his chair as if he were aristocracy himself. 'A genius, a royal genius with green fingers!'

'Lancelot Parker!' He laughed at the thought.

'I don't think it'll be Parker,' ventured Amber, realising they hadn't talked about things like last names.

'Lancelot Delaunay,' tried Jack. 'Even better! And I shall be Jack Parker, father!'

It was hard to know which bit of all this tipped Stevie over the edge. She got up, even though she was under instructions to rest.

'There's not going to be a fucking child,' she shouted.

No pregnancy had been confirmed. There was no need to yell. Amber stood up to calm her wife down.

'Stevie!'

Stevie looked at her and said quietly, 'I've changed my mind. I don't want a kid.'

Amber took Stevie's arm and tried to get her to sit down. 'Look, maybe let's have this conversation just the two of us … I was going to tell you—'

'I don't want to talk about it. I can make up my own mind. I had a blow to the head not a lobotomy. Stop fussing. Amber, you cannot keep saving me. It was enough when we met. All of you, just go!'

Dorothy looked at her and said quietly, 'Family meeting!'

'You what?'

'It's time we all said a few things. Amber! Jack! Sit down at the table. You too, Stevie. Come over here. Don't tell me you can't manage a few yards with St John hanging round your neck.'

Without another word everyone gathered around the table. Dorothy could not have been firmer.

'Stevie, all of us, every single one of us, feel bad for you but it's enough. You can't just say whatever you like. This family meeting is where we are all going to try and work out how to help you without being wrecked in the process.'

'Only one problem with that brilliant idea, Dorothy,' replied Stevie through gritted teeth as she went back to the sofa and shut her eyes.

'We are *not* a fucking family.'

22

'I'm going home,' Amber announced the next morning. 'Back to Dudley. My mum is home for a bit and ... Dotty is here. She'll look after you ... and Jack and everyone. I don't know you any more.'

Stevie didn't even look up so Amber left.

Dorothy left it a while before coming down to find Stevie still lying in silent rage on the sofa. Her fury filled the room.

'Stevie ...' Dorothy began.

Stevie looked up and said with even more venom than usual,

'What is it with you? I told you to leave! I keep telling you to go and you never do. You shouldn't fucking be here. This is not your house.'

'No,' agreed Dorothy, 'and I'll go. I'll go when you tell me what is going on.'

Stevie looked away like a small child who cannot tell the truth. Dorothy moved to sit on the end of the sofa. She put her hand gently on Stevie's outstretched leg and waited for her to speak. Stevie moved her leg but not very far and began fiddling with the holy medal which hung round her neck.

'Aren't you going to make some joke about saints?' she snapped. 'Tell me about, I don't know, the patron saint of venereal disease?'

'Saint Vitalis of Assisi,' replied Dorothy, quick as a flash.

Stevie held back a small snigger. 'Seriously?'

Dorothy nodded. 'I feel bad for him. Not a great gig,' she admitted.

They sat for a bit longer. Dorothy did not push her.

'Amber and fucking Jack keep talking about the baby being like him or like her and their fucking ancestors and I'm ... I'm nowhere,' Stevie whispered, breaking the stillness. 'I'm no fucking where. I'm nothing and I keep telling myself that's fine because that just about sums me up. Stevie Baxter! The Baxters! That's my family! Can you fucking imagine? Probably decades of paperware distribution and disappointment. Parker because you work in a park, Baxter because you are a fucking—'

'That's enough. Don't you dare,' said Dorothy, surprising Stevie with her fury. 'Don't you dare. Feel sorry for yourself, sure. What happened to you was horrific, but you are alive and believe me I know what the relief of that is. And now that I have finally found something worth living for—'

'Worth living for?' interrupted Stevie. `What the fuck is worth living for?'

'You, you prat.'

It was not the answer Stevie had been expecting.

'Will you wake up, please?' continued Dorothy. 'You love Amber, and she loves you and God help me, I love you too. Those are not words I have said in decades so you had better make them worth my while.'

Stevie looked up at Dorothy. They held each other's gaze for a moment before Stevie turned away. Dorothy softened her tone.

281

'Do not let something as trivial as who came before you in your family dictate how you live your life. I've told you, it's not where you came from but where you're going that matters. You must live your own life: "If I fail, if I succeed. At least I'll live as I believe ..."'

Stevie stopped her. 'Whitney Houston?' she asked. 'Are you quoting Whitney Houston. "The Greatest Love of All"?'

'Yup,' said Dorothy. 'Look, I don't have a big speech for you because I don't think we've got time plus most of my education has come via the top ten. You're a wonderful human being, Stevie, it'll be enough for any child if you just pass on what you know. Who you are. Have a family. Make a family who love you. What the fuck are you thinking, letting that woman go? Amber! Literally the kindest person I have ever met. Thank your lucky stars she chose you. She *is* your greatest love of all.'

Stevie looked at Dorothy and mumbled,

'I don't know what's wrong with me. I'm just angry all the time.'

'And frightened,' suggested Dorothy, 'and I get that, but you will know real terror if you let Amber leave your life. She is the best thing that ever happened to you. And ...'

Stevie was listening now. Really listening. 'Yes?'

'Not bad looking, which is a bonus.'

Dorothy smiled and Stevie gave a tiny grin of acknowledgement.

'I do want a family,' she said.

'Well, one step at a time,' replied Dorothy in practical mode. 'I suggest you get your wife back first.'

Stevie sat up and looked at her watch.

'How long has she been gone?'

'She went off just under an hour ago.'

'We have to get to the station!'

'I'll drive!' volunteered Dorothy.

Neither of them could move very quickly to get across the square to the pub. Dorothy still had some pain and Stevie was on crutches. Jack appeared in the doorway as they hobbled toward him.

'I didn't know where to go. I didn't want to be too far away,' he explained. 'Agnes has gone. All her stuff – and Frank's. I'd never thought to ask if she was married,' Jack whispered shamefacedly to Dorothy.

'Yes,' she replied. 'You don't always cover yourself in glory, but we haven't got time now.' Dorothy headed for the garages round the back.

'Where are you two going?' Jack asked.

'To stop Amber,' Stevie replied. 'I've been a complete idiot.'

'Never a good look,' said Jack, falling in step with her. The two friends rounded the corner to find Dorothy trying to open the heavy garage door.

'Let me!' cried Stevie, trying to move forward quickly but stopping mid-stride with a groan. The two women looked at Jack.

'You're kidding?' he said. 'Suddenly I'm the butch one?' He shrugged, moved to the garage and lifted the metal shutter instantly. He smiled, admitting, 'That felt pretty good, actually.'

Dorothy unlocked the car. 'Get in, you slowcoaches,' she called.

Jack leapt to get in the back seat which was a squeeze.

'Christ, thank god you weren't there at Dunkirk,' groused Dorothy. 'We'd never have won the fucking war. Stevie, you wait there!'

Dorothy put the car in reverse and swept out, with Stevie throwing herself and her crutches into the front seat while the car was moving.

Dorothy even surprised herself with the speed with which she headed for the station. It was the perfect time for all her honed driving skills to come to the fore. There did not seem to be a short cut or traffic-free route she didn't know. At one point there was a build-up of cars on the main road, and she suddenly pulled onto a petrol station forecourt and waved through the window at the man behind the till, who pressed a button to open a garage door. Dorothy shot into the garage.

'Dorothy!' yelled Jack, clinging on to the seat in front.

'Pillar!' shouted Stevie as a large concrete post veered into view.

'Hang on!' roared Dorothy as she slammed on the brakes and pulled on the wheel. Her action caused the car to skid round the column and head straight for a closed door at the end. Certain he was going to die, Jack closed his eyes and almost prayed. Seconds before they got to the door it opened and the car zoomed back onto the open road. It was like being in a movie.

She screeched to a halt in front of the railway station, not worrying about niceties like permitted parking zones as she and her two very shaken passengers spilled from the car.

The station was a large city hub and trains were heading all over the country.

'She's going to Dudley,' shouted Stevie, hobbling behind him. 'Look for the Birmingham train.'

The giant departure board had dozens of trains listed and the three of them scanned it looking for the right destination.

'Platform six!' cried Jack and they were off again, with Jack leading as fast as he could and Stevie and Dorothy bringing up the rear, weaving between waiting passengers and their luggage.

Dorothy saw her first. Amber was walking dejectedly to the platform gate.

'There!' she cried.

'Amber!' called Stevie.

Amber turned and saw her wife and two friends heading toward her. Amber was in a terrible state and just wanted to leave them all behind. She held up her hand to stop them.

'I'm going home,' called Amber quietly. 'I'm going back to Dudley.'

'You can't even get a train from here to Dudley,' replied Stevie.

'I can change.'

'Please don't change. I love everything about you. Look . . .'

Stevie reached into her pocket and took out her wallet. She brought out a very flat dried dandelion.

'What is that?'

'It's the dandelion from in front of our house. That first day. You remember. It means faithfulness. I kept it.'

'I love you, Stevie, but I need some time,' said Amber. 'I don't know what's happening with you.' She turned to move away.

Dorothy hovered near by, watching. She knew she should leave it to Stevie, but it just wasn't her nature. Between platforms six and seven she spied the very thing that was needed.

'The piano!' cried Dorothy, pushing Jack towards the musical instrument which stood available on the concourse for public use.

Jack ran, calling over his shoulder, 'I don't know what to play.'

'Rachmaninov!' cried Stevie.

'Second piano concerto!' instructed Dorothy.

Jack threw himself down and began to play. The sweeping chords of the theme from *Brief Encounter* swelled into the air. Stevie slowly followed Amber as the music took hold.

'I love you, Amber,' she began, almost afraid to speak in case

285

she said the wrong thing. 'I love you with a passion which I didn't think possible. I'll behave and whatever happens with the baby, we can sort it.'

'I'm going back to Dudley ...' Amber tried.

Several people stopped to listen to the music and then to watch the unfolding scene. A young woman began to record it all on her phone while two elderly sisters drinking takeaway coffee on a bench were enthralled. Stevie's awkward movement on her crutches toward her runaway wife continued one tiny pace at a time. It was as if she were trying to capture a bird about to fly away. Nearly at Amber's side and possibly overwhelmed by the music, she began to quote:

'I'm an ordinary woman. I didn't think such violent things could happen to ordinary people.'

Dorothy stood biting her lip and watching as Jack brought the music to a great crescendo. Amber began to laugh. She put down her bag and turned to grab Stevie round the waist. Stevie dropped her crutches and clung on for dear life. It was beautiful. It was perfect. They kissed. Jack finished playing and a few people applauded. He hugged Amber, Dorothy hugged her, they all hugged each other and then slowly the four of them went back to Dorothy's car, which was now festooned with parking tickets.

The sisters on the bench finished their coffee before one remarked to the other, 'That was nice, although I do think if Dudley *is* the father of that baby, then maybe she *should* have gone back to him.'

The drive home was much calmer, with Jack failing to get Dorothy to do the petrol station shortcut again. Amber and Stevie sat in the back and held each other. When they got home Jack and Dorothy went to visit Birdie, giving the married couple time to themselves. The real owners of Number 4 went up to their room and shut the door.

'You scared me,' admitted Stevie. Amber held her hand as they lay on their bed.

'Not as scared as I was when I thought you were going to die.'

'No.'

'What finally got you off that sofa?' asked Amber.

'Dorothy told me off. Said she loved me.'

'How terrifying for you.'

Stevie smiled. 'Ambs, did you know she thought she was going to die?'

'Yes.'

'Did you talk about it?'

'There was no need.'

They lay side by side, looking at the ceiling and holding hands.

'I . . . we . . . need to find a different way to do this,' said Stevie.

'Yes,' agreed Amber. She turned to stroke her gorgeous wife's cheek. 'Stevie, I'm not pregnant.'

'It didn't work?'

'No. I tried to tell you but . . .'

'I was busy being a twat. Are you OK?'

'I'm fine,' said Amber and she was.

23

The next evening Arun, Jack, Stevie and Amber had their first proper conversation about babies and about what might be best for everyone. Amber told the men that the first attempt had not succeeded. Stevie had predicted Jack berating himself and his 'second-class sperm' but there was general relief all round.

'We can't thank you enough, Jack, but something doesn't feel right,' said Amber. 'What we are doing is wonderful, but this is huge. I want it to be perfect.'

'If you want to do this, Jack, I am on board. One hundred per cent,' declared Arun.

Jack looked at him and smiled before shaking his head.

'The truth is,' he said, 'I know you'll be wonderful parents, Amber and Stevie. Who could doubt? But I wouldn't want to just watch from the sidelines. It would be too hard, and I don't think I'm ready for a child. I don't know anything about having a family. I mean, I have Nan, but my mother doesn't speak to me. I have no idea who my dad was, but it's not just that. I don't know anything about just being me. I don't know who I want to be when I grow up, except that I want to be with Arun. I've been looking after Nan since I was fifteen and maybe it sounds selfish, but I don't want to have any more responsibility for a while.' Jack continued, 'I'm not saying I don't want a family, just not now, and, honestly, I think even a dog might be too much.'

'A dog?' queried Arun. 'You mean a cat, right?' and laughed. 'Jack and I are new to each other,' Arun ventured. 'I think we both just want to enjoy it for a while. My family don't know about him, and they won't be pleased when I tell them. Not about Jack but the whole gay thing. We'll have to deal with that. You know how much he loves you, Stevie, but I'm not sure about more complications right now.'

'It's completely fair enough,' agreed Stevie. She smiled at Jack. 'Besides, we might never agree on parenting.'

'I believe in brightly coloured sweets just before bedtime,' said Jack earnestly as Stevie pretended to smack him with the back of her hand.

'This is about me and Stevie,' Amber said. 'As much as possible I just want this to be us and no one else. I get that lots of people create a child with someone they know and that's great but I'm not sure it's right for us.'

'I didn't know it would make me so jealous,' admitted Stevie.

It was honest and it was better.

After that Stevie did some of her excellent research and booked them in at a clinic. A clinic with the Danish sperm Amber had wanted all along. Once the date was set Stevie began finding the next thing to worry about.

She and Dorothy were having tea on the red sofa.

'The sperm will arrive at the clinic by specialist courier,' Stevie explained.

'Oh good,' replied Dorothy, 'I hate to think of it taking an Uber.'

Stevie carried on. 'It will arrive, and we go in and they take care of everything. It's all set: April 8th.'

'I should have found somewhere by then.'

'You are waiting for your all-clear and that's all there is to it. Anyway, that's not why I'm telling you. The thing is, I want to make it perfect for Amber. I want to make up for everything, but I don't really know what to do.'

'Why don't you take her for a romantic meal the night before?' suggested Dorothy. 'That's what loved-up people do before they make a baby.'

Stevie shook her head. 'I don't know,' she said. 'It's hit and miss in restaurants for the two of us. It can be fine, but you have no idea how many times some bloke has come over and said something like "What are you two ladies doing out on your own?" or the waiter is weird with us.'

Dorothy had had no idea and was horrified. So, unable to stay out of it, she concocted a plan. It involved Jack.

After a month of recovery Stevie had gone back to work at a desk job until her physio was complete but Jack was still at a loose end.

The day before their appointment at the clinic, both Stevie and Amber made sure they had the night off. Dorothy was very clear in her instructions. 'You both go for a walk,' she said. 'Come back at seven p.m. precisely.'

Stevie and Amber had learnt to do as they were told.

They had a lovely stroll and at seven were back at Number 4. The paper star still shone in the window. It seemed to have become a permanent fixture, but the curtains were drawn behind it. Jack opened the door before they could put the key in the lock. He was wearing an old dinner jacket he'd found in the pub loft. He bowed and murmured, 'Good evening,' before walking backwards to show Amber and Stevie into the sitting room. The room was transformed, with the card table from Christmas now immaculately set for dinner for two. There were candles everywhere and a curtain had been hung to hide any view of the kitchen. Arun appeared, also dressed for the occasion, although nothing Dorothy owned had fitted him, so his outfit was a little more hit and miss. A white shirt, a bow tie and Hawaiian shorts. He carried two offerings of champagne in immaculate glasses. He handed them over saying,

'Vera Wang.'

'Language!' admonished Jack in his maître d' voice.

The meal was perfection. The service divine. Even Amber had a bit of champagne. It was utterly romantic.

Once everything was served, Arun and Jack left and Dorothy appeared wearing her coat.

'Right, kitchen's all done. I'm off to spend the night with Birdie. You two have some time to yourselves.'

'It's been wonderful, Dorothy,' said Stevie, getting up. 'Thank you.'

'I won't let anything spoil your perfect moment,' said Dorothy, just as there was a noise in the hall and the front door could be heard opening.

The three women looked to the door as a strange man entered. He was in his seventies with faded good looks, his grey hair still thick. He wore a sheepskin coat with the collar up, loafers and a pair of unpleasantly tight jeans. He bowled in with an entitled air but then stopped, clearly astonished by the restaurant scene playing out in front of him.

'What the fuck are you doing in my house?' he boomed at Stevie and Amber.

291

Dorothy stood stock still. Instinctively Stevie went to stand by her side.

'What's happening?' she asked, looking at the man and then at Dorothy's unnaturally pale appearance.

Dorothy took a deep breath and said, 'Amber, Stevie ... this is Tony.'

'And he is?' asked Amber.

Dorothy paused before replying. 'My husband.'

24

'Hello Dots,' said Tony, cocking his head and smiling as if he were just a bit late back from the pub. He reached into his pocket and pulled out a cigarette case, apparently confident that he had all the time in the world. Dorothy looked at him and then, without a word, disappeared into the kitchen. Seconds later she came back out through the temporary curtain. She was carrying a gun and pointing it straight at him.

'Fuck!' cried Stevie.

'Dorothy . . .' warned Amber, getting up slowly.

'It's fine,' said Dorothy calmly. 'You two just sit down and let me deal with him.' She held the gun level with both hands and didn't take her eyes off Tony. 'You were supposed to be here months ago. You said you were on your way.'

Tony had put his hands up, but he was also trying to look as though it was all rather funny.

'Yeah, you know what it's like,' he grinned. 'Everything took a bit longer than I thought. You remember my life? Ducking and diving. Come on, Dots. We can talk about this,' he protested. He moved to get out a cigarette. 'Let me just light my fag and—'

'Talk?' screamed Dorothy, losing her rag and waving the gun in earnest. 'Is that what you did with Connie? Talk?'

Dorothy stepped closer to her husband, pointing the gun right at him. There was little doubt that she was not at all worried about using it.

'It wasn't my fault,' he jabbered, dropping his cigarette case. 'She was keen, you know what young girls are like . . .'

Dorothy raised the weapon up and without another word fired a shot into the ceiling. Tony ducked as plaster and dust rained down on his head.

'Christ!' shouted Stevie and tried to move but the sudden action was too much for the not quite healed injury to her side and she fell back onto the sofa. Amber's instinct was to protect her wife by standing in front of her.

'Do not ever talk about Connie like that!' hissed Dorothy.

'Sorry, sorry,' said Tony, crouched down and looking for a way out. He reached for his cigarette case and stood up.

'Look, Dots, I know you're upset but—'

'Oh no, I'm not upset. That doesn't really cover it.'

Dorothy's hands were shaking but she managed to level the gun once more at Tony, who tried to regain his cool. He put his cigarettes away and tried to dust the plaster off his coat. 'I think there's been a misunderstanding,' he said. He turned and tried to charm his way with Amber and Stevie. Giving them a broad smile he explained, 'I'm married to the, uh, joy that is Dorothy. Still married, which is why I'm here. I find myself in a tiny spot of uh . . .' – he gave a slight cough – 'financial embarrassment and as this house is still half mine I wrote to say I was coming back to, uh, have a chat about it. Settle matters.' He turned to Dorothy, holding up both his hands in defence and saying, 'You said yes. You said I should come.'

'And this is me settling matters!' She waved the gun at him again. 'I am going to kill you,' she said incredibly slowly in case anyone was not following. 'I just can't decide whether you should depart this life with or without your dick.'

'Hang on, this *is* my house!' Tony yelled at Dorothy. 'We never got divorced,' he protested to the two young women.

'That's because I couldn't fucking find you!' said Dorothy.

'Dorothy, I think we ...' tried both Amber and Stevie.

Dorothy glanced at them out of the corner of her eye. 'Not now!' she commanded.

There was no doubting her seriousness.

Tony swallowed hard as he tried to steady his voice and move on to some of the conversation he had clearly rehearsed. 'This is my house,' he began. 'I want what's coming to me.'

'Coming to you?' repeated Dorothy. 'Coming to you?' Her voice began to rise to a crescendo. 'I'll give you what's coming to you, you prick.'

She raised the gun again and no one in the house was in any doubt that she intended to use it on something other than plaster. Tony turned and ran. He pelted across the square with Dorothy following after him to the door. She was still slow since the operation. A shot rang out in the darkness. Dorothy stood on the doorstep, holding the gun in her shaking hands. Amber raced to get Dorothy back into the sitting room, where Stevie stood in a state of shock. Within seconds Mrs Haggerston was at her door and peering out into the night.

'Give Stevie the gun, Dorothy,' Amber demanded.

'I don't want the gun,' protested Stevie.

'You did gun training!' insisted her wife.

Stevie put her hand out for the fired piece. Dorothy obeyed without another word.

'What the fuck, Dorothy?' Stevie managed, looking at the gun in her hand and trying to work out how to make it safe.

Amber helped Dorothy to sit down and then summoned all her professionalism as she tried to be calm.

'Where did you get a gun?' she asked, sitting opposite the elderly would-be assassin.

'It's all right,' mumbled Dorothy. 'Just blanks.'

'Nooo,' said Stevie slowly, removing four live bullets from the chamber. She put them down on the card table as if they might go off by themselves.

The sound of police sirens could be heard. Mrs Haggerston had clearly made a call. Since the trouble at the Onion patrol cars had been including Grimaldi Square more often in their nightly rounds. They were not far away.

Dorothy was no longer functioning properly. She sat on the sofa shaking.

'What if she's killed him?' whispered Amber to Stevie as the sound of the sirens gathered momentum.

Suddenly Stevie got up and moved as quickly as she could to the stairs.

'What are you doing?' demanded Amber.

'Hiding the gun. I'm going to put it with the money.'

'Oh great. Half a million quid and a potential murder weapon. You're a police officer! And you can't even move quickly either. I'll take it!'

'I know, but it's . . . Dorothy. We need a minute! I'll get the door when they ring. Dorothy, shift yourself!' urged Stevie. 'Hide the bullets!'

Fortunately, the police started with Mrs Haggerston. While Amber raced upstairs Stevie hid by the front window, listening to Mrs H talking on her front step.

'About time you came,' she was saying. 'I don't know how many times I've called. Do you have any ID?'

The two male police officers had arrived in a patrol car and were in full uniform so a request for ID seemed excessive. But they got out their warrant cards and showed her. It all took time because Mrs Haggerston hadn't got her glasses. Once she was satisfied, one of the men got out a small notebook and pencil. Mrs Haggerston spoke slowly, wanting to make sure he got every word.

'There's a woman next door who claims to be a police officer,' she began, 'and I've already reported it. Then someone burnt down Notre-Dame and no one did anything about it. Did you know about that?'

'Yes ...' replied the officer slowly. 'Notre-Dame was burnt down, but I don't think that's really in our jurisdiction.'

'Well, whose jurisdiction is it?'

'Uhm ... somebody in ... Paris?'

The second officer had paused in his note-taking.

'You say you heard a gunshot,' he tried.

Meanwhile at Number 4 Dorothy was starting to come round from her daze. She grabbed Stevie by the arm just as Amber returned from hiding the gun.

'Don't let them go in the garden!' Dorothy pleaded.

Stevie's head was already in turmoil and she was further bewildered by this new request. 'Why?'

'Jack and I are growing weed in the shed.'

'What?'

There was a knock at the door.

'Oh my god,' said Amber, going to answer.

The police came in and sat down in the sitting room, but they did not stay long. It turned out Stevie *was* a police officer.

'Constable Baxter,' she said, showing her ID.

'And Mrs Haggerston, have you known her long?'

'A w-while,' stammered Amber.

'Do you have any concerns about her?'

'Some.'

'She's upset about Notre-Dame burning down,' said one of the officers.

'Is she?' managed Amber.

No one had ever fired a gun near Grimaldi Square, and it seemed an unlikely occurrence. No, they didn't need to investigate further. Yes, it was likely Mrs H had fallen asleep in front of a crime programme or a car had backfired. Dorothy sat meekly, not speaking. The police tried to engage her in some light questioning, but she just sat on the sofa making gurgling sounds and refused to look at them.

'She all right?' asked one of the officers.

'Alzheimer's,' blurted Amber. 'She doesn't speak.'

By the time the door closed on the brief investigation the three residents of Number 4 were in a state of shock.

'Why didn't you say anything?' Stevie asked Dorothy, who explained by opening her mouth and removing the four remaining bullets. Stevie lost her rag.

'What the ... what is wrong with you?' she shouted.

'You told me to hide them,' said Dorothy defensively.

'Not in your fucking mouth! Do you know how dangerous that is? Who are you?'

'I just lied to the police,' muttered Amber.

'*I* am the fucking police!' exploded Stevie. 'How the fuck have we ended up here? I just want a normal life and everything with you, Dorothy, is one drama after another. I don't even know you!' Stevie suddenly stopped mid-rant. 'Weed! Did you say there is weed in my shed?'

Stevie went out to the back garden with Amber and Dorothy not far behind. It was dark yet a bright glow was emanating from the shed. Stevie opened the shed door and was immediately hit by a shaft of light. Heat lamps had been rigged right across the ceiling and shone down on row upon row of hemp growing on very neat wooden shelves.

'First of all can I say I am still recovering and . . .'

'Do not try that with me,' replied Stevie slowly. She looked over the fence and saw Mrs Haggerston staring out of her kitchen window. 'Get inside,' she ordered.

The three women returned to the sitting room. Amber and Dorothy sat down at the table while Stevie clapped her hands.

'OK, I can explain this,' said Dorothy, trying to sound entirely reasonable. 'The weed, although extensive, is a good thing. Jack and I are running a joint care club for the elderly!' She smiled as if everyone was going to be delighted. 'We make brownies for them, to help with their pain. It's terrific. One of the women has made a remarkable—'

'It's illegal!' yelled Stevie.

'We don't charge,' said Dorothy, looking hurt.

'Will you two keep it down!' said Amber. 'Somebody might be listening.'

'Never mind that,' replied her wife, looking out the window into the dark square. 'Somebody might be dead.'

Amber went out with a torch, but she couldn't see anyone. There was nothing but the usual rubbish. By the time she came back Stevie was shaking.

'What have I done?' she kept repeating.

Dorothy was the quietest she had ever been. She didn't even drink her tea from her *Hygge* mug but just sat letting it go cold. Stevie was in pain from all the racing about. Amber got her her

299

medication and eventually she and Stevie fell asleep on the sofa. In the morning the two women were woken by the sound of a throbbing engine outside in the street. Stevie got up and looked out.

'It's Dorothy,' she said to her waking wife. 'She's in the car. Wants us to come out. I don't think we should do one more thing she suggests.'

'What time is it?' asked Amber.

Stevie checked her watch. 'Seven.'

Amber stood up and looked out the window. 'We need to find a way forward,' she said. 'It's Dorothy. We can't just abandon her. Plus . . .' Amber sighed. 'I think we may be in too deep.'

No one spoke as Dorothy drove, until at last she came to a stop at the entrance to a large Victorian graveyard. It was a deserted place with collapsed and collapsing slabs of grey stone bearing the names of the departed.

'Dorothy, what are we . . .' tried Amber.

'I need to show you something,' said Dorothy.

They walked in silence for some time, before at last Dorothy stopped in front of a rare well looked after plot. A rough-hewn stone bore the name *Connie* the inscription *Beloved Daughter* and the dates *1962–1984*. The lawn around the stone was carefully kept but the edges were a little freer, with a frame of wild grasses. Dorothy bent down to wipe the top of the grave. Stevie began to speak but Amber put out her hand and indicated to wait.

'Give her a minute,' she said.

There was a wooden bench opposite the grave and the two shellshocked women retreated to sit down. It was early April and one of those spring mornings where the world feels as though it is waking up again. They sat and watched Dorothy tend to her child's resting place. The sun was rising and the light glistened on the dewdrops. Birds were singing and it was strangely peaceful.

After a while Dorothy stepped back from the grave. She looked at it again and then walked over to Amber and Stevie. They made a space for her to sit between them. There was a long hush.

'How the hell have we ended up here?' said Stevie at last.

It was Amber who started to try to unpick the story. 'Where did you get the gun, Dorothy?' she asked.

'I told you, One-eyed Billy left it in the back of my cab,' replied Dorothy.

'You didn't tell me you kept it.' Amber looked at her. 'Anyway, I don't believe you. It was Bobby, wasn't it? You got it from Bobby.'

'Don't be daft,' snorted Dorothy.

'I don't believe anything you say any more,' declared Stevie, wincing as she turned too quickly. 'Why didn't you tell us?'

'Oh, I'd just drop it into the chat that I was hanging around the house waiting for Tony to turn up so I could kill him?' retorted Dorothy.

'You knew he was coming?'

'Yes, but he didn't arrive when he said he would. I thought it would have been sorted by the time you arrived. I know I should have left but he and I had unfinished business.'

'You cannot go around killing people, Dorothy,' said Amber evenly. 'And now you've involved us.'

Dorothy looked shamefaced. 'I know. I am sorry about that.'

'I can't believe we hid the gun and I lied!' groaned Stevie, putting her head in her hands.

'I am sorry you got caught up in this, but I need you to know that he does deserve to die,' said Dorothy emphatically, suddenly ready to tell them everything. 'I loved him. Really loved him. You should have seen him. Always turning up with some mad, exciting thing – a car, a jukebox. He was handsome then. Young. Younger than me. In my heart I always knew Tony was a wrong 'un but it felt like something out of a film. He was so charming. I wanted that . . . romance, a man to grow old with. I even thought we might have a baby. Idiot!'

Dorothy paused and stared with a great yearning at her child's grave.

'I had Connie when I was practically a child myself. She was just eighteen by the time I found Tony. That's all – eighteen. I thought he was going to be a dad to her. She'd never had a dad and fact is she didn't need one, but I should just have been a better mum. Looked out for her but I didn't want to see what was happening. My dad wasn't well, so I worked almost every night at the Onion. He needed the help.'

Dorothy could hardly control her voice. Amber stroked her arm while Stevie looked away at the gravestone.

'We moved into Number 4. Dad's wedding present and Connie spent most nights there with Tony. I thought it was nice she had the company. Birdie saw it coming. She wasn't surprised when they ran off. Went to Greece. We chased after them, me and Birdie, but we never found them. No internet then. Just a lot of buses.'

'I'm sorry,' interrupted Stevie. 'Tony ran off with your teenage daughter?'

'Almost exactly a year after our wedding.'

'Oh my god!'

'Fucker!'

Dorothy paused in her story and all three women looked at Connie's gravestone.

'What happened to her?' asked Amber quietly.

Dorothy took a deep breath before continuing.

'She was killed on the road to the airport in Athens. I got a message from the local police. Birdie helped me. We brought Connie home and laid her here.'

'And Tony?' asked Stevie.

'I never saw him again. Until now.'

Stevie's enquiring mind had a million questions. 'Where was Connie going that day? Heading for the airport?'

'I don't know. I like to think she was coming home. I thought Tony might tell me but now that I tried to kill him . . .'

'Is that why you wanted to stay in the house?' asked Amber. 'Because you miss Connie?'

Dorothy shook her head. 'I don't need to be there to miss her. There's not a day . . . Out of the blue I had a letter from Tony. He said he was coming back. He wrote and said he wanted half the house. Wanted me to buy him out. It was dated the tenth of August. I couldn't believe it. I don't think he had even noticed.'

'Noticed what?' asked Stevie.

'The date. It was our wedding day. The cheek of it, but that's him all over. After everything. Well, he wasn't getting anything from me, so I put the house up for sale. I didn't want him to have any bit of it. I kept waiting but he didn't come, and the house didn't sell until nearly a year later when you came along.'

'The tenth of August. That's when we saw the house,' said Amber quietly.

'You made an offer and I said yes straight away. It seemed like fate and I just wanted out but then I didn't know what to do with the money. I thought if it was in the bank he might still get it somehow so I took the cash and then I couldn't think what to do with it so I just carried it around. I was going to leave with the cash but then the doctor wrote about the cancer and I thought, well, if I'm dying anyway, I'll just wait till he comes. Look him in the face. Kill him. He killed me. Yes. It was a perfect storm and then . . . well, you were so nice so I just . . . stayed.'

'Why didn't you tell us?' asked Amber.

'Because what I did is mad. It was mad not to leave the house.' Dorothy turned to Amber and Stevie saying, 'And to be fair, you were mad to let me stay.'

'So all that stuff about you deciding to sell up because you were bored and wanting to go backpacking,' asked Amber, 'that's just nonsense?'

Dorothy shrugged. 'Not entirely. I do think that programme *Tipping Point* is enough to make you want to top yourself.'

Stevie had been quiet until then.

'I wasn't ready,' she said softly, 'I wasn't ready for a house and marriage even though we had planned and planned and then suddenly Amber started talking about babies. I used to dream about a house of our own but when it happened I think it was too much. Focusing on you, Dorothy, arguing about you, was easier than sitting down and talking about what was really happening. You were a terrific distraction.'

'Do you want a baby now?' asked Amber gently.

'I think I do. Yes, I do. I just didn't want my DNA anywhere near it.'

'It's not your father who would be bringing the child up,' admonished Dorothy. 'It would be you.'

'Possible accessory to murder,' added Stevie.

'Maybe keep that to yourself,' suggested Dorothy.

The three of them sat through another more comfortable silence until Amber said,

'Stevie, you seem to forget that Delaunay is not my real name. Remember, it was the name of the first children's home my grandmother was in as a baby. It was run by nuns. If no one knew anything about a kid, they were given the surname Delaunay. There is no past. I had a sort of donor father too. I'm fine. It's fine.'

Stevie looked at her wife. 'I do want a baby with you. I don't care about anything else.'

Dorothy, sitting between them, took one hand each and brought them together, resting her own on top.

'You two will make lovely babies which' – she looked at her watch – 'I seem to remember is supposed to be happening this morning.'

Despite being present at a possible homicide, helping to hide a potential murder weapon and discovering a dope farm in the garden, Amber and Stevie were due at their first fertility clinic appointment that morning. Dorothy drove them from the cemetery to the clinic.

'I'm sorry it hasn't been quite the romantic dinner followed by baby-making which you'd planned,' she said as she pulled up outside.

'The dinner idea was lovely,' said Amber.

'Yes,' agreed Stevie. 'You possibly killing your husband, less perfect. Have you got a saint for today?'

Dorothy shrugged. 'Today I don't think we need one.'

She waited outside and then drove them all home full of expectation.

'It never takes first time,' Amber kept repeating. 'We mustn't get our hopes up.'

When they got back to the house Tony was waiting, not dead, on the doorstep, smoking a cigarette. With him was a man in a very ill-fitting grey suit. Tony's rage from the night before had only grown. Eyeing Dorothy to check she was not carrying a gun, he squared up to her with his usual cocky confidence.

'Dorothy, this is my solicitor, Graham. Graham, this is my wife. We've come to talk about my settlement. There won't be a lot of negotiating. I haven't been to the police about last night, but I will if I have to.'

'Yes, indeed,' agreed Graham. Stevie realised it was the same man she had seen at her cousin Maisie's place in his underpants. She had not seen him fully dressed before.

Dorothy couldn't speak. The sight of Tony, even the smell of him, made her feel sick. He was still smoking those foul roll-up cigarettes. He dragged on one now and she noticed his once mes-merising hands were stained yellow with nicotine. How could she ever have fallen for him? How could he have ever touched her beloved child?

'I gather you fired a gun at my client,' said Graham.

Stevie laughed too loud. 'A gun? She's nearly eighty years old.'

Tony was in no mood for this. He had spent the night on a bench at the bus station, opposite the GOAT Pizza shop. They were just opening when Tony went looking for both a lawyer and a place to stay. Weirdly the owner knew where he could find both. Now Tony had hired Graham and he was out for revenge.

'Don't push me, Dorothy,' he said with quiet fury. 'I will get what I am owed.'

'We will be fair,' Graham intoned in his nasal whine, 'but shall require, without discussion, at a minimum, half the house money and half the value of the pub.'

'The pub?' said Amber and Stevie at the same moment.

Dorothy looked at Tony. Years' worth of hurt and rage filled her eyes before she nodded and looked across the square. 'The Onion,' she said. 'It still belongs to me. I should have sold that too.'

25

Possibly one day pregnant or not, Amber went to work the next morning. Even though it was a terrible idea Stevie went to see Maisie and, leaving out the unfortunate shooting, explained what had happened. She staggered up the stairs and sank into a chair.

'So Tony is back, and they're still married. He says he's going to sue her for everything she's got. I need you to ask your friend Graham not to help him.'

Maisie was busy dealing with quite specific pizza toppings on an order for downstairs and not at all helpful.

'You know I'm sleeping with Graham?' she asked, banging on the pipe.

'Yes. Do you like sleeping with him?' Stevie asked, amazed that it was something anyone would do by choice.

'Not particularly,' admitted Maisie. 'He makes some odd bedroom requests.'

'Then don't do it. Tell him to back off.'

Maisie banged on the pipe again and took another call. When she had finished, she sat down, eating tuna straight from the tin.

'I could, but honestly if it's not him then Tony will find someone else,' she said between mouthfuls. 'And the truth is, Stevie, I don't know if Dorothy's got a very good case.'

'Is that your legal opinion?'

'No. When I say I don't know, I really have no idea. I've not studied this kind of thing.'

'He ran off with her teenage daughter!'

'I don't think the law cares about that.' Maisie lowered her voice and looked to the bedroom. 'Anyway, we can't talk about this here.'

'But you don't have an office,' Stevie pointed out. 'We have to do it here.'

'I know, but Tony is staying here now.'

'What?'

'My Airbnb?' Maisie reminded her.

'Oh my god.' Stevie got up to go. 'What is wrong with you?'

'Graham brought him,' muttered Maisie, digging into the sides of the tin she was eating from with a teaspoon. Stevie looked at the label.

'Maisie, is that cat food?'

'I don't have a cat.'

'Nevertheless ...'

Stevie knew she wasn't getting anywhere. She headed home in a taxi but not before the Greek woman in GOAT Pizza persuaded her to buy a two-for-one special.

Stevie was carrying two boxes of margarita with pepperoni into Number 4 when she heard shouts from across the square. Jack was pushing his nan in her wheelchair, with Birdie yelling as they approached. Stevie had never seen her in such an agitated state of excitement.

'We have news!' she shouted as soon as they saw Stevie.

'Me too,' said Stevie, looking at Jack, who was breathless. 'Apparently I'm running a dope farm and didn't know.'

'Oh that,' tutted Jack as if it were nothing, 'I meant to tell you.' He took one of the boxes from his friend and began eating a slice of pizza.

The old Nordic walking poles woman strutted past without her sticks and waved. She looked terrific, almost upright and needing no help at all with walking.

Stevie couldn't help but comment. 'She looks great.'

'Very good brownies,' explained Jack between mouthfuls.

Birdie was almost levitating.

'*Step into the Spotlight!*' she trilled. '*Step into the Spotlight!*'

Stevie looked at Jack and his grandmother, who were both beaming. 'Is there something in the water round here, so no one ever just has a calm day?'

Mrs Haggerston's curtains flapped in her front window and she could be seen peering out. Stevie gave a small wave before ushering Jack and Birdie inside.

'Come in, come in.'

'Yes Jack, stop eating in the street,' scolded Birdie.

'That was my big worry,' said Stevie.

They went into the house, where Dorothy was just coming down the stairs with her suitcase and the gun. The case was heavy and caused her to wave the gun as she bumped her way down.

'I'm getting rid of the gun and hiding the money,' she declared. 'I can't risk you and Amber landing in hot water.'

'The money and the *gun*!' echoed Jack. 'Suddenly I feel my two pence worth of illegal weed fading in importance.'

'You told them about the gun, then,' said Birdie matter of factly to Dorothy.

'You knew about the . . .' began Stevie.

Birdie waved her away. 'Never mind that! Jack has news!'

Stevie wasn't sure she could cope with any more. She flopped down on the sofa, too exhausted to even try to take the illegal weapon.

'I do!' said Jack, plonking himself down in the sitting room while Dorothy remained standing in the doorway next to her suitcase, still clutching the gun.

'You know when I played the piano at the train station?' he began. 'Well, someone filmed it and put it up online and—'

'It's a virus!' shouted Birdie.

'It's gone viral!' corrected Jack.

'He's a sensation,' beamed his nan.

'Well, I think we knew that,' said Dorothy.

'The people . . .' Birdie paused, almost unable to say the words. 'The people from *Step into the Spotlight* have been in touch.'

Dorothy clapped her hands. 'I love that show. Will you be a ventriloquist? That would please your nan. We could ask Mrs Haggerston to be the dummy.'

'No! Piano. They want me to go on the show and play.'

Jack's piano-playing and the romantic scene which he had accompanied had entranced the internet. A member of the *Spotlight* talent team would be down later in the week to speak to him.

'He could be famous,' dreamed Birdie out loud, 'or rich or both.'

'Excellent,' said Dorothy. 'You can help me pay Tony off.'

'You need a proper lawyer,' said Stevie for the umpteenth time as Dorothy put down the gun and got plates for the rest of the takeaway.

Afterwards Birdie insisted on taking Jack off up the high

street to seek a possible outfit for his audition despite his protests that no local shop would have what was required. Dorothy left shortly afterwards.

'Where are you taking that?' demanded Stevie, pointing to the suitcase of money.

'I'm not telling you,' replied Dorothy. 'I don't want you in any more trouble.'

'Well, at least put the gun away in your pocket,' insisted Stevie.

She was left in a terrible state of agitation, so resorted to her usual coping mechanism and tried to make a plan. Perhaps she could find proper legal representation for Dorothy. She tried half a dozen different law firms and had finally found someone qualified when Dorothy returned empty-handed.

Stevie put her phone against her chest as she whispered to Dorothy, 'I'm getting you a lawyer!'

'Stop interfering,' replied Dorothy but she did at least sit down to listen.

'Yes,' said the smart, actual lawyer on speakerphone. 'I'm afraid the law is not entirely clear about who owns what if a married couple has failed to divorce but have lived separately for years. There is no simple, one-size-fits-all answer to the question. Would that there were. It all depends on each couple's individual circumstances and history. What does the husband own in the way of assets?'

'Nothing!' said Dorothy.

She, on the other hand, on paper at least, was quite well off but the lawyer found getting to the bottom of her finances hard work.

'You sold the house?' she asked.

'Yes,' agreed Dorothy.

'And what did you do with the money?'

'I spent a bit of it.'

'On what?'

'Marijuana plants, mainly. Some lighting and a couple of trestle tables.'

'I don't think we need to share that,' said Stevie.

It didn't take long to prove that Dorothy's money could not be found. Stevie was thrilled to be able to say absolutely truthfully that she had no idea where it was.

'He ran off with my daughter,' Dorothy wailed to the lawyer for the umpteenth time.

'Yes,' replied her counsel yet again, 'I understand she was a teenager but I'm afraid the law doesn't really care about that.'

Birdie was adamant about the whole situation. She and Jack had come back to show off his new suit and Dorothy updated them about the lawyer.

'You must not give in, Dot,' insisted Birdie. 'Do not give that reprobate one single penny.' Mostly Birdie wanted to talk about the forthcoming audition, but not before she had laid into Tony. She did not have a single good word to say about the man.

'And another thing,' she told Jack. 'It's his fault there's no ABBA in the jukebox. He hated them with a bizarre passion. Seemed personally affronted that they won Eurovision in '74 and never got over it. "Who did they think they were, taking that prize?" he would say. "Europeans," I'd say but he'd just mutter "Fucking Swedes". I don't know why he hated them so much. I think he had a dodgy Saab at the time. Kept saying we'd made a terrible mistake with Olivia Newton-John and needed Cliff back. "Cliff Richard," he'd say. "He's the man. Handsome. Proper man. That's a man's man."'

'No ABBA,' repeated Jack in shock. 'He is way worse than I thought.'

All of Dorothy's friends were on her side and wanted her to stay strong, but Tony had begun walking past the house at all hours. He'd go by slowly. Sometimes stop and smoke a cigarette outside on the street, staring at the house. If he saw Dorothy he would leer at her and say, 'You can't hide from me, Dot. I'm going to get my money.'

Dorothy always replied with a smart remark, but each incident left her more fragile. She felt she had been enough trouble, so she tried not to bother Stevie or Amber. Instead she found herself spending more and more time at Birdie's flat.

'You always said he was wrong 'un,' said Dorothy.

'I told you that at your wedding,' Birdie reminded her. 'He came on to me just after the service.'

'Prick.'

Birdie wanted to help her old pal but she was finding it hard to think of anything other than Jack's exciting turn of events. It was the most thrilling thing that had ever happened to her. The talent agent came and heard Jack play and was sufficiently impressed to announce that he would bring a film crew some time in the summer to capture Jack's audition. There was every chance that Adam Anderson himself might attend. Birdie was beside herself at the thought.

'The audition can't be here in the flat,' she declared. 'I've watched the show. It needs to be a bit showbiz. It has to be on a stage. It has to be at the Onion. That's perfect – a little bit glitz but also a little bit shit, so everyone can see he has been on a journey.'

'A little bit shit?' repeated Dorothy.

'You know what I mean,' said Birdie defensively. 'It's not exactly the Palladium, is it?'

It wasn't exactly anything. The pub was in a terrible state. The hooligans had done quite a job. All glass, decorative or otherwise, was smashed, the curtains ripped and even the piano was missing a couple of keys. Dorothy brought Birdie down to see the devastation.

'It's been more than two months and I'm still waiting on the insurance,' explained Dorothy, thinking Birdie might stop going on about the audition being held there but all she said was, 'We'd better get a broom and start tackling this mess.'

'Oh and are you doing that?' asked Dorothy.

Birdie spun round in her chair to look at her. 'Don't be ridiculous. What is the matter with you? I'm going to do the garden!'

'What?'

Birdie had been to the square several times lately and was appalled at the neglected state of it.

'What happened to all the flowers?' she asked Dorothy. 'And the nice benches? There's nothing but old vape pens.'

'I saw a condom,' added Dorothy.

'Can I just remind you that Adam Anderson himself might approach the Onion through this squalid mess? Something needs to be done.'

'Like what?'

'I'll do the place up,' Birdie said with determination.

Dorothy looked at her and shook her head.

'Birdie, you are seventy-eight and in a wheelchair with rheumatism. Which bit of that do you think might get in the way of using a shovel?'

'Nothing,' replied Birdie. 'You say you're still driving a mini-cab. Who are you to underestimate the power of old birds? It's spring. Perfect time to get going.'

'I thought you were going to have to move house,' tried Dorothy. 'Shouldn't you be packing?'

'I've got plenty of time before August.'

'What happens then?'

'They're knocking the tower down.'

'That'll focus you.'

Birdie looked at the square with fresh eyes. 'Now, my only problem is going to be money.'

'How much do you need?' asked Dorothy. 'I've got cash.'

Birdie grasped the new square renovation project with all the vigour of a much younger, fitter woman. In fact, she was stronger than she had been in years. Since she had begun coming out again and more conscientiously taking her medicine, her health had improved dramatically. Birdie was now wheeling her own chair whenever possible and refusing most offers of help. She sat outside the Onion with paper and pencil and considered what needed to be done. She had been growing plants in her flat for decades and had the greenest fingers in the neighbourhood. She drew up extensive plans before getting Jack to order plants. Soon she was out in the open air directing a team comprised entirely of ancient women.

'Who are they all?' asked Stevie.

'Joint care club,' replied Dorothy.

'Are all of them being supplied from our weed farm?'

Dorothy looked at her suspiciously. 'Are you looking for a cut?'

'No, just an explanation.'

Dorothy nodded. 'All these women,' she said, 'are past a certain age and suffering with one kind of ache or another. The NHS is bankrupt so I'm helping out. It's nothing. We get together, we eat a bit of cannabis cake and everyone feels better.'

Stevie eyed the energetic octogenarians. 'They're all stoned?' she asked.

'Don't be silly,' said Dorothy. They both turned to watch one of the women stand completely still, transfixed by the floral pattern on her gardening gloves. 'Well, not all the time.'

'Your trees have arrived!' announced Jack, bringing over some potted plants.

'Excellent!' declared Birdie, rubbing her hands. She looked at her grandson. She knew that the night of the fight had had a terrible impact on Jack. Even the exciting television news had not quite brought back his spirit.

'Right, let's get these in,' she called to her team. 'And you, Jack? What are you going to do?' she asked.

'Me, Nan? I was thinking of growing up, but it seems like quite hard work.'

'Yes, well, while we're waiting, what are you doing this minute? Last I looked you worked at the pub and that's not going to carry on unless you shift yourself. That place is not going to fix itself.'

Jack looked through the door to the mess inside.

'I'm not ready.'

'You can't let them win, Jack,' said Birdie with utter conviction.

'I don't know where to start.'

'Order a skip.'

That seemed like a simple start, so he did and the work began. Soon Jack found just clearing out the mess made him feel better. Each day Arun came after work and helped, and before long Mimi also arrived with some friends to muck in. Jack tried to get Stevie to help but every time she got to the pub she found she just stood in the doorway and did nothing.

One afternoon Dorothy was in the Onion, making tea for the garden brigade. She saw Stevie hovering at the door and brought over a cup. Together they looked in at the rooms Dorothy knew so well.

'I couldn't come in here for a long time,' said Dorothy, 'which is a shame. There is nothing wrong with the place, Stevie. Come on, let's bite the bullet together.'

'Not a good expression for you,' replied Stevie evenly. She turned to her friend. 'Dotty . . .'

'Yes?'

'I don't think I can be a police officer any more,' she confessed, 'and I can't tell Amber. They've got me tied to a desk and keep asking when I'll go back out on patrol but I just – I don't think I want to. When she has the baby, then . . .'

'Well, let's not jump the gun.'

'Another poor turn of phrase. We'll need my job and . . .'

'One thing at a time,' soothed Dorothy.

Ever interfering, later that day Dorothy texted Amber to come to the Onion at the end of her shift. She took her by the hand, saying, 'Come on, I'll show you something.'

She led her young friend round the back and up the steep stairs to the first floor. Amber was amazed. There was no sense of its size from downstairs. It was huge. Several bedrooms, a couple of bathrooms, a big kitchen, sitting room, office.

'What is this?' she asked.

'This was my home when I was growing up. We lived here. Years ago it was a hotel but not in my time. Sometimes Dad rented out a room. There's another floor above.'

'Why didn't you tell us you owned it?'

Dorothy shrugged. 'Tony and I met downstairs. He was such

317

a breath of fresh air. Swept into the place and took over. Always arriving with some mad present or other.'

'The jukebox?' Dorothy nodded.

'The car?'

'The car! I never asked but he probably nicked it. After Tony left and my father died, I didn't want anything to do with the place. I'd lost everything. I hated it here but somehow I just couldn't let it go. I hired people to keep it ticking over and then didn't come back. It was never going to be what it was.'

Amber wandered round the rooms.

'It's massive. Bigger than our house.'

'Connie grew up here. Ran about. Learnt to talk and never stopped ... Ooh she was a chatterbox ... but what's that got to do with the price of onions?'

'What?'

'It's what my dad used to say. All the time. About anything really. We all got drunk after he died and renamed the place. Anyway, when you have, you know, a scare it makes you think. Then I came up here with Jack before the party and I was surprised. It didn't seem so terrible after all. Anyway ...' Dorothy took a deep breath, turned and took Amber's hand.

'I've had the all clear, Amber. Cancer bloody free. They will keep watching me but for now ...'

Amber could not speak but hugged Dorothy close.

'It's a fresh start,' continued Dorothy. 'I don't know that I deserve it, but you'll be delighted to know that I was thinking about moving on. I thought I might live up here again. I think I'm OK with it now.'

'But you live ...' Amber stopped herself and smiled.

Dorothy sat down on a small pouffe. 'I did want to kill him,

318

you know. He ruined my life. He took everything. My dreams, my future, my daughter, my chance of a family.'

'The crib? Was there a baby?'

'No. That was just a fantasy.' Dorothy smiled. 'But now it doesn't need to be. Maybe that wicker basket was always for your baby. I wasted so much time hating Tony. I used to imagine tracking him down but now he's here . . . All I know is that I need to make some changes. I need to leave you and Stevie alone.'

'Yeah, well, that's not happening. You have a new family,' said Amber quietly. 'You have us and we're not going anywhere.' She looked around the large Victorian room. A cast iron fireplace was just visible behind a stack of boxes. 'I think living here could be wonderful. We'll be just across the square.'

Amber suddenly moved to sit down.

'Nauseous?' asked Dorothy and Amber nodded. 'Have you told Stevie?'

'She knows. It's already making her crazy.'

26

Seeing the double red lines on the small plastic pregnancy test had been the first thing to galvanise Stevie in a long time. She had leapt to her feet at the news.

'Oh my god, oh my god! Can I get you anything? Do anything?' She was off and wouldn't let up.

'Apart from needing to do something for herself, she'll drive me mad "looking after the baby" if we don't keep her busy,' Amber told Dorothy. 'She's made a colour-coded chart of vitamins I have to take and keeps making me have scheduled naps when I come home from work.'

Dorothy looked at the piles of furniture and detritus. 'Send Stevie up here,' she suggested.

When Stevie turned up she found Dorothy trying to lift a large trunk of clothes.

Stevie rushed to help her. 'What are you doing?' she asked. 'That weighs a ton. You'll hurt yourself. Here, let me.'

Stevie lifted the trunk, pleased to notice most of her strength had returned, as Dorothy directed her into the next room.

'Amber and I have agreed that I'm going to live here,' said Dorothy, 'so I need to do the place up.'

'Jesus, Dorothy,' wheezed Stevie from the exertion.

'I am going to move back home.'

Stevie looked around at the piles of stuff everywhere. 'You can't do this by yourself,' she said.

'And who is going to help me?' asked Dorothy. 'Amber is pregnant.'

Stevie smiled. 'She told you.'

'Jack is busy downstairs and you don't seem to want to come back to us.'

'I could help a bit, I guess,' suggested Stevie slowly. 'I'm back on shifts and . . .'

Dorothy gave a show of trying to leap in the air but lacked the vigour. They both grinned. Dorothy stood with her legs apart and put her hands on her hips before enquiring, 'Where shall we start?' She looked down at her stance and sniggered, 'Christ, I think I'm turning into Jack.'

Stevie looked in admiration at the old woman. 'How can you carry on being cheerful when Tony hangs about threatening you every day?' she marvelled.

'I won't let him win,' said Dorothy without hesitation.

Once the plan to move Dorothy back into the pub was hatched, Dave de Van came and took any unwanted furniture to auction or charity. Skip after skip arrived, was filled and departed from the courtyard at the back. In her spare time Stevie started on the basic DIY work upstairs and found it soothed her. Downstairs she could hear the sound of the pub being brought back to life with Arun working every spare hour repairing the bar with Jack. Bobby fixed the plasterwork in the pub, and also the ceiling of Number 4, from which he quietly removed a bullet.

Stevie became relentless in her determination to make Dorothy's new home as fine a residence as anyone had ever seen. Naturally she made a folder of plans and ideas. Young Justin was supposed to help but mostly sat on the side of the pub stage, playing his guitar from Argos. It provided a nice soundtrack to what everyone was doing.

Dorothy was just coming down the stairs to the courtyard with some pieces for the skip when she found Tony trying to open one of the garage doors. He turned as she approached.

'Hello, Dotty Dot.'

'Don't call me that. What are you doing here?'

'I'm retired now. I can do what I like.'

'Retired from what, you lazy fuck? Stealing other people's lives?'

'Look, you don't know what my life has been like in Greece. Moving boats. Always busy. Some rich bastard has a yacht in the wrong place then Tony's your man.'

'Well, go back and don't mind the high tide. You just might drown.'

Tony clicked his cigarette case open and shut in a restless rhythm.

'Love to,' he declared, 'but the knees have gone.' He looked at Dorothy and gave one of his old grins. 'Getting a bit old, aren't we? Too old to fight. Dots, come on. Can't we forget about the lawyers and sort this out?' He smiled and put his arms out as if to welcome her into them. 'I know you. You're so angry anyone would think you still love me.'

'I don't. I never loved you.'

'You were mad for me. Absolutely mad. Remember that time we snuck off and—'

'Stop it!'

322

'Look, I am sorry about Connie. I know it wasn't right, but she was all over me.'

'She was a child.'

Tony held his hands up in self-defence. 'Legal, perfectly legal. The truth is, I don't think she liked Greece. Look, Dots, I'm not saying I was perfect, but you know my life, bobbing and weaving, doing my best. What can I tell you? Women fall for me.'

Dorothy looked at him.

'Where was she going?' she asked.

'When?'

'She was on her way to the airport.'

'Oh that. She got mad coz I'd moved on with someone else and—'

'You moved on?' said Dorothy, incredulous.

'Yeah, well, Connie was very young. We didn't even like the same music and it's not like we were married. I've told you: it wasn't my fault. Like mother like daughter and ...'

Dorothy looked around for something heavy to throw at him. As she looked down he turned and wrenched open the garage door. There stood the bright orange convertible Ford Cortina from 1978. Tony whistled.

'Well, well, if it isn't my car.'

Tony didn't ask. He just took it. Hotwired the old vehicle and then got a dubious mate to make him a key. After that he was like the proverbial cat with the cream. He drove about the square with the top down, his sheepskin collar up, looking for all the world as if he owned the place or was about to. He would sit revving the engine or at other times park up outside Number 4 and stroll into the square to flirt with the women doing up the gardens. It was grotesque. Often he just sat on a bench smoking and drinking lager out of a can, saying things like, 'I love how

323

you pull those weeds! I bet you're not too old to pull something else! Know what I mean?'

Amber and Stevie watched him do it.

'Be nice to think those creepy men don't exist any more,' commented Amber.

'But they do,' replied Stevie.

'Be even nicer to think women don't fall for it but sadly they do that too.'

They watched him hold court with some of the old birds who giggled and brought him biscuits.

As he motored or messed about, Birdie ploughed on in the square directing the progress of the flower beds. She was loving being outside. The fresh air was wonderful and she berated herself for having stayed in her high-altitude nest for so long. Having started on creating a setting worthy of the arrival of Adam Anderson, Birdie couldn't stop. Bulbs and bushes were planted, rubbish cleared and Bobby brought wood to rebuild the benches. He got Arun to carve flowers on them. The place was becoming stunning. Old Nordic sticks even laid a small mosaic of a sundial, with the arrow pointing straight at Soros Tower.

Birdie worked ridiculous hours. She was there from first thing in the morning until dusk. One evening, Dorothy brought her a cup of tea just as Bobby and Arun had finished their final seating arrangement. Birdie was in her wheelchair, admiring the work.

'The police were here,' said Birdie, not looking up.

'Oh yes?'

'Looking round the square. I think they found something near that bench.' Birdie pointed. It was the one directly opposite Number 4.

Dorothy handed her the tea. 'Did they say what?'

'No.'

Birdie began cutting away a load of ivy to reveal an old Victorian street sign which read 'Grimaldi Square'. 'Who's Grimaldi?' she asked as Jack came over.

'Clown, I think,' he replied, wiping his warm face with his sleeve. 'Grimaldi. I only know coz I seem to remember Agnes had some kind of enquiry about a party here for some clowns. I'm sure there was an email.'

'Clowns!' exclaimed Birdie. 'You're kidding! Adam loves a clown.'

'Adam?'

'Adam Anderson. We should get clowns!'

Dorothy frowned at her. 'This is going too far, Birdie. It's not an actual television show that Jack is in. Not yet, anyway. It's just an audition. I doubt Adam Anderson himself will even come.'

Birdie wasn't listening. 'We definitely need clowns,' she declared, 'and we need them soon. Jack, see if you can find that email.'

'Soon?' asked Dorothy.

Birdie nodded. 'They've set a date for the audition. I think the whole neighbourhood, past and present – well, possibly not the hippies on the third floor – should—'

'Birdie! Could you slow down? Have one of your cakes or something. What is wrong with you?' asked Dorothy, slightly alarmed at what was happening.

Birdie looked down into her mug of tea as if looking to the future.

'The date of the audition ...'

'Yes?'

Jack interrupted. 'It's the same day the council says the tower will come down.'

'Same day? How?' asked Dorothy. 'How is the tower coming down?'

325

'Explosives.'

Dorothy was appalled. 'We can't have a piano audition in the pub while Armageddon is happening next door!'

'It's fine. I've spoken to them,' reassured Birdie. 'Grimaldi Square is just outside the exclusion zone. We'll hear it and feel it, but nothing will happen here. It's perfect. Don't you see, Dorothy? It's an ending and a beginning and we need to mark it.'

'When is it exactly?'

Birdie gave a half smile. 'Actually they were nice about it and said I could choose the date. That it didn't matter to them.'

'What did you choose?'

'The tenth of August.'

'Birdie . . .'

'It's time, Dot. Let's blow that particular day up.'

And with that she went back to beautifying the square.

'Nan, you're working too hard,' called Jack after her. 'And I want to talk to you about the whole audition thing.'

'Jack,' shouted his grandmother, wheeling away, 'let me do this. This is a great chance for you, and I want you to take it. Listen to me, and I don't want any discussion. We've got to crack on. Do you have any idea how long I need to grow sunflowers from seed?'

'No,' replied Dorothy and Jack.

They sat and watched her as she moved to command her troops.

Jack sighed. 'Dorothy.'

'Yes?'

'Can I tell you something?'

'You will anyway.'

'I don't know if I want this, this whole telly thing, and I can't tell Nan. She is so excited, but I don't know. Something changed

326

the night of the fight. I like playing music but it's not everything. I don't think I want to be famous. I think actually I want something more ordinary. Just because I'm gay doesn't mean I want to be in showbusiness. Nan's in a wheelchair but she's not champing at the bit for the Paralympics.'

'I wouldn't mention the possibility to her at the moment,' replied Dorothy. 'I can just see her taking up the high jump.'

Jack went back to work.

He and Arun worked well together and really enjoyed doing up the pub. They did far more than just repair the place. The floorboards of the stage were stripped back and sanded. The jukebox was fitted with a permanent plug and all the old drink posters Jim had once stored in his office came out, were dusted down and reframed. Jack had worked in the pub for over a year but had never really taken the time to think about the place. As they worked, locals stopped in and said how much they missed it being open. There had been some news reports about the attack and what had happened. Since then people from all over had called the Onion to give support and ask when *Fabulous Friday* would be back. It was clear that the place meant a great deal to a lot of people. Mimi Beaverhousen and her friends supplied the fabric for new red velvet theatrical curtains and even had the piano overhauled.

Arun was still working for Bobby, who also lent a hand when possible. One day he turned up in his van and shuffled in speaking in a gruff, businesslike tone.

'All right, lads? Uhm, here's the thing – I was up at the old reclamation yard, you know, by the station, just by chance, not for any reason ... and I found some old stained-glass panels.' He motioned toward the missing section of glass between the two large rooms. 'Thought they might do for the ones that got broken.'

327

Upstairs, in every spare minute, Stevie was also hard at work. She had cleared the rooms of everything except the few pieces of furniture which she and Dorothy agreed might make a good starting point for the new home. Stevie had done DIY before but never this much.

'Fuck!' she cried out just as Young Justin appeared in the door with his guitar. He had never been upstairs.

'You all right?' Stevie asked.

'Noisy!' he replied, indicating downstairs.

'Aren't you supposed to be helping Bobby?'

Perhaps he was but instead he sat down and began to play.

Stevie went back to her work. She was trying to rehang an old door and kept pinching her hand in the hinge. 'Fuck!' she said again.

Young Justin stopped for a moment and said, 'YouTube.' As he rarely spoke, Stevie stopped to pay attention.

'YouTube?'

Young Justin got out his phone and speedily tapped something in. Then he held it up to Stevie. It was a video showing exactly how to rehang a door. It was perfect. Stevie smiled, watched it several times and got the job done. All the while Young Justin played. After that he arrived most days, combining his music with research for Stevie, who watched and learned. Soon she could do pretty much anything required.

'Turns out a lot of those jobs men seem so pleased with themselves about aren't actually all that difficult,' she said to Dorothy while stepping back to admire a new skirting board. Young Justin played quietly behind them.

'You don't say,' replied Dorothy, who had just moved a load of bedding and was now bending over to take some measurements in the hall with a metal tape measure.

'What you doing?' Stevie asked.

Dorothy seemed entirely focused on her work as she casually said, 'I thought we'd put in a lift from downstairs. I've had a look and I think the end of the hall up here is just above the kitchen and there's room.'

'A lift?'

'Yeah, you know, wheelchair access.' She snapped the tape measure shut and stood up as if this substantial idea would be the work of a moment. 'Prams. Things on wheels,' she added. This was not an idea which had occurred to Stevie, who frowned. It sounded like a lot of expensive work.

'Just in case,' smiled Dorothy reassuringly.

Stevie smiled back as she picked up a rag to shine the finger-prints off the new hinges on the sitting-room door.

'Thank you, Dorothy. Amber says I needed this. Needed something to take my mind off everything.'

'Does she now?' replied Dorothy.

Stevie gave a short laugh as a realisation hit her. 'Oh my god! You did this on purpose! This was you, you old bat. Stop sorting all of us out and get on with your own life! Make that fucking Tony go away and then we can all relax.'

Dorothy nodded. 'You're right,' she said.

The next morning Dorothy called a meeting with Tony and his lawyer.

She took no one with her and wasted no time in stating her case.

'I'm ready to make a settlement,' she announced. 'No more arguing.' She turned to face her estranged husband. He began to smirk but there was something about her which suggested now was not a good time. He made himself sit still.

'Tony, I'll give you £250,000 in cash but once you have your money, you have to go away and never come back. You cannot live anywhere near here.'

Graham began to make lawyerly noises, saying the pub was worth a great deal more than that and he was sure they were on very firm footing with ...

Tony held up his hand. He had his car. He felt he still had his looks. He had never had any intention of staying. With a quarter of a million pounds he could make quite a nice fresh start. In exchange for the cash Tony agreed to give up all claim to any other property.

'How will I get my money?' he asked.

'I'll deliver it,' replied Dorothy.

'When?'

'The tenth of August.'

As the great day approached, Grimaldi Square had never been busier. Strings of fairy lights were being hung in the gardens when a large van arrived and the new lift connecting the lower and upper floors of the Onion was installed.

'Do you think it's big enough?' asked Dorothy anxiously.

'You could put a donkey in there,' Bobby laughed.

'Yes, well, let's just stick to old ladies, shall we?'

The rehoming of the last residents at Soros had finally picked up pace. The local TV news had done a piece about the appalling conditions they were living in, and the poor publicity had at last galvanised the council into completing the rehousing programme. Ida Kovak, the woman with stage four cancer, was moved into an assisted-living flat and even Harry and his Monopoly mob were sorted out after a single, never to be forgotten visit to the council offices by Dorothy. She managed to exhaust everyone who worked there and get free coffee while she waited for a solution to be found. Which it was. The Ukrainians decided it was safer to return to Lviv then spend one more minute with local English officialdom.

Dorothy had also been relentless on Birdie's behalf in her now infamous attacks on the system and its unfortunate operatives. Because of her medical needs, a room in some sheltered accommodation had been found but it was several miles away, far from everything Birdie knew. She had declined and was still hoping for something better. Birdie and Jack were now living at the top of the great concrete and glass building all by themselves.

Dorothy could not believe she had not been able to sort the problem. At night she paced up and down, unable to sleep. Stevie would sometimes wake and find her cuckoo friend sitting in the kitchen, endlessly trying to google solutions. It was painful to watch.

'She'll have no choice,' repeated Dorothy. 'It's miles away. Miles away!'

Two nights before demolition day, Dorothy came down into the hall carrying a single half full bin liner. Stevie and Amber were sitting arm in arm on the sofa in the sitting room.

'Right, I'm off,' called Dorothy.

Stevie got to her feet, bemused. 'Off where?' she asked, feeling suddenly anxious.

Dorothy smiled. 'It's Birdie's last night in the tower. I'll go stay with her, then Jack can go to Arun's.'

'It's late,' said Stevie, trying to find a reason for this not to be happening. 'And dark. You can see her in the morning. We'll all go.'

Dorothy took Stevie's hand and held it for a second. 'It's nine o'clock and I've been wandering about these streets all my life. Anyway, I do have a gun.'

331

Now it was Amber's turn to be distressed and move to stop Dorothy. 'Please tell me you are not carrying . . .'

Dorothy laughed. 'I'm just going to Birdie's.'

She picked up the binbag and opened the front door.

'Let me come with you,' begged Stevie.

'No,' replied Dorothy firmly and turned to leave. 'I've left everything laid out for breakfast,' she called as she walked down the path.

'Oh thank god,' replied Amber.

'Right,' said Stevie quietly as Dorothy headed off. 'Night, Dotty!' she called into the dark.

Stevie watched Dorothy's shadow all the way from the front step until she disappeared into the night. She shut the door before sighing a very deep sigh and sitting back down. At nearly four months pregnant, Amber's belly was just beginning to show. Stevie took Amber's hand, kissed the growing bump and sat silently until at last she said, 'Quiet, isn't it?'

27

'I've lived most of my life here,' Birdie said as she watched Dave and his gang take the last of her possessions.

Stevie came over to lend a hand and everyone checked and double checked that nothing had been overlooked. It was painful for Birdie.

'I lost my husband in here. Sitting right there. He was only watching *Blankety Blank*.'

'Happy times,' murmured Dorothy.

Boxes and boxes of plants had left the place. Gone was the green oasis, replaced by something grey and miserable. Birdie looked around and moved to wheel herself out into the hall.

'I got you!' called Dorothy, grabbing the handles of the chair.

'I can manage,' insisted Birdie.

'I know, I need something to lean on,' claimed her old friend. 'I've been very ill, you know.'

'Oh, it's all about you!'

Dorothy took her time as she pushed her pal out into the hall for the final time. Jack was tearful and stood pressing and re-pressing the button for the lift as if that might speed things along. Stevie brought up the rear carrying a final forgotten hemp plant without giving it a second thought. Dave waited below in his van, ready to make the transition as smooth as possible.

The lift screeched and complained as it crawled its way one last time to the top floor. Stevie, Dorothy, Jack and Birdie listened in silence. The doors had just opened when Birdie suddenly grabbed the wheels of her chair and turned herself around.

'Nan!' cried Jack.

'Birdie!' yelled Dorothy, but she was off, off to the corridor window which looked out onto the world below. She paused by a filthy pane of glass and stared out. Her flaming red hair a beacon of colour in the drab corridor. She gazed down toward Grimaldi Square. The lift pinged open but her three companions knew it would have to wait. They went to stand beside Birdie, who had begun to cry.

'It's a shithole,' comforted Dorothy.

'Yes,' agreed Birdie, 'but it's my shithole. It's my home.'

Dorothy put her hand on her old friend's shoulder before speaking.

'You know, Birdie, I thought I was too ancient to learn new things but the last few months I feel like I might even have grown up a little.'

Birdie smiled. 'Seems very unlikely,' she managed as tears fell from her eyes.

Jack was in pieces and could not console his grandmother.

'I'll sort something. I promise,' he said.

'This place,' said Dorothy, indicating the broken corridor they stood in, 'this was your home, and we'll always remember it, but a real home isn't any one building. It's actually the place where the people you love are living.'

'Nice,' said Jack. 'I mean, schmaltzy, but nice.'

The four of them stood huddled amongst the devastation.

Birdie reached out for Jack's hand.

'Oh, my lovely boy, we used to fly up here,' she whispered. 'I don't know if we'll have that again.'

Dorothy smiled before saying quietly, 'Of course you will, Birdie. In fact, you will find it in the strangest places.'

Jack interrupted. 'I'm going to stop you there, Dorothy. Are you about to quote Westlife?' he asked.

Dorothy nodded. 'Four of us,' she said, indicating Stevie, Jack, Birdie and herself. 'Thought we looked a bit like a boy band. Come on. Enough moping.'

Dorothy grabbed the handles of Birdie's wheelchair and propelled her toward the lift with Jack and Stevie following. As they got into the lift, they all turned to face the corridor down to the old flat for the last time and Jack began to lead them in quiet Irish song.

The doors juddered closed and, incredibly softly, the gang of four could just be heard harmonising that they were flying without wings.

The day of the big audition, the people of Grimaldi Square woke up to a brilliant day. Up above the sky was blue and below Birdie and her old birds had done a superb job. Lavender and roses had blossomed, and the new benches provided the perfect spot to appreciate the vibrant colour. Balloons in rainbow colours hung from the lamp posts alongside fairy lights and there was even a red and white striped stand for serving beer and lemonade. A large banner proclaimed *Welcome, Adam Anderson!*

At 8 a.m. the residents and a vast number of others from Soros and the surrounding area gathered in the centre of the square. They waited by the new sundial and faced the empty tower. From the square, above the rooftops of the surrounding buildings, the top of it could be seen. It was high enough for Grimaldi to sit in shadow. Bobby was there, and Arun with Jack, Dave and his friends, Mrs Haggerston, the entire congregation from St Mary the Virgin, with the kind vicar standing alongside Mimi Beaverhousen and the drag queens. Dorothy had her hand on Birdie's shoulder while Amber and Stevie stood beside them. Young Justin had brought his guitar, ready to accompany the moment. He strummed a few dramatic chords as Birdie looked at her watch and called out the seconds:

'Three, two, one.'

Nothing. At first nothing but then a low rumble followed by the sound of timed explosions. The crowd looked up. The top of Soros stood tall against the sky. To the naked eye it appeared invincible but slowly it began to crumble. Crumble and then fall neatly down in layers. No one in the square was close enough to see the final tumble, but they heard it as the tower collapsed and, after all those years, the thing no one had expected: the sun finally shone down on Grimaldi Square. The shadows disappeared. There was silence and then cheers and hugs and tears.

Amber and Dorothy made breakfast together in the pub kitchen. They sang along to old tunes before serving up splendid bacon sandwiches on trestle tables outside. Jack had several.

'Right, action time!' called Birdie and every person there began an allocated task which Stevie checked off on a chart. Clowns arrived and began setting up small brightly coloured cannons in the square. There was face painting. Even Mrs Haggerston came out with sausage rolls.

The Onion looked better than it had ever done. Welcoming. 'A proper local,' as Jim would have said. Two vans with camera crew arrived and heralded the moment when Adam Anderson might grace their presence.

'He's here! He's here!' cried Birdie, jumping up and down in her wheelchair.

'Steady on,' advised Dorothy. 'Those incontinence pants won't last all day.'

Adam Anderson came round the square in a shiny limo and was cheered, and despite years of showbusiness cynicism he was overwhelmed and declared that everything was a 'duhlite'. Birdie was beside herself.

'We'll need cameras here, here and here,' yelled a bossy woman in headphones. 'Audience please! Inside!'

'I think she means us,' said Dorothy, pushing Birdie into the pub.

The piano, the curtains, even the floorboards looked magnificent. The stage was literally set.

'Standing by!' someone shouted. 'Mr Anderson, please!'

Adam Anderson entered and took a seat at the back as if it were all very casual and not planned at all. A man just dropping in to a pub. Birdie had thought he would be at the front and was astonished to find him right behind her.

Mimi Beaverhousen walked out onto the stage. She had crafted a very fine new outfit made of rainbow ribbons and took it upon herself to introduce the show. This was, after all, the home of her *Fabulous Friday*. It was Mimi's first time in front of professional cameras, but this did not deter her. She was born for this moment and took her time.

337

'Ladies and gentlemen, non-binaries and all others as they choose to express themselves, this is a very special occasion when one of our own steps into the spotlight. We are proud to be part of his family . . .'

Birdie began to sob loudly with pride, and Dorothy had to pretend she had something in her eye as she dabbed it with a tissue. Arun was nowhere to be seen but Stevie stood beaming beside Amber. She helped her wife onto a stool and carried on fussing as Mimi continued with as much hyperbole as she could muster.

'He was one of us but now we give him to the world. Please welcome the genius that is Jack Parker!'

There was wild applause and then, rather like the moment in *The Sound of Music* when the von Trapps are announced as winners of the Nazi music competition and don't come on to the stage, nothing happened. Mimi said Jack's name again but still there was no sign of him.

Arun moved away from the curtain and awkwardly took centre stage.

'I'm very sorry everyone but . . . Jack doesn't want to play. He doesn't really want this. We should have said.'

Arun disappeared backstage, Birdie gasped and the room erupted in chatter.

'Stevie! Stevie!' Birdie whispered urgently, knowing Adam Anderson was right behind her. 'You have to find him! Make him do it.'

Stevie looked at Amber, who almost pushed her to go backstage.

Birdie dared to look behind her. Adam Anderson did not look pleased. It was awkward. A lot of people had gathered for this moment, and it was all on camera.

Dorothy scanned the room before alighting on Young Justin standing still holding his guitar.

'Young Justin,' she called, 'give us a tune!'

With the casualness of youth, Young Justin stepped up and began to play.

It was to the accompaniment of guitar music that Stevie found Jack and Arun holding hands in the miniature dressing room. There was hardly space for all three of them.

'Is she angry?' Jack asked.

'Who?' said Stevie.

'Nan? Dorothy? Everyone, I guess.'

'What happened?'

'I don't know. I had to think a lot when you got hurt. When we had to move house and the thing is, I like it here, Stevie.' Jack looked round the world's smallest backstage space. 'It's enough. I'm fine here with you and Dorothy, Amber and the baby.' He then smiled at his lover. 'Arun. I'm so lucky. It's enough. I don't want any more.'

Stevie looked at her childhood friend and smiled. 'That's fine,' she said. 'I don't want any more either.'

Back in the hall the tension of Jack not appearing and Young Justin taking his place meant it took a second for everyone to realise that the youthful guitarist was actually very good. No, not good, brilliant. He played one song and the place erupted with demands for another. Adam Anderson and the team were bowled over.

The host of *Step into the Spotlight* leant over to Birdie, who was swallowing her disappointment bravely, and whispered,

'What type of guitar is that he's playing?'

'Argos,' she replied.

'So he's got no money?' commented Adam.

'Poor as a church mouse,' agreed Birdie.

'And does the boy have family?'

'His mum died of cancer.'

'Excellent,' said Adam. 'This is all excellent.'

When a 'duhlighted' Adam Anderson departed the entire party went out into the sunlit square to wave him goodbye. The clowns' cannon sprayed confetti over everyone. Stevie and Amber walked hand in hand through the square chatting with everyone as if they had lived there all their lives. They stopped in front of their own house and Stevie was surprised to see her work partner Kevin arrive dressed in civvies.

'Come for the party?' she asked him.

He shook his head. 'I wanted a word. On the quiet. It's awkward. You remember the gunshot your neighbour said she heard?'

'It was nonsense. She's old,' she replied, rather flustered.

'We've been looking around. I'm afraid we found a bullet.'

'Can't you just let it go?' asked Stevie but Kevin shook his head.

Stevie and Amber turned back to the pub where they could see Birdie and Dorothy standing in the doorway, watching.

'You all right about Jack?' asked Dotty.

'I just want him to be happy,' came the honest reply.

'How's your new place?'

'Shit.'

A child ran past laughing with a balloon animal from one of the clowns.

'You did good today, Birdie.'

340

'You too, Dotty. People round here have so little so why not make what we can be the best? We all need a party every now and then. It's not much. Not like it's raining money, is it?'

'Now that would be nice,' said Dorothy.

Tony pulled up in his car. He had been drinking. He swayed toward her with his usual leering grin while Stevie watched with concern from across the square.

'You shouldn't be driving,' Dorothy pointed out.

'Not worried about it. That landlady at my Airbnb says she can get me off. I want my money. Tenth of August, you said. That's today.'

Dorothy looked at him. 'Do you know why I said this day?'

'I have no fucking idea and I couldn't care less. Just give me my fucking money.'

'It was our wedding day,' said Dorothy.

'OK,' replied Tony. He looked baffled. 'Is that it?'

'Yes,' said Dorothy. 'That's it.'

She walked over to one of the clowns, said something and the two of them went inside. She was gone for a while but when she returned her hands were still empty.

Tony was pulling on a cigarette. 'Where the fuck is it?' he demanded as his yellowed fingers drummed on the back of a bench. He smelled of decay and she almost felt sorry for him.

'You were never patient, Tony. Quarter of a million pounds, was it? I said I'd deliver. Just watch,' she said, 'it's over there,' and pointed to where a clown was putting a fresh pint down on the ground and fiddling with the theatrical confetti cannon. The red-nosed fellow pressed a button and the toy weapon fired ... ten-pound notes. The money filled the sky and floated down into the crowd.

Dorothy smiled before continuing, 'Your money is over there

and over there and some here . . .' She waved her arms in the air as cash drifted down from the sky. The crowd went mad. People began leaping, grabbing money which seemed to have appeared from thin air. Ida Kovak, who was sitting on one of the new benches, found ten notes just fell in her lap.

'What the fuck?' cried Tony.

'That's your money,' grinned Dorothy. 'I said I'd give it to you, I just never said how.'

Now Tony ran toward the money. He tried to grab it in the air, off the ground, while cursing at everyone to get out of his way.

Stevie came over to Dorothy and couldn't stop laughing.

'Did you just fire a quarter of a million pounds down on people's heads?' she asked.

'Don't be ridiculous,' whispered Dorothy. 'It was only ten thousand. I'm not completely mad.'

'Where have you been keeping it?'

'Inside the *Star Wars* stormtrooper. Tony could have asked me for that. It was his.' She turned and looked at Birdie, who was clapping her hands with joy as her former neighbours finally had unexpected good fortune.

'Oh Dorothy!' she cried excitedly.

'Well,' replied her friend matter of factly, 'I thought for once it *should* rain money on everyone who lives here, and it might just give the bastard a fright.'

It had indeed caused a fright. Dorothy looked for Tony to see how he was coping. It wasn't good. As he ran about trying to stop the cash cascade into other people's hands his many years of smoking and drinking caught up with him. He stopped running. First he appeared to look confused, which was not surprising, then he had some kind of spasm before both his right arm and

342

the right side of his face appeared to droop and he fell to the floor.

Amber was quick. 'Call an ambulance,' she shouted. Despite being more than four months pregnant she rushed to kneel down beside him and help open his airways.

Tony had had a stroke.

It was Dorothy who went to the hospital with Amber.

'Who is his next of kin?' asked the nurse.

'It's me,' Dorothy heard herself say.

'What's his address?'

'I don't know. Number 4 Grimaldi Square, I guess.'

'I'm afraid the stroke has affected parts of his brain,' said the doctor. 'I doubt he'll speak again. He can have physio, but it's a long road.'

Dorothy and Amber exchanged a glance.

Tony was in hospital for a few weeks and Dorothy visited him most days. Despite excellent treatment none of it helped bring back his voice or movement. Constable Kevin came to see him. He had some questions about the night the gun was fired in the square, but it was pointless.

'Let me know if he starts to talk,' he ordered as he departed.

Dorothy carried on spending her days with him.

'You don't have to see him,' Stevie kept saying.

'I'm thinking,' replied Dorothy.

'There's nothing we can do,' explained the doctor. 'He'll need to go into care.'

'It's not your responsibility,' Stevie tried.

Sometimes Stevie went with her. She had become a demon on

343

the internet and spent time helping to look up the best possible care options.

'I can't believe it, but I do think he might get the best care at Jane Topper. It's just very expensive. Has he got any money?'

'He has a quarter of a million pounds,' replied Dorothy. 'Well, minus ten grand the clown shot into the air.'

Stevie looked at her. 'You don't have to do this.'

Dorothy eyed her silent but awake husband. 'Let's kill him with kindness.'

'So much better than a gun,' murmured Stevie. 'Where is that, by the way?'

Dorothy never said.

It was the last day in August when Tony moved into the Jane Topper Care Home. Rochelle was there to welcome him as Stevie pushed the rather collapsed man in the door in a very strange wheelchair. It was a curious wooden contraption. Edwardian, by the look of it.

'He likes clapping,' Dorothy said as she was leaving. 'Oh, and if he gets agitated there's nothing like a bit of ABBA to calm him down.'

Stevie said as they got in the car, 'What happened to kindness?'

'There's a limit,' replied Dorothy.

28

'You're free, Dotty! Let's go see your new place!' yelled Stevie, ready to race off, but Dorothy suddenly pulled over and got out of the car. Stevie watched as she walked round the front of the car and opened the passenger door.

'Get out!' ordered Dorothy.

'What?'

'Out! I am not driving someone else's car.'

'What are you talking about?'

'God, Stevie, sometimes you take your own sweet meandering way to get anywhere. You are having twins. Amber told me. Congratulations. I am giving you this car. You will need a car.'

Dorothy held out the keys. Stevie started to protest but Dorothy held up her hand.

'Don't you dare!'

Slowly Stevie got out of the car and took the keys. The women swapped seats and Stevie started the ignition. The engine revved and without another word Stevie put her foot down on the accelerator and the two of them roared back to Grimaldi Square.

Stevie whooped with excitement. All that manual labour on the renovations had done her good both physically and mentally. She was back to her old self and couldn't stop smiling. Twins! She was also thrilled with what she had created. Her hard work had created a vast space. Enough to make two flats, one with four bedrooms on the first floor and another with two up in the eaves. Each was self-contained but they were connected to each other and to the pub below by the excellent lift.

Stevie screeched into the pub courtyard. The two women sat for a moment grinning.

As they reached the sitting room of Dorothy's new flat a great cheer went up. Jack, Arun, Amber, Stevie, Birdie and Bobby were all there, waiting for them. The small red sofa with its Pride cushion was in place but so too were newly polished pieces of furniture from the past. The place looked like home. A champagne cork popped and Jack handed Dorothy a glass of fizz.

'What the hell is this?' she said.

'Time to celebrate,' declared Birdie.

'It's ready. Ready for you,' beamed Stevie.

'Speech!' cried Bobby, smiling at his old sparring partner.

Dorothy stood, glass in hand, and thought about what she wanted to say. 'I have waited a long time for today. I thought if I got revenge then it would make me happy but all I realised is how much of my life I have wasted. Wasted being angry and feeling impotent. Well, it's enough. I'm getting too old to squander any more time so, if we all agree, I want to suggest that we, this group of us, ought to make some changes. I've been thinking. I've been thinking a lot.'

'Uh-oh,' said Bobby.

'First of all, Birdie.' She turned to her friend. 'You can't live

346

in that shithole they've put you in so why not come and live here with me?'

'I don't want any charity,' Birdie muttered.

'And you're not getting any,' replied Dorothy. 'I plan to make you garden in the square for the rest of your life.'

'I bet you snore.'

'There's two bedrooms and you're deaf as a post. Next, the pub.' Dorothy nodded to Jack, Arun and Bobby. 'You boys have done a wonderful job. It is looking so nice. Thank you, everyone, but now the place needs running and running properly. The Onion used to be wonderful in its heyday and Jack and Arun's *Fabulous Friday* showed us that it can be again. It's a lot of work for one person – trust me, I know. Stevie and Jack have always been good together so I would like to give the whole place to you two.'

'*Give* it?' repeated Jack as Stevie turned open-mouthed to Amber.

'Yes. Give it.'

'What is wrong with you?' laughed Bobby.

'Nothing. I got the idea from Harry at the tower. I played Monopoly with him, and I thought, how great to just give houses away if you like. What the hell do I need with a boozer? I suggest, Stevie, that you and Jack run it between you. That way Jack will have time for Arun and Stevie for the babies.'

'Wait! What about the police?' asked Stevie, startled by the speed with which things were happening.

'No one wants you to go back to that,' said Dorothy. 'It's dangerous. Am I right? Let's vote.'

She was right. No one did. 'You will need time at home, Stevie, so that Amber can go back to her studies.'

'Dare I ask what I'm studying?' asked Amber, almost laughing at Dorothy's breathtakingly thorough planning.

347

Dorothy smiled at everyone. 'I'm proud to announce that our Amber is going to become *Dr* Amber Delaunay. She is going to medical school because that is what she should have done in the first place. She was born to be a doctor. This works for everyone because neither Birdie nor I can ever get an appointment at the GP and would appreciate having someone on tap.'

Arun surprised everyone by getting to his feet. 'Dorothy, you can't just sort everyone's lives out. We have to do a bit of it ourselves.'

'Oh, I've not left you out, Arun. I've been thinking about Bobby's business. He's not getting any younger.'

'Thanks,' said Bobby.

'I think he should bring you on as partner and you can run it together.'

Bobby nodded slightly. 'I don't mind that.'

'I'd like that,' said Arun. 'Maybe we could call it Pride Builders.'

Bobby nodded. 'Yeah, don't push it.'

He put out a hand for a shake and the two men solemnly agreed to their new partnership.

Arun cleared a small frog from his throat and stayed standing. 'But I do want to say something.'

'Well crack on, Arun,' said Dorothy as Jack made space for her to sit down.

Having gained everyone's attention Arun felt shy. It took him a moment to begin. 'I want you all to know that Jack and I are serious . . .'

There was mock surprise from everyone.

Arun turned to Jack. 'I was so proud of you with that TV thing. I know you'll also make the right decision if I ask you, in front of all our friends, to please move in with me.'

Jack looked shy. 'Really? You might hate my bathroom habits. I've been known to lie in the bath fully clothed.'

'Is that a refusal?' asked Arun.

'No.'

'Good, because otherwise I would have had to write it down as a micro-aggression in my notebook.'

'And where are you going to live?' asked Birdie.

Bobby clapped his hands together as if he were about to be brilliant.

'Amber and Stevie's house,' he declared.

'What the hell is wrong with everyone? Our house?' asked Stevie, wondering if she had misheard. 'There isn't room.'

'Not with you,' assured Bobby. 'On their own.'

'And where are we supposed to live?' asked Amber.

Dorothy smiled at Bobby. 'He's right. Here, of course. You'll need more room with the twins. At least another bedroom, so you ought to have the other flat. Up here at the pub. It's got four bedrooms, and someone has made it very beautiful indeed.'

Birdie clapped her hands in delight. 'That's brilliant. Dorothy and I will be right next door. That way we can babysit, and you can have more space.'

'But we've only just moved in!' protested Stevie. 'We have to live at Number 4.'

'*I am no bird; and no net ensnares me*,' quoted Bobby.

Amber grinned. 'Charlotte Brontë!' She began to laugh. 'It is kind of perfect as a solution. Give up, Stevie. Stop thinking you and I are in charge.'

Amber and Stevie's babies were born on December 16th.
'Same day as Jane Austen,' said Dorothy.

'What happened to the saints?' asked Stevie.

'I thought we'd move on.'

At just thirty-six weeks, they were tiny, and fitted just nicely end to end in Dorothy's beautiful lace-trimmed crib.

Jack was among the first to hold them.

'Have you chosen names?'

'Daisy and Jack.'

'Little Jack,' he blubbed, cradling the child.

'I wanted Dandelion for the girl,' said Stevie, 'but Amber said it was too weird.'

They had sent word to Stevie's parents but got no reply and Amber's mum was in America. She had a first edition of *The Road to Oz* from 1909 delivered to celebrate, which Dorothy thought was a bit odd.

'It's the book where the phrase "Friends of Dorothy" comes

from,' explained Amber. 'It an old euphemism for gay people and it's funny because your name is ...'

But Dorothy was busy arranging for Little Jack and Daisy to be christened at St Mary the Virgin in the new year.

'I thought you weren't religious?' said Amber.

'I'm not but I've had my brush with death and reckon you might as well hedge your bets. Besides, it makes a nice party.'

The nice woman vicar said she would happily conduct the service and everyone pretended they had never been to her church before.

Mrs Haggerston didn't change much because this is not a fairy tale. Having had a lesbian couple next door for a while, she now had gay boys and didn't think she liked it any better until Arun offered to rebuild her beloved bird feeder.

'I can make it just like Notre-Dame,' he offered.

'Why would you do that?' she replied, almost coy and unused to such kindness.

'Just being a good neighbour,' Arun assured her as Jack kicked him gently in the shins.

Jack learnt the name of every tool in the building trade and Arun set about bringing his family on board with his life.

'I love them and I'm too happy not to share it,' he said with determination.

Dorothy carried on running the joint care club. She decided to hold future meetings in the garage with the fairy-tale characters on the wall. The decrepit women loved sitting there, eating brownies and feeling the magic.

'I think Peter Pan is smiling at me,' old Nordic sticks would say, and Dorothy would always agree.

Birdie and Dorothy settled in to their new home. During the day Birdie supervised the garden while Dorothy tried to run everything else. At night they would watch television together and chat.

'I called Jack's mum,' Dorothy said one night. 'I explained about him running the pub and being so happy with Arun, and she actually listened. I think she might be ready to see him soon.'

Birdie muted the sound on the TV and looked at her. 'Will you ever stop interfering?' she asked.

'No,' replied Dorothy.

They bickered quietly and it made them both feel alive and not at all lonely.

Birdie and Dorothy went to watch *Step into the Spotlight* be recorded and they learned that television takes for ever to make and that Adam Anderson was a knob. It didn't matter, because Young Justin won and became quite the star. Neither of the women ever stopped bragging about it.

Over at Jane Toppen, Tony remained silent, much to the frustration of the police.

Fabulous Friday resumed with Bobby and a group of local allies keeping an eye out for trouble. Bobby made a sign for Number 4 which read 'Cuckoo House'.

Amber applied for medical school and got in.

Stevie worked her notice on the force and then got a dog on the day she left. A cockerpoo named Wilhelmina.

The lift at the Onion proved very useful, both for Birdie's wheelchair and the babies' pram. It ran from the pub kitchen to the end of the hall outside the two flats. Even during a busy shift Stevie could quickly pop up to check on Amber and the twins.

The gardens in the square stayed splendid and the following year won an urban gardening award. Something about the renovations and the new lease of life at the pub caused others in Grimaldi Square to decide to smarten their own places up.

352

'It's been on the telly, you know,' they would tell anyone who would listen.

Now that he was in charge, Jack began to enjoy running the pub. They had to hire more staff and he became quite bossy, allowing no one to slack during work hours. He was standing behind the counter when two young men came in together for a glass of wine.

'We've just bought Number 12 here in the square,' they confided excitedly.

Jack grinned.

'Welcome to the gaybourhood,' he replied.

Christmas Eve

It was the second annual fancy dress Christmas party. Arun and Jack were having yet another triumphant evening providing the entertainment and customers spilling in and out the front door of the Onion could be heard laughing in the night air. The Carpenters crooning that they would be home for the holidays swayed smoothly from the jukebox. A heavy fall of snow the night before had covered everything in a blanket of white. A giant Christmas tree dominated the centre of the square and every house appeared to have taken up a directive for festive lights. It was like a picture postcard for Yuletide cheer.

Stevie and Amber were in their upstairs flat, marvelling at their sleeping babies.

'They're so tiny,' Stevie whispered for the umpteenth time.

'So perfect,' said Amber.

A light scent of lily of the valley caused them both to look up as Dorothy appeared in the doorway.

'Party sounds good downstairs,' she commented.

354

'What did Jack and Arun go as in the end?' asked Amber, smiling.

'St George and the dragon. Not ideal. Jack keeps knocking the tonic bottles off the bottom shelf with his tail.'

Stevie moved to fuss over one of the children. 'Do you think Daisy is too hot?'

Amber raised an eyebrow at Dorothy, who smiled and said,

'I know Jack was hoping you'd pop down for ten minutes. He's worried he'll forget something.'

'I made him a chart,' replied Stevie. 'Do you think we should wake them for their feed?'

'I think you should go down to the party for a bit,' repeated Dorothy, looking at Amber.

Stevie shook her head. 'No, I need to be here.'

'Stevie!' said Dorothy. 'You have to go down because Jack has written a song about you. It's supposed to be a surprise, but it won't be anything if you hang about here.'

'But I don't have a costume.'

'You can go as Prince Charming from last year.'

'I don't know where it is.'

'I laid it out on your bed.'

Stevie looked at the two women. 'It's an ambush, isn't it?'

She went and got changed, and when she returned Amber was holding Little Jack and Granny Dotty had Daisy. All four looked entirely happy.

'Have fun, my love,' said Amber.

Stevie was leaning against the doorframe, tired and smiling at the happy scene, when she heard the lift rising up from below. She looked down the corridor as the doors opened to reveal her mother, her hair long again, with a giant suitcase. Backlit by the harsh light of the lift, she looked tiny. Prince Charming walked toward her, and they hugged as Stevie asked, 'Come to see your grandchildren?'

'Yes,' whispered Barbara before pulling back to look at her daughter. 'I've left your father,' she announced.

Stevie looked at her mother before turning her head back to the nursery, calling out, 'Dotty!'

'Yes?' Dorothy replied, looking up from her cooing.

'Family meeting!'

Acknowledgements

This book would not have happened without the guiding hand of my editor, the legendary Lennie Goodings; the kindness of Clare Alexander, my literary agent; the Team Toksvig Curtis Brown agency gang of Alastair Lindsey-Renton, Helen Clarkson and Gena Davies; eagle-eyed and thoughtful copy-editor Zoe Gullen; proof-readers extraordinaire Debbie Toksvig and Jon Appleton; PR guru and kindly shepherd Susan de Soissons; and the impossible to thank enough Mary Hepworth.

Credits

48 and 49   'Pink' lyrics by Andrew Wyatt, Eric Frederic, Mark Ronson and Melissa Jefferson. Copyright © Concord Music Publishing LLC, Kobalt Music Publishing Ltd, Sony/ATV Music Publishing LLC, Universal Music Publishing Group, Warner Chappell Music, Inc.

101 and 286   *Brief Encounter* (1945). Screenplay by Noël Coward, Anthony Havelock-Allan, David Lean and Ronald Neame

109   Ursula K. Le Guin, *The Farthest Shore* (New York: Atheneum Books, 1972)

112   Dr Seuss, *Oh, the Places You'll Go!* (New York: Random House, 1980)

149   Simone de Beauvoir, *The Coming of Age*, trans. Patrick O'Brian (New York: W. W. Norton, 1996)

160–1   'Seventy-Six Trombones' lyrics by Meredith Willson. Copyright © Frank Music Corp. and Meredith Willson Music

Sandi Toksvig was born in Denmark, brought up in Africa, then America and moved to the UK when she was fourteen. She has been on British stage, screen and radio for over forty years and was awarded an OBE for services to broadcasting. She is the mother of three children, married and lives deep in the woods.